Published by: Gulf Book Services LTD
20-22 Wenlock Road,
London N1 7GU
U.K

Email: Info@gulfbooks.co.uk

ISBN : 978-81-902679-2-2

Table of Contents

Dedication

This fiction is dedicated to the Almighty, who kindled my passion to write novels.

The next dedication is to the dominant stakeholders – "The Audience"

"Not everyone can become a celebrity, but a celebrity can never exist without everyone. Who is this 'everyone'?"

Yes, the community of audience is that every one, who make or break the life of celebrities.

The Trigger

Millions of aspiring youths go into depression when results do not align with their expectations. This electrifying tale does not answer, but attempts to awaken you, whenever deviations from results upset you ………..

Acknowledgements

At the outset, I have to thank the Almighty for having kindled my passion to write fiction. This thought came from nowhere and I trace it to divine inspiration. What did not occur to me in the last four decades suddenly arose in my mind as a spark one fine morning. This spark has lit flames of unbridled passion in me..

I register my gratitude to my core think tank, which tolerated my constant intrusion into their personal time. They supported me in terms of perfecting the story design, smooth flow of the story and screenplay and the promotional aspects of the book. The main brain power of this core think tank is Ms. Priyanka Das (USA), who deserves to be designated as a co-author of this book. In spite of her strenuous schedule at Stanford University, she gave it her best. The other key members of this core think tank, who walked along with me shoulder to shoulder are Mr. Padmanabh Diwanji (Paddy – UAE) and Ms. Jyothsna (UAE).

There was a supporting think tank that relentlessly assisted me in terms of the research, conversion of manuscripts into digital files and playing the role of critics. They are Mr. Chandramouli Raman (USA), Ms. Janani Ramaswamy (USA), Ms. Shreya Gupta (UAE), Ms. Mansi Iyer (UAE), Ms. Rupali Bhatia (UAE) and Mr.Vijayakumaran (UAE).

I am grateful to our publishers, Palm tree books, for showing confidence from inception to completion of the book._I would like to register my gratitude to Mr. Madhavan Menon (UAE) whose enthusiastic guidance helped convert my dream into reality. In addition to serving as an advisory board member on this project along with Ms. Priyanka Das and Mr. Padmanabh Diwanji, he was also instrumental in helping with the publication.

A special thanks to my media partner IBD (India) Pvt. Ltd, represented by Mr. Rajagopal, Mr. Gilbert and Ms. Neeti Agnihotri (Chennai) for giving me a 24/7 promotional support.

Above all, I could not have spent quality time on this project but for the key support of my wife Ms. Gowri Durgadoss. In addition, I owe my gratitude to Mr. Suresh Bhatia and Mr. Rajeev Bhatia (UAE), the businessmen who support me in every one of my projects.

I also thank Mr. Shiv Iyer (UAE) who initially helped me to commence my social media campaign. Further, I thank all my well-wishers who are following my Facebook pages (www.facebook.com/theshacklesofthewarrior), (www.facebook.com/drdurgadoss), (www.facebook.com/asaintintheboardroom) , my website (www.drdd.co.in) and my Twitter page.

This book relies on a vast body of research and artistic work from a number of scholars, books, articles, journals and websites. We thank all these sources and have cited them wherever possible.

Finally, I am not able to individually thank all my well-wishers. I register my debt of gratitude to all of them collectively.

With Warm Regards,

Dr. R. Durgadoss

A Disclaimer

The Author hereby registers his disclaimer on this fiction – The Shackles of The Warrior. The disclaimer relates to the following:

1. This work is a fiction and the characters are imaginary. Any character resembling a real life character is only coincidental and the author does not own any responsibility for such resemblance.
2. The author does not claim the accuracy of the mythological/historical facts used in this fiction which relates to the Mahabharata era.
3. The imaginary characters in this fiction live along with the mythological/ historical heroes already documented in the public domain. But the author does not claim any authenticity for these facts used in this book.
4. In order to enhance the smooth flow of the story, the timeline/mythology or historical facts already available in the public domain have at times been tweaked a little wherever necessary.
5. The author strongly recommends reading this book only as a fiction and does not support the views expressed by the characters in this fiction.
6. Finally, the author unhesitatingly adds that no character or message of this fiction is intended to hurt any segment of our society.

Author,
Dr.R.Durgadoss

Shackles of the Warrior

Prologue

26.11.2008

Mumbai

Taj Mahal Palace Hotel – Colaba

It was 2:30 in the afternoon. The waves of the Arabian Sea kissed the Mumbai shoreline with unceasing continuity. The passersby were caressed by the gentle sea breeze. The rhythmic sounds of waves, loud chatter of tourists and a buzzing breeze created a kind of orchestra witnessed in the symphonies of the Budapest Festival.

The Taj hotel, commanding an impressive view of the Gateway of India, set against the backdrop of the Arabian Sea and the harbour, was a delicious treat to the eye. When the Gateway of India was built, it symbolised the city's openness to visitors. The builders of the Gateway- never realised that one day, such openness would attract terrorists from an alien shore.

Shivshankar Narayan had just attained extensive global visibility for his heroic deed of annihilating cyber terrorists who had tried to destroy global networks. These terrorists were sending viruses through satellites around the planet. Shiv, at just 28, was the youngest and most sought-after crisis management specialist in NASA. He alighted from his black limousine along with his colleague Mike Pedro.

Shiv was a tall man with a well-toned physique and sharp facial features. Though he was very young, he had deep set eyes that exuded seriousness beyond his age. He had been born in America to Indian parents who had been settled in Seattle for over 40 years. The dimples in his cheeks and chin shone when the late afternoon sunlight caressed his face. He brushed aside a strand of silky hair that fell on his face. He looked at his friend Mike. Mike was a Hispanic American and nearly the same age as Shiv. Unlike Shiv, he was a short, white man with a boyish face that bubbled with energy and curiosity. His eyes shone with excitement as he set foot on the land that he had heard so much about, but never had the chance to visit till this day.

Mike and Shiv were not just colleagues but thick friends who had developed an excellent bond over the last five years. Mike was a part of the crisis management team at NASA, headed by the tech wizard Shiv. Shiv had completed his Masters at Stanford University and displayed extraordinary creative sparks in the burgeoning field of Information Technology during his project assignments with NASA. Given his academic credentials, it was a cakewalk for Shiv to land a plum position at NASA.

Shiv and Mike were received at the entrance to the hotel by a reception team comprising of the general manager of Taj, Mr. Kanwar Singh, and Kishore Rathod, the president of the Peace Lovers Association (PLA). PLA, an NGO, had organised a felicitation function for Shiv to celebrate his recent heroic deed at NASA.

1. – The Rewind...

Two beautiful girls, from the guest relations of Taj Palace Hotel, clad in a gracefully designed ***Banarasi saris*** came forward to garland Shiv and applied a vermillion mark in the shape of a ***Tilak*** on his forehead.

Mike raised his eyebrow, rolled his eyes and asked Shiv "What is this red mark applied to your forehead, Shiv?"

"Mikey, this is the traditional welcome that you receive on Indian soil. Would you like to have one on your forehead too?" Shiv asked.

Mike suppressed a grin and said, "Yes Shiv, this tradition seems interesting, especially with these beautiful women doing it."

"Mikey, be careful, I cannot shield you from the attack of beautiful Indian girls. Remember that these Indian girls have respectable and conservative etiquette. So, please don't try to display your smartness to them."

"Yes boss, I will cause no problems for you," answered Mike.

After this, the women garlanded Mike and applied the ***tilak*** on his forehead. Both of them continued to walk without removing the garland or the ***tilak***. They enjoyed their new look.

"Welcome to our hotel sir," said Mr. Kanwar Singh.

Shiv had been the darling of the Indian media for the past one week. It was no wonder that the other guests in the lobby recognised him and smiled at him. Shiv's talk on how he had successfully carried out "Operation Cyber Cleaning," the heroic task mandated by NASA, had been posted on YouTube. It had gained more than a 100 million views.

His success at annihilating the cyber terrorists, who had sought to plant viruses through satellites, was a deed that received global appreciation. Hence it was no wonder that he was very popular across all continents and easily recognised. Being a person of Indian origin, the people of India passionately followed his award functions. He had also been honoured with the ***Padma Bhushan*** by the Government of India. Mike also thoroughly enjoyed the celebrity status accorded to Shiv.

Shiv had read extensively about the Tata DNA and how employees across the firms strictly behaved as per set traditions. Today, he witnessed it firsthand in the warmth that was exuded by the reception staff. After completing the usual check-in formalities, the lady at the

Reception desk told Shiv, “Sir we have allocated sea-facing rooms 629 and 631 to you and your colleague, Mr. Mike.”

“Thank you. But can't you give us adjoining rooms? I need Mike, my walking encyclopaedia, to be close to me at all times!”

“Sorry sir, the hotel is fully booked today. We don’t have adjoining rooms available.”

“Ok, but can't you speak to the guest in 630 and make a request? Or maybe I can try it. Could you tell me the name of the guest in 630?”

“Sir, as per hotel policy, we can't reveal the names of any of our guests.”

“Forgive me dear lady. I am only trying to understand whether he is from the United States. If he is, then I can personally request my fellow countryman to make a small adjustment.”

The lady at the reception smiled and recognized the genuine intention behind the question and said, “Sir, he's not from the USA. The guest in Room 630 is Mr Omar Khayyam, a student. I am sorry but it is against our policy to request any of our guests to shift rooms.”

Little did the reception lady or Shiv realise that the person in room 630 under the false name of Omar Khayyam was Azmal Amir Kasab. It would be this man who would change their lives forever.

“Boss, let’s move on. Let’s not get finicky about small issues today,” Mike joked. “I am always going to be there for you anytime, anywhere.”

They moved into their rooms. Kishore Rathod and the general manager escorted them and insisted they rest for sometime. He said that he would return to fetch them at 5 p.m. Shiv asked, “Kishore, I am floored by the beauty and grandeur of this hotel. Could we see the complete property?”

“Don't worry sir, I will be glad to join Kishore and give you a hotel tour,” replied the general manager.

After taking a quick nap and hot shower, Shiv and Mike were ready for the in-house tour. As promised, both Kishore and Kanwar came to the rooms. Without wasting time they proceeded to the lobby to start the tour.

“By the way, when was this hotel built? What is the history of this hotel?” asked Mike.

“Oh, it has a long and interesting story which goes back to the 1890s. Security men denied J.N. Tata entry into the Royal Navy Yacht Club and poined to a board that read, ‘No Entry for Indians and Dogs’. At that moment, J.N. Tata knew that he had to create a world-class hotel in Bombay. The Taj hotel was his gift to the city that he loved so dearly, just as the Taj Mahal of Agra was Shah Jahan's memorial to the woman he loved. Back then, it costed Rs. 25 lakhs and was the first building in the city to have electricity. The day it was opened, it had a large staff of waiters but only seven guests. Can you believe it?”

"When this hotel was first built, there must barely have been any other good hotels in India. Is that so?"

"Yes, you are right Mike. The hotels during in days were in a rundown condition and mostly overcrowded and dirty. Even the best hotel at that time, Watsons Esplanade Hotel was pretty old. This prompted Tata to announce grand plans of building the Taj Palace hotel in Bombay.

"But he faced many questions from his community. They said, 'You are building an Institute of Science in Bangalore, a state-of-the-art iron and steel factory in Jamshedpur and planning a hydroelectric power project in another Indian city. Why are you building a boarding house - does this fit your stature?' Tata brushed aside these remarks, went ahead and commissioned this hotel on 16 December 1903. This hotel became a symbol of Indian affluence and sophistication. The Maharajas became patrons. In fact, the hotel has turned out to be an architectural marvel bringing together Moorish, Oriental and Florentine styles along with contemporary Indian influences and European ideas. The distinctive onion domes and pointed arches constitute a jewel in the crown."

Both Shiv and Mike noted the overflowing passion in every word that Kanwar uttered.

"By the way, why is this building constructed the wrong way around? What should have been in the rear is in the front and vice versa," enquired the inquisitive Mike.

"Mike, your observation is right. Tata was once asked this question, and he replied that he wanted the majority of the hotel guests to have access to the breathtaking view of the Arabian Sea.

"No wonder then that the hotel has attracted the who's who of the world. Various kings, presidents, legends, performers, religious heads and entertainers have stayed here. Well known personalities including George Bernard Shaw, Irving Stone, Barbara Courtland, Margaret Thatcher, Prince Charles, Bill Clinton, David Rockefeller, Duke Ellington and Lord Mountbatten have all stayed here."

Mike winked and said, "And now you can add Mike Pedro and Shivshankar Narayan to this list."

Kanwar smiled and said, "By the way, your inquisitive nature is very infectious, Mike. Now it is my turn to ask you a question. What is this bright orange pen-like instrument that you and Shiv hold in your shirt pockets?"

Mike looked down at his pocket, beamed and said, "Oh! This is a special gadget used by the crisis management group at NASA. This is the NASA VGN 009. With this device, we can communicate with all CMG members located across the world. We can intercept any frequency and crystallise the convergence of voice, data and image. In certain territories, there is no access to communication towers. But this device operates on a private network and keeps us connected at all times. In fact, it is a hi-tech device that has separate buttons for film recording, voice interception, transmission and so on. In many ways, it is like the black box of an aircraft - it has a battery back-up of two full weeks, cannot be broken and if it is lost, it can be recovered by following the signal frequencies it emits."

A thrilled Kanwar said, "That's very nice, Mike. It looks like a modern James Bond gadget!"

As they walked, Mike noticed several event banners in the lobby for various functions. Apart from Shiv's felicitation, he saw the "Hindustan Unilever - Farewell Dinner for the outgoing CEO," "International Trade Delegation Conference - European Parliamentary member committee," "***Bohra*** Wedding" and few more high profile corporate meetings.

While his mind registered the events, he said, "I have heard that Indian weddings are very interesting. I am very keen to attend one."

The workaholic Shiv intervened, "Mikey, we have a flight to America tomorrow. We need to report the day after tomorrow for another important assignment at headquarters. So, please try not to overindulge in Indian weddings and feasts."

An amused Mike said, "Boss, you are the one who always says that we do not know what is in store for us in the next hour. So how can you ask me to worry about tomorrow?"

In an attempt to please the foreigner, Kishore intervened. "The crackers at Indian wedding processions are a treat to watch. The hotel entrance will stage dances, crackers and a whole range of festivities tonight. You can definitely join in, Mike."

All four of them continued to walk around the hotel. None of them knew that the sounds of bombs, not firecrackers, and horror, not festivity, were awaiting them.

"The hotel still looks fresh in spite of its hundred-year-old history behind it. How is that?"

Kanwar answered, "Mike, we recently carried out an extensive renovation and refurbishment programme. International architects worked hand-in-hand with local to complete the beautiful restoration. Mr. Tata believes in keeping the hotel as fresh as possible while retaining the antique architecture."

"Nice to know that, Kanwar, but tell me how the hotel assembled so many of these fine artefacts?"

A proud Kanwar explained, "Our hotel amassed a diverse collection of paintings and works of art. From massive Belgian chandeliers to the finest ***Bastar*** tribal art, from Anglo Indian inlaid chairs and tables to Goan artefacts, from Mogul-inspired ***jaali*** designs to contemporary sculpture, the hotel incorporates different styles and tastes."

"That's very interesting. The interiors include onyx columns, vaulted alabaster ceilings, cantilever stairways and collections of Indian furnishings and art. I must say, it is lovely and amazing," Mike said.

"Hold your breath, Mike. We're now going to take you through our delicacies," Kanwar chipped in.

"Boss, can we indulge in the delicacies at Taj since our function is much later in the evening?"

Shiv laughed and said, "Mike you are known for overindulgence at parties. Make sure you can stand straight at the function this evening. I'll be busy attending to the dignitaries and won't be able to lend physical support!"

The enthusiastic Kanwar continued with his lecture. "We have more than ten grand banquet rooms with state-of-the-art facilities. The catering service is overseen by a special executive chef. All events are managed by an array of specialised banquet planners and hospitality personnel. We are very proud of them."

Mike noticed some of the younger staff wearing a sky blue uniform with a tag that said "Hospitality Trainees." Mike knew of training in other industries, but had never seen a trainee in a hotel and was quick to point at them and ask Kanwar about them.

"Well, these are our apprentice trainees. We train them in-house. Apart from the plethora of training programmes they attend, we also try to inject the theme '***Atithi devo Bhava***' which means 'The guest has to be delighted' and make it part of their cultural DNA. And the rest falls into place. Everyone from a waiter to the hotel head will respect the hospitality profession that they have selected. In this way, there is no need to supervise or give incentives to boost performance. Respect and empathy are the basic traits of our people."

Shiv was appreciative of the Tata touch and the success story of the Indian entrepreneur's approach. He said, "Oh! It is nice to learn about auto-performers in today's world, where we hear so many theories about inducing superior performance through human behavioural motivation. I must say you are part of a splendid culture, Kanwar."

Kishore and Kanwar led them through the various banquet halls. While Shiv gave the halls a cursory glance, Mike was mentally noting everything he saw. They were first shown through a ***Crystal Room*** used for high-profile launches and lavish cocktail receptions. Then they moved on to the ***Aalam Ballroom***, which had been the venue for the most historic meetings, including Shiv's function. Next to the Ballroom was the ***Rendezvous*** banquet hall that had four glass walls and provided a 360° view of the city.

Shiv and Mike forgot that they were in a hotel and eagerly walked into the next banquet hall as though they were moving from one room in a high raised viewing tower to another. The entrance to the next banquet hall displayed the name ***The Gateway***. True to its name, it offered an impressive view of the Gateway of India against the backdrop of the Arabian Sea.

Soon after, they walked into ***The Golden Banquet Room*** which was tastefully decorated with golden chandeliers and had a complete golden theme against which to set an evening of exotic wining and dining. They were then shown into ***The Emerald and Jade Room*** which was artistically designed with deep green walls and soft brown carpets with muted gold curtains that created a relaxed ambience.

After they finished touring the banquet halls, the playful Mike said, "Mr.Kanwar, these are lovely banquet halls designed to suit every possible occasion. Can we go over to the restaurants, already my favourite part of the hotel?"

Kanwar laughed and answered, "Oh yes, why not? We will go to each of the restaurants Mike."

They walked to the restaurants and passed through each one. They crossed the ***Zodiac Grill*** that served French cuisine. Mike walked across to the exquisitely designed leather encased menu card placed on a wooden stand and read out the signature dishes: New French goose liver and selections from the house of caviar. He rolled his eyes and they all laughed.

They stopped in front of another restaurant named ***Masala Craft***. A beautiful lady in a white cotton sari with a golden border folded her hands in a sign of welcome. When Kanwar told her that he was giving the guests a tour of the hotel, she smiled and introduced some of the dishes on the menu she held.

Apart from eyeing the woman, Mike managed to notice a piping hot ***Phulka*** trolley, seafood station, Mumbai Tiffins - non-vegetarian ***Bohri***, Parsee and Vegetarian delicacies on the menu. Then they moved over to the next restaurant, The Golden Gate. The architecture and the faint sound of the Han music made it clear that the place was a Chinese restaurant. Kanwar told them that this restaurant was famous for Peking duck and the Song of the Dragon.

They moved on and passed ***La Patisserie***, which served delicious pastries and confectioneries along with mango spice cheesecakes, brown onion ***zoff*** breads and ***ciabatta*** sandwiches. Next was a Lebanese restaurant named Souk that served delicacies including ***mezzes, humus, baba ganoush, falafel, sheesh taouk***, Moroccan vegetarian ***tagine*** and rose petal ice cream. Next came the Sea Lounge which was a high tea venue offering hot snacks, ***dim sum***, kebabs, scones and pastries with jazz music in the evening. Mike savoured the aromas from the restaurants.

Then they came across the Wasabi by ***Morimoto*** that served Japanese delicacies including the famous ***Enoki tempura Shimaji*** mushrooms along with mouth watering ***Sushis***. As they reached the end of the line of restaurants, they were shown to the Harbour Bar, which offered creative dining with guacamole ***Pani Puri,*** Crab ***samosas, Paya*** crockets and a large selection of single malts and wines. Mike pointed at the bar, winked at Shiv, but refrained from grabbing a drink. They visited the Star Board Bar last, which offered the finest selection of creative cocktails and European and Cuban fusion snacks.

Shiv looked at his watch and noticed that it was close to 6:30 p.m. He thanked Kishore and Kanwar for the tour. Mike could not resist the temptation and asked Shiv, "Boss what is the point of seeing the restaurants without tasting the food? Why don't we get some drinks and a quick bite right here at the Star Board Bar?" Before anyone could answer, Mike took a seat at the bar and the others had to join him.

Kanwar suggested that they opt for the Stormy Nights cocktail. It was so smooth that the first one disappeared and they were already on to their third before they realized it. Mike was drawn to the finest selection of single malts, cognac and Armagnac and the array of wines on the list. Shiv warned him to stop with his third peg of Stormy Nights. Mike obliged and they decided to have a quick bite.

Mike's preference was ***Wasabi by Morimoto***, the Japanese restaurant, and he led them towards it. The ***sushi*** counter and the ***teppanyaki*** kitchen were attractions for all the guests. They were given an intimate private experience of the restaurant with a personal chef and exclusive preparations.

A tall, dark and handsome waiter attended to them. Mike, being friendly as usual, asked him, "Hi! What is your name?"

"Sir, I am Thomas Kurian, senior waiter at this restaurant. It is a pleasure and privilege to attend to your group. We understand that there is a felicitation for Mr. Shiv, the new world hero, today."

For the next half hour, Thomas Kurian served them various exotic Japanese delicacies. Shiv and Mike enjoyed the service and the food immensely.

An euphoric Mike asked Thomas Kurian, "Thanks Thomas, we were thoroughly delighted. We would like to give you something as a memento. What would you like?"

"Sir, your pleasure is our privilege. I do not need anything other than the guest's happiness."

Noticing that the guest was interested in hearing more, Thomas continued, "Actually my daughter's marriage has been scheduled for the day after. I overlooked it and came in today just to greet the hero Shiv, who is the pride of the planet. I am very glad that I had the opportunity to serve all of you today. Tomorrow morning I will have to go off duty to organise my daughter's wedding."

Shiv looked at his watch again. It was already 7:30 p.m. Shiv suggested that they go straight to the ballroom where his function was to be held. They reached the ballroom, which was all set for the event. A young banquet manager, wearing a badge with the name "Mallika," was attending to the details. Kanwar introduced her to the guests and said, "When Mallika handles the event, I can be sure that it is in safe hands and I have nothing to worry about."

Shiv tested the acoustic systems and found the arrangements to be perfect. He was now on project operation mode and gave orders to everyone. "Mike it is 8 p.m. Let us refresh ourselves and come back at 9:15, well before the event begins. Once again, thank you very much, Kanwar and Kishore. We will see you later."

Kanwar said, "Sir, I have a conference at 9 p.m. at another Tata property. I will be a little late in joining you for the function." They bade their goodbyes and departed from the ballroom.

On the way back to their room, in the elevator, Mike bumped into an old acquaintance, Zane Henry, a security specialist from South Africa.

"Hi Zane! What a pleasant surprise. How come you are here? Do you remember our 12 hour flight from London to San Francisco last year? It is a pleasure to see you again today. We all can sleep well knowing that a top security expert is staying with us in the hotel. After all, you are known to handle several security assignments and protect Hollywood's stars."

Zane laughed and said, "Mike, It is my pleasure to meet you too. I am here to offer security cover for the cricket stars participating in the champions' league scheduled to take place this week. And let me tell you that we are not comforting you anymore. It is your boss and your team at NASA who saved the planet from cyber terrorists after all!"

Meanwhile, the elevator had reached the sixth floor. Little did they all know that every one of them would be saving more people on this very day!

At 9:15 p.m., Shiv and Mike reached the ballroom. The festive atmosphere had already set in. They could see the technology at its best in the room: state-of-the-art A/V systems waiting to commence at the click of a button. The digital banners, the high-tech podium and the exquisitely decorated stage were clearly indicative of the festive tone. The graceful arches, scalloped pillars and crystal chandeliers gave the banquet hall an air of regal elegance.

"Felicitation to the Cyber Hero!" declared the digital banners. The guests had started taking their seats. A number of European parliamentarians, who were at the Taj hotel for an International Trade Delegation, were also present. British Conservative Members of the European Parliament, Social Democrat MEPs, Spanish MEPs, Polish MEPs, Hungarian MEPs, Indian MPs from Kerala, a few of the top executives of the Hindustan Unilever Company and many other captains of corporate India were already among the guests.The US ambassador to India and the Indian Ambassador to the US were the chief guests.

Kishore Rathod gave a quick welcome address. While welcoming the dignitaries, he paid tributes to Shiv and his "Operation cyber cleaning." Hackers from a rogue state had obtained access to satellite controls and had been on the verge of damaging various satellites and manipulating transmissions. Landsat 7, jointly managed by NASA and the US geological survey, had been their first targets.

The cyber-terrorists planned to take control of the satellites, corrupt the information flow and plant viruses across networks. This could have disrupted air traffic systems, interfered with the control systems for water and electricity, blocked and falsified commercial communications, crashed various network systems, accessed military information and defaced various websites. Further, it could have completely disrupted the energy systems, emergency services, telecommunication, banking and finance, transportation and water systems. The world would have faced a chaotic situation.

NASA deployed the CMG crisis management group, headed by the young 28-year-old captain, "Shivshankar Narayan," who skilfully defused the crisis with his extraordinary god-gifted software brain. We are proud to honour Shiv in this event today. We request the chief guests, His Excellency the US ambassador to India to give away the golden plate with carvings that read "Cyber Freedom" to Mr Shiv."

As Shiv walked up to the podium to collect his award, all 250 special guests gave him a standing ovation. There was a video clipping of US President George Bush and India's Prime Minister Dr. Manmohan Singh offering their appreciations and hearty congratulations to Shiv as well.

Shiv looked at his watch once again. It was 10:15. He took a deep breath and rose to deliver his speech. "At the outset, let me thank you all for honouring me with this award." After more clapping, he continued. "Let me tell you something. One might think that in the 21st century, people are sitting on a summit of happiness and are much happier than all their predecessors in human history. People of today have high income levels, high life expectancy and reduced infant mortality, but the reality is different…."

At that moment, there were violent sounds of explosions outside the banquet hall. There was a whisper among the audience. They all thought it was the sound of the crackers from a wedding procession. As the sound subsided, everyone focused their attention back on the speaker and Shiv continued.

"Unfortunately, there is a flip side to today's society. While our planet can produce food for everyone, 800 million people continue to remain malnourished. Life expectancy has increased globally, but HIV/AIDS is wreaking chaos in Africa, India and China.

"The world's capacity to produce increases, but only at the cost of the environment. Agriculture is putting pressure on water supplies, fish stocks and forests. There is still a portion of the world that has never used telephone or television. This has caused a gap, as some parts of the planet are oblivious to vital information that affects their self-interest. Such a divide has aided a new breed of terrorism…"

While he was talking, two men entered the room and there was a sudden indiscriminate shooting and flurry of bullets from the AK-47 rifles they carried. Pandemonium broke out. Shiv ducked under the podium to escape the gunshots. When the bullets were being splashed all around the room, Mallika, the banquet manager, ran to the switch board and turned off the lights. The room was in complete darkness for ten long minutes. A flood of bullets and confusing noises followed. After that there was pin drop silence.

The shocked and petrified crowd slowly realised that the two terrorists had left the hall. The banquet manager mustered courage and switched on the lights for a minute. My God, what a scene it was! Shiv could see 30-odd bullet-riddled bodies. He could hardly recognise the bloody faces on the floor.

He closed his eyes when he saw the body of Kishore Rathod, who lay dead near the stage. It was a vision of horror. The next thought that came to Shiv's mind was one of Mike. A chill ran down his spine and he called out in a low, whispering voice, "Mikeeey...." Mike slowly came out from behind the podium, where he had been hiding. Shiv breathed a sigh of relief on seeing that his friend was safe.

The banquet manager was trying to calm the guests and telling them to lie low on the floor. She advised the families to split up and take positions at different places to minimise the risks of entire families being shot.

Before the lights were turned off again, Shiv asked Mike to go to the lobby along with the Black Cat security commandos who had been shielding the ambassadors. Commandos manning other areas in the hotel passed on the information that it was safe to evacuate the ambassadors through the lobby. As they were about to leave to the lobby, Shiv instructed Mike –

"You stay hidden in the lobby, as we have to operate from different places. Listen Mikey, we are used to handling crisis situations. Cyber terrorism was easy to handle, but this is physical terrorism. Keep your instrument with you. Stay in regular touch with me. It looks like it is going to be a long night. The gunmen may turn off the electricity. But we will be able to operate, intercept, view the television through our instrument. Good luck and stay safe."

For the first time, Shiv saw a very serious and alarmed look on Mike's face. Mike blurted out, "Yes boss, I'll keep moving. I'll reach the lobby along with the Z-security commandos and the ambassadors. You take care."

Soon after their exit, Mallika ran to the door, bolted it and turned off the lights again. The group stayed there all night, listening to terrorists rampaging through the hotel, hurling grenades, firing automatic weapons and tearing the place apart. Shiv noticed that even at this hour of crisis, the banquet manager stepped out of the hall into the kitchen and got the right wine glasses for the guests.

He used his instrument to access the news. He tuned into NDTV and silently watched a live report..

Breaking News from Mumbai -

At 4 p.m. yesterday evening, a trawler approached the shores of Mumbai. The leader of the crew, apparently from Pakistan, contacted his handlers. When darkness set in, the men killed the captain of the trawler and boarded a dinghy with an engine that investigators now report bore marks from a Lahore-based importing company.

The men reached Mumbai at about 8:30 p.m. and split up into five teams of two each and set upon their targets: **Chhatrapati Shivaji** Terminus, the city's main train terminus, and several other sites in Mumbai. India's financial capital was hit on a Wednesday night by a wave of terror attacks, reportedly aimed at Americans and Britons. These attacks have left dozens dead and potentially hundreds injured, as Indian forces battle with terrorist gunmen to free hostages from two luxury hotels. Several staff members were killed at the Taj Mahal hotel and gunfire continues to erupt at the site as part of an ongoing hostage situation. It is reported that there could still be three or four terrorists inside the hotel.

Gunmen have reportedly taken hostages elsewhere in the city, including the Oberoi hotel and a hospital. The exact status of those locations is not completely known.

Casualty figures vary with the Associated Press reporting at least 82 dead. Reuters report 86 dead including 11 police officers, and 250 people are injured. The Associated Press quoted a senior police official who said that the Chief of Mumbai Antiterrorist Squad was one of those declared dead. It is still not clear what motivated the attacks of the terrorist group, which has also targeted a popular restaurant. Eyewitnesses say the gunmen mainly sought American and British passport holders.

Mumbai has frequently been targeted in terrorist attacks blamed on religious extremists, including a series of bombings in July 2007 that killed 187 people. A terrorist organisation claimed it was behind those attacks. Some analysts suggest that the little-known group is actually an amalgam of existing Indian terror groups. The terrorists, in this latest attack, have used automatic weapons and in some places grenades, Maharashtra police Commissioner B. N. Shenoy said.

The White House has condemned the attacks. "President Bush offers his condolences to the Indian people and the families of the innocent civilians killed and injured in the Mumbai attacks. He will continue to stand with the people of India in this time of tragedy," press secretary Dana Perino said in a written statement. "The US government continues to monitor the situation including the safety and security of our citizens and stands ready to assist and support the Indian government."

Shiv realised that the matter was much more serious than he had believed. He called Mike on his instrument and asked him what was happening in the hotel lobby. Mike whispered into his instrument.

"Boss, the situation here is alarming. The terrorists burst into the lobby shooting at everything that moved. I can see more than 20 bullet-riddled bodies lying all over the lobby floor. I just watched Zakir, a reporter at CNN, reporting important information about this attack." He transmitted the news recording to Shiv.

"The first events were detailed around 20:00 hours Indian Standard Time last night when ten Urdu speaking men in inflatable speedboats stepped onto Indian shores at two locations in ***Colaba***. They reportedly split up and headed in different directions. The ***Chhatrapati Shivaji*** Terminus (CST) was attacked by two of these gunmen. One of them was later caught alive by the police after being identified by eyewitnesses.

"The attacks began at close to 9:30 p.m. The two men entered the passenger hall and opened fire, using AK-47 rifles. In the 15-minute assault that followed, the attackers killed 58 people and injured 104 others. The two gunmen fled the scene and fired at pedestrians and police officers on the streets, killing eight officers.

"The terrorists then headed towards Cama hospital and attempted to enter the patient ward, but the hospital staff managed to lock them down. When the local police arrived, they threw grenades and shot an officer before fleeing. A Mumbai Antiterrorist Squad led by police chief Hemant Wagle searched CST and then headed out in pursuit of the terrorists who opened fire on the pursuing vehicle.

"Chief Officer Wagle and four other officers were killed and the only survivor was wounded. The terrorists ran into a police roadblock. A wounded police officer radioed for help. This lead to a gun battle, in which one terrorist was killed and another was wounded and arrested.

"The Leopold Café was one of the first sites to be attacked in which at least 10 people were killed. There were two explosions in taxis caused by time bombs, one at ***Vile Parle***, killing the driver and a passenger and another at ***Wadi Bunder***, killing three people and injuring 15 others.

"Two hotels, the Taj Mahal Palace and the Oberoi Trident, were among the four locations targeted. Explosions were reported at the Taj Hotel and at the Oberoi Trident."

When the CNN news transmission from Mike ended, Shiv said, "Mike, the terrorists seem to have a bag in front of them and their fingers on the phone at all times. My instinct is that they are receiving instructions from elsewhere. We should intercept their lines. Do you have any idea how many of them are there?"

"No boss, I am not sure. But I will intercept their lines."

While Mike was trying to intercept their lines, Shiv found another news report from NDTV. He spoke into his device, "Mike listen to this reporting by Krish Shrinivas from NDTV. We may get more clues from this."

Krish Shrinivas reporting from NDTV...

"Blood smeared the floor of ***Chhatrapati Shivaji*** rail station, where attackers sprayed bullets into the crowded terminal. Press Trust of India quoted the Chief of the Mumbai railway police, KK Varun, who said that several men armed with rifles and grenades were holed up at the station. Other gunmen attacked Leopold restaurant and the police headquarters in southern Mumbai.

"The restaurant was riddled with bullet holes and there was blood on the floor and shoes left by fleeing customers. Officials also reported attacks at **Cama & Albless** hospital and GT Hospital.

"A British citizen who was dining at the Oberoi hotel told Sky News that the gunmen singled out Britons and Americans. Another tourist said, 'The gunman, a young man of 22 or 23, ushered 30 to 40 people from the restaurant into a stairway and ordered everyone to raise their hands. The gunmen spoke in either Hindi or Urdu. They were specifically talking about Britishers and Americans. There was an Italian guy, who, you know, they asked "Where are you from?" and he answered he was from Italy and they left him alone and I thought: "Fine, they're going to shoot me next if they asked me anything. But, thank God they didn't."' He said he managed to slip away as the patrons were forced to walk upstairs. But he thought much of the group was still being held hostage.

"The British foreign office said it was advising all British citizens in Mumbai to stay indoors. Britain's Foreign Secretary David Milliband strongly condemned the attacks. 'Today's attacks in Mumbai, which have claimed many innocent victims, remind us yet again of the threat we face from violent extremists,' Milliband said in a statement.

"Since May, a militant group has taken credit for a string of blasts that have killed more than 130 people. The most recent attack was in September, when a series of explosions erupted in a park and crowded shopping areas in New Delhi, killing 21 people and wounding about a 100 more. We will update you more as and when we receive new information" the NDTV reporter concluded.

Shiv switched to the communication mode and said, "Mike, did you gather any clues from this?"

"Boss, we do not know the exact number of terrorists at Taj from these reports. We do not know their staying power yet. I have gotten hold of their telephone intercepts. Let me transmit this to you. I must say that the exchanges are extremely chilling."

A horror-struck Shiv listened to the intercepted calls. One of the leaders operating from an external location instructed the gunmen, "The hostages are useful only as long as you do not come under fire."

He added: "If you're still threatened, then don't saddle yourself with the burden of the hostages. Kill them immediately."

This was followed by a reply from one of the gunmen, "Yes, we shall do accordingly, God willing."

"The media is recording every single action. You must therefore inflict maximum damage. Keep fighting. Make sure that you are not caught alive."

Another instruction to a gunman inside the Taj Hotel said, "Throw one or two grenades at the Navy and police teams that are outside. Keep a minimum level of explosives and three grenades aside and spend the rest of your ammunition."

At one point, the councillors who were passing intermittent instructions over telephone to the gunmen enquired whether they had set the hotel on fire. One attacker said he was preparing to set the hotel ablaze.

Another gunman asked whether to spare the women in the hotel. In response to his question came the chilling reply, "No, don't spare anyone. If hostages from foreign countries are killed on Indian soil, it will desecrate relationships between India and the others. So, kill them all."

Shiv swallowed hard and spoke into the device.

"Mike, the sole purpose of this attack seems to be to create chaos. What I can interpret from their conversations is that they are few in number and are not working together at the same time. They keep moving in small groups; two or three of these groups should be inside our hotel. They seem to be keen on destroying the hotel at large. They may even set fire to this property. Do one thing, Mike. Try to locate the exit with the help of the hotel staff. Take as many hostages outside with you as possible. The terrorists are using the hostages as shields to protect themselves. We must try our best to minimise the killings and save as many hostages as we can."

A flustered Mike interrupted, "But Boss, what about you?"

"Stay calm Mikey, and move the hostages out. You must get out of this place with them. I will come later with the other guests who are with me in the Ballroom. Wait outside and if my plan goes well, I will join you."

Mike listened to him carefully. When Shiv had finished speaking, Mike looked around and spotted Zane Henry sitting under the reception desk and desperately trying to fix his walkie-talkie.

He crawled to Zane and whispered into his ears, "Hello Zane, this is such a nasty way to see you again. Anyway, there is no time left for you to try and gather radio signals on your walkie-talkie. We really need to do something quickly to save the guests."

"Mike, I have a few guards supporting me. Unfortunately, they are only armed with knives and meat cleavers. We have managed to barricade the doors to the conference centre from the lobby. We are now watching the lift Sachin Jha(DOB 25.12.71) is an engineer(IIT Delhi) by training. He runs a chemical manufacturing business in Rajasthan and is an avid reader. This is his second book (the first being 'It all adds up', which was published by Penguin).

s to see if the gunmen are coming our way. We have instructed the security manager of the hotel to tell the police not to shoot, as we are trying to stealthily walk everyone down the fire exit at the back of the hotel."

Mike spoke in a husky voice, just enough to be audible to the 200 guests in the lobby. "All of you, listen to me carefully. Try to drive the fear out of your minds and think about getting out of this place. If you remember in the 9/11 crisis in New York, it was only those who acted quickly and tried to get out of the building who are alive today. The rest who were scared to move ultimately died. So come and hurry up now. Mr. Zane here will be leading all of us through the back door."

Zane had spotted the exit door and signalled to everyone to follow him, one after the other. Mike stood at the other end of the lobby and kept a watch on the elevators while the guests moved out. Once they had all been ushered out, Zane screamed, "Mike, come out now, all of us are outside. Don't delay any longer."

Mike glanced around the empty lobby and decided to update Shiv. He tuned into his device and spoke. "Boss, we have moved everyone in the lobby to the outside through a hidden exit door. I am leaving too. I just came to know that the TV footage has now been banned from telecast, since the terrorists have also gained access to these live updates. You may not be able to watch any more footage of the attack. Take care and plan your escape soon. Hope to see you outside!"

Just as he said his goodbye, there was a gunshot. Shiv could hear Mike's screams blaring through his gadget. A few seconds later, a loud voice spoke: "***Kuthey, kaminey, tumhara aadmi mar gaya. Abhi tumhara instrument bhi marega. Abey gora***, watch me shoot your instrument in front of your eyes. Now, your man will never hear your voice again."

Boom! The sounds reverberated through the gadget at Shiv's end. Shiv understood that his closest friend had been shot dead. Tears rolled from from his eyes. He writhed in agony, hiding on the third floor, while his friend died in the lobby. "What an irony! The man who could save the world from cyber terrorism can do nothing in the face of physical terrorism!"

Shiv sat there listening to more sounds of gunshots. He looked at his watch and saw that it was now 3 in the morning. As he looked around, he saw the ***Wasabi*** restaurant's senior waiter, Thomas Kurian walking towards him.

"I think the only way out is to make a few sacrifices. My colleagues will form a human cordon around all of you. If a bullet is fired, it will hit us and we promise we will walk you through to the exit. Please do not worry about us; just stay with us as we form a human chain around all of you."

Thomas led them near a spiral staircase behind the makeshift stage. He told them that the staircase led outside the hotel. He sent the guests out one by one. While they were moving out, Shiv received information on his gadget from Twitter. Kanwar, the general manager, had taken charge of one of the hotel wings and was supervising the evacuation of the guests.

Meanwhile, Thomas Kurian called to Shiv, "Sir, please hurry up. We are the last left. Let us get out quickly, as there is no time left."

They ran down the spiral staircase and neared the exit. Boom! There was a series of gunshots; Thomas Kurian and Shiv were the last victims. The force of the gunshots had thrown them out of the open exit door. Shiv did not know what happened afterwards.

NDTV's Sarita Bhat reported live from Breach Candy Hospital, Mumbai. "We have breaking news. Mr. Shivshankar Narayan, the NASA scientist who destroyed the cyber terrorist network, was shot today alongside Taj Hotel's senior waiter Thomas Kurian. Mr. Kurian succumbed to his injuries, but Mr. Shiv has been admitted at Breach Candy Hospital with serious head wounds. The doctors are working to remove the bullets in his skull. We will keep you posted as and when we receive further information."

Breach Candy housed several victims of the terrorist attack. The grieving relatives and families were waiting to see their injured kith and kin.

Breaking news again, on another station. "Shiv, the cyber hero from NASA, was operated on a few hours ago. Doctors say that he has slipped into a state of coma. They say that his vital functions are fine but he is in a state of deep coma. He has suffered cerebral palsy, physical disability, stiff muscles and quadriplegia due to the severe impact of the gunshots on his head.

"Currently, he is being administered liquefied nutrition through tubes inserted into his body. He is said to be suffering clinical death. Doctors say that he may not come back to his normal senses for a very long time. They continue to keep him under medical observation in the ICU."

The domes of Taj were burning and a third of the staff had laid down their lives as a sacrifice to help the 1,200 guests escape. Two cyber-war heroes had suffered gruesome deaths. Mike Pedro lay dead at the back of the hotel lobby, while Shivshankar Narayan was lying in a state of unconsciousness, fighting death.

The heroes who had saved the planet from the cyber terrorists could not avoid succumbing to physical terrorism. Why? Why? Shiv's unconscious mind asked.

Memories from the time in coma were inexplicable. They were like a patchwork quilt, with no apparent sequence nor temporal relationship to one another. The purest and most extraordinary part of his journey commenced deep in his state of coma. In the midst of his coma, his cerebrum unleashed a quest to unravel his past. Then all of a sudden, everything opened up. His mind navigated its way into a valley, so crisp and beautiful.

He could see waterfalls, pools of water, and indescribable colours with arcs of silver and gold light and beautiful hymns emanating from them. Boom! Suddenly the serene image shifted into images of war, weapons and weeping widows. He saw himself on the mast of a tall ship, he saw himself in a missile silo, and he saw himself on the watchtower of a mammooth fort, guiding the cannons of a great warship. And then he saw images of himself swiftly move out of the earth and then out of the universe. He had lost awareness of his physical body. In the process of this deep search, his mind realized many of his previous states by breaking the shackles of all his earlier births.

His mind was filled with the chorus of a great army crying out the name Sagar, Sagar, Sagar….. He was lying on the battlefield as a wounded solider with deep cuts inflicted by sharp weapons. It was bloodbath all around.

He was holding his last breath, waiting for his beloved wife and newly born son. It was the land of the battle between the Kauravas and Pandavas, the land that was situated between the two rivers Sarasvati and Drishadvati, the land where Manu wrote his Manu-smriti and the land where the Rig and Sama vedas had been compiled.

"This battleground is not the land of my birth or my beloved kingdom," he thought. "This is not the place where I spent my joyful childhood. This is not the beautiful place I come from. I need to trace the origin of my birth."

His comatose mind continued to wander further into the past. It now flashed images of the spectacular city of his birth. The golden fort of the city threw its yellow glitter on the surrounding waters, making it look like flames rising from the riverbed. There was a township with six sectors along the banks of the river. It was connected to the mainland by floating bridges, which could be withdrawn whenever there was an attack from enemies. The floating bridges and the design of the city was truly a marvel.

Having identified his the city of his birth, he stumbled upon his colourful life in his first birth as "Sagar," the great warrior of the Kingdom of Krishna in 3083 BC!

*** ***

2. The Kingdom of Krishna

First, let me talk about my leader – the charismatic Lord Krishna. Though he is not the designated king of this kingdom, Krishna has always been the real ruler. The Yadav clan was the first modern democratic society. The Yadav clan is a federation of six tribes who elect their leader, but retain their old king Ugrasena as head of the state with no real powers. Lord Krishna is the elected leader who has actual control and he makes all the key decisions.

As a fighter, he is without rival, as a statesman most shrewd, as a social thinker very liberal, as a teacher the most eloquent, as a friend never failing and as a householder the most ideal. He is a grand mystery and everyone tries to understand him in their own way. The yogis consider him to be the absolute truth, the Gopis the highest object of love, the warriors the ideal hero, Kamsa an object of fear and Krishna's other nephew Sisupala an object of hate. Is he a human or a divine god? To me, he is a fascinating hero.

Moving on, let me also tell you about Dwarka, my beloved city.

Dwarka is a federation of many republics rather than a kingdom ruled by a single king. The federation of Dwarka includes the states of ***Andhakas, Vrishnis*** and the ***Bhojas***. ***Dwarka*** was founded by a clan of *Yadu* chiefs who fled from the *Surasena* kingdom because of their fear of King Jarasandha, the king of *Mahada. Jarasandha* wanted to avenge himself on the *Yadavas*, who had killed his son-in-law Kamsa. The territory of Dwarka also includes the Dwarka Island, seven neighboring islands including Antar Dwipa and the mainland area of the neighboring *Anarta* kingdom.

Many prominent Yadava chiefs, including Vasudev Krishna, Balaram, Satyaki, Kritravarma, Uddhava and Akrura under the king Ugrasena, live in Dwarka. There are other kingdoms in west central Bharat including Surasena (Mathura district in Uttar Pradesh, also known as Vraja), Dasarna (south to Chedi Kingdom), Gurjara (southern Rajastan), Heheya (Narmada valley around the city Maheshwar in Madhya Pradesh), Saurashtra (southern Gujarat) and Vidarba (north-eastern Maharashtra) among 150 others spread across ***Bharatvarsha***.

You might wonder what is so great about the city of Dwarka. The name Dwarka means a gateway. It is also known as a multi-gated city. It is situated at the western point of ***Bharatavarsha*** and faces the sea. It is the land of *Ekalavya*, who considered *Dhronacharya* to be his ***manasa guru***. Having faced the attack of King *Jarasandha*, the native ***yadavas*** fled Mathura and arrived at the coast of *Saurashtra*.

However, Lord Krishna was not one to run away from the battlefield. It was his audacious retreat that changed the fate of his clan. Under Lord Krishna's leadership, they decided to build their capital on the coast and invoke Lord Vishwakarma, the deity of construction. Lord Vishwakarma materialized in front of them, only to tell them that the task could be completed only if the Lord of the sea provided the land for construction. Shri Krishna intently worshipped the Sea Lord, who was pleased with his prayers and offered his clan the reclaimed land measuring ***12 yojans***. With Lord Vishwakarma's blessings, the *Yadavas* built Dwarka, the city of gold.

This geographical marvel is situated at a point where River Gomti meets the ***Sindh Sagar*** (Arabian Sea). This fertile land is known as the gateway to eternal happiness. It is also the western gateway of Bharath, through which trade enters the country and hence continues to be known for its wealth and prosperity.

It does not end here; Dwarka has many more wonders. The most expensive, luxurious materials have been used in the city's construction. It is quite common to use precious stones, gold and silver as construction materials. Royalty and rich nobles invariably use gold; those who cannot afford it use silver or metal.

However, *Dwarka* is a rare city of rose and gold. The palaces and many of the mansions are built of gold, over which pink lotus domes tower, topped by soaring golden spires. The floors are made of emeralds. Precious stones stud the walls and crystal arches cruve overhead, inlaid with gold. The houses are beautifully decorated and sculptures adorn the walls. Even the cowsheds are made of silver, brass and iron. *Dwarka* is a very well planned city that has clearly followed the highly developed science of town planning.

Interestingly enough, *Vishwakarma* first mapped out all the highways, lanes, gates and parks. He sectioned off the plots and divided the city into six zones, residential and commercial. He planned the port and created the bridges, gateways and the fortifications. Everything was laid out in detail before the construction began. Today, his foresight has fructified into a large, well fortified city with an excellent drainage system and massive gates. The city stretches over about 180 miles.

Dwarka is decorated with 900,000 extraordinary mansions built of first-class marble, with gates and doors made of silver and jewels. The residents of these mansions are all pure devotees of our beloved leader, Krishna. Another element that adds beauty to this city is its innumerable gardens and parks that display a variety of rare flowers. Fruit, flowering trees and shade-giving trees line the roads and fragrance from the flowers gives the city an everlasting perfume.

The city's lakes and ponds are abundantly decorated with lotuses, while the fountains and waterfalls delight the eye. Even the heavenly ***parijaat*** trees have been planted in abundance. Beautiful chirping birds, intoxicating peacocks and ponds filled with lilies and lotuses delight the senses. The residents decorate every lane and sidewalk with water pots, banana trees and fragrant flowers.

The safety element that has been included in the city's planning is commendable. The fortifications of Dwarka make it hard to attack. Two lines of massive fort walls built from huge stone blocks run all around the city and the surrounding sea serves as a natural moat. The island is cut off from the mainland and can only be reached by boat. Several floating bridges connecting the island to the mainland can be withdrawn in case of attack. The walls are furnished with watch towers and machines to fling fire, inflammable liquids and missiles. The structure and location of the city makes it almost inaccessible to its enemies.

I must also add that Dwarka is the epitome of cleanliness. When Lord Krishna returns to Dwarka, women stand on the top floors of mansions and drop rose petals and lotus garlands on the procession below. The roads are a festive sight filled with music and dancing. The citizens of this kingdom of Krishna enjoy eternal joy and happiness.

Another interesting aspect of the city is that it has a passport system. The citizens are issued with a clay seal which has to be presented when they enter or leave its massive gates. The seal of Dwarka is a mythical three headed dog. This system ensures that adequate protection is given to their citizens from attacks.

Yet, in spite of all this, Dwarka has been attacked many times. Unable to attack from land and sea, aerial attack has been used on Dwarka. King Salwa, agitated by Krishna's nephew Sisupala's death, used an air chariot that could fly at great speeds and at such high altitudes that it was not visible to the human eye. He destroyed the city from the sky and took the defenders by surprise.

Lord Krishna had to use unique weapons to destroy Salwa and his air chariot. It was a rare attack on the city of Dwarka, which is otherwise always alert. It is a city that never sleeps. Since then, the aerial attacks have also been factored into our safety mechanisms.

In this beautiful Kingdom of Krishna, I was born in dramatic circumstances.

*** ***

3. The Birth of the Trio

It was the ***Maagha*** month of the Vyaya year. It was an Amavasya, new moon day. On this day, the priests and their wards perform religious rites for their ancestors. The rites were performed at the extreme western tip of Kathiawar peninsula, where the serene river Gomati meets the Sindhu Sagar.

On this day, one could take in the breathtaking sight of more than 500 people bathing in the confluence of Gomati and the mighty sea. It was a day marked by the gods for religious rituals.The sounds of the waves were dwarfed by the sacred sound of the hymns, as prayers were offered for the departed souls of the ancestors of those gathered.

Suddenly, the crowd collectively chanted "***Amavasya Punyakala Snanam Karishye***!" and took a dip in the flowing water. Priest Bharadwaj was one among them. After his holy dip, he emerged from the water with open hands. When he looked down, he was astonished to see a small child in his palms. He realized that it was a new born baby…one that had entered this world less than a few hours ago! Bharadwaj immediately walked to the shore and stopped his chants. Thirty of his wards also stopped their chanting and walked out of the water. They reached the shore and stared in surprise at the baby.

A few metres away, a crowd had gathered around an unconscious couple who had been swept away by the waves. The priest bent over them and saw that they had consumed too much water. He handed the baby to a person standing nearby and along with some of his wards, tried to pump the water from their bodies.

Within a few minutes, the unconscious man opened his eyes and looked around. He looked like he was no more than 35 years old. Noticing that the man was in a state of shock, Priest Bharadwaj calmed him down. He said, "Gentleman, what is your name? Calm down first, we are all here to help you. I am Bharadwaj, a priest in the Kingdom of Shri Krishna."

The man looked at Bharadwaj and noticed a ***Brahmanic*** look on his face that exuded spirituality and tranquility. The priest looked like someone in his mid thirties. A tuft of hair at the back of his head was clearly visible. He wore a sacred thread across his shoulders and was dressed in an eight yard ***dhoti*** with a wet towel on his hip. One look at him and anyone could easily tell that he was a priest.

The man slowly got up and turned to the priest with folded hands. '*Panditji*, I am grateful to you. The newborn baby in your hands is our son.'

Pointing at the unconscious woman lying near him, he said, 'My wife, Yamini, is yet to regain consciousness. She was heavily pregnant and must have delivered the child in the last few hours in the deep sea.'

As the shocked crowd looked on, Bharadwaj spoke. 'What? Do you mean the baby was born in the middle of the sea? What is your name? Where are you coming from? It is quite unusual for us to welcome a guest from the sea into the kingdom of Dwarka. Who are you?'

The man answered the questions, his head bent in shame. '*Panditji*, my name is Matsya Rajan. I am a ***Sudhputra***. I hail from the fishing community. My journey through the high seas is a long story. We are part of a deprived society. We are sinners.'

Priest Bharadwaj interjected, 'In the eyes of the Almighty, no one is classified as low or high. However, society might have put us in separate ranks in the name of caste. Come on, get up and have some water. Don't be afraid. We are all here to support you. Tell me more about what happened, Matsya.'

After regaining some strength, Matsya looked at his wife. He looked back at Bharadwaj and said, 'Panditji, you are so kind. Let me tell you my tale of sorrow. We belong to Antar Dwipa, the neighboring island of Dwarka. We hail from a very poor community. I head a group of 500 fishermen on my island. From time to time, we borrow money from the famous usurer Dhana Vysya. We live at the mercy of the sea. The ***varsha ritu*** (monsoon) affects our livelihood. We borrow to make our ends meet during the lean seasons. But we could not pay our loan on time and the loan shark instructed his men to throw us all out of our colony, while he confiscated our land and houses.

'With all our possessions taken and nowhere to go, my community got into our ***Katamarans*** and moved into the sea last night. We did not know where to go and decided to follow the direction of the wind with the hope of reaching land. It being an ***Amavasya*** day, the tidal waves were at their peak. Sadly, the peak of my bad fortune came during my wife's advanced stage of pregnancy. Looking at our ill-fortune, she was extremely upset. While travelling the high seas, she vocalized her feelings and asked me – "Why do we need this child? Are our current sufferings not enough? Why should our child also suffer?" I had no idea that these would be her final words to me, as she jumped into the sea to kill herself.

'At that instant, our katamaran also rammed into a big ship. There was a loud noise. I was shocked and didn't know what to do, but to jump in to the sea after her in an attempt to save her. This happened in the early hours. My fellow fishermen who had been following us in separate boats lost track of us and might have proceeded to the next island.

'Once I plunged into the sea, I did not know what happened. Now I realize that Yamini might have given birth to this child in the deep sea. We landed in an unconscious state on the shores of Dwarka. This is our story.'

After recounting his story, Matsya made an emotional appeal to Bharadwaj. Bharadwaj could not refuse him, but both of them did not know the enormity of the consequences this action would bring.

Meanwhile, his wife slowly opened her eyes.. With tears in his eyes, Matsya told her, 'Yamini, you have given birth to our son. The boy is safe in the hands of this priest. The sea has brought us to Dwarka, the kingdom of Krishna.'

Bharadwaj helped them to their feet. As the crowd thinned, the newborn was shown to his parents, whose joy was beyond description. Their treasure of pleasure was beyond measure!

Coming back from seventh heaven to reality, Matsya said, "*Panditji*, you are so kind. The birth of the boy is good news. My wife did not end her life in haste. God saved us and this means he has something waiting for us. But the reality scares me. Where can we go? What can we do for our food and living? I do not know anything other than fishing.'

Bharadwaj intervened. 'Do not worry. When you are in the kingdom of Krishna, everything will be taken care of by Krishna. Let me take you to my home.'

Walking home with the new parents and their son, the priest said, 'Your son was born at sunrise on an ***Amavasya*** day in the ***Mrigashirsha*** star. He was born amidst the tidal waves of the sea and the oscillatory mental waves of your wife. Matysa, a calm sea never brings out the best mariner. Nothing worthwhile comes without a struggle. Your son was born amidst chaos. I can tell you without looking at his birth chart that he will show courage in crisis and humility in success. My intuition tells me that he will be a great strategist warrior – don't worry Matsya. He will conquer many seas, as he is a ***samudra putra.*** He will be extraordinarily proficient in matters related to the sea. Cheer up, Matsya.'

A comforted Matsya replied, '***Panditji***, you do not even know us properly. You have volunteered to take us with you. The glow in your eyes and look of tranquility on your face tell me that you are a true Brahmin. But how did you believe every word I said without even questioning me? I am perplexed by your limitless kindness.'

'Matsya, do not elevate me to the status of God. I am an ordinary man like you. I am a priest in the ***Samudhra Narayana*** temple in this land. Matysa, the Vedas say that man lives individually, but he survives collectively. I not only preach the Vedas, I also make it a point to practice them. First, let us reach home and then we will plan what to do next. The newborn baby needs some urgent care. Let us move quickly now.'

They reached the priest's small house near the Samudhra Narayana temple. The temple management had allotted this house to the priest and his family.

Bharadwaj had been married to Shakuntala for twenty years. Unfortunately, they had not been blessed with children. His wife's unmarried sisters Shyamala and Sharmila also lived with them. Apart from being a priest at the Samudhra Narayana temple, the Brahmin was also a well respected Vedic scholar and followed a service approach to everything that he did. He was known to speak very calmly and no one had ever seen him raise his voice, even in stressful situations.

He lived a life of attachment with detachment. He periodically visited orphanages and tutored poor children. Money, fame, name and accumulation of material possessions by others did not bother him. He treated prosperity and adversity alike. Many people had heard him say that unhappiness is only an interval between two happy events and vice-versa. He always insisted that joy and sorrow are cycles like day and night and we should learn to accept them as they unfold.

As they approached his home, his wife greeted him. 'Today you have come with some guests. Who are these people? Did you finish your holy bath in the Gomati River?'

'Shakuntala, you are right. Today I have brought three new guests, including this newborn child.'

He looked at the adoring look on her face and said, 'I know you are fond of children, even though we are not blessed with any.'

'What a lovely child. Let me invite them to our home.'

But she quickly took one step backwards and said, 'They are not Brahmins, are they?'

'Shakuntala, I told you to look at the guest first and not their caste. First, invite them into our house and give them something to eat. The child needs to be fed by the mother. Facilitate that first, before shooting your questions at me.'

Turning around to Matsya, Bharadwaj said, 'We have a small outhouse meant to be a cowshed. We have no cows now, as we receive milk from the temple. You can stay in the cowshed for the time being. As far as your livelihood is concerned, I will take you to the fisherman street tomorrow. You can practice your profession with them, catch fish and sell them at the ***Mandi***, or you can teach the children at the ***Gurukul*** the art of swimming in the sea. But before that, I have to make arrangements to get you an identification seal.

'Meanwhile, take rest for the day. We will make sure you are fed well. My wife will provide milk for the newborn. She bought a cradle for the child we never had. She will give you all of it for your son. Make your stay comfortable as our ***atithi***. Once we make your identification seal, we will think about your other issues.'

'We have no words to thank you for your kind gesture. This is a second life you have given us. We will go and freshen up and come back later.'

'Matsya, shed your inhibitions, and treat this as your home. The outhouse is yours till we find you something else. Be ready in the next few hours, I have to take you to the Dwarka Administrative office for your ***Mudhra***.'

As Bharadwaj was about to step outside for his morning prayers, he heard the sounds of horses outside his house. He wondered which royal family member was crossing this poor man's street in the morning. To his surprise, he saw some of the horsemen alight right outside his home and walk towards him. His wife whispered, 'Some palace members are coming in. I do not know what mistake we have committed. I am afraid.'

'Shakuntala, you are always worrying too much. The position of the moon in the twelfth house in your birth chart is your biggest weakness. You get perturbed and tense for everything. Come, let us see what this is all about.'

'Ji, you always brush me aside by quoting my astrological dispositions. But I am really afraid of the royal family.'

Meanwhile, three men wearing royal attire stepped into Bharadwaj's small home. '***Pandit Ji, Namaskar***.... I am Krita Verma from the Palace of Shri Krishna. We have come with good news. Early this morning, King Arjuna was blessed with a boy. As per custom, we want to have the naming function on the thirtieth day from the day of the birth. We want to hold this function at the ***Samudra Narayana Temple*** with your Vedic recital. We request you to conduct the naming ceremony in the temple. Please accept the fruits, flowers and the gifts from the palace.'

At that very moment, a thought crossed the priest's mind. Today, at around the same hour, yet another boy had been born in the sea under miraculous circumstances. Both the boys were born in the same star on the same day. Quickly, his mind came back to the present and he realized that the Royal Palace was honouring him by requesting his services.

He said, 'It is a great honor to be informed that a new prince has arrived in the royal palace. We will carry out the naming function and pray to the Almighty to bless the child. Please convey our ***Pranams*** to his Majesty Shri Krishna and Balarama. We are poor Brahmins. Having a Royal guest in our home is a great blessing.'

Krita Verma intervened. '***Panditji***, we may fight wars on the battlefield. But it is people like you who teach us how to fight the greatest wars in the silent chambers of our soul. Our physical battle is relatively easier than the battle of the minds. You are a Vedic pandit. We worship you just as we worship the holy cow. Moreover, ego is an anesthesia (***Nizvetana***) that deadens the pain of stupidity. Showing respect to a Vedic Brahmin like you serves as an ego-buster for us and puts us on the right path of dharma. It is our honor to invite you.'

As they took their leave, Bharadwaj addressed his wife. 'I told you, your fear has no basis. Learn to think of positive outcomes. Don't speculate on negative scenarios. Now, please understand that I am not using any astrological jargons, I am only trying to clear your mind.'

As they were talking, once again they heard the noise of voices outside their house. 'Ji, I am worried again. More people are coming. They also look like wealthy and influential people. What a day this is turning out to be!' shouted Shakuntala as she peeped from the window.

A smiling Bharadwaj said, 'Yet again, my doubting queen, you have started speculating and conjuring up confused, adverse scenarios. Stay calm, Shakuntala. Let us first receive them.'

Four well dressed men came in. '***Priest-ji***, we come from the house of Dhana Vaisya,' they said.

Suddenly a spark hit Bharadwaj's brain. 'I have heard this name Dhana Vaisya somewhere. Where did I hear it?' he asked himself.

‘Ji, our head is the President of ***Vani vaishya*** community.’

The priest smiled and said, ‘Oh, he is a ***Vani*** and lends money. Now, please tell me what I can do for you?’

‘Ji, our community head has had a baby boy this morning. He wants to have the naming ceremony done at the ***Samudhra Narayana*** Temple on the thirtieth day from today. He sent us to invite you to conduct the function at the temple. Please accept the gifts sent by our community head.’

Now Bharadwaj’s mind set to work again. Oh, this third new father was the same man who had evicted Matsya from his home. He did not want to share any knowledge that he had on Dhana Vaisya with these guests. He agreed to conduct the naming ceremony and upon his consent the guests took their leave.

‘Three boys came into the kingdom of Krishna on the same day and at the same time. What a coincidence! All three boys will have very similar birth charts,’ he thought.

‘It is getting late ji, please have your lunch.’ Shakuntala’s voice brought him back from his thoughts.

‘Have our guests had their food?’ Bharadwaj asked.

‘They had their food. I sent food to the outhouse.’

‘Where are Shymala and Sharmila?’

‘They have gone out.’

Bharadwaj finished his food. Suddenly, the identification seal issue crossed his mind and he said, ‘Shakuntala, I have to go with Matsya to the downtown Dwarka Royal Administrative Office.’ Saying this, he spotted Matsya and both of them proceeded towards the Royal Administrative Office.

On entering the office, he walked straight to the concerned ***Adhikari*** in-charge of the citizen identification seal and said, ‘***Namaskar*** Ji, I have come here to get an identification seal for my guest Matsya.’

The ***Adhikari*** looked up and asked, ‘Is it a guest seal or a citizen seal that you want?’

‘It is the citizen seal. He was earlier a resident of Anarta Dwipa Island which comes within our federation.’

‘Do you have any proof of the seal of Anarta Dwipa Island? When did he come to Dwarka?’ the ***Adhikari*** asked him.

‘Ji, he came this morning.’ Bharadwaj did not want to explain the circumstances under which Matsya had come to Dwarka. Instead he simply said, ‘Matysa lost his seal and other identification documents on his island, where he lost his home and belongings. Therefore, he now has no proof of his seal.'

The ***Adhikari*** was unconvinced and said in an angry tone, 'Look here, Panditji, what is your name you said? Bharadwaj? With no past track record or past identification seal, we cannot give your guest a new citizen identification seal. Your request is rejected. As per the laws of this kingdom, anyone without an identification seal has to vacate this kingdom within a day. Therefore, your guest has to leave before sunset today.'

Bharadwaj and Matsya were confused. With tears in his eyes, Matysa asked Bharadwaj, 'What do we do now? How do we vacate this kingdom before sunset? We should have lost our lives in the sea. Our bad luck continues… Why do we have to live like this, ji? You said the kingdom of Krishna will not deprive us of our right to life. But, with this ***Adhikari***'s new order, where do we go now?'

They looked at each other and the priest prayed to God to come to their rescue. As if to answer his prayers, God sent a miracle man to save them. Outside the Administrative office building, their eyes witnessed the miracle man.

*** ***

4. The Voyage Disaster

As the dejected Bharadwaj walked out of the Royal Administrative Office along with Matsya, a powerful voice called out his name. 'Panditji, ***Namaskar***... How are you?'

Bharadwaj turned and came face to face with a tall youth dressed in royal attire. The man had the deep eyes of a visionary. He smiled and said, 'I am Sahadeva, the youngest of the Pandavas. I came to the ***Samudhra Narayana*** temple and met you at the time of ***dharshan*** of Shri. Narayana.' When he saw the confused expression on the priest's face, the young man's smile widened. '***Panditji***, you have already forgotten me!'

Bharadwaj was pleasantly surprised. Goosepimples erupted all over his body. What a great moment this was. His strong astrological inclinations attracted him to Sahadeva, who was another well known astrological wizard.

'Your highness, meeting you is such a great encounter for me. I am always fascinated by the extent of your astrological knowledge and your conquest of the entire ***dakshin*** (south) ***Bharath***. You are a rare warrior with astronomical and astrological knowledge – an extraordinary combination. It is truly a blessing to meet a member of the royal family.'

Sahadev gladly accepted the praises and said, 'Thank you for your kind words. But what has happened to you? You seem to be in considerable dejection. What is the matter?'

'Your Highness, this gentleman accompanying me is Matsya. He has come to this kingdom under very difficult circumstances. I promised him that the Kingdom of Krishna would embrace anyone who seeks shelter. But unfortunately his request for citizenship was rejected and he has to leave before sunset. This poor man has a newborn baby and a wife and has no place to go. Now, I do not know what to do to help him.'

Sahadev caught a glimpse of Matsya and immediately decided to help the priest. He said, 'So, this is the problem. You can now stop worrying; I will talk to the ***adhikari***.'

He took them back to the Mudhra section. He told the ***adhikari***, 'Look, I am a permanent guest of the country with citizenship conferred on me. I am Sahadeva, the youngest brother of the Pandavas and if you don't know, I am also the nephew of His Highness Shri Krishna. You can give this poor man temporary citizenship under the ***Mudhra*** of Priest Bharadwaj who will take responsibility for his good conduct. And after one ***varsh*** (year), you can issue him his permanent citizenship ***mudhra***. ***Adhikari***, don't you know about the rules of temporary citizenship?'

The ***Adhikari*** stood up as a mark of respect and spoke in a quivering voice. 'Your Highness, I am sorry, I had not offered him this solution and I have also been rude to them. Please pardon me for this.'

'You cannot have one set of rules for the powerful members of society and another set of rules for the commoners. In the kingdom of Krishna, everyone has equal rights. Don't you know this?' Sahadeva thundered in a cold fury.

Then the ***adhikari*** quickly created a temporary ***Mudhra*** for Matsya. Matysa's name was written on the clay seal. He filled out the name of Bharadwaj in the caretaker reference column and wrote out the number three in 'the number of persons' column. The mud seal, coated with turmeric paint, was handed over to Matsya.

A curious Matsya, who had been silent all this while, raised his inquisitive questions. 'Ji, what is this three headed dog on the seal?'

'This is ***Saram***a, the watchdog of ***Yama*** - the demigod of death,' Bharadwaj explained. 'In the kingdom of Krishna, the three headed dog seal is a depiction adapted from the Vedas. The ***Yadavas*** are always under attack from the Jarasandha – the King of Magadh. Every individual citizen entering Krishna's kingdom is guarded by this '***hree murthy*** representing the creator Brahma, the preserver Vishnu and the destroyer Shiva. This is what is reflected by the three headed dog seal, Matsya.'

Matsya probed further with his questions. 'Ji, are there other kinds of seals? I remember the ***adhikari*** mentioned a guest seal and a citizen seal. Are there others?'

Bharadwaj was happy to share his knowledge of the different seals with the new member of the kingdom. 'Matsya, there are different kinds of seals in our kingdom. We have a Permanent Citizen Mudhra for the principal family member. It is a green clay seal. Similarly, we have a seal for each of the sub members of the family – brown (male), blue (female) and black (children less than 12 years). Matsya, you are holding the Temporary Mudra (yellow) at present given under the strength of my permanent mudhra as caretaker. In addition, there is Permanent Guest Mudhra with multiple entries (white) and Temporary Guest Mudra valid for one month (red).'

Permanent Citizen Mudra (Main Principal Family Member) –  Clay seal with green colur

Permanent Citizen Mudra (Sub Members)

Male -  Brown colour

Female -  Blue colour

Children (Less than 12 years) -  Black colour

Temporary Citizen Mudra -  Yellow colour (Turmeric)
(To be regularized within one year)

Permanent Guest Mudra -  White colour
(Multiple Entries)

Temporary Guest Mudra - 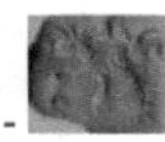 Red colour
(Valid for one month)

Matsya said 'Oh! It is an impressive and well-drafted concept.' Then with gratitude in his eyes, he said, 'I really admire your hospitality, priest. It is rare that a priest like you offers to sponsor the temporary citizenship of a poor man like me. Even though you don't know me, it is heart-warming to see a pure Brahmin assist a ***Sudhputra*** from a lower community. ***Panditji***, from your explanation, I could see that there is much logic in this seal. I never realized this. Had I known its importance, I would have protected my earlier seal.'

Meanwhile, Sahadev returned. Bharadwaj thanked him and invited him to visit the Samudhra Narayana temple. Sahadev said, 'Today, my brother Arjun and my sister in law Subadhra have had a new baby. You must have already received the invitation from the Royal Palace to the naming ceremony. We are very happy that you will be heading the ceremony. I will meet you there on that auspicious occasion.'

At that instant, a messenger came running and handed over a scroll to Sahadev. Sahadev quietly read the news and informed Bharadwaj, 'I just received news that the ship carrying the Royal Prince of the Pandiya Kingdom (Maran) collided with another. Maran was rescused and is in now receiving treatment in our Ayurvedic hospital. He is in a deep state of shock. I shall take leave from you now to visit him.'

Bharadwaj asked, 'You mean Maran, who does not believe in God and sought answers from me for several questions?'

'Yes, you are right.'

'Oh my god. My sister-in-law's husband Brigu Maharaj was also traveling on the same ship. Did you receive information about the others on board?'

'I was only told that Maran had been found on the shore and was immediately rushed to the Ayuverdic clinic. There were no traces of other passengers and our Rapid Action Force is still searching for them. The exact details will be known only by tomorrow.' Saying this, Sahadev immediately rushed to the Ayurvedic clinic.

Ayurveda relies on clinical observation, including the ancient art of diagnosing a patient's ailment by feeling his pulse to identify any imbalance of Nature's three basic forces known as ***Vata, Pitta and Kapha***. It also involves understanding how these forces relate to one's personality and skilfully diagnosing and treating possible ailments. People from different kingdoms came and received treatment in the Ayurvedic clinic of the kingdom of Krishna.

The Ayurvedic clinic where Maran had been admitted was run by special Brahmins from ***Shakdivipa***. They were worshippers of the Sun and specialized in astronomy, astrology and Ayurveda. These ***Shakdivipiya Brahmins*** were also called ***Magi Brahmins*** and their Ayurveda had become the official healthcare process of the kingdom. These centers could diagnose and treat any disaease that affected a man. Lord Krishna's son Samb had been cured of leprosy at the same clinic. Even Maran, who could not be cured anywhere else, had been treated for similar aliments in this clinic before sailing back to his kingdom.

When Sahadev reached the clinic, there seemed to be an intensive care treatment going on. Maran had been admitted to the surgical division. Due to collision of the ship, some pieces had pierced through his body and were being removed on an emergency basis. After treatment, he was brought out of the surgical area to the secluded post-care hut. He was regaining his consciousness from the effect of aneasthetia (Nizvetana).

Sahadev asked the ayurvedic doctor Dhanvantri, 'Doctor, How is Maran doing now? Is this a serious injury?'

The doctor replied, 'We had to surgically operate to remove the external particles that had pierced his body. Moreover, we had to apply neem tree-based healing lotions to cure foul sores and ulcers. He also needed some antiseptic dressing with tulsi plant extracts. We had to treat him both through ***shamana*** (medicines for internal consumption) and ***shodana*** (external treatments). He is now out of danger but is still under our close observation. To get over any allergy effects, we have to administer a few mantras (invocations) involving ***atharvan hymns.*** He is yet to come out of the state of shock.'

'Can I go and see him now?' asked Sahadev.

'Yes, of course,' replied the doctor.

With his permission, Sahadev went into the hut and whispered, 'Maran, how are you doing?'

Maran slowly opened his eyes and stared at Sahadev.

'Sahadev, I lost the love of my life, Kanchana, right in front of my eyes. As we travelled back to my kingdom, there was a terrible storm and our ship was wobbling due to the heavy winds. Suddenly, something rammed into our ship and there was a big noise. There was a heavy inflow of water into our ship through a big hole caused by the collision. We tried our best to fix the hole but the ship started sinking into the deep waters. At the last minute, we had to jettison our ship and everyone jumped into the sea in the darkness. I was holding Kanchana's hands as we jumped in together. Unfortunately, I lost consciousness and when I woke up, I was alone on the shore of Dwarka. I think I have lost Kanchana. I cannot live without her.'

Saying this, he fainted.

Dr. Dhanvantri rushed in and checked his pulse. By definition, ***Vata*** is responsible for both physical and psychological movements, both muscle tone and moodiness. People dominated by ***Vata*** are high strung, restless and prone to high blood pressure. The next force, ***Pitta*** governs heat and metabolism. People dominated by ***Pitta*** are intense, have sharp intellects and are quick to anger. Skin rashes and ulcers may result from too much of this force. The third force, ***Kapha***, maintains structure and stability. ***Kapha*** types are strong, tend to gain weight easily.

'Doctor, is he alright?' asked Sahadev.

'Very soon, he will be alright,' replied the doctor.

As Sahadev waited a little longer, Maran opened his eyes again and looked around. He started talking again. 'Sahadev, you introduced me to one of the most attractive courtesans of your kingdeom. Do you remember the time when all the three of us met at the darbar hall of the Royal Palace at Dwarka?' Stating this, he remembered the sweet interactions of the past….

*** ***

It was a Guruvaar (Thursday). The darbar hall of the Royal Palace was heavily crowded. Everyone had come to watch the 'Natya Nritya' (Dance Drama) program. The start of the program had been delayed by two hours since the chief guest of the function, Balarama, was yet to emerge from an urgent cabinet meeting. In this crowded hall, Sahadeva met Maran and the beautiful courtesan Kanchana.

As they were seated together, Sahadeva asked, 'Your Excellency, how did you enjoy your stay in the kingdom of Krishna? I hope our Ayurvedic doctors are treating you well. Where have you reached in terms of your treatment at our Ayurvedic Centre?'

Maran began to narrate his experiences in Dwarka to Sahadev. 'Firstly, thank you for inviting me here as a royal guest and getting the best healers to attend to me. I had a perennial skin disease that could not be cured anywhere else and today I have been declared completely cured.'

He looked down at his hands and feet and said, 'I am also particularly happy that Kanchana has stayed by my side and has constantly encouraged and supported me. Sahadev, I must say that everything about this kingdom is so impressive that I want to learn more and more about it. I am now spending time with Kanchana to try to understand the physical and social infrastructure of this great kingdom. I also intend to extend my stay here till the forthcoming ***Amavasya*** (New Moon).'

Sahadev wanted to quench Maran's intellectual curiosity. He asked him, 'Maran, let me understand – what have you already learnt about the physical infrastructure of Dwarka, the kingdom of Krishna? What are the places you have visited in Dwarka with Kanchana?'

'That is a very strategic question Sahadev. I see the marks of your intelligence all over this question. You are ensuring that I do not carry any wrong impressions of this kingdom and hence you have raised this question.

'I understand your concern Sahadev. Well, in the last few days, I have learnt about the origin and the physical infrastructure of this kingdom by way of visiting various places here and talking to various people. Kanchana has played an important role as well. Let me share my understanding on this subject so far…'

Observing this, Sahadev said, 'Excellent Maran, you have a wonderful understanding of our kingdom.'

He then turned his attention to Kanchana.

'Kanchana, how are you taking care of our dignified guest, Maran, the Crown Prince of the Pandiya Kingdom? You are the best courtesan in this kingdom and have been specially designated to take care of our guest. If you do not take excellent care of him, I am afraid we will soon earn the wrath of the fiery Pandiyas.'

'Come on, ***Yuvraaj***…. You are a man with many achievements under your belt and you seem to be praising me. You are the bravest Pandava who conquered the ***Dakshin*** (South) Bharat. You vanquished numerous kings including those of the ***Mlechchha*** tribe living on the sea coast, ***Nishaadas*** - the cannibals and the ***Karnapravarna*s**. You defeated the ***Kalanukha*** tribes, a dangerous community composed of a human and ***Rakshasa*** hybrid. You brought under your control King Timingla, the leader of a wild tribe known as ***Kerakas***, who were perilous men with one leg. You also conquered the ***Paundrayas***, the ***Dravidas***, the ***Udra-keralas***, ***Andhras*** the ***Telingas*** and the ***Kaalingas***. You conquered many islands and you are well known for your expertise on water. Sahadev ji, while you praise my small, humble conquests, I can talk about your acts of bravery for many years to come.'

Sahadev smiled and saw Maran exchange a loving glance with Kanchana. When he probed in a friendly manner, Maran said, 'Sahadev-ji, Kanchana is doing an extremely good job. She has offered me wonderful companionship over the last month of my stay.'

Sahadeva waved his hand at Maran and said, 'Maran, it is now time that you stop addressing me with the suffix ji after my name. We have become intimate friends and you can address me informally.'

Sahadeva continued, 'Maran, from what you say, I now understand that you will most definitely request an extension of your guest seal beyond the designated one month. Kanchana has captivated you so much, hasn't she?'

With twinkling eyes, Maran replied, 'Sahadev, you hit the nail on its head. I am going to steal this beauty from the Kingdom of Krishna. In fact, your own brother Arjun is my role model. He is known to be the one who stole Subadhra ji from her palace. Why shouldn't I follow his example and bring Kanchana to my kingdom?' He teased further and said, 'I simply obey and follow my role models, Sahadev.'

A laughing Sahadev turned his attention to Kanchana and said, 'Hey Kanchana, better be careful. This man here seems to have a hidden agenda.'

He then looked at Maran and said, 'Maran, Kanchana is one of the most beautiful courtesans in the kingdom. As you know, we assign a higher status to these courtesans who are well respected in our society. ***Rigvedha*** calls them ***Sadhbarani***. Earlier, during the Vedic era, they were only dressed in red. Even their gold jewellery was reddened since the red colour scared demons away and offered protection to those whom they accompanied.

'In our kingdom, they are employed by the state. They belong to the superior ***Ganika*** class whose members are proficient in various art forms. There is another class called the ***Rupajiva***s who accompany royal guests and the army and provide entertainment to the army guards on the warfronts. The courtesans of our kingdom are in fact more talented than the famous courtesans of ***Indrapuri*** like *Urvashi*, *Menaka, Tilothama* and *Rambha*. Therefore, don't underestimate this woman, Maran.'

Kanchana began blushing, her face turning the colour of a fresly bloomed rose. With shyness evident all over her face, she said, 'Your Excellency, Sahadev, you are praising me so much. I only hope I am doing a fine job of keeping our guest happy.'

Maran smiled at Kanchana as an affirmation of her statement.

Sahadeva added, 'Maran, Kanchana is a beauty with incredible intelligence. This gifted woman used her intelligence to save herself from great danger when she was accompanying me during one of my conquests. Did she tell you about that?'

'Well Sahadeva, lately I have been learning more about Kanchana than about your city.'

'Maran, I suppose you are referring to your discovery of her dangerously attractive curves. However, I am talking about her intelligence!'

'Sahadev, you are back to pulling my leg again.'

He looked at Kanchana in admiration and asked her to elaborate on the incident that Sahadev was referring to.

A blushing Kanchana replied, 'Fine, Your Excellency, I will explain. As you are aware, I accompanied His Excellency Sahadev on his expedition. He had already conquered many cities and islands in ***Dakshin Bharat*** before we reached Copper Island on the south western side. As we entered the island, we saw a small ***kaali*** temple close to the shore. Sahadev created temporary shelter and settled all our military men close to the shore. Since they were all tired and it was nightfall, I took to my role as an entertainer. On the beach, I performed a ***Natya Nritya*** on the love story of Dhushyanth and Shakuntala. My co-artists played musical instruments.

'The whole battalion of soldiers watched the performance. We were unaware that some locals from the nearby enemy camp, well hidden from our view, were also watching our dance. The next day, Sahadev ordered a scheduled attack on the local wild tribes called *Kerakas*, who were men with one leg. As planned, after sunrise, the war started. The fight took place on the open grounds. The girls, mainly courtesans and artists, stayed back at the temporary shelter near the shore. I think in the mid afternoon, a few of our soldiers came running back to me and said, "His Excellency Sahadev ji wants you to come deeper into the island!"

'I simply assumed that the battle had ended quickly and Sahadev ji was calling me for a celebratory dance performance. I went with our soldiers. Suddenly a small group of the Kerakas circled us. I realized that they had used our soldiers, who were prisoners of war, to catch me. However, I did not understand why they were more interested in catching me than fighting on the battlefield. Later, I came to know that they had been mesmerized by my dance performance and hence wanted to take me as a captive.

'They took me to their hideout in the forest. In the light of the burning lamps, I saw a few one-legged men sitting below a huge tree. One of them was supposed to be the head of the tribe. The men watched every move I made. I could not understand their language, but I could grasp the broad content of their discussion. They were perverts, making ugly gestures at me and calling me provocative and sexually alluring. They shamelessly stared at my bosom. They even tried to touch and feel me. I think this behaviour was due to desperation, as they rarely came in contact with two-legged feminine creatures. The head of the group shouted, "Tonight, my dear voluptuous woman, I will claim you as my lady."'

With horror still alive in her eyes, she recollected more details of the incident. 'At this point, an elderly tribesman joined them. Contrary to most tribal men, this old man was sober looking and as he approached the group, all the five tribesmen stood up as a sign of respect. As I stared a little longer at him, I noticed a big vermilion mark on his forehead and his priestly gestures and I could tell that he was the '***pujari***' of their temple.

'The priest stared at me for a few seconds before he vehemently told his men that I was an evil spirit. He then instructed them to take me to the ***Kaali*** temple at night. Suddenly I realized that they are referring to the temple on the beach where our army shelters were located. I watched and listened intently to grasp the details of their conversation. I was aghast when the priest instructed them to strip me naked and make me dance in front of their goddess.

'The orders did not stop at that. He then ordered the five tribal leaders to consume the locally made alcoholic drink called ***Sura-ras***. With perversion in his eyes, he said whosoever drank the most and still retained his composure should take me and sexually enjoy me. After that, the other four should offer me as ***Nara Bali*** (human sacrifice) to the goddess. He ordered them to present my blood to the goddess to appease her and then eat my body parts to gain strength. As I listened to his instructions, I trembled with fear.'

She sighed and continued, 'I had no chance to beg for mercy, as I knew these heartless cannibals would never listen to me. At that instant, I prayed to God to give me the mental agility and courage to escape. As darkness filled the sky, the men carried me to the temple. I volunteered to brew the Sura drink for them. They were little surprised by my cooperative attitude. During times of war, we courtesans always keep a small quantity of poision hidden in our rings. I opened my ring and put a little poison into their drinks. I knew the small quantity of poison would render the men unconscious and then slowly kill them.

'The five tribesmen downed one drink after another, with the sole intention of emerging the winner. Midway through their drinking, they fell unconscious as the poison spread to their brain. Luckily for me, the men had decided not to involve anyone else in their secret party. They soon fell to the floor one after the other. I looked around and quickly gathered that our campsite was located on the opposite side of the Kaali temple. I ran to our camp and met with a surprised Sahadev and all our soldiers, who had noticed my absence by then.'

Kanchana shuddered as she said, 'Even today, when I think about those heartless, wild cannibals, I shiver.'

But, her highly expressive face immediately registered shyness when Sahadev said, 'The next day, the war ended as their leaders were wiped out one by one and the tribes surrendered. From that very day, we began to call her Beauty queen with incredible intelligence. Her presence of mind and courage should be an example to all women. Maran, now that I have exposed a secret side of your lovable escort, I am eager to ask you about your plan for the day.'

'Sahadev, after this dance programme, I am taking Kanchana with me to the festival at the Ravatika Mountain. Our chariot is ready. We intend to move shortly, so that we reach in time for the festival.'

'Oh dear, has Kanchana told you that Ravatika is the mountain of love? I am sure you are going to have a wonderful time. Have a great time, Maran. Kanchana - take good care of the prince of the Pandiya Kingdom. Make his stay at Ravatika Mountain lively.'

As they bid farewell, Maran and Kanchana commenced their journey up the mountain.

Ravatika is a mountain resort on the mainland close to Dwarka. The picturesque mountain is a treat to the eye, another one of Nature's gifts to the kingdom of Krishna. That day was the Ravatika Festival - a grand festival for the local ***Vrishnis*** and ***Andakhas***. Adorned with many beautiful decorations and covered with diverse ***koshas*** made of jewels and gems, the Ravatika Mountain shone in great splendor. The path up the mountain was decorated with golden poles with lighted lamps. The lighting was brilliant and it made the journey through the caves and fountains during the twilight hours a truly memorable one.

On all sides, beautiful flags colored the skies and jingles from little bells filled the air. Shops selling exquisite clothes and stalls selling garlands lined the roads. Melodious music from veenas and mridangas could be heard in the background. Food accompanied with wines of different kinds was distributed for people to enjoy on this festive day.

There was a display of wealth all around. There was no dearth of gifts being offered to those who were blind or helpless. As Maran reached the festival venue, he was fascinated to observe that the enjoyment being shared by the haves and have-nots, a perfect embodiment of an egalitarian society.

As the festivities commenced, the musicians gave concerts and the dancers began to perform. The local youth ***Vrishnis***, adorned with the finest ornaments and riding their gold chariots, looked extremely handsome. The citizens - some on foot, some on chariots, many with their wives and followers--were there in the hundreds and thousands. The air of festivity was contagious.

Beautiful girls with slim waists and broad, shapely hips began to perform various dances. They exhibited attractive postures and attitudes, stealing the hearts and resolutions of the spectators.

Unable to resist the temptation, the natural dancer in Kanchana took over and she joined in with the others. Watching her dance, Maran thought, 'What a beautiful woman she is. She is endowed with the best of the features that the ***Samudhriga Lakshna*** specifies as the grammar for beauty.'

His obsession with her increased manifold as he thought to himself, 'I think I am deeply in love with her. I am not going to delay the proposal any longer. Tonight, in this beautiful mountain cave where we are going to rest, I shall convey my love to her.'

As his mind drifted from the lovely festivity in front of him, he thought about the society of the Kingdom of Krishna. He thought that Dwarka was home to people who enjoyed many pleasures but still remained philosophical. It was home to people who were happy but had not lost sight of seriousness. The people were wealthy but not filthy in the display of wealth. He thought what a perfect blend they were, an outgoing society that had never lost sight of inward search. On the whole, he concluded that it was the ideal society to live in.

As his mind came flashing back to the dancers, he observed that even the women participated in most public performances without any hesitation. They enjoyed a high status in the society. Subconsciously, Maran began comparing his kingdom with the kingdom of Krishna. He saw quite a few interesting contrasts. The openness, happiness, joint celebrations, women's role in society, and the notion of simple happy living – all these lifted his respect for the society of the Kingdom of Krishna.

He witnessed the concerts, ***Natya Nritya*** (dance drama), ***Roop Nritya*** (Abhinaya and dance), ***Bhav Nritya*** (Emotion through dance) staged on the public platform. Kanchana also gave her dance drama performance, the love story of Dhushyanth and Shakuntala.

Everyone performed well but the audience was spellbound by Kanchana's performance. It was the first time that Maran had seen her dancing skills at close quarters. With love dripping from every vein in his body, he thought 'Who says the ***apsaras*** of Indrapuri are the greatest dancers? Here is my Kanchana – the ***apsara*** of the Kingdom of Krishna - the best of all the dancers in the universe.'

He suddenly realized that he was referring to her as 'my Kanchana.' The realization filled him with deep love and an obsession towards her that was beyond imagination. As she finished her performance and walked towards Maran, he greeted his new ound love and hailed her performance from the bottom of his heart.

'Kanchana, your dance was truly a treat to the audience! Now I understand why the tribal ***Kerakas*** stole you....Your beauty and grace is such that it leaves no one untouched. In a way, I don't blame them, Kanchana....You are such a wonderful dancer, and I have no words.'

Kanchana blushed as she said, 'Your Excellency, you are flattering me. This is Dwarka, where our leader lord Krishna used to perform the ***Raas Nritya*** with ***Gopis*** (village women). His performance would captivate everyone in the audience so much that they would all go into a state of a trance. No wonder even the leaves in this kingdom rustle with grace and poise, reminding us of Lord Krishna's dance. In this environment, my dancing is a very small thing, Your Excellency.'

'I appreciate your humility, my dear. It is definitely a great quality. But the humility need not extend to your addressing me as "Your Excellency." I think we have reached a stage of addressing one another with love rather than with respect. Kanchana, I think it is now time to tell you my true feelings. I prefer that we talk about it when we reach the cave reserved for us atop this wonderful mountain.'

Kanchana noted the change in his tone and realized that the distance between them was thinning. Suppressing their love, they enjoyed the food of the Ravatika Mountain and retired to their reserved cave for the night. It was a beautiful cave from where they could see the Island floating in the sea.

Inside, the cave was furnished like a room within a palace. The intensity of the cold was sealed off by the walls, which were beautifully decorated by many *artificers*. A scented waterbed had been placed in the centre of the cave. Fruits, flowers, sweets and variety of wines filled the table near the bed. The aroma of the flowers was so exhilarating that Maran felt as though he were in the paradise of pleasure.

As Maran's mood was aroused, he softly called out to her, 'Kanchanaaa.....'

He paused as he stared deep into her eyes and then continued, 'Love isn't something that you consciously seek and find. Love is something that finds you. It makes your soul crawl out from its hiding place. It is a game that two can play and both can win. I am in love with you, my lovely Kanchana.... Should I have the power to fly, I would have plucked all the stars in the sky and laid them at your feet. I am cursing my inability to fly Kanchana!'

As Kanchana sat there engulfed in his love and smiling back at him warmly, the quotes of many books on love came to his mind. Words can melt barriers between lovers. He could now see how simple yet truthful words could so easily stimulate pleasure centres in their minds and body. These words had the power to lift lovers to the heights of unbridled passion, he thought.

In a soft voice, he said, 'You know, darling, I love the way you are looking at me right now.' Both of them felt a sudden rush of energy in their bodies.

Kanchana slowly revealed her mind and spoke about her true feelings for the very first time. 'Maran,' she said, breaking the remaining barriers in her mind and addressing him by his name. 'You have mesmerized me. You are killing me with the deep look of love in your eyes. Your eyes are so powerful and engaging that I too have fallen in love with you and have implicitly surrendered to you over the last few days.'

As love enveloped their hearts and their intimacy and bond strengthened further, words of love came to them more naturally.

'I am so lucky to have you as my lover. I feel you have pleasured every bit of me!' cried Maran.

As Maran reached out to gently stroke her hair, she closed her eyes and shyly said, 'Yes Maran, every nerve in my body now chants only one name – and that is yours.'

They stared at each other for a long time,. Then, suddenly, Maran held her hand and walked out of the cave to enjoy the pleasant breeze outside. With the glittering stars shining in the sky, the green mountain casting a beautiful reflection on the sea below and Dwarka Island in the background, they strolled for a while. They sat in the well landscaped garden just outside the cave.

As Maran enjoyed the experience of staring at her openly, he noticed a look of concern on her face. Upon enquiring and probing a little, Kanchana told Maran, 'Maran, there is one important issue that has to be discussed.'

She hesitated, but when Maran held her hand as a show of ceaseless support, she continued, 'You are the first man I have truly loved. Being with you brings me a lot of happiness. I want to ensure that you don't consider this to be a one-night stand. I want to lead a life with you forever…. And I only hope it will come in the form of decent living with long term stability.'

A shocked Maran said, 'Kanchana, what are you saying? I love you with everything that I have. I have plans of marrying you. You are coming back with me to my kingdom. You are going to be the Queen of the Pandiya kingdom, Kanchana.

'In fact, I have many plans for you in our kingdom. You will take care of two issues. You will head the dance and arts institute. You will help our people learn these things. There are many male-biased societies that either kill or desert female children as soon as they are born. Our kingdom wants to adopt these children and educate them to take up the career of their choice – to become courtesans, dancers, and artists or lead life as married women. You are the right person to head this project.

'Kanchana, I have come here to pick up some good inputs and implement them in my kingdom. I also intend to invite your doctors, a few of your ***Gurukul*** teachers, and take them back with me in a ship in a few days. You have a great role ahead of you, Kanchana. You were born to play a great role in my kingdom – our kingdom.'

As Kanchana looked at him with tears of joy in her eyes, he said, 'Kanchana, you are someone who is deeply committed to the roles assigned to you. Now, apart from your role of addressing these issues, you must also play the role of my wife, meeting the typical needs of every husband. Kanchana, do not forget to pamper your husband, once you assume your new role.'

Kanchana lifted her beautifully curved eyebrows and her smile widened at Maran's taunts of love. She planted a kiss on his forehead in a sign of agreement. As they lay side by side, lost in thought, Kanchana asked, 'Maran, what is the plan for tomorrow?'

Maran, amazed by her dutiful nature, said 'Kanchana darling, I am yet to get a feel of the socio-cultural dimensions of this kingdom. I want to know more about the level of social integrity, the caste system, the ***Vedic*** astrology and the method of god worship that this great kingdom adopts. I have my reservations on these subjects. But this time I want to assume a camouflaged identity, and not reveal my true self. I wish to go and mingle with the common man and find answers to these questions. The commoners are the key. Will you accompany me in disguise?'

Kanchana smiled at her lover and expressed her willingness to help in every possible way.

Maran asked her, 'Kanchana, what kind of identities do you think we can adopt for tomorrow's mission?'

The mentally agile Kanchana said, 'Maran, I have an idea. We can go as a dancer and artist couple. Tomorrow morning, we can leave under this new identity and reach Dwarka.

As Maran's concerns were taken care of, his feelings of love came gushing back and with a serious face, he said, 'Kanchana, but what we do tonight? The night is still young. I want to celebrate this night as it is the first night we have openly discussed our feelings for each other and agreed to marriage. Do you have to seek anyone's permission to marry me?'

'No Maran, in our kingdom, considerable freedom is given to youngsters to select their partners. Approval from a parent is not essential but preferred, as the blessing of elders is given high importance. Inter-caste marriages face a lot of objections, which you will learn about when you meet the commoners. As far as I am concerned, I have no one from whom to seek permission. My mother died when she gave birth to me and I was brought up by the Royal Girl Care Taker Foundation. I took up the courtesan role by choice, driven my proven competence. I only have to resign and come with you. That is all I have to do,' replied Kanchana.

He took her hand in his and said, 'Kanchana, looking at you, words flow into me.... Thinking about you, words pour into me like a flood... There is a saying that if you want to be a poet, you should experience true love. With your love, I have turned into a poet today, Kanchana....' In a romantic tone, he recited....

The pleasing curve of your frame projects images in my brain,

The sound of your voice is pleasant to my ears
The softness of your touch puts to rest all my fears
You make me speechless with your voluptuous radiance –
I long for the day when I taste the sweetness of your lips,
While my hands caress your nice wide hips,
Your ruby lips and your nice hips
Your dimple cheeks and your blue eyes,
The soft touch of yours with your
Luscious body raises my temperatures, honey!
Should I die this day – I'd be the
Happiest man on earth – because
I am privileged to be with a
Beautiful woman of priceless worth
But I am not going to die that easily
Because I plan to court you Kanchana
And make you mine to enjoy
Your sweetness and sensuality forever and ever!
I will convert you into a
Beautiful queen – as I will become
The man, who will be your only King!
Tonight at this moment – I
Declare my true love and place
it at your feet, my dear.
Tonight I will claim you
as my lady forever.

Kanchana clapped her hands in admiration and said, 'Maran, I had no idea that you had such excellent poetic skills. I thoroughly enjoyed it.' Saying this, she affectionately lifted his hands and pressed his palms to her cheeks. She slowly moved them to her lips and planted a warm passionate kiss on them.

He tried to embrace her to reciprocate her warmth, but she playfully ran out of his reach and walked out into the open. Maran tried to catch her and the chase went on for a while. Meanwhile, the strong mountain winds blew parts of her garments away. Seeing her partially disrobed, Maran could control himself no longer and abandoned all his restrictions. What followed was a ***Sangamam*** of the North and South, a complete union of two souls in a single body.

The trees and the stars surrounding the open cave were shy to witness their sexual union. The twinkling stars and the breezy winds blanketed the couple, who were oblivious to the outside world. They forgot that they were outside the cave while lust conquered them.

After melting into oneness for hours together, they came back to their senses only to realize that they had been making love outside. They quickly gathered their clothing and walked into the cave. They fell into deep, sound sleep together.

The next day, they donned their new avatars. In their new attire, they began their journey back to Dwarka. But when they reached the city, a horrific scene was waiting for them.....

*** ***

5. Cultural Echoes from the commoners

As Maran and Kanchana entered Dwarka from the east, they were horrified by the sight of blazing flames. A house in the Brahmin Residential zone was burning. A Rapid Action Army force was fighting the blaze. From inside the burning house, they had carried three charred bodies into the open. A few children who had been playing near the house had suffered burns and were being treated by the Ayurvedic team. The whole street was in a state of chaos.

Many passersby were trying to help the victims. As Maran alighted from his chariot, he noticed a twelve-year-old boy with severe burns on his hands and face. Several people were crowding around the boy. Maran walked closer and enquired of one of the passersby what had happened. The man told him that a fire had broken out early in the morning in the house. He revealed that the apparent cause of fire had been the lamps placed close to flammable materials stocked in the house. Maran was shocked to hear that the house was a ***Gurukul*** that educated boys between ages five and fifteen.

The man also mentioned that the Guru had been away when the fire began and that there had been more than fifteen students in the house at the time, along with the Guru's family.

The man pointed to the small boy and said, 'Twelve year old Mahendra was one of them. While trying to escape from the flames, Mahendra heard the cries of four other young students who were caught inside. Mahendra immediately jumped into the flames and rescued them one by one and brought them outside the house. Even the Rapid Action Army Force, known for its timely action, was surprised by the young boy's bravery.'

A surprised and awestruck Maran turned around and asked Kanchana, 'What is this Rapid Action Army Force?'

'Given the possibilities of external attack , Lord Krishna constituted the Rapid Action Force. They are commandos who spring into play and are known for their intelligent, smart and brave actions,' replied Kanchana.

Maran's eyes landed again on the young boy standing nearby. With Kanchana following, he walked to the boy who was receiving treatment from the Ayurvedic team. Many questions ran through Maran's mind – how could this twelve year old boy have no fear? Where did he get these brave qualities? Unable to control his curiosity, he asked Mahendra, 'My dear boy! What crossed your mind when you went inside the house to rescue the others? Were you not afraid?'

Mahendra looked eyes with Maran and replied, 'Ji, our ***Guruji*** – Shri Brighu Maharaj-- has taught us that society comes first, self safety comes next. He used to say that when a ship is sinking, saving a co-passenger's life is more important than retrieving one's personal belongings.

When the young students were in danger, my Guru's teachings came to mind. I could not let them die while I myself ran to safety. At that moment, I did not think about my personal safety or any other consequences. Since I am older than those boys, it is my job to protect them. Since my ***Guruji*** was away, I had the added responsibility of defending them at any cost. Everyone here has been patting my back and praising my actions as bravery, but I consider this an act of responsibility,' Mahendra answered.

A stunned Maran thought, 'Oh my God! This small boy speaks like a great leader. He does not speak like a twelve year old. The kingdom of Krishna is blessed with a responsible younger generation. How do they develop such leadership skills at such an early age? I should meet his ***Guruji***.'

Meanwhile ***Guruji*** reached the scene. He looked like someone who was no more than twenty five years old. The designation had made Maran assume that he would be at least forty. Maran approached the ***Guruji*** and struck up a conversation.

'***Namaste Guruj***i. It is extremely unfortunate that the fire has victimized your family and students. Please accept my heartfelt condolences.'

When the ***Guruji*** nodded his acceptance, Maran continued, 'I want to speak to you about your student, Mahendra, who has saved four others. He acted in haste, unmindful of the dangers that he faced. When I spoke to him, he answered me like a responsible leader. How did you build such responsibility-consciousness in the minds of young children? I am unable to control my curiosity and want to know more about your education system. You may wonder why a dancer like me asks about your education system. But ***Guruji***, as an artist, I strongly believe that the education system moulds the individuals of a society. I apologize for asking this question at this hour of grief, but I request you to kindly answer me, ***Guruji***.'

Guruji answered, 'Yes, you said it right...This is a grevious occasion. I am shocked to see three of my young boys lose their lives today. The cries of the parents, when they claim their children's bodies, will haunt me for the rest of my life. But still, responsibilities can not be abdicated on the premise of brooding over past incidents. Life has to move on.'

Taking a closer look at Maran, the Guruji said, 'So, you said you are a dancer, right? I am happy you raised the question, because the world should know the superiority of the kingdom of Krishna. Hence, even though I am in mourning for the loss of my students, I shall answer your question.'

He took a deep breath and continued, 'As part of our education system, we have a ***Gurukul***, accredited by the Royal Palace. Depending upon the grading of the ***Gurukul***, the federal government of Dwarka pays us. The admission of every child takes place at the age of five and the child completes his education by fifteen. Parents have to make their choice of ***Gurukul*** and seek admission. If they do not receive admission at their school of choice, then they can admit their sons to the Royal Palace ***Gurukul***, which is run by the government. This ***Gurukul*** is one such centre. I am employed by the government and I am on their payroll.

However, privately-run ***Gurukuls*** receive grants on a quarterly basis based on their grades and provide education from their homes.'

Maran interjected, 'You have addressed my question on student admission. Can you also tell me about how the actual teaching happens?'

'Yes I am coming to that,' ***Guruji*** answered. 'Our education focuses on three modules – soul, mind and body. The first soul searching module enables the student to understand the concept of bringing out the insider. This module is taught to students aged between five and eight. Topics covered in this phase include the evolution of the universe, the philosophies of life, meditation and "knowing yourself" sessions.

'The second, mind-oriented module starts when students turn eight and ends at the age of ten. Students learn about the kinds of worldly affairs that they will face in lives, how they should react to these situations and other worldly things.

'The third module focuses on the body and is taught between the ages of eleven and fifteen. In these three years, students go through a compulsory bravery and yoga session. The last two years of education are more flexible. Based on the student's outlook and interests, the ***Guru*** and the student make elective choices. They can either opt to continue the bravery sessions to achieve military or trade proficiency, or choose other subjects that will enable the student to excel in other occupations of interest. At fifteen, they complete their education and take up an occupation certified by the system.

'The education system doesn't end there; there is an ongoing one that administers tests every five years between the ages of fifteen to thirty, and once every ten years between thirty and fifty. Anyone seeking to migrate to another occupation will have to perform excellently in these mid-life proficiency tests.

'At every phase in one's life, the citizens of this kingdom face proficiency tests and need to repeatedly exhibit their qualifications. Young man, you know something – in our kingdom, the mother's womb does not decide the fate of the child. We believe that every child comes into this world with his own agenda and our role is to guide them to realize and pursue the same.'

'The system is very detailed and fair ***Guruji.*** But still, you have only talked about male children. What about the girl child?' asked Maran.

'That is an excellent question! Let me tell you about it....There is a similar education system for young girls, but the teaching is rendered by qualified women teachers. Girl students also go through the soul and mind module. However, instead of the bravery phase, the girls go through an arts and dance phase. Depending upon their proficiency and capabilities, they take up professions such as royal courtesans, common courtesans, dance artists or become home makers. In short, our education system ensures that one's competence and not their birth determines their occupation,' concluded Brighu Maharaj.

'Wow! What an excellent system,' Maran thought. Several questions about the ***Varna*** and the caste system crossed his mind. But he decided to hold back given the scene in front of him. He decided to ask some of the questions to the others he would meet over the day. Maran mentally made a note to invite Brighu Maharaj and Mahendra to his kingdom to pioneer a similar education system.

Before leaving, Maran asked his final question, 'One more question, Brighu Ji. How did the parents of the three dead children react to the death of their loved ones?'

Brighu Ji replied, 'My dear young man, these parents definitely do not blame the ***Gurukul*** and accept this incident as a part of their lives. This is because every one of us is trained to accept externalities during the soul searching module at an early phase of our lives. But you may be surprised to learn that tomorrow, these parents are scheduled to visit our Royal Caretaker Centre to adopt orphans and raise them as their own children. Our kingdom is highly proactive in understanding the needs and emotions of its citizens.'

Maran was stunned. This initiative would give the parents a child and bring them solace in the long term. It also relieved some burden of the caretaker's budget. For every situation, the kingdom of Krishna has an answer, thought Maran. He thanked Brighu Ji for his answers.

He and Kanchana proceeded back to the guest house. Maran wanted to rest for a while and take Kanchana out to the ***mandi*** (bazar) to buy several special articles from the kingdom – jewels, emeralds, clothes, musical instruments and so on. After all, he intended to take a full shipload of materials on his voyage back to his own kingdom.

But Maran could not sleep as more questions about the kingdom haunted him. He tossed and turned and an understanding Kanchana asked him, 'What is the matter, my dear? You seem to be facing difficulty in falling asleep. Are you wondering about the answers to more of your questions?'

Maran felt blessed that Kanchana understood him so well. He kissed her on the forehead and said, 'Yes, my love. I have some questions about the system of marriage practiced in this kingdom. Would you tell me little about it?'

Kanchana laughed before saying, 'Maran, your curiosity about every aspect of this kingdom makes me wonder if you plan to take over it. Before I explain our system of marriage to you, I am curious to know which system you will choose for our wedding. Your kingdom's system of marriage, I suppose?'

'No, no, you are mistaken Kanchana. I value you and the kingdom you come from.' As he played with her hair, he teased, 'Gor all you know, I may decide to have a dual format wedding which will incorporate both styles of rituals. But I would prefer to keep it as a surprise! Tell me about it.'

Kanchana smiled shyly and said, 'Maran, we believe that marriages are still made in heaven for the average Arya couple in our kingdom. We regard the institution of marriage as sacrosanct and not simply a contract between two members of the opposite sex. What is matchless about this alliance is that it is as much a union of two families as that between two individuals. It is a lifelong commitment and the strongest social bond between a man and a woman. We also believe that marriage is not only a means of continuing the family but a way of repaying one's debt to one's ancestors. The ***Vedas*** also affirm that a person, after the completion of his student life, should enter the second stage of life, that is the Grihastha or life of a householder.

'Most people tend to equate this system of ***Vedic*** marriage with arranged marriage. The parents prepare themselves mentally and, more importantly, financially when their child reaches marriageable age. They search for a suitable partner, keeping in mind the societal rules regarding caste, creed, natal chart, and financial and social status of the family. Traditionally, it is the girl's parents who bear the cost of the wedding and to jumpstart their daughter's married life, they shower her with gifts and ornaments to take to her in-laws. An arranged Brahmin marriage involves a number of ceremonies. These ceremonies are indispensable, highly religious and significant.'

Maran interrupted, 'But what if the girl or the boy refuses to marry the person chosen by the parents? What if they choose a partner of their own liking and opt for a love marriage? Would your society rule out such a marriage?'

'The average person anchored to the age-old rules of an arranged marriage would hardly embark on a love marriage. Love marriage is looked down upon and the orthodox priests preach against it. This is mainly because such unions often defy the barriers of caste, creed and age. Ironically, ours will be a love marriage, Maran. Hopefully your parents will approve of me.'

Maran took her palm in his hands, kissed it and reassured her that their marriage would be a blissful one with everyone's acceptance and blessings. He then asked her how the royal family chose their partners.

'Our princesses choose their mates in a ***Swayamvaras*** – an occasion where princes and noble men from all parts of the kingdom are invited to assemble in a choosing ceremony.'

As she finished her explanation, she said, 'Maran, you should let your mind relax now and sleep. We have to go shopping tomorrow.'

*** ***

Recalling his loving interactions with Kanchana, Maran began weeping. 'Sahadev, Kanchana was instrumental in helping me understand the culture and the ethos of the residents of Kingdom of Krishna. She stole my heart and we decided to marry but alas! Now she is no more with me. I wonder what the purpose of my life is now.'

Sahadev intervened. 'Maran, don't lose hope. The mind that gives you the power of thought and reminiscence can also give you the power to forget. Time is a great healer. You will soon come out of it. Rest now.'

While Sahadev was leaving, Bharadwaj stepped in and asked Doctor Dhanvantri about Maran's health.

The doctor replied, 'He is recovering quickly. His external injuries are healing but he is suffering from a short-term memory loss known as ***smriti nasaha,*** which is caused by vitiated ***vata dosha*** in the body. The abode of intellect, which is the carrier of the three types of gunas - ***satvik, rajasik and tamasi***k--has been disturbed and the balance lost. We provide herbal treatment with herbs such as ***brahmi, vacha and amalki*** to prevent memory loss. However apart from the medical treatments, it is imperative that people meeting him help him recall the events of the past. This alone can help him to come back to normalcy. You may go and meet him now.'

Bharadwaj went in. 'How are you, Yuvraaj Maran?'

The moment Maran looked at Bharadwaj, his eyes brightened. He began recalling his past interactions with him.

'Bharadwaj ji, you predicted it correct. You warned me to be careful during sea voyages. I lost everything in my disastrous sea journey. I am very sorry that I could not save Brighu Maharaj. I have also lost my beloved Kanchana. From my horoscope, you predicted that guru mangala yoga (marriage phase) had begun. But sadly, before it could start, my marriage has ended miserably,' he said with tears in his eyes.

Bharadwaj tried to console him 'Yuvraaj, the good and bad things follow us like day and night. I know it is difficult to accept your fate now, but your mind will soon learn to live with it.'

Recalling the doctor's words, Bharadwaj wondered how visual connection with someone from the past had the power ro make the patient recall events. 'This is a sort of recall therapy,' he thought. He decided to probe further and play his part.

'Yuvraaj, do you remember when we first met at the Samudhra Narayana temple? I met you in your disguised form as an artist?'

'Yes, how can I forget that great interaction we had?'

*** ***

Kanchana and Maran had reached the temple. It was guruvaar (Thursday). There were close to a hundred devotees gathered there to mark the auspicious morning. Maran decided that this would be the ideal place to test the integrity of the public. As he looked around, an idea struck him and he said, 'Kanchana, I want to leave my diamond-studded ***haar*** (chain) here on the floor of this sacred sanctorum. Let us go around the temple and come back. Let us see what happens.'

Fifteen minutes later, they returned to the sacred sanctorum of the temple. Someone called him and said 'I saw you here a little while ago. Are you looking for something?'

Maran turned around and came face to face with the priest of the temple. Maran immediately recalled Sahadeva's advice to meet the priest of the ***Samudhra Narayana*** temple to obtain clarifications on various customs and practices of the people of Kingdom of Krishna. Maran was labelled a non-believer and atheist by Sahadev. Hence, he always insisted that Maran meet the priest so that he could clear all his doubts. Now, he was meeting the priest, but in a disguised identity.

'Yes, ***Panditji***, I am looking for my ***haar***. I guess it must have fallen somewhere. I seem to have lost it,' Maran said.

The priest smiled and said, 'Not to worry. One of the devotees found a ***haar*** right here and gave it to me and asked me to hand it to the owner. Can you please establish the identity of your ***haar***?'

Based on the exact description Maran provided, the priest handed the chain to him. However, the priest stunned Maran with his follow up question, 'By the way, I somehow get this feeling that you are testing me.'

A shocked Maran struggled for words before he said, 'Why do you feel that?'

The priest grinned and said, 'Well, your actions made me think it. I saw no anxiety on your face for your missing chain. You seemed to be quite casual about it. Moreover, when I examined the ***haar*** closely, I noticed a tiger engraved on it. The embossed tiger looks like the symbol of the Pandiya kingdom.'

He looked deeply into Maran's eyes and said, 'Tell me, who exactly are you?'

Astonished by the priest's acumen, Maran decided to reveal his true identity. The priest's expression did not change when Maran said he was a prince of the Pandiya kingdom. The priest did not tremble with fear or seem interested in pleasing him.

Maran was pleased to see that the priest treated a king and commoner alike and offered the same level of respect to him that he would have shown to any other devotee. Maran's respect for Bharadwaj increased manifold. He admitted to the priest his true intentions and elaborated upon his reasons for testing the integrity of the commoners of the kingdom.

The priest nodded his head and said, 'Now, are you satisfied with what you have learnt about our integrity, Yuvraaj Maran? "Society first, self anxiety next" is our belief.'

This rang familiar bells in Maran's mind. He remembered the young boy, Mahendra, having quoted the same saying that morning. Maran thought, the Kingdom of Krishna has a homogeneous population with unified thinking. How has the kingdom managed to achieve such unification of minds and souls? Could it be the education system?

At that very moment, Sahadev entered the temple. He was surprised to see Maran in disguise. However, he understood the situation and realised that the intelligent priest had already seen through it. Sahadeva decided to break the ice and formally introduced Maran to the priest.

'Maran, I hope by now you know that this is Shri Bharadwaj. He is a true Brahmin who treats prosperity and adversity alike. He is also well versed in Vedic astrology and is an interesting man who does not know his own strengths, or rather does not like to exhibit his proficiencies to the outside world. In this world of external display of strengths, he is a rare soul.'

Turning to Bharadwaj, Sahadev said, 'Bharadwaj ji, here is Yuvraaj Maran of the Pandiya kingdom. He is a hardcore atheist and he questions every ancient custom and practice followed by our people. I understand you were successful in tearing apart his disguised form and bringing out his true identity. In the same way, you are the only man who can remove the clutter in his mind by answering his rebellious questions.'

'Bharadwaj ji, Sahadev is presenting me as a rebellious person who is against the social customs of this kingdom. But that is a very strong statement. I am not trying to question the social practices, I just want to understand and feel the pulse of the commoners in this kingdom. So far, my stay in this kingdom has been a great experience.

'I came here to receive treatment for my disease, but now I am more fascinated by the harmonious society and want to learn as much about it as possible. I also have many unanswered questions relating to astrology, cultural ethos and the caste system here. Some of my questions have already been answered, but a few more await. I understand from my good friend Sahadeva that you are a great astrologer, scholar and the right person to clear some of my doubts.'

'Oh! His Highness always speaks very high about me. Sometimes, I wonder if all that is really true. I am happy to answer your questions to the extent of my abilities,' Bharadwaj answered.

The two men moved to a corner of the temple and began their question and answer session. Meanwhile, Sahadev bid them farewell and moved on.

'Bharadwaj ji, the subject of Vedic astrology is very intriguing. I have always wanted to learn about its intricacies. Unfortunately, though we have some talented astrologers in our kingdom, they have not been able to answer basic questions that have haunted me from my childhood. I know that Dwarka is the land of knowledge and the people of Dwarka are the only ones who can unravel many mysteries.' Saying this, Maran posed his first question.

Q: Bharadwaj ji, what exactly is Vedic astrology? Is everything in this universe predetermined? If everything is predetermined, can we stop chasing our dreams? Can we sit back and relax with the assumption everything will happen as per fate?

A: Many texts attribute the origin of ***Vedic*** astrology to various ***Rishis*** – Parashara, Garga, Jaimini and others. It is futile to attempt to ascertain the originator of ***Vedic*** Astrology. Our ancient astrologers used their divine intuition to record planetary movements and their effects on us. Astrology has a twofold purpose.

On one hand, it is used as a tool to select the right month, the right date and the right time to undertake various auspicious rituals, so that the best results ensue. On the other hand, it is used as a guide to study the destiny of an individual.

According to ***Vedic*** astrology, a person is born at a given place, on a given day and at a given moment when his individual fate is in perfect mathematical harmony with the progress of the stars. However, ***Vedic*** Astrology does not preach total dependence on fate. Astrology lets you know what you were born with, what your possibilities are, what limitations you will face and what your strong points and your drawbacks are.

Astrology is the roadmap of your destiny. However, your fate is in your hands. The scriptures guide us by telling us what is good and what is bad; what to do and what not to do; how to do and how not to do it. Fate is like a game of cards where you cannot influence what will be thrown at you, but how to play them is in your hands. You may get good cards but if you play badly, you will lose and you may get bad cards and may win if you play carefully. The roadmap is to give you direction, but it is you who should take the right turns at the right times!

Q:- Bharadwaj Ji, can you also tell me about how our life is connected to these planetary movements?

A:- Crown prince, that is an interesting question. Well, the moment one is born into this world, the strong pulling force of the planets starts to control the newly born. Thereafter, the planetary movements and the newborn's movements go in tandem. This is the law of the universe. From the position of the planets at the time of birth, the future of the newborn can be predicted. In expectation of the forthcoming occurrences, we have to proceed with the present. We are driven by nine planets.

Q:- Why are we born at the right or wrong planetary positions at the time of our birth?

A:- The science of Astrology is based on the principle of evolution of time. The accumulated results of our past incarnations are brought to the present. Human ego has undergone many previous births and still has to pass through many incarnations before it can become one with the 'Supreme being.'

In the course of its evolution, it seeks higher or lower forms of terrestrial existence, according to the good or bad deeds (***karma***) of its previous birth. Planets indicate the results of our past actions and the science of Astrology divines our future.

Q:- How do we predict a birth chart, Bharadwaj Ji?

A:- Each birth chart is divided into 12 houses. Each house is ruled by a planet which is called the Lord of the house. Each of the twelve houses signifies certain important events and incidents such as appearance, family, intelligence, bravery and so on. The human lifespan is considered to be 120 years for this ***Yuga*** and is divided into several periods or ***Dashas***. Each ***Dasha*** is governed by a particular planet. The exact ***Dasha*** that was running when you were born depends on the date, time and place of birth. Each ***Dasha*** has certain beneficial and detrimental effects.

And lastly, the ***lagna*** is your birth sign. It is the constellation that covered the sky in the eastern horizon at the place and time of your birth. Many people confuse ***Lagna*** with ***Rasi***. ***Rasi*** is the constellation where the moon was at the time of one's birth. The rising sign – the ascendant or ***Lagna--*** describes one's characteristics.

Q:- Can you predict my birth chart, Bharadwaj Ji? I was born in *Dhanusha Lagna, Khumba Rasi* and *Poorvabhadra Nakshatra* at 6 *Nazigas* after sunset in the late evening hours in Madurai.

A:- Based on the details that you have given me, I can see that ***Guru Mangala Yoga*** or marriage phase has started in your life. You might have recently finalized or come very close to finalizing the lady of your life.

The path of your marriage shows considerable turbulence. A difficult period lies ahead of you. Be extremely careful during sea voyages. Pray to our Lord ***Samudhra Narayana***, and everything will happen for the good.

Maran thanked the priest for his predictions, warnings and blessings. Having gathered an understanding on the basics of ***Vedic*** Astrology, he decided to move on to his questions on cultural ethos. He said, 'Bharadwaj ji, I would like you to answer some questions on the cultural and religious practices that are followed here. Even in the Pandiya kingdom, we follow most of these practices, but I am curious to know the basis for the same.'

Q:- Why do we chant mantras 108 times? What is the significance of the number 108? Why not 150? Why not 100?

A:- Ancientastronomers have calculated and deduced that the diameter of the sun is 108 times the diameter of the earth. The nine planets go round the twelve signs 108 times. This number is therefore a powerful one and chanting mantras 108 times dissipates energy to all parts of the universe. Even the lotus flower has 108 petals.

Q:- All married women wear vermillion on their foreheads, I never understood why this is necessary. Is it not a discriminatory practice?

A:- In Vedic culture, married women apply red vermillion (***Sindoor***) in the parting of their hair, while widows refrain from doing so. This is actually a very sentimental act. After all, marriage is the union of two hearts, and is a very intimate affair. The ***Sindoor*** is a symbolic of expression of love and the groom applies it on the wife's forehead for the first time during the wedding. Thereafter, the wife applies it every day. It is not possible to express love openly with words on every occasion in a joint family system and therefore, symbols play a role in the expression of these intimate feelings.

Q:- I never got a good answer for an intriguing question, *Panditji Ji.* Can you explain why we choose different directions for different rites? Is it necessary?

A:- The East and West are related to the sun and its energies. North and South poles are the poles of magnetic forces. East is the perfect setting for devotional exercises, as the waves of positive energy of our body are charged from dawn to the noon in the eastern space. According to the ***Shastras***, the god of death resides in the southern direction. Therefore, all rites for dead ancestors are performed facing the south.

During marriages, the groom faces the east because he needs all the energy to protect his new family from the sun. The bride faces the west as a woman is the daughter of darkness. She will be bold in darkness but during daylight she is coy and prudent. Thus, the ***Shastras*** provide the order of directions based on the scientific logic regarding physiology and psychology.

Q:- Another question that I have is in regard to the practice of blowing through conch shells.

A:- In our tradition, the conch shell is blown on many occasions, including times of worship, ***Yajna***, birth, funerals and other ceremonies. It is also the boggle of war. His Excellency Arjuna uses ***Panchjanya*** to announce his intention to do battle. The blower is required to concentrate his mind and blow a lungful of air with measured force into the shell. The sound that erupts from the shell is like a long drawn ***Om***, which is the most revered chant of our ***dharma***. It is also symbolic of the humming echo of ***Brahm*** (big bang) that still hangs in space as a cosmic vibration.

Maran looked at the priest with newfound respect and said, 'Bharadwaj ji, you are a true scholar who answers my questions with ease and clarity. I also have few unresolved doubts about the genesis of our planet that I would like you to answer.'

Q:- Is the planet due for extinction in this *yuga*?

A:- Maran Ji, the evolution of our world has been described in our scriptures. Who said the world is coming to an end now? That is a myth; there is still a long way to go. Lord *Bramha's* day and night determines the state of our universe. One day and one night for *Bramha* consists of one thousand ***chaturyugas*** each. When it is *Bramha's* night there is no activity in the universe. When it is *Bramha's* day, (denoted as one ***Kalpa***) the universe is active. One ***kalpa*** consisting of a thousand **chaturyugas** are further divided into 14 ***Manvantras***. Hence one ***Manvantra*** represents 71 ***chaturyugas*** (1000 divided by 14). We are now in the seventh ***Manvantra*** and in the

28th ***chaturyuga*** of the 71 ***chaturyugas*** of this ***Manvantra***. Therefore, our planet has balance life left:

Balance of 7 ***Manvataras*** viz., 497 (7 x 71) ***Chaturyugas*** plus balance in this current running ***Manvantaras*** viz., 43 (71-28) ***Chaturyugas***. Thus we have 540 (497+43) ***Chaturyugas*** left. Our planet has still a long way to go.

Q: So many *Chaturyugas* sound good but how long is one *chaturyuga*?

A:- To answer you quickly, one *chaturyuga* is 4,320,000 earth years. But it is called ***chaturyuga*** or four **yugas** for a reason. Each ***chaturyuga*** is further divided into four ***yugas*** namely, ***Satya, Treta, Dwapara*** and ***Kali***. In the same order of listing, these ***yugas*** follow a time line of total years in the ratio of 4:3:2:1. ***Satya Yuga*** had 1,728,000 years, ***Treta Yuga*** had 1,296,000 years, present ***Dwapara Yuga*** had 864,000 and the future ***Kali Yuga*** has 432,000 years. Even the number of avatars of Vishnu follow the timeline of the *yugas* i.e. 4,3,2,1 avatar in each ***yuga***.

The cycles are repeated like the seasons, waxing and waning within a greater time-cycle of creation and destruction of the universe. All the planets will be absorbed by the Lord, from whom they initially emerged, at the end of 1000 ***chathur yugas***. We still have 540 more ***chaturyugas*** to go, at which point we will face a ***Maha Pralaya*** or a universal disaster. You and I should not worry about the end of earth any time soon.

Q:- I have seen that the Kingdom of Krishna practices a unique caste system with color codifications for each class. Can you explain the basis of this?

A:- Before, I go into details, let me tell you about Varna. Varna literally means color. It refers to the distinct qualities (***guna***) that the four functional classes possess in their hearts and minds. There are four different ***varnas*** for human beings – white, red, yellow and black.

White (***Sattva*** = truthful) represents the quality of purity, love, faith and detachment. Those belonging to this ***varna*** seek true knowledge and often possess a spiritual temperament. They belong to the ***Brahman*** class.

Red (***rajas*** = energetic) represents the quality of action, will, aggression and energy. Those belonging to this ***varna*** seek honor, power and status and are often people with martial and political temperament. They belong to the **Kshatriya** class.

Yellow (***rajas***) represents the same qualities as red but these people seek communication, interchange, trade and business. This color exists in those of commercial temperament. They make up the ***Vaishya*** class.

Black (***tamas*** = inert, solid) represents ignorance and inertia. Those belonging to this color are dependent on the others for motivation and seek nothing. They have a servile disposition and make up the ***Shudra*** class.

Q:- But Bharadwaj ji, this system is based on discrimination. All humans are equal, is it not?

A:- ***Varna*** also means veil. It shows the four different ways in which the Divine self is hidden in human beings. It refers to the ways in which the god's four body parts make up the four classes, depending on the nature or values that the human holds. The ***Brahmans*** hold spiritual and intellectual values and are in charge of teaching ***Vedic Sanskrit***, and thus represent the lord's head. The ***Kshatriyas*** are the warriors who protect their kingdoms and thus represent the lord's arms. The ***Vaishyas*** are the farmers and merchants and represent the Almighty's belly, while the ***Shudras*** are the laborers who perform manual labour and thus symbolize His legs.

Q:- But this is still discrimination, Bharadwaj Ji. Ekalyva was refused admission by Dronacharya on the ground of caste – is this not discrimination?

A:- ***Brahmins*** have the attribute of goodness (***sattwa***), the Kshatriyas have the attribute of passion (***Rajaas***), the third have a mixture of the two – goodness and passion (***Sattwa*** and ***Rajaas***), while the lowest order possess the remaining attribute viz, darkness (***Tamas***).

But note this key line – A ***Sudhra*** is not a ***Sudhra*** by birth alone, **Brahmin** is not a **Brahmin** by birth alone. If the virtue of goodness is not prevalent in a **Brahmin**, he is considered as ***Sudhra***.

Varna is character-driven, while caste (***jathi***) is birth driven. Our education system determines the ***varna***. A **Brahmin** by ***jathi*** may adopt a warrior's role. Look at Dhronacharya - a **Brahmin** who took up a warrior's role. His ***varna*** is that of a warrior, but by ***jathi*** he is a Brahmin. Depending upon the characteristics tested and certified by the ***Gurukul*** and endorsed by the education council, citizens of this kingdom take up a position in life. The qualities of people as tested are matched with their profession. Aligning profession and skill is not discrimination.

If we say that a member of the ***Kshatriya*** caste can only be a warrior all his life, then we are definitely discriminating. However, this kingdom believes that the father's occupation need not be pursued by the son. In fact, even on the political front, the kingdom elects its leader; while King Ugrasena is the ceremonial king, our elected leader is Lord Krishna, who has been chosen by the people. Where is the discrimination here, Yuvraaj Maran?

Let me give you more examples. Saint Vyasadeva was the grandson of a fisherman. His father Parashara was born from a woman who was a dog-eater. Vashishtha was the son of prostitute. Other sages like *Kanada, Shringi*, *Mandapala*, and *Mandavya* have all had questionable births, and yet all of them are highly qualified brahmins and recognized as such.

Likewise, several historical instances are known where the ***varna*** of an individual changed due to circumstances such as adoption. Though of the brahmin ***jathi***, *Rishi* Bharadwaj became a ***Kshatriya*** when he was adopted by King Bharata. His descendants were also considered Kshatriyas and were called ***Bharata Kshatriyas***. King Vishvamitra was a ***Kshatriya*** but became a brahmin as a result of his spiritual austerities.

As to your question of Ekalyva's admission, please note that individual liberty cannot be overruled as long as it does not affect social justice. A master has liberty in choosing his students. The teacher and a prospective students' communications, the student's limitations and other factors matter in the admission process. It is a personal liberty issue.

Had Dhronacharya admitted Ekalyva and not given equal education to all his wards; it would have been a social justice issue. But not admitting Ekalyva is an individual liberty issue. Following that incident, the Kingdom of Krishna has recently set up the Royal Gurukul Centres to admit those students who are unable to gain entry into a private ***Gurukul.*** Now the state takes care of such issues, Yuvraaj Maran.

Q:- Now I know there is a justification for the division, but how are the codes different for these four *varnas*?

A:- Here is a list of attributes, Yuvraaj Maran.

BRAHMIN

Role: Teach Vedas, officiate religious ceremonies, receive charity, and provide advice to kings

Beliefs: Truth, Ahimsa, Purity, contentment, austerity and simplicity

Eating Habits: Vegetarian

Mark: Sacred thread made of munja grass

Demigods worshipped: Agni, Prajapati and Brahaspati

KSHATRIYAS

Role: Wield weapons protect and administer the people and country.

Beliefs: Valor, passion, fights righteous wars, justice, and courage.

Eating Habits: ***Rajasika*** food including meat

Mark: Sacred thread made of bow strings

Demigods worshipped: Indra, Varuna, Soma, Rudra, Yama and Mrtyu

VAISHYA

Role: Agriculture, dairy farming, trade, money-lending.

Beliefs: Financial acumen, generosity, honesty in financial transactions.

Eating Habits: Vegetarian

Mark: Sacred thread made of hemp or wool

Demigods worshipped: Vasu, Aditya Maruti

SHUDRA

Role: Artisanship, labor and construction.

Beliefs: Attachment to material and physical pleasures and indifference

Eating Habits: Non-vegetarian ***Rajasika*** foods including meat

Mark: No Sacred thread

Demigods worshipped: ***Ashivn Pushan***

Q:- But Bharadwaj ji, who monitors this *varna* or *jaati*?

A:- We have a council that settles disputes on inter-caste issues. Caste is determined by birth but it is only a family identity. The ***varna*** council endorses the true ***varna*** after the completion of education, based on certain proficiency tests that assess the suitability of each person for a specific profession.

Every male in this kingdom belongs to a designated varna from ages fifteen to sixty. At sixty, their occupation comes to an end and thereafter they can opt for ***vanprastha***. No ***varna*** applies to individuals after turning sixty. Moreover, in this kingdom, there is no ***varna*** for women and children. Their caste is determined by their parent's caste. If any inter-caste marriage takes place, we have a mixed caste category; in short we have a very flexible caste system. Much like the citizenship seal identification, we have an armband that identifies a person's ***varna*** and ***jathi***. The metal and colour of the armband is different for every ***jathi***. Everyone in this kingdom has to wear this as identification at all times.

Q:- Pandit ji, You say that every soul undergoes rebirth. But the population in this Dwapara Yuga is much greater than the last Treta Yuga. How did the people multiply when one soul can take only one new birth? Is it not a contradiction?

A:- Maran ji, your question is correct. But the question is based on half information. You know there are more than 64 bilion species in the planet. Some which existed in the last Yuga have become extinct today. A soul may take the birth of any species – why do you think that the soul of a man only takes the rebirth as a human? How do you know whether that total population of all 64 billion species remains the same between the Yugas?

The priest's extent of knowledge and clarity of communication left Maran spellbound. He added, 'Bharadwaj Ji, you have answered all my questions and have enhanced my understanding of various topics. I am grateful to you. I shall take your leave now.'

Bharadwaj asked, 'So, have you become a "believer" now?'

'No, not yet; But I have moved from being a non-believer. I am now in transition. Earlier, I said there was no God. Now I feel that it would be good if God exists.'

'Eventually, you will change,' replied Bharadwaj.

Saying goodbye, Maran left the temple with Kanchana. They boarded their chariot and moved towards the royal guesthouse. Maran told Kanchana that since he had found the answers to all his questions, it was time to put off their disguise. They rested for a while and then took a short walk into the residential zone of the city. The casual walk however turned more eventful.

They saw a small gathering under a tree. The setting looked like a ***Panchayat*** court and one of the three people standing in the 'accused box' was none other than Priest Bharadwaj, whom they had met a couple of hours ago. He stood there with his hands folded and face pointed at the floor. Shame was written all over his face.

Kanchana and Maran stared in disbelief and looked at each other, wondering, ‘What has happened? How can a person of high values, and someone who is an embodiment of discipline, one who religiously follows the Vedic scriptures, be an accused?’

**** ****

6. The bonds of matrimony

It was a caste council hearing. A man and woman in their mid-twenties stood along with Priest Bharadwaj in the accused box. Three senior citizens sat on a raised platform beneath a banyan tree and nearly one hundred onlookers squatted on the ground. Maran and Kanchana moved closer to the scene.

The judge opened the proceedings. He listed the charges against Bharadwaj.

The accused were a women named Parvathi, a Brahmin widow and the man next to her, a barber named Kalpak. The inter-caste marriage had been solemnized by Priest Bharadwaj. The case had come up for hearing by the caste council.

The judge asked the accused, 'Do you accept your offence?' The accused couple stayed silent, while Bharadwaj said, 'I do not accept the offence charged against me.'

Judge: And why is that so?

Bharadwaj: Of late, the condition of widows in our society has been deteriorating. They are being subjected to a lot of restrictions. They are expected to live a pious life after their husbands die and are not even granted entry to a celebration. Their presence at any auspicious function is considered to be a bad omen. They are also asked to shave their long hair and are not allowed to remarry. I strongly believe that living as a widow, in this society, is a curse.

Judge: Does that mean that you have chosen to question society and its beliefs?

Bharadwaj: Well, society should live happily - that is the theme of this kingdom. When there is a section of society that is suffering and devoid of happiness, we have to question the system. Your Honor, the two counts of accusation that we are discussing today are-

Widow Remarriage and Inter-caste Marriage

Let me take up widow remarriage first. The idea of widow remarriage was practiced without any hindrance in ancient society. This can be testified to by the various references to it in our ancient literature. Three kinds of remarriages have been referenced in ***Narada purana*** –

- Remarriage after the death of husband,

- When the woman fulfilled the rituals of marriage but did not live with her husband for a single day,

- When the woman comes back to her first husband after parting from the her second husband.

In fact, the ***Rigveda*** prescribes that the widow give up her late husband and accept the proposal of a person who is willing to marry her. The ***Dharmasutras*** appended to various ***Vedic*** schools also permit widow remarriage.

Today, unfortunately, widows are a highly frowned-upon lot. The ideal widow is now expected to resign herself to a life of piety, austerity and self-abnegation.

Judge: Bharadwaj, We are not here to listen to your analysis. We have to evaluate this case in today's context, not yesterday's dharma.

Bharadwaj: I beg to disagree, Your Honor. ***Dharma*** is static; it is only the ethical codes that change over time. I can cite several examples of widow remarriage from ancient literature. In ***Harivarmsa Purana***, Ugaryudha proposes to Sathyavati, the widow of Shanthanu, indicating that it was not a taboo to marry a widow. Arjuna, the archer extraordinaire and the brother in law of our beloved Krishna, is married to Ullopi, the widowed daughter of the Naga king.

Why should a widow of a young age spend the remainder of her life in misery and sorrow? Why should she give up all the comforts of life? Why do they only wear plain clothes? Why do they have to tonsure their heads? Why should they stay separately and have bland food?

This woman, Parvathi, was isolated for over three years after her husband passed away. She has been kept away from everything, including talking to the male folk, and had her head tonsured every fortnight. Fortunately for her, it is this man who was assigned to shave her head. Your Honor, isn't it paradoxical that a man was chosen to shave her head, when society has banned her from seeing or interacting with any man?

With no one to talk to, the lady found solace with this man. As their conversations became intimate, a strong bond formed between them. Now, Your Honor, do you think this is wrong? I believe that giving a widow the option of remarrying someone who is willing to share his life with her is far better than ***Sati*** or leading the life of an ascetic at such a young age.

Judge: Before we proceed further, what do you say about the second charge?

Bharadwaj: Your Honor, today we find men of lower castes ascending to positions of eminence and authority. Only three ofVishnu's incarnations are from the high caste; most of his incarnations are animals. God does not discriminate between his own creations. Many ancient sages come from a humble background as well. Sage Viswamitra was a warrior by birth but practiced austerities like a Brahmin and was recognized as a great rishi. Sage Vysya was born to a fisherwoman, and Valmiki came from a family of hunters. Drona, the great guru of the Pandavas, was a Brahmin by caste but excelled in marital arts.

I can go on citing examples from our rich past. However, lately, the flexible caste system is slowly giving way to a more rigid one. A man from a higher caste marrying a woman from a lower caste is less objectionable, but a lower caste man marrying a higher caste woman is considered an offence. This is precisely the reason why we have all assembled here today.

Your Honor, I have quoted many examples from our own society. Our ***Sanatan dharma*** is about setting up an egalitarian society and these manmade rules are against the intentions of our dharma.

Judge: You have lectured to all of us about the past. However, you do not confine yourself to the current code of conduct that the council has set out. Unfortunately, I have to base my judgment on the current code.

The council hereby gives the verdict:

Parvathi and Kalpak are banned from society. They have to surrender their citizenship identification cards, leave the kingdom and live in exile in the deep forests. They have to vacate this place within thirty days. The council issues a warning to Priest Bharadwaj and advises him to refrain from solemnizing such inter-caste marriages in the future. The council is now adjourned.

With this the council members left and the public dispersed.

*** ***

Maran came back to himself. The doctors at the clinic were waiting to check his health as per their routine.

Maran told Bharadwaj, 'You are a social reformer. Your knowledge of our ancient ***sastras*** and ***puranas*** is commendable. Even though the council did not pass a judgment favoring you, you raised several thought-provoking questions. I am positive that the caste system in your kingdom will soon be refined, as the Kingdom of Krishna does not tolerate discrimination. The rules have been interpreted overlooking the true intentions of the laws. These will definitely change with more appeals coming to the ***Varna*** council as the Royal court oversees this council and is indirectly in charge of administration of justice. I also intend to share this with Sahadeva, who may convey it to Lord Krishna.

'By the way, your predictions about me were absolutely correct. Earlier, you asked me whether I had become a believer. I can't say I have done so. But I can confess that I'm moving towards it. One thing is for sure: I am going to live in the land of my beloved Kanchana forever. I'm not mature enough to become a saint, since I can never erase Kanchana from my mind.

'I am very impressed by the Ayurveda treatments of your kingdom. I also owe much to the community of Ayurvedic doctors here, as they cured my skin affliction. In fact, I came to this kingdom to get the treatment. I also took experts from here with me on my ship. They lost their lives in the disaster. I am the lone survivor. I am guilty of having killed the experts of this kingdom. As a mark of respect to them, I intend to start a new clinic here. I want to carry out research in the field of herbal treatments. In addition, I want to impart the techniques to the young students here.'

*** ***

The ship that had set sail from the Kingdom of Krishna with the crown Prince of the Pandiya kingdom, Kanchana and the others had been hit by a terrible storm. By the time the rescue fleet from Dwarka's navy reached the site, all they could find were broken pieces of the ship and some floating bodies. All the sailors had lost their lives in the accident. Maran was the lone survivor.

Dwarka was grieving after receiving this devastating news. The entire city was talking about it and everyone was curious to know more about the incident. While the public was busy analyzing the causes and consequences, the house of Bharadwaj wore a gloomy look. It was a glaring contrast to the festive environment that the house had worn just a few days ago.

Sharmila cried uncontrollably and refrained from touching food or water. The sudden end to her three-day old marriage had left her in a state of shock. Unable to watch her sister writhe in mental agony, Shakuntala asked, 'How long are you going to deny yourself food and water, Sharmila?'

With tears in her eyes, Sharmila answered, 'Why do I have to eat food? Why do I have to live? My marriage lasted only three days. Now, I am left with nothing. I think it is written in my fate that I should also die. I had a very short but pleasant association with my husband, Brighu Maharaj.'

She began recalling the pleasant memories shared with him and the interactions they had had with their guests during their marriage.

*** ***

Sharmila had been happy that day. Her marriage to Brighu Maharaj had been fixed. His father had come to their house the previous week, stating that the birth charts of Sharmila and Brighu had matched well. Brighu's parents decided that their son was making a decent living by working as the Guru in the Royal ***Gurukul*** and that it was time to get him married.

Normally, the girl's side would approach the boy's to initiate the alliance. However, in this case, the boy's parents had taken the first step. Bharadwaj and Shakunthala felt that Sharmila's good fortunes were at play. It was then that Shakunthala realised that in order to complete her third sister's marriage, they would have to get the second sister, Shyamala, married. Shakunthala decided to take the matter up with Bharadwaj

Sitting inside the house, Bharadwaj was thinking about the forthcoming marriage. His wife had brought up her long-held grievance, that she had not been able to give birth to a child in the last twelve years of their wedlock. She insisted that he marry Shyamala so that there would be opportunities to extend the lineage of their family. Bharadwaj did not agree to the plan. But Shakunthala would not give up. She wanted to see the wedding of both her sisters happen at the same time. She countered Bharadwaj's concerns by saying –

'Shyamala is well versed in Vedic astrology, just like you. Both of you feel so comfortable discussing this subject for hours together. Moreover, Shymala's birth chart conveys that she will be blessed with many children after marriage. I think she will make an ideal match for you. You must marry her.' There were prolonged arguments between husband and wife. After considerable thought, Bharadwaj agreed to the marriage with Shyamala.

Both marriages were to be held in the ***Samudhra Narayana*** Temple's main hall. The bride's side usually bore the wedding expenses and hence Bharadwaj was busy making the wedding arrangements for his second wedding and that of his other sister-in-law.

Finally, on the day of the wedding, there was a large crowd gathered in the hall. Just at that instant, the prince of the Pandiya kingdom entered. He invited Brighu Maharaj, the bridegroom, to come with him to his kingdom to set up a Gurukul. And so the prince himself attended the marriage.

There were two decorated stages for the solemnizations. Maran thought that the dual marriage celebration had been initiated to allow economically backward classes to share marriage expenses. But when he went near the stage to bless Brighu Maharaj, he was surprised to see none other than Bharadwaj as the other groom.

At that time, the prince heard some one calling him. 'Your Excellency, Prince of the Pandiya Kingdom, on behalf of the kingdom of Krishna, I welcome you!'

Maran turned and saw his friend Sahadev.

He smiled and said, 'Thanks for your welcome, my dear friend. You seem to be the key host at this function. It appears that you are hosting this marriage?'

'Yes, Maran ji. Bharadwaj is one of the people I respect a lot. We share interests in Vedic astrology. And, as you already know, the other groom is an educationist in the Royal ***Gurukul*** and hence I am personally overseeing all the marriage proceedings today.'

Maran was impressed by the commitment shown by Sahadev. Sahadev was aware that Maran would be leaving the kingdom in the next couple of days.

He said, 'Maran, I was told that your ship is full of goods bought here in our kingdom. You are also taking with you many of our Ayurvedic pandits and educationists. I hope this one month in our kingdom has been fruitful for you.'

'Sahadev, you are right, I am carrying a number of things to my kingdom. But you forgot to mention one thing. As you must have rightly guessed by now, I have fallen deeply in love with Kanchana. Hence, she is also accompanying me. I plan to conduct our wedding within a month's time. I will send the wedding invitation soon. You must come with your respected brothers, the other Pandavas.'

'Congratulations, the cat is finally out of the bag. I have to be more courteous to you now Maran Ji, because you are now a bridegroom of the Kingdom of Krishna.'

He turned around and spoke to Kanchana with a new respect. 'Congratulations, Your Majesty, the future Queen of the Pandiya kingdom!'

Your Excellency, do not embarrass me. I am always a citizen and an employee of our beloved Kingdom of Krishna. I consider this to be the happiest place on the planet. Nothing on earth can take away my affection for our kingdom, Your Excellency,' Kanchana said.

Maran envied the attachment that Kanchana felt for her kingdom.

Sahadev added, 'Maran ji, I am sure you have seen enough of the attachment shown by our citizens to this kingdom. Our leader is a magnetic force, a towering king with an inclusive approach. He does not meet everyone in the kingdom, but he makes them feel that he will be there for them whenever they need him.

'Maran ji, I will definitely be there for your wedding. I want to witness the Pandiya kingdom's style of marriage.'

Maran looked lovingly at Kanchana and added, 'Sahadev, I have planned a two style marriage ceremony. I know the strong bond that Kanchana has to this kingdom. I do not want to deprive her of her cultural beliefs on an important day. Therefore, we will have two ceremonies - one our way, the other your way.'

Sahadev addressed Kanchana, 'Your Majesty, future Queen, you are lucky to have found a loving husband. It is better to marry the one who truly loves you than someone whom you love.'

Kanchana replied earnestly, 'Your Excellency, you are right. Fortunately, in this case, it is mutual love with a meeting of minds. I know that our culture states that a bride walks into a groom's family like the river joining the sea. I, the product of the Gomati River, will soon be joining the Pandiya sea. I will make sure I live up to their expectations and ensure that the pride of our kingdom flies high.'

Maran was keen to learn about the rituals involved in the marriage, and Kanchana happily explained them to him. Meanwhile, Sahadev moved around the hall, ensuring that all the guests were being taken care of. Sharmila was watching them closely as well. Since Kanchana and Maran wanted to understand all of the rituals, they stayed near the wedding stage, taking position just behind Sharmila, the bride. Hence, Sharmila could listen to the all the explanations provided by Kanchana to Maran.

Kanchana explained, 'Maran, most ***brahmins*** celebrate their weddings with great fanfare. Their marriages are tradition-bound and have a lot of poojas and rituals. The marriages are held around the holy fire with Lord Agni as the witness. ***Brahmins*** uphold the tradition of ***Kanyadhan*** or giving away the daughter. The groom takes up responsibility for the bride from her parents. He vows to stay with her in joy and sorrow, in this life and thereafter. In Brahmin marriages, the tying of the ***mangalsutra*** has a lot of significance. It means the groom and his bride are bonded together for life.'

As more questions came to his mind, Maran asked, 'Oh, there seem to be quite a few interesting rituals. What exactly is Kanyadhan, Kanchana?'

"***Kanyadhan*** or offering the daughter as a gift to the groom is akin to offering a gift to god. The daughter may be very dear to her parents, but they have to part with her after marriage. It is in fact the best gift that a man can ever give. However much a father might love his daughter, he will not be able to keep her.

'Generally speaking, most marriages are performed at auspicious hours in the morning. They take place in a decorated mandap like this with a sacred fire. The bride wears a silk saree, flowers in her hair and jewels given to her by her parents and the groom's family.

'The father of the bride welcomes the groom and washes his feet. The groom's family presents the bride with a nine-yard marriage sari, which symbolizes energy, passion and fertility. The action also states that "henceforth in this lifetime, I (groom) will buy you all your clothes."

'The girl's father is made to sit on a sack of paddy which symbolizes material and spiritual plentitude in the marriage. The girl is seated on her father's lap. Then the yoke of a plough is touched to the bride's forehead. This symbolizes that just as two bullocks are required to carry the plough and work and till the fields, she and her husband will remain side by side to go through life. The bride's father gives her to the groom. This is called the ***Kanyadhan***.'

She looked at Maran and guessing his next question, she volunteered to answer it before he asked. 'Maran, the next ritual is ***Mangalya-Dharanam***. When the ***Thirumangalya*** (a sacred thread with a golden pendent) is tied around the neck of the bride, they normally put three knots. The three knots symbolize Brahma, Vishnu and Rudhra.

'After that, the next ritual is called ***Sapthapadi*** which constitutes the chief element of the marriage. The groom holds the bride's right hand in his right, his shawl is tied to the threads in the corner of her saree and they walk around the sacred fire seven times. He then takes hold of her right foot and makes her take seven consecutive steps, after which the bride touches her feet to a grinding stone. This symbolizes that their union will be as stoic, solid and steadfast as stone.

'This is an interesting part of the ceremony because the couple vows that if one ***is Rig Veda***, the other will represent ***Sama Veda***. If one is ***Booloka*** (earth), the other will represent heaven. If one is bright, the other will wear the rays from his or her brilliance. Pledging this, they agree to be united and to bring very good progeny to this world. This declaration is the whole theme behind ***Sapthapadi***.

'Then the bride is taken to the north side of the sacred fire and asked to put her right foot on the ***sil***, a hard, flat stone used for grinding in the house. The groom holds her right toe and puts on the toe rings. Then the groom applies sindoor on her forehead. The newlyweds then prostrate themselves before their parents and elders to receive their blessings to have good progeny and long life.'

As she narrated the significance of each ritual, they reached the ***Mangala Aarti***, which marked the conclusion of the marriage. She continued her explanation. 'At the conclusion of the marriage, they take the ***Mangala Arti*** for the wedded couple. They mix lime and turmeric powder in water and take it around the couple three times. This is supposed to ward off any evil cast on the couple.'

Then came the time for wishes and blessings from the audience. Maran and Kanchana also walked up to the couple, gave them gifts and congratulated them. Brighu introduced the prince to his newly wedded wife Sharmila, and informed her that he would soon be leaving with the Prince to his kingdom.

Sharmila told him that the prince and Kanchana had been sitting behind her. She could see the prince's interest in every single ritual. She said she had listened to each question raised by the prince and the excellent answers given by Kanchana. After enjoying the feast at the wedding, Maran and Kanchana retired to their guesthouse to prepare for their voyage the next day.

That the, nuptials for the newly wedded Brighu and Sharmila started off on a sober note. The usually bubbly and enthusiastic Sharmila was silent, her head bent and cheeks red from crying.

A tense Brighu asked her, 'Sharmila, the love of my life - you seem to be so nervous. What is the matter? From now on, you can share all your worries and concerns with me.'

She looked up and controlling her tears answered, 'Ji, I am thinking of tomorrow night. I will be alone and will miss you. It will only be one day after our wedding and you will be gone. The separation will kill me.'

Brighu Maharaj looked at his new wife lovingly and said, 'Sharmila, I understand your concerns and feel happy to have a loving wife like you. Now that we are together and the time is limited, let us enjoy the moments that we share. Do not take tomorrows' worries and spoil today's happiness. I am going to the Pandiya kingdom for a good cause. In six months' time, I will return and take you with me. With your permission, I gave my consent to the prince of Pandiya. Sharmila, let us enjoy this happy moment of our union instead of brooding over our forthcoming separation.'

After the exchange, like a river joining the sea, the two souls unified into a single body. The sunrise brought them back to this world from their joyful journey.

Brighu Maharaj's first words were –

‘Sharmila, I have to get ready now. I have to leave for the ship in two nazhiga.’

Brighu Magaraj got ready, offered his respects to his elders and bid farewell to Sharmila. With tears in her eyes, Sharmila watched him leave.

Everyone assembled on the ship. Accompanying Prince Maran were Kanchana, four ***Ayurvedic pandits***, Brighu Magaraj, and a few servants. The flag of the Pandiya kingdom waved high on the mainmast of the ship.

Meanwhile, in Dwarka, Sharmila had already started feeling lonely. One day passed like a year for her. At sea, the men in the ship had successfully completed one day of sailing. But soon, disaster struck. The shocking news hit the shores of the kingdom of Krishna. It was a great tragedy that shook the entire kingdom.

*** ***

Shakuntala had no words to console the unfortunate widow. She vented out her distress at Bharadwaj.

‘Ji, you are supposed to be a great astrologer who can predict forthcoming events from birth-charts. You are the one who matched the horoscopes of Sharmila and Brighu Magaraj. Did you not see this coming? Or have your predictions lost their accuracy?’

Bharadwaj, who was also terribly upset by the change of events, replied –

‘Shakuntala, I know that our family now faces the worst time in our lives. But that should not lead you to question the accuracy of my astrology. Astrology is a divine gift. In certain cases, fate closes the eyes of the foreteller – man proposes while God disposes. The foreteller can never take the role of God to narrate all future events with complete precision. There are several issues here – the casting of the birth chart is one of the key elements. Had the time of birth been wrongly casted by one ***Naazhiga*** (2½ ***Naazhiga*** is one hour), the complexion of the horoscope would change completely. We do not know for sure whether the birth charts were accurate in the first place.

‘Another thing you should note here and something I have told you before is that Sharmila has a ***Manglik dhosha***. This means that she will have a disharmonious relationship with her spouse in her first marriage. The planet Mars is located in the second house of her birth chart. To counter this dhosha, we tried two things –

‘One, we made her marry a banana tree before marriage. We were of the belief that this ***Kumbh vivah*** (a symbolic marriage) would make the banana tree her first husband and thereby nullify the effect of the ***dosha***.

'Second, we selected the horoscope of Brighu Magaraj whose stars strongly conveyed the presence of peace and patience. We believed that his horoscope would dominate and do its part in eliminating situations of disharmony.

'Shakunthala, we have tried some corrective measures that we believed could cure her ***dosha***. But there is an Almighty above us. We can never alter the pre-determined fates of people,' concluded Bharadwaj.

Shakunthala was not convinced by this answer.

'Ji, you are philosophical man; you can take such things in your stride and retain your composure. But we are emotional women and cannot take things that way. What will my sister do now? Why should she face this?' Having said this, Shakuntala sobbed uncontrollably.

Meanwhile, the neighbors began pouring in. In the name of sharing grief, most of them ended up designating Sharmila as the most unlucky woman. Their hushed conversations did nothing but add more fuel to the fire. Sharmila could no longer control her emotions and sobbed hysterically. With no food or water, she grew weaker.

As the family mourned Brighu's death, the ***Brahmin*** community head visited Bharadwaj. He told him, 'We have to accept the reality, Bharadwaj. You have to follow the traditional ten-day mourning period. On the tenth day, you have to tonsure Sharmila's head, remove the vermilion ***thilak*** and ***mangalsutra***. She should start wearing a white saree and cover her head. She should not attend any festive occasions from now on. She should spend all her time performing services to God and seclude herself from society. We have to follow the conventions Bharadwaj, even though it is difficult. On behalf of the entire community, I stand before you today to convey our heartfelt condolences to your family.'

The moment he left, Shakuntala voiced her views to Bharadwaj.

'Ji, we cannot implement the traditional rituals for Sharmila. She is a child who grew up in front of me. I cannot see her following these awful rituals. I can never witness her putting on the white saree, just two days after being dressed in the beautiful bride's attire.'

Bharadwaj consoled his first wife.

'Shakuntala, hold on. Let us not worry. We will do what is best for Sharmila. When all the doors are closed, God will open a window. Stay calm, we will work out something for her.'

Meanwhile, her other sister, Shyamala, who had recently married Bharadwaj as his second wife, also joined the conversation.

'Society denounces a widow. It is very unfortunate that society does not allow widows to re-marry and have the opportunity to lead a happy second life.'

Bharadwaj, who strongly opposed ill-treatment of widows, firmly said, 'On the tenth day, when the community assembles to perform the atrocious rituals on Sharmila, I am not going to allow them to go forth.'

'Ji, are you serious? Are you going to antagonize our community by rejecting the accepted norms?'

'Yes. Why not? I have given it some thought and I have reached the conclusion that I will not let Sharmila become a victim of these rituals. At this time, she needs mental rejuvenation, not ill-treatment,' Bharadwaj said.

'Ji, what can we do for her? As per her horoscope, she is a ***manglik***. Now she is a widow and wears the stamp of bad luck. No one will come forward to marry her. I really do not know how can we help her,' Shakunthala said sadly.

At this juncture, Shyamala intervened and spoke to Bharadwaj, 'Given the situation and the long life indicated in your birth chart, I suggest that you consider marrying her, ji.'

A shocked Bharadwaj replied, 'What? Have you lost your mind? You well know that I reluctantly agreed to marry you as my second wife. It took eight years for your elder sister to convince me and now we are already discussing a third marriage?'

Shakuntala voiced her views. 'Ji, she is right. We cannot find anyone else at this point to willingly marry Sharmila. We cannot make her live a life of complete seclusion. I therefore, endorse Shymala's suggestion. Please ji, you have to agree to this and save my youngest sister's life.'

On hearing the views of both his wives, Bharadwaj thought about it for a while. The objective was correct, but he wondered whether it was right to agree to a third marriage. Looking at the grieving Sharmila, he was confused. Then he said, 'Alright, I will consider this proposal only if Sharmila wholeheartedly agrees to it.'

Shyamala and Shakuntala decided to broach this subject with their sister after three days. They knew it would be too early to raise it now.

As the days passed, Shakuntala and Shyamala spent more time with their sister. When the time was right, they broached the subject. 'Sharmila, you should slowly come out of the grief. The disaster has taken place and we cannot bring back what has already been lost. We have to look ahead. We want to see you as the same happy and lively character you've always been.'

'It is not easy to get over my feelings so quickly, Shakuntala. Looking ahead, I do not know why I have to live any longer. I should end my life. But I don't seem to have the courage or strength to do that. I feel so confused and lost,' said Sharmila.

'No, no, don't say that, my dear. You were born to live happily. Don't jump to conclusions based on events. Both of us have decided to get you married to our own patidev as his third wife, after the ten-day mourning period. What do you say?' asked Shakuntala.

In a state of shock, Sharmila said, 'What? How did such a thought cross your minds? Your husband is like an uncle to me. He has provided everything for me since childhood. It is impossible to think of such a marriage.'

Shymala intervened, 'But why not, Sharmila? It is not a hasty decision that Shakuntala and I have reached. We have given it thought. We can understand your feelings. But, the sad truth is that we can no longer expect any good man to come forward to marry you. You know how society brands widows. Let us face it, this is the reality. But, as your loving sisters, we cannot allow our dear sister, the bubbly young Sharmila, to suffer for a lifetime for no fault of her own. Hence, we believe that this is the best course.'

'I know that both of you always want the best for me. Therefore, if you feel that this is the only solution, then I will abide by your decision.'

'Thank you Sharmila, we are relieved. We will organize the marriage as a simple family function in the temple after the completion of the ten-day mourning period,' said Shakuntala.

The mourning period finally came to an end. Bharadwaj did not carry out any of the traditional rituals that marked the widow as an outcaste. People living nearby gossiped at length about the family not conforming to traditions. A few more days passed without much activity. Finally, after several rounds of deliberation, Bharadwaj tied the knot for the third time on an auspicious day, in the temple with his two other wives witnessing. The community soon came to know about this and a summons was issued by the caste panchayat. The hearing was to be held a month later.

*** ***

7. The Naming Ceremony

It was the thirtieth day since the birth of the three children. The naming ceremony fo was being held at Samudra Narayana temple. There was a big crowd. The members of the royal family - Subhadra, her newborn son, Sahadev, Pradiyumna (Krishna's son), Satyaki, Kritaverma, a host of other ministers and many other members of the royal court were present. The general public was also there. Everyone was looking for Lord Krishna and Arjuna, whom they considered to be their heroes. They soon learnt that they were in Indraprastha and would not be attending the function.

Apart from Subhadra's son, two other babies were placed in front of the deity. The babies in the golden cradles were Subhadra's son and the son of the wealthy Dhana Vaisya. Another baby was wrapped in a plain white cloth and placed on the floor, next to the golden cradle. That baby must have been born to poor parents. There was festivity all around. Bharadwaj was very busy with various tasks related to the function. Three whole pots filled with water, mango leaves and coconuts called ***Purnakumba*** caught everyone's attention.

The mango fruit is a symbol of love and fertility. The leaves of the mango tree are used during many religious and social ceremonies. The ***Purnakumba*** pot is considered to be the ***sthapna*** (sacred placement) of the puja. The pot symbolizes Mother Earth, the water contained in it represents the life giver, the coconut represents divine consciousness and the mango leaves symbolize life. The whole taken together symbolizes Goddess Lakshmi and good fortune. On various auspicious occasions, mango leaves are used to adorn entrances to signify good fortune.

Everything was in place for the ***Ayushya Homa***, which is conducted for the wellbeing and longevity of the child. ***Vedic pandits*** recited hymns and ***Agni*** was invoked. Ghee, fruits and cooked rice were poured into the fire.

As preparations were being made for the pooja, the third child's father, a wealthy looking man, came out of the sanctorum shouting, 'What is this? Why does my child have to undergo the naming ceremony along with a fisherman's son?'

As everyone looked around, the wealthy man shouted, 'This fisherman ran away without paying my dues. ***Panditji***. You did not tell me that this idiot's son is going to be named at the same function. I do not want to see this cheater here. Please ask them to get out!'

Bharadwaj momentarily halted his tasks, looked up and said, 'Dhana Vaisya ji, in the kingdom of Krishna, when the naming ceremony occurs on any given day, there is no discrimination based on ***varna*** or caste. Even the royal family is celebrating the naming of Subadhra's son today and they have no hesitation in having the ceremony along with a ***Sudhpudra***.

'Vaisya Ji, God does not acknowledge or accept these discriminations. Your wealth may be displayed outside but not inside this temple. In fact, as an extension of your concerns, even the royal family could raise objections against having their naming ceremony with your Vaishya son. Please understand and do not create a commotion here.'

'***Panditji***, whatever you may say, this man cheated me and scurried away from the scene. And now he has no right to be considered on par with me.' Dana Vaishya continued his shouting.

'Dhana Vaishya ji, I wish to inform you that I have brought Matsya and his family under my identity seal. I am now his designated caretaker. I name this child as a Brahmin's. He is now my son. What can you do now?'

Witnessing the scene, the youngest Pandava prince Sahadev came out and pacified Dana Vaishya. Decorum was soon restored. Everyone walked back inside the sanctorum to join the naming of the trio – a ***Kshatriya, Vaishya*** and a ***Sudhpudra***.

'Naming a baby is considered to be sacred and therefore is an important tradition. The people involved in the naming ceremony are the parents of the newborn, the paternal and maternal grandparents and few close relatives and friends. Traditionally known as ***Namakaran Sanskar***, this ceremony is conducted in an elaborate form. This ceremony is usually held after the first 30 days of a baby's delivery.' Bharadwaj explained to all those gathered.

'These 30 post-natal days are considered to be inauspicious as the mother and child are considered to be impure. After those 30 days, the house is cleaned and sanctified for the ceremony. The mother and child are bathed traditionally and prepared for the ceremony. Relatives and close friends are invited to be part of this occasion and bless the child. Priests are called and an elaborate ritual takes place. Therefore we are all here to bless these lovely children.'

The formalities followed. The children were dressed in new clothes. The mothers wet the heads of their babies with a bit of water as a symbol of purifying the child. The baby was then handed over to the paternal grandmother or the father who sat near the priest during the ritual. The sacred fire was lit and the priest chanted hymns to invoke the blessings of the gods.

The child's eyes were lined with ***mayye*** or ***kanmashi*** (kohl). A black spot was placed on one cheek or asymmetrically on the forehead, to ward off the evil eye. According to the date and time of birth of the child, a particular letter of the Sanskrit alphabet was chosen which would prove lucky for the baby. The baby was given a name starting with that letter. The father whispered the name in the child's right ear three times while the left ear was covered with a betel leaf. This was then repeated with the left ear. A mixture of ***ghee*** and honey was given to the infant as a base for its various foods in the future. The father touched the nose and felt the breath of the child so as to awaken its consciousness and to draw its attention towards the ceremony.

An elaborate feast was being made ready for the priests and guests and this marked the closing event of the ceremony. This feast would be a ***Samapandhi Bhojan*** where the wealthy and poor sat across from each other and ate at the same time, without any discrimination.

The rituals were now over and the priest started to cast the birth charts of the children and offer his broad predictions. He generally refrained from indulging in micro-level predictions; it was strongly believed that astrology should not offer too much detail. Only broad roadmaps of the child's life were predicted in the birth charts and conveyed by the priest.

Priest Bharadwaj came out of the sanctorum. He addressed the gathering. '***Aryajan***, today we have completed the naming ceremony with the grace of Lord Samudhra Narayana. Three children, one each from the royal family, a trader family and a fisherman family have been named today. While casting their birth charts, I witnessed a strange coincidence - all three children were born at more or less the same time, share the same star ***Mriga Shirsha*** and have the same rasi of Taurus.

'All three are likely to emerge as great warriors and are also likely to work together. Their fates are aligned, even though they come from different backgrounds. May Lord Samudhra Narayana bless them with many green pastures. Now, let me announce their names and my predictions of their individual skills –

Abhimanyu – H.E Arjuna and Subadhra's son, will be an embodiment of bravery and perfection in archery like his father.

Aryavaishya – Dana Vaishya's son, will be a great military tactician and excellent mobilizer of military resources.

Sagar Matsya – Matsya's son was born in the midst of a chaos, but he will show courage and calm in any crisis. He will display extraordinary skills in military strategies.'

Dana Vaishya shook his head disapprovingly when he heard the predictions. He did not want his son to interact with the fisherman's. But he did not know that the fate had other plans for them.

After the ceremony, it was time for the ***Samapandhi Bhojan***, where the princes, priests, traders, workers and others were served food. What a scene it was! Clearly the kingdom of Krishna was an egalitarian society with no room for caste, creed, colour – all were treated on par and all lived happily.

As the lunch proceedings were taking place, suddenly an ***astra*** (missile) pierced the hall and parts of the flooring caught fire. Pandemonium was unleashed. The diners hurried out through various exits. What came next was shocking…

8. The Exile: A Stateless Status...

At the time that the ***astra*** set the hall on fire, piercing sounds from a conch shell, blowing at a distance, reverberated through the sky. Everyone thought it was a siren. Everything happened in a matter of seconds. People moved out of the hall through several emergency exits. The Rapid Action Force of the Royal Guards stepped in, put out the fire and performed quick restorations.

As the initial fears passed, it was seen that no casualties had occurred and no one had been injured. Calm was soon restored. The damaged portion of the hall was repaired by the Rapid Action Force. An outsider would have been surprised by the quick recovery. Many of the guests washed their hands after having partly eaten their lunch and dispersed as though nothing out of the ordinary had happened.

Subadhra asked the priest, 'Bharadwaj ji, was this fire a bad omen? Does my child have a long and safe future?'

Bharadwaj replied, 'No, no, do not read into this incident, Your Excellency. Difficulties arise in day to day life. Today, it has happened after the naming ceremony and these issues have been managed without any loss. This is an indication that the children will pass through many clouds in their lives, but they will handle situations calmly. Did you notice that none of the three children cried when the commotion happened? Their observation of the crisis is a sign that they will show courage in such times and exhibit heroic skills on the warfront. You do not have to worry too much about their future. Turbulence will fill their lives, especially once they reach the age of sixteen, but Lord *Samudhra Narayana* will help them to pass through it all. May God bless them!'

One of the guests from a neighbouring kingdom asked Bharadwaj, 'Priest ji, do you have any idea where this sudden attack came from? And why did it stop after a single astra being fired? Who are the people behind it?'

'Ji, it is well known that Jarasandha, Kamsa's father-in-law, has an everlasting grudge against Krishna's community. For years, he has been waiting to avenge himself on Krishna and his followers. Unable to win conventional wars, he resorts to guerilla wars against the kingdom. He pursues cross-border terrorism from the border state of Avanti. He sends ***Agni astras*** (missiles) from the neighboring state.

'But when an ***astra*** hits this kingdom, there are sensors that detect them and set the conch shell blowing. When these siren-like sounds are heard, the counter ***astras*** are fired in the direction of the incoming astra, and the source is destroyed. In most cases, those firing the destructive ***astras*** are found dead at the borders. Also, the siren serves to alert the public, the

Rapid Action Force, and the rest of the kingdom. This is one of the main reasons why no one was wounded today.'

'Oh! It left me spellbound to watch the incident handled so quickly. It baffles me to see how people in this kingdom are so alert,' the guest said.

'Ji, now that you have seen an important aspect of our kingdom, let me narrate another incident that showcases the preparedness of our people in an emergency.'

Watching the guest listen intently, the priest continued, 'During the Raivataka festival, Arjun fell in love with Krishna's sister Subhadra. He whisked the maiden away, with the secret consent of Krishna, but provoked the anger of the other Yadava heroes. The armed attendants of Subhadra, feeling defeated, ran crying to the city of Dwarka. They headed straight to the Yadava court, popularly known as the ***Sudharma***. They spoke of the prowess of Arjuna to the chief officer of the court. The chief officer blew his gold-decked trumpet, calling all to fight.

'Stirred by the sound, the ***Bhojas***, ***Vrishnis***, and the ***Andhakas*** began to pour in from all sides. Those who were eating left their food, and those who were drinking left their drink and flooded the courtroom. Those tigers among men, those great warriors of the ***Vrishni*** and the ***Andhaka*** tribes, took their seats upon their thousand thrones. The chief officer of the court, assisted by those that stood at his back, spoke of the conduct of Arjuna. The proud Vrishni heroes rose from their seats, unable to brook what Arjuna had done. Some amongst them said. "Yoke our chariots," and some, "Bring our weapons" while others loudly called upon their charioteers to harness their chariots.

'As the commotion built up, Lord Krishna advised Subadhra to drive her chariot herself to indicate that she was the one to abduct Arjuna, and thereby pacify the angry Yadavas. Those pleasant conclusions to the story apart, look at the preparedness of the warriors of the kingdom. On hearing the conch shells, all the warriors assembled in minutes. I am narrating this incident so that you are aware of the preparedness of our warriors. Moreover, for many years, we have been facing attacks from Jarasandha, and hence our kingdom is always ready to fight. This is a city that never sleeps; someone or the other will always guard our society, ji.'

*** ***

It was a ***Somavar***, Monday morning. People assembled under the shadow of the banyan tree, the usual place for the caste Panchayat. The head of the ***Panchayat*** was the very same old man who had conducted the proceedings on an earlier day, when Bharadwaj had been involved as a witness. Today, Bharadwaj and Sharmila stood in the accused box.

'Priest Bharadwaj, are you aware of why we have convened this ***Panchayat*** today?'

'Yes, Your Honor.'

'Do you know you have a double crime charged against you? As the head of the house, you have not carried out the traditional rituals for a widow. And you have also married the widow, against caste norms. Do you accept your offence?'

Bharadwaj spoke with no feeling of guilt in his voice. 'Your Honor, before I accept or reject the offence, let me place certain facts before you. In an earlier deliberation as a witness, I presented the case for widow re-marriage. Let me present the case in proper perspective again.'

When no one objected, he continued. 'The dependency of a woman on her husband and her inability to find a new husband after the death of the first leaves the widow with a very undesirable and cruel life. The choice was always between death with honour or life as a destitute. The decision to die, however vile, becomes more appealing when the widow does not have sons to support her. But how can I be a party to nipping a blossoming bud?

'***Sati*** (self immolation) could be an option for some, but I do not subscribe to this view. The dharmic scriptures support my view. The Vedas do not encourage the performance of ***sati***. Passages in the **Rigveda** encourage the widow to leave the side of her dead husband and find another life partner amongst the living. The epics do not advocate sati, but women who have committed it are highly regarded.

'The most famous is the death of Her Highness Queen Madri. Her devotion to her husband is praised and immortalized and such a role model might encourage this practice amongst women of high birth and nobility. But Madri's ***sati*** was not one that was encouraged. She was asked by ***rishis*** and others not to go ahead with it. In fact, Her Highness Kunti did not opt for sati in order to bring up her children. Therefore, ***sati*** is not an option that I can impose on the budding flower that has faced just one day of married life.

'I did not want Sharmila to be a useless member of the household and be considered inauspicious, ineligible for invitations and celebrations. I didn't want her to spend the remainder of her life in sorrow and misery.

'The next option was remarriage. ***The Rigveda*** and ***Adarvana veda*** (10.40.2 and 9.5.27 respectively) indicate that widow remarriage is allowed. In fact, the *Rig* ***veda*** even prescribes that the widow give up thinking of her late husband and accept the marriage proposal of the person who wants to marry her. Both Tara and Mandodari married their brother-in-law after the death of their husbands during Rama's rule.

'Today, we do not allow widow remarriage and neither do we allow these women to live as members of society. Bearing all these factors in mind, we decided to have Sharmila remarried. But given the stamp of bad luck and since she was a ***manglik*** , we realized no one would come forward to marry her. Hence, with the consent and persistence of my other wives, who are her sisters, I decided to marry her. Therefore, I feel I am not guilty of a crime,' concluded Bharadwaj.

The judge had different views. In an authoritative tone, he said, 'Bharadwaj, you have started lecturing us yet again. I am sure you are aware that each one of us is governed by caste

Panchayat rules and we have to operate within this framework. You had received a warning in the earlier case. This is now your second offence. Therefore, the caste ***Panchayat*** declares that you and your newly wedded wife Sharmila shall be banished and live as outcastes hereafter – ***Jati Bahishkar*** is ordered. Your occupation as the priest at the temple also stands forfeited. You are asked to move out of the community locality. The ***Panchayat*** also announces that no one will have any relationship with you or your family any longer. You have to vacate your house in the next seven days.'

The court was adjourned.

Bharadwaj came home with his wives. Shakuntala was furious and spoke at the top of her voice. 'Ji, you should appeal the case to the ***Varna*** Council under the Royal court's jurisdiction. You should take the matter up through your well wisher Sahadev. We should not accept this verdict, given the circumstances that led to this marriage.'

'Shakuntala, calm down. I do not want to seek favors from Sahadev. I know that he respects me. But that does not mean that I have permission to ask for favors. Let us face the verdict. Everything happens as per God's wish. We have to repent for our past ***karma***,' replied Bharadwaj, retaining his composure.

'Ji, I don't know how you can retain your calm even in such stormy situations. But where can we go now and what can we do for a living?' asked Shakuntala.

Bharadwaj took a deep breath, looked at each of his wives and said, 'For now, I can only think of moving to the border of our kingdom, near the forest. We can take the help of Matsya Rajan and build a ***pharnasala*** (hut) for ourselves. We will have to learn to eat the fruits of the forest and live our lives in such a manner. Let us see what God has decided for us.'

Reluctantly, they left their home. Matsya Rajan was kind enough to help them build a thatched hut. He was now a swimming instructor at the royal ***Gurukul***. Due to this, he no longer needed the temporary seal of citizenship sponsored by Bharadwaj. The ***Gurukul*** had made him a full citizen of Dwarka.

He said, '***Pandit Ji***, it is you who gave me shelter in this kingdom. It makes me miserable that today I have to help you to build your own shelter. But do not worry. I promise you that I will supply you and your family with food grains and vegetables. You are the one who gave me a new life. For me, you are God. Will you accept a small service from this ***Sudhputra***?'

Bharadwaj took Matsya's hands in his and thanked him.

Days passed. Living in seclusion, with nothing to do, the troubled sisters played games with their minds. Shakuntala could not control her anger. Sharmila blamed her bad luck as the cause of all their miseries. Grief and sorrow filled their daily lives.

Days passed without much activity. One morning, they saw a band of well-dressed royal personnel riding towards their ***pharnasala***. As usual, the paranoid Shakuntala screamed, 'Ji, I can see few royal staff coming towards our hut. What do they want from us now? We have left everything and come here. Why does the caste ***panchayat*** want to cause us more trouble? Can't we live peacefully, ji?'

As usual, Bharadwaj was unperturbed. As he waited for the royal staff to walk into the hut, he comforted Shakuntala.

The men on horses walked in and asked, 'Ji, are you Bharadwaj? We have come from Indraprastha, the kingdom of the Pandavas. His Excellency Sahadev sent us. We visited your old house, but did not find you. We then went to the identification card office and came to know of the unfortunate ***Jathiprashta***. We came here to see you.'

'What is the matter?' Bharadwaj asked, looking a little confused.

'Ji, His Excellency Sahadev has given strict instructions to bring you for the ***Rajasuya Yagna*** to be performed by his elder brother, our Emperor Dharma ***Putra***. He wanted us to bring you and your family to the occasion as special invitees. We can leave tomorrow morning.'

Watching Bharadwaj nod his head in confirmation, the royal staff continued, 'We will come back to fetch you then.'

As soon as they left the hut, Shakuntala, who wore her emotions on her sleeve, said, 'Ji, I always knew that we will have good future. God is with us and will not let us down. This is an excellent opportunity to settle down in the kingdom of the Pandavas.'

'Shakuntala, don't go overboard with your emotions. We are only going there as guests. I advise you not to imagine any further,' said Bharadwaj.

The next morning, they departed in the special chariot that had been sent by His Excellency Sahadeva. The sisters prayed that this journey would reverse their fortune and they would see better days ahead. Little did they know that misfortune would continue to haunt them.

*** ***

9. The unending miseries

Bharadwaj and his wives commenced their journey to Indraprastha, the land of the Pandavas. They travelled in a brightly coloured royal chariot driven by four shining horses.

Shakuntala was ecstatic.'What a change of fortune! Never did I imagine that we would be invited as royal guests to the ***Rajasuya Yagna*** performed by Dharmaraja. I simply cannot contain my excitement!'

'Shakuntala, you are too quick to reach conclusions. There is no reason to conclude that this journey will end all our sorrows. Do not dream too much,' warned Bharadwaj.

'Ji, you are always like this. You don't know how to enjoy the moment. But, unlike you, if I am happy I enjoy myself thoroughly and if I am sad, I mourn deeply. Now, let me enjoy the moment like any ordinary person would. I am not a saintly character like you.'

Their journey took them through various forests and kingdoms. After crossing *Saurashtra, Narmada Valley, Malava, Avanti* and the Kingdom of *Gurjara*, they reached *Indraprastha* that next morning.

Indraprastha was the new land of the Pandavas. They had initially been given the *Khandarva Prastha* or the unclaimed forest. Although it fell under the area ruled by *Hastinapur*, the forest did not have any major villages or cities and was filled only with ***asuras***, tribals, hermits and animals. They had been allotted this unwanted and useless land by Dhritarashtra, the king of Hastinapura, as a settlement.

The story was that the Pandavas originally had the right to rule Hastinapura, which was being temporarily ruled by their uncle Dhritarashtra. But when their father died and they were still very young, Dhritarashtra tricked them into taking the forest as barter for the kingdom of Hastinapura. The Pandavas did not want to argue with their uncle and obliged. They then took up their abode in *Khandava Prastha.*

The *Khandava* forest had its own history. After they were granted the land, the forests had been burnt by Lord Krishna and Arjuna. Arjuna had covered the forests with innumerable arrow,s leaving no living creature a chance to escape from the onslaught. It so happened that while the forest was burning, Takshaka, the chief of the Nagas, was busy fighting another war and not present.

However, his mighty son Aswasena, who was guarding the forest, was burnt alive by the fire from Arjuna's arrows. The other inhabitants including the ***Nagas, Asuras*** and the ***Rakshasas*** offered stiff resistance. Armed with machines, iron balls and bullets, catapults for propelling huge stones and rockets, they fought Lord Krishna and Arjuna. Their energy and strength increased with their wrath. Though they rained a perfect shower of weapons, Arjuna struck off every one of their heads with his own sharp arrows.

One of the asuras by the name of Maya became an ally of the Pandavas. To show his gratitude for sparing his life, Maya cleared the land. The Pandavas planned and constructed the city on this land. The city, so formed, came to be called *Indraprastha* (Indra's city).

The chariot carrying Bharadwaj and his family passed through this great city. They noticed numerous gardens adorned with trees bearing colorful fruits and flowers. There were varieties of trees bearing fruits ranging from mangos to blackberries.

They saw colorful birds with wide and beautiful feathers pecking at the fruits. These verdant groves resounded with the notes of maddened peacocks and ***kokilas*** (blackbirds). They also saw many bright pleasure-houses, numerous bowers of creepers, green hillocks, and lakes filled with water shining like crystals. They rode past water tanks fragrant with lotuses and lilies and adorned with swans, ducks and ***chakravakas*** (brahminy ducks).

Shakuntala and her sisters were stupefied by the beauty around them. The chariot passed through the magnificent streets and finally came to a halt at a large mansion. The royal guards announced that this would be their guesthouse.

Once inside the guesthouse, the sisters noticed that they were not alone and were accompanied by many other guests from different kingdoms. The Bharadwaj family were escorted to their allotted room. They rested for a while. They rose in the evening, just in time to watch the beautiful sunset from the banks of the ***Yamuna*** River.

They walked back to the guesthouse. On their way back, while the sisters looked on, Shakuntala asked Bharadwaj, 'Ji, what is this ***Rajasuya Yagna***?'

Bharadwaj replied, 'Rajasuya is a sacrifice performed by the kings of the land of Bharath, those who consider themselves powerful enough to be emperors. Generally, Rajasuya is performed after the return of the generals from successful military conquests. In the case of Pandavas, the Dharmaraja or the King sent his four brothers as generals, one in each direction. They conquered many kingdoms and now Dharmaraja is being crowned as the emperor. The kings of the vanquished kingdoms are invited here for the ceremony and from now on, they will all bow down to Dharmaraja as their emperor. The ***Rajasuya Yagna*** is a confirmation of this process.'

'Ji, how does this Rajasuya Yagna differ from ***Ashwamedha yagna***?' asked Shakuntala.

Bharadwaj replied, 'In the case of the ***Ashwamedha yagna***, the army is led by a wandering horse which has been let loose from the capital. Whichever land the horse goes to and passes through unchallenged will belong to the King to whom the horse belongs. In the case of Rajasuya, there is no horse involved, but the generals plan the route. I hope that answers your question, Shakuntala.'

Shymala asked, 'Shall we all go out again and see more of the city?'

As they stepped out again, they were welcomed by a festive atmosphere. The streets were decorated with temporary shops. They sold goods ranging from pearls and expensive gold ornaments to decorative mud products.

As they walked near the shops, they overheard conversations from other guests who had arrived a few days earlier. From their conversations, the Bharadwaj family came to know that many ***rishis*** and kings from various kingdoms had come to Indraprastha for the ***Yagna***.

Virtuous and learned rishis with senses and souls under complete control and many others skilled in the Vedas and conversant with rules of morality had also gathered for the ***Yagna*** at Indraprastha. Many wealthy and well-armed ***kshatriyas*** endowed with great might had come as well. Artists skilled in vocal and instrumental music and those with the ability to sing to celestial tunes in charming voices had reached to showcase their brilliant performances.

What caught everyone's attention was the magnificent palace of the Pandavas. Like a mass of new clouds conspicuous in the sky, the palace rose up, coming into view. It was supported by columns of gold and the area it covered measured close to five thousand cubits. It shone in great splendor, and by its brilliance seemed to darken even the bright rays of the sun. With its effulgence, which was a mixture of both celestial and terrestrial light, the palace looked as if it were a sea of flaming torches. Eight thousand ***rakshasas*** called ***Kinkaras*** guarded the palace. They were fierce, huge-bodied and endowed with great strength, coppery-eyed with pointed ears and well armed.

Within the palace was placed a peerless tank, and in that tank were lotuses with leaves of dark-colored gems and stalks of bright jewels, and other flowers with golden leaves. Aquatic fowl of various species sported in this tank. Variegated with full-blown lotuses and stocked with fishes and tortoises of golden hue, its bottom was without mud and its water crystal clear. There was a flight of crystal stairs leading from the banks to the edge of the water. The gentle breeze that swept along its bosom softly shook the flowers that studded the water.

The banks of the tank were overlaid with slabs of costly marble set with pearls. Beholding the tank adorned with jewels and precious stones, many kings who came there mistook it for land and fell into it with eyes open.

Many tall trees of various kinds were planted all around the palace. Of green foliage and cool shade, and ever blossoming, they were all very charming to look upon.

Artificial woods were laid around, always emitting a delicious fragrance. And there were many other ponds adorned with swans, ***Karandavas*** and ***Chakravakas*** (ducks) in the surrounding grounds of the mansion. The breeze bearing the fragrance of lotuses growing in water and ministered unto the pleasure and happiness of the Pandavas.

'Oh, my God, is this a celestial world? A place full of fairy tales,' murmured Bharadwaj.

Another guest from Khoshala Raj spoke of the way the Rajasuya Yagna was being managed. He applauded the clear delegation of work from the royal palace with rights and responsibilities carved out for each of the portfolio managers. Bharadwaj wondered how the king of Pandavas commanded such a high level of respect that could cut across barriers.

As Bharadwaj listened, the Khoshala guest described the brilliance of the delegation process adopted by the King, the Emperor Dharmaraja. 'King Dharmaraja is a great soul. His congenial disposition attracts everyone as his friend, and therefore he is known as ***ajatasatru*** - one who never created an enemy. He has engaged all the members of his ***Kuru*** dynasty in taking charge of different departments for the management of the **yagna**. For instance, his brother Bhimasena has been put in charge of the kitchen, Sahadeva in charge of the reception, Nakula in charge of the stores, and Arjuna entrusted with the duty of looking after the comforts of the elderly.

'Not only this, he has also managed to get Duryodhana to take care of the treasury. The most astonishing feature is that Krishna, the Supreme Personality of Godhead, has taken charge of washing the feet of all the incoming guests. The Queen, the goddess of fortune, Draupadi, is in charge of administering the distribution of food, and because Karna is famous for giving charity, he has been placed in charge of the charity department. Similarly, the others including Satyaki, Vikarna, Hardikya, Vidura, Bhurisrava, and Santardana are all engaged as well. They are all so keen to show their affection for King Dharmaraja.'

As more conversations flew in the air and as Bharadwaj and his family dwelled in the festive atmosphere, they noticed a middle aged woman curiously looking at Shakuntala. After a while she came up to her and said:

'I am Karthika. I work as a helper in the team of girls serving Queen Draupadi. I saw the mehndi on your hand. You have drawn your husband's face on your palm. I think it is very beautifully done. Our dear queen is very fond of ***mehndi***. I want to take you tomorrow to the palace to apply it on the queen's palm. Will you come with me?'

Shakuntala was surprised by this question. She said, 'Yes, it is an honor. I will come with you. But, I don't have any materials for the mehndi.'

'Oh, no worries, we have everything in the palace. Our queen wants a unique artistic design on her hand. Till date, no one has managed to impress her with their drawings. Something tells me that your work will have a positive impact on her. Tomorrow morning, I will come and take you.'

Noticing two more women standing by Shakuntala's side, Karthika said, 'Do you want these two ladies with you to accompany you to the palace?' When Shakuntala nodded, she continued, 'No issues, you can bring them along. By the way, where are you staying?'

Shakuntala agreed to the request after consulting Bharadwaj. Bharadwaj encouraged his wives to go, while he said he preferred to stay back in the guesthouse to recite his hymns. The sisters were excited and happy, talking among themselves. Bharadwaj socialized and talked to more guests. The ***Yagna*** was a rare occurrence. The more experienced ***pandits*** were elaborating on the way the ***Yagna*** would be conducted. Bharadwaj soon learnt that the ***Rajasuya Yagna*** had two distinct aspects to it: the spiritual part and the pleasure part. After listening to details of the ***Yagna*** and spending more time on the streets of the city, he went back to the guesthouse.

The next day, two ***Nazhigas*** (2½ ***Nazhiga*** is one hour) after sunrise, Karthika came to the guesthouse. Shakuntala and Shyamala were ready. They went to the Queen's palace with Karthika. Sharmila decided to stay back with Bharadwaj.

As they entered the palace, they were awestruck by the glittering, rich environment. This was the first time they had visited a palace. They were mesmerized by the posh, graceful ambience. They have never seen anything like this before, not even in their dreams.

While they were enjoying the ambience, beautiful Queen Draupadi walked up to them. Draupadi wore a large and glistening pearl necklace draped across her breasts, a golden belt around her waist, glittering diamond earrings dangling from her ears and ruby studded clips encasing her flowing hair. The Queen's perfumes spread their aroma all over the palace. The queen was of a dark complexion but with her glowing face, she looked like a celestial beauty from whom no man could escape. Shakuntala could not stop staring at Queen Draupadi.

In her melodious voice, the Queen said, 'Karthika, whom have you brought with you today?' The voice though melodious and sweet still had an element of authority. Yet the words were graceful and far from arrogant.

'Your Excellency, I have brought two of my new friends from Dwarka. They are here for the ***Yagna***. I met them in the market. Shakuntala and Shyamala are sisters and are excellent at applying mehndi. I believe you will love their designs and I brought them to you for this purpose.'

The Queen smiled at the sisters and said to Karthika, 'Karthika, let me see what they can do for me.' The observant queen noticed the mehndi on Shakuntala's hand and asked, 'Lady, who is this person you have drawn on your hand?'

A slightly trembling Shakuntala said, 'He is my husband. I can draw the face of your husband on your hand, if you wish, Your Excellency.'

'Ha! Ha!' The Queen laughed. 'I was won in a contest by Arjuna. When my mother-in-law was told by Dharmaraja that they had brought the best bhiksha alms for that day, she asked him to share the alms between the five brothers. I thus became the wife of the five Pandavas. So, dear lady, whose face will you draw on my hand?'

Shakuntala thought for a while and said, 'Yes, Your Excellency, I can draw all five faces. When you look at the mehndi from every angle, you will be able to see the face of each of your husbands.'

'Really? Is that possible? I love the idea!' beamed the queen.

'Yes, Your Excellency. The only problem is that I have not seen any of them. How can I draw their faces without seeing them?' asked Shakuntala.

'Is that a problem? No worries. I will allow to see them. In fact, you can see them from the balcony right now. They are all together, discussing the plan for ***yagna***.'

She took Shakuntala to the balcony and pointed to the five Pandavas sitting below.

'Your Excellency, we can sit here. I can draw their faces while looking at them from here.' Shakuntala said.

For the next three hours, Shakuntala concentrated on her job, while Shyamala played a supporting role. At the end of it, Draupadi got just what she wanted: something very unique that she had never seen before. When she looked at her hands from different angles, she saw the faces of her five husbands.

Draupadi liked Shakuntala's work very much. As a token of her appreciation, she gave Shakuntala a golden necklace. Shakuntala was happy and thanked the queen. The queen also invited her to witness the ***Rajasuya Yagna***. Shakuntala's gratitude knew no bounds. The sisters left the palace feeling very happy.

In her excitement, Shakuntala talked about the incident all night and Bharadwaj could do nothing to bring her back to reality. He finally decided to leave her in her own fairytale, rather than trying hard to inject philosophical thoughts into her mind.

Then came the day of the Rajasuya Yagna. Bharadwaj woke up very early in the morning. Shakuntala was at the peak of her excitement.

They were dressed up and ready by sunrise, and they started for the palace. The people they met on the way seemed ecstatic. There was singing and dancing on the streets. The earth, the rivers and hills, the winds and mountains had come alive to celebrate the crowning of their new emperor.

King Dharmaraja and Queen Draupadi were taking their holy bath in Ganga. There was a huge crowd and the ambience was charged with a festive mood. The sounds of different musical instruments – mridangas, conch shells, drums and bugles--vibrated through the sky. To add to the festivity, the ankle bells of the dancing girls jingled.

Many groups of professional singers played veenas, flutes, gongs and cymbals. The princely guests were present with their different flags and gorgeously decorated elephants, chariots, horses and soldiers. Every one of them was waiting to follow King Dharmaraja's procession. The citizens of Indraprastha began to beat drums and blow the trumpets in their feelings of happiness. There was a shower of flowers from the sky.

After the King and the Queen had finished bathing, all the other citizens followed their footsteps into the river. Meanwhile, the King dressed himself in a new silken garment and put on valuable beaded chains and other jewelry. He gave away all the ornaments and exquisite clothing that he had worn before the bath.

By then everyone had dipped themselves in the holy waters and dressed up in colorful clothing with jeweled earrings, flower garlands, turbans, long wrappers and pearl necklaces. All the women were finely dressed. Each of them wore a golden belt around their waist and a wide smile on their faces.

King Dharmaraja boarded his royal chariot with Queen Draupadi. All the other kings from nearby states, generals and soldiers followed the chariot in a procession. Priests and other brahmins followed chanting Vedic hymns. Behind them were the men and women of Hastinapura and Indraprastha.

All of them were thoroughly enjoying the procession and threw liquids like water, oil, milk and yogurt on each other. The liquids had been mixed with turmeric and saffron and everyone was painted with a lustrous yellow. The beautiful courtesans were also part of the procession and were at their very best on that day. They accompanied the royal guests and swayed gently from side to side in a rhythmic fashion.

The other queens and princesses of the royal family arrived in their gorgeous palanquins, surrounded by their bodyguards. The perfumed liquids were thrown at them causing them to become bashful, but their beautiful smiles lightened up their faces. The whole procession as well as the grandness of the Yagna was such that it almost felt as if the gods themselves would come down to watch it.

This side of the Yagna was the pleasure part, where a display of wealth and beauty reaffirmed the position of the emperor. But the display by Dharmaraja was always in the best taste possible. Even the ample display of beauty evoked wonder rather than lust in the watchers. The procession inched forward and finally reached the palace.

After all the pomp and festivity had ended, the stage was set for spiritual affairs. Vyasa was the chief priest of the sacrifice. Many rishis from far off lands had assembled as well. Rishi Susharma chanted the hymns of Sama Veda - the musical Veda. Rishi Yagna recited slokas and mantras. Rishi Dhaumya poured libations into the sacred fire. With the brahmin pandits reciting the Vedic hymns in the background, Dharmaraja was crowned emperor and consecrated with the ultimate authority.

Bharadwaj tried to meet Sahadeva, who had invited him to this grand occasion. He was glad that his Vedic knowledge had received recognition in the form of this invitation. But he could not meet him, given the huge crowd. He walked into the group of brahmin pandits who were reciting hymns. But when he joined them, the head pandit did not recognize him and noticing Bharadwaj's simple attire, mistook him to be someone who had just come looking for food. Bharadwaj did not hold with self-proclamation and therefore did not elaborate on his knowledge. Lack of recognition caused the other pandits to bar him from joining their group and Bharadwaj was left in a state of shock for a while.

He then decided that he would not fight with pandits who only recognized scholars dressed in glittering silk angavastras, displaying layers of gold chains on their necks. Bharadwaj kept himself aloof from this crowd and sat meditating in a corner. His cold behavior elicited anger from the other pandits, who mocked him for coming there only to receive free gifts, and not possessing any real knowledge of Vedas. The head of the pandits decided to use Bharadwaj for odd jobs and ordered him to prepare the sandal paste for the yagna.

Bharadwaj did not complain, as he was always philosophical in his outlook. He started making sandal paste while silently reciting sacred hymns. Suddenly, he remembered the Agni Suktam and subconsciously began reciting the powerful hymn. He son finished making the sandal paste and handed it over to the other pandits. The paste was to be offered to all the brahmins during the function. They would apply the paste on their stomachs after eating food since it was thought to have a cooling effect and help with digestion.

Later, when the sandal paste was passed around, things turned out very different from what was expected. Instead of being cooled by the paste, all the brahmins shouted 'Burning, burning!' followed by a huge commotion. Sahadev came running to the scene to figure out what had gone wrong. He noticed the paste on the brahmins' stomachs and from the corner of his eye, saw Bharadwaj sitting with the mortar and pestle used for grinding the paste.

He walked up to Bharadwaj and said, 'Bharadwaj ji, welcome to Indraprastha. Forgive me for not noticing you till now, even though I was the one who invited you here. I am sorry; I have been extremely preoccupied with the function. Now that I have spotted you, I will see to it that you are treated well. What is this confusion with the sandal paste? Everyone seems to be pointing fingers at you!'

By then, the other pandits were even more jealous of Bharadwaj, the new person who was having a private conversation with Sahadev. They pointed at Bharadwaj and shouted, 'He did this job and he is the one who created all the confusion. He simply wanted to enjoy himself while we struggled with this burning sensation.'

Bharadwaj could not properly react to the warm reception from Sahadev. His mind was focused on the sandal paste that had caused the confusion. He asked himself, 'What could have gone wrong?' He realized that he had recited the Fire God prayer. He immediately took to the stone on which the sandal paste had been prepared and started making a new paste, reciting the Varuna Suktam (hymn in praise of the Rain God). When everyone applied this paste to their stomachs, their bodies cooled down.

Everyone knew that only great souls had the power to invoke the gods with their prayers. Bharadwaj was one among them. The Brahmin pandits who had hitherto mocked Bharadwaj fell silent. They looked at him with awe and immense respect. At that very moment, the newly crowned Emperor Dharmaraja walked into the room and prostrated himself at his feet and said –

'You were born for a noble cause.'

Bharadwaj was shocked and cried out--

'Your Highness, it is a blessing that I am here today. His Excellency Sahadev invited me to this grand function. I am only an ordinary brahmin. Please forgive me if I have done anything wrong.'

‘No, no, we are honored to have invited you,’ said Sahadev and introduced him to the Emperor Dharmaraja. He elaborated further and said Bharadwaj was someone who took prosperity and adversity with the same equanimity. He pursued passion in reciting Vedic hymns and practicing astrology.

The emperor announced on the spot that Bharadwaj would henceforth be the head of the pandits in the Royal Palace. He invited him to start his new assignment the very next day. He instructed Sahadev to take care of his comforts.

A thought crossed the stunned Bharadwaj’s mind. ‘What an irony – one group banished me from society, while another kingdom is giving me a warm welcome. This is life – the most certain about it is its uncertaint.’

Bharadwaj returned to the guesthouse with his wives, who were extremely happy. Shakuntala was ecstatic at their elevation.

Everyone elese went happily back to their residences. While going home, they praised the work and actions of King Dharmaraja. For the king himself, the completion of the yagna had satiated an ocean of desire.

Even a common man cannot overcome all his desires, but by the grace of Lord Krishna, King Dharmaraja was able to cross over it very easily, and thus he was freed of all his anxieties.

Soon, the king’s cousin, Duryodhana, noticed that Maharaja Dharma had become very famous after the ***Rajasuya yagna*** and was fully satisfied in every respect. Duryodhana began to burn with the fire of envy, true to his poisonous mind. For one, he envied them their imperial palace. In that great palace, the Pandavas lived with their families, and Queen Draupadi served her five husbands peacefully. Lord Krishna also frequented the palace, because of which it was decorated by thousands of his gopikas.

When these gopikas moved within the palace, and their ankle bells sounded melodiously, the whole palace appeared more opulent than any heavenly kingdom. After looking at such beauties in the palace, Duryodhana became envious. He became especially envious and lustful upon seeing the beauty of Draupadi because he had cherished a special attraction to her from the very beginning of her marriage to the Pandavas. In her marriage selection assembly, Duryodhana had also been present, and along with the other princes, he had been captivated by the beauty of Draupadi. But he had failed to win her and since then had been envious of the Pandavas.

Duryodhana was always in an irate mood, and therefore, even on the slightest provocation, he would speak sharply even with the doorkeepers. He was irritated because he failed to distinguish between water and land in the palace. Dharmaraja’s palace was so well decorated in some places that anyone who did not know the tricks would be confused.

Duryodhana often slipped and fell into the waters. The women in the palace giggled among themselves every time he made a fool of himself. King Dharma could understand his feelings, and he tried to restrain the queens, princesses and other women, and keep them from laughing.

One such day, after being laughed at and feeling insulted, Duryodhana immediately left the palace with his head hung low. He chose to take his insult in silence and did not protest or shout. When he left, everyone regretted the incident, and King Dharma also felt sorry. But despite all these occurrences, Lord Krishna remained silent. He did not say anything against or in favor of the incident. It appeared that Duryodhana had been put into an illusion by the supreme will of Lord Krishna, and this was the beginning of the enmity between the two sects of the Kuru dynasty.

After the Rajasuya Yagna had been completed to everyone's satisfaction, Emperor Dharmaraja resumed his routine. Bharadwaj also reported for duty as the head of the Vedic Pandits. He was well received by Sahadeva and after a brief meeting with Dharma Raja, Bharadwaj started interacting with the other Vedic Pandits. Shakuntala and Shyamala, having already established their connections with Queen Draupadi, joined the queen's regular mehndi panel. They were allotted a comfortable house inside the palace. Things moved smoothly for the next two weeks.

Two weeks later, the inauspicious occurrences began. Bharadwaj noticed some bad omens. He observed that the planetary configurations did not look good. He noted two comets with red heads in the sky. Another rare occurrence took place – three eclipses, two lunar and one solar within a lunar month of 27 days. Being a Vedic astrologer who knew the impact of the planetary movements, Bharadwaj was worried. He mentioned his worries to Sahadev, who in turn conveyed them to Emperor Dharma. These astronomical occurrences signalled war, destruction, loss of life and enmity among people.

Even though the worries lingered in their minds, no one knew what exactly might happen next. They tried to forget their anxieties, but within a week, they had found form.

*** ***

10. The Great Chase

The news of the Pandavas' exit from the town was spreading like wild fire in the city of Indraprastha.

Duryodhana had invited Dharmaraja to participate in a game of dice. Bharadwaj had warned him against accepting the invitation, but the king had said that it was his duty and he must follow protocol and accept the invitation. The worst had happened.

'The Pandavas have lost the game of dice to Duryodhana. This has forced them to leave Indraprastha on a Vanavaas (going to forest) for 12 years and Adnyatvaas (living in disguise) for one year. If they are found by anyone during the thirteenth year, they have to redo the Vanavaas.'

Everyone in the city of Indraprastha was talking about this. Shakuntala came running from the street and asked Bharadwaj, 'Ji, Do you know this? We are entering a dark phase. Our bad luck has touched the Royal Palace. We were born to suffer. How can we tolerate these ever continuing difficulties?'

'Shakuntala, you have begun crying. I always tell you to treat these miseries as a part of your life. You jump to conclusions once you sight a good occurrence. Both misery and good things occur to us like a day and night, Shakuntala, Calm your nerves, let me check what is happening,' Bharadwaj said.

'Ji, the day and night is equally divided. But for us, miseries occupy the major portion of our lives. We do not have an equal taste of prosperity and adversity. The adversity hits us more.'

Bharadwaj preferred not to pick arguments with her. Instead, he proceeded to the palace to find out what was happening. He met Sahadeva. Grim-faced, Sahadeva told him the whole story.

'Following the great ceremony, all the guests left with great appreciation for the Pandavas. But our jealous cousin and his maternal uncle Shakuni extended their stay as special guests in order to enjoy the grandeur of the beautiful palace longer. The Palace was full of illusionary things. Duryodhana was repeatedly fooled and his appreciation soon turned into jealousy. He said to Shakuni, "Uncle, I cannot bear the prosperity of the Pandavas. I feel like attacking them and take away all their wealth."

'"I know a way by which they can be ripped off and sent to exile," replied Shakuni in his cunning voice.

'Duryodhana was impatient to know more about Shakuni's trick. Shakuni asked him to wait until they go out of the charming palace. "Who knows, the walls may have ears," Shakuni said in agitation.

'After reaching their Hasthinapura, Shakuni unveiled his plan. "We can invite the head of the Pandavas for a game of dice. The king does not play well, but he will not refuse your father's invitation. I will play for you as I have mastered the art of the game of dice. You must convince your father to invite the king for the game."

'Everything happened as per the cunning plan. King Dharma played and lost his empire, his brothers and his wife. We younger brothers did not question our elder brother. Everyone was taken aback.

'King Dharma then lost our wife. She was dragged into the palace of Hasthinapura. She was ridiculed as a harlot and other abusive language was used against her. To top it all, Duryodhana's brother was asked to disrobe her. She cried for help from the elder ministers. No one came to her rescue, but when she cried for help from Lord Krishna, her saree went on rolling with no traces of ending. Everyone was stunned by the miracle.

'Draupadi took the oath of not tying her hair till Duryodhana's is destroyed in a war. Bhima, the strongest of us, and Arjuna, the greatest archer on the planet took an oath to kill him and his brothers for this shameful act of disrobing.

'Draupadi was given three boons by Dhridarashtra, Duryodhana's panicked father. Using these boons, Draupadi managed to free us, and our kingdom.

'Duryodhana and his uncle then forced Dhridarashtra to invite Dharma to play just one more game of dice. Dharma always obeyed our uncle. This time the condition was that if he lost, we would go into the forest for twelve years, and live one year in disguise. If we are discovered, we will have to repeat the exercise all over again. Dharma lost the game.

'And now we must leave, Bharadwaj Ji. We intend to leave our mother here with our uncle, due to her old age. The rest of us are ready to go.'

Bharadwaj said, 'We have nothing to do here. Wherever the Pandavas are, that is the place for us to live. I will accompany you with my wives. Please do not try to stop me, Your Excellency.'

He began following the Pandavas, along with waves of people who came out of their homes. Not a man, woman or child stayed inside. They followed their kings like a river, reaching out to comfort them. King Dharma begged them not to follow him. They wept, sobbed like children and stood on the roads, gazing after the Pandavas long after they were out of sight.

But many continued to follow the Pandavas into the forest, and Bharadwaj and his three wives were among them.

The Pandavas made their way to the banks of the Ganga. They drank the water and refreshed themselves. They took rest under an immense banyah tree at the water's edge. The Brahmin Pandits who had insisted on coming with them lit a fire the next morning and chanted hymns. There was nothing to eat and the fruits and the stalks of lotuses floating in the river Ganga could not satisfy their hunger.

The dethroned Emperor turned sadly to the brahmins who followed him. 'The forest is worse, full of serpents and poisonous insects. I am touched by your gesture of coming with us. But I cannot feed you. We will have to hunt, and when we find nothing, we will have to subsist on roots and fruits. I plead with you to go back. I cannot watch you all suffering. It is our destiny to have to go through this process, but we do not want all of you suffering with us.'

'Don't turn us away, Dharma Ji. We are devoted to you. We will watch over you in the jungle with prayers and lighten yours spirits with the stories from our puranas. You need us, don't send us away,' they answered.

Bharadwaj intervened at this stage. 'Your Excellency, Surya Deva (Sun God) is a lord of foods of this earth. If you worship him, you will find a solution to feed all the brahmanas.' Dhaumya *Rishi*, a noble saint amongst them also echoed a similar thought.

The next morning, standing in waist-deep water, King Dharma performed ***Surya Namaskar***. He prayed for the blessings of the god.

The god appeared in front of King Dharma. He was holding a copper platter in his hand. He said to him, 'This platter I am giving you will feed you all. Whenever you want to eat, it will fill with food and remain full until Draupadi has eaten. For the thirteen years of your exile, this plate will feed you. In the fourteenth year, you will get your kingdom back and you shall be the lord of the earth again.'

He vanished. Dharma took the plate and came back to the banyan where the others waited. He thanked Rishi Dhaumya and Bharadwaj. He told the others about the plate and asked Draupadi to prepare food for all of them. He said, 'We will not starve any longer. The others can stay with us now.'

Even as Draupadi served, the food on the platter never diminished, delighting all of them. When Draupadi finished eating, the platter became clean and the food was no more. After a day of staying there, they moved into the deep jungle. They came to the jungle on the banks of the river Saraswati.

'This is ***Kamyaka Vana***,' said Dharma. They built thatched wooden huts and began living there. Bharadwaj stayed in a hut adjacent to that of the Pandavas, along with his three wives.

Very soon, the jungle inmates – its wild denizens, the rishis who lived in ***Tapasya*** praying for the world--became familiar to them.

When Krishna heard what happened, he came to ***Kamyaka Vana*** to meet the Pandavas. He came with the host of kings. He assured them that they would win back their Palace. When Dharma said he would complete the thirteen years of exile and only then stake his claim, Lord Krishna blessed him. He assured them of his help and went back to Dwarka.

One day, the Pandavas went hunting in the deep forest. Jayadratha, the king of Sindhu, the only brother-in-law of Duryodhana, was passing through the forest on his way to Hastinapura. He saw the Pandava's ashram. He saw Draupadi standing at the door. He did not know who she was, so he sent an emissary to find out. Her beauty struck him, and he wanted to have her more than anything in the world.

He went to her and told her, 'I am the King of Sindhu, brother-in-law of Duryodhana. The forest is no place for you. Is this the kind of life your husbands have given you? I will keep you as a queen. Come with me.'

'Aren't you ashamed?' Draupaid asked. 'You should be like a brother to me. Won't you fear for your life when the Pandavas hear about this? They will not spare you.'

But he cried, 'I don't care. I want you now, this moment!' He seized her, flung her across his shoulder and moved towards his chariot.

Draupadi cried, 'Let me down! Let me go!'

Hearing the cries, Bharadwaj came out of his hut and tried to intervene.

'Who are you?' he asked, 'What are you doing?'

The king replied, 'I am Jayadratha, king of Sindhu. Get out of my away. Don't stand in the way of a Kshatriya king.'

He kicked him from the chariot, and Bharadwaj fell down. Draupadi was in tears as Jayadratha took her to the chariot and drove away. Bharadwaj ran behind the chariot, but could not catch up. He knew that they were moving eastwards.

He knew he had to find the Pandavas, but he did not know where they were. As he ran through the forest, he saw a rishi meditating under a huge mango tree.

He shouted, 'Ji, did you see the Pandavas come through here? Help me please, their wife has been abducted. They have already suffered enough. I cannot see them suffering anymore. I would give my life to stop their suffering. Please help me, Ji.'

The *Rishi* opened his eyes. He looked at this panicked Brahmin, realized that there was a grave problem, and showed him the place where Pandavas had been hunting. Thanking him, Bharadwaj reached them.

The Pandavas saw Bharadwaj crying. 'Draupadi has been abducted by the Sindhu King, Jayadratha!' he sobbed.

He showed them the direction in which Jayadratha had gone. Since the Pandavas were very familiar with the forest by now, they ran though short cuts and secret trails. Bharadwaj followed them. They spotted the chariot of the Sindhu King. The Pandavas' arrows flared out from the trees, and from the sky.

Jayadratha could not cope with this situation. Leaving Draupadi, he fled. Bharadwaj roared in anger. Dharma saw him losing the temper like this for the first time. He saw the red eyes of the Brahmin priest, a rage that is only witnessed in the eyes of the brave warrior on the battlefield.

Bharadwaj told the Pandavas, 'Had we been late, the matter would have gotten worse. Had the Queen not been saved, I would have ended my life, as I cannot see you all suffering anymore.'

Sahadeva cut away the ropes on Draupadi and freed her. She clung to him and then came to her other husbands, sobbing with relief.

Bhima shouted, 'I will go after that wretch. He won't live after what he did.'

Dharma said, 'He is the husband of our cousin. Don't kill him. I will not allow you to do that.'

But Draupadi cried, 'If you love me at all, kill that beast.'

After hearing this, nothing could control Bhima. He went into the jungle, got hold of Jayadratha and brought him back.

Bhima shouted at him, 'Do you fight only women? What kind of Kshatriya are you? You are a useless coward.' He pushed Jayadratha down and shaved his head, leaving only five tufts.

He made him shout, 'I am the Pandavas' slave! I am the Pandavas' slave!' Bhima pushed him so he fell at the queen's feet.

'Is it enough, Draupadi?' Bhima asked.

'That will do, you have humiliated him. I am satisfied, spare his life,' she said.

Jayadratha was ashamed. He came to the banks of the Ganga and pursued a tough ***tapasya,*** worshipping Lord Shiva. Later, Shiva gave him a boon, by which he could hold the Pandavas other than Arjuna when he met them in a battle.

After releasing Jayadratha, the Pandavas, Draupadi and Bharadwaj started back towards their ashram. On the way, they came across the Rishi under the mango tree.

The Rishi looked very calm. Peace and tranquility was written all over his face. Any one who saw him would automatically solicit his blessings. The Pandavas fell at his feet and thanked him for giving them timely directions.

The Rishi said, 'Pandavas, I am *Markandeya Rishi* and have been doing ***tapasya*** for the last ten years under this tree. Your priest Bharadwaj is very attached to you. He cried that he would not live a minute longer if anything happened to Draupadi. He has so much respect for you.'

The Pandavas were elated when they heard this. They were all thankful to Bharadwaj for his timely action.

A monkey took the ***astras*** from Arjuna and climbed up the mango tree. Bhima followed the monkey. Both reached the top. The branches of the trees were entwined here, and flowers and mango fruits were plentiful. Bhima realized the monkey was an ancient of his kind. His golden face was covered in wrinkles. It was not possible to tell how old he was. Bhima growled. The monkey raised his head. To his astonishment, the monkey spoke in perfect human speech.

'Young man, what do you want? Why are you after me? Don't you know this is a dangerous place? What are you doing here?'

Bhima cried, 'You are the strangest monkey I have ever seen. You speak like a man in the old language. Are you a monkey at all? You have taken the astras of my brother. If you do not give them back to me, I will jump above you like Hanuman, who crossed the sea and snatched those astras that are in your custody now. Give them back.'

'Who is Hanuman? His very name raises your passion. Who is he?' asked the monkey.

Bhima got wild. 'You are a monkey and you do not know the immortal Hanuman? He fought at Lord Rama's side. It was he who found Seetha in the Asokavana in Ravana's palace. He leapt across the sea to give Lord Rama's message to Sita. We worship him. You have not heard of him? What a shame!'

On hearing this, the monkey said, 'Bhima, my brother, I am your Hanuman.' They hugged each other.

Hanuman cried, 'Ah! When you embraced me, I felt the same thrill of love that I received when I first touched Lord Rama in the last Yuga. Take the ***astras*** with my blessings. Give them to your brother. Tell him that I will sit on his banner during the Great War to follow. You will win.'

When the monkey moved, Bhima saw a glittering triple mango. The fruit was shining, inviting him to eat it. There were more fruits all over, but the triplet mangos were unique. Hanuman saw the look in Bhima's eyes.

'Bhima, don't pluck the triplet mangoes. They have a sacred history. Go and seek the answers from Rishi Markandeya, who is sitting below the tree. He will guide you.' Saying this, Hanuman vanished like a dream.

Bhima came down with the astras, handed them over to Arjuna and told his brothers what had happened at the top of the tree. They were curious to know about the triplet mango. They went to Rishi Markandeya.

'Rishi, Bhima was told of a unique triplet mango. Hanuman advised him not to pluck it but to heed your advice. Kindly tell us about it,' Dharma requested Rishi Markandeya.

The Rishi said, 'The triplet mango in this tree blooms only once every ***Yuga***. The Krita is the immaculate age, when there is no trace of evil on the earth. Every creature is content. There is only one ***varna***, the 'Brahmin,' in this yuga. The importance of this triplet is visible to the ordinary person on earth in this ***Yuga***. The benefit of eating this fruit is to feel god in this ***Yuga***. Prahalad could see this and ate this fruit in the first ***Yuga***. This kindled his deep devotion to Narayana.

'In the ***Yuga treta***, evil enters the world. There are three portions of ***dharma*** and one of ***adharma*** which starts showing its ugly face. Avarice and passion arise, violence erupts. Hence to rule the earth a new ***varna*** called ***Kshatriyas*** is created. During this ***yuga***, the governance of the kingdom is key and the triplet mango gives that power of governance.

'During this ***treta yuga***, Lord Rama, Bharatha and Lakshmana were resting under this tree. Bharatha made a last attempt to bring Rama back to the kingdom. Lord Rama could see this triplet mango on the tree and gave it to Bharatha, so that the mango could give him the power of governance in his absence.

'Now, this ***Dvapara Yuga*** is an age of conflict and men doubt the very nature of truth. ***Dharma*** and ***adharma*** are equally divided. A great war will dominate this ***yuga***. The triplet mango in this ***yuga*** can give the man who consumes it extraordinary war skills on land, sea and sky. A lady has to eat this so that she bears a son with great competence in land, water and sky.

'Three of the ***Pancha bhoodas*** – land, water and sky--will obey this boy and he will also be able to invoke the other two, namely fire and air. The land proficiency comes from the fruit portion, the surface of the mango; the water proficiency comes from the juice of the mango and the sky proficiency comes from the smell of the mango. The first mango's surface has to be eaten from the left, the second one's juice has to be drunk and the third one's aroma has to be smelt. This is the way the fruit must be consumed by the lady who is blessed to have it in this ***Yuga***.

'The secrets of this triplet mango in this ***yuga*** must be unveiled by a Rishi like me. You cannot pluck it. You have to use a blessed arrow and make the fruit fall in my lap. Once I give it to you, the benefits will accrue.

'Going forward, the last ***Kali Yuga*** will be filled with wrath and darkness. ***Adharma*** will dominate. In that ***yuga,*** a person will be blessed by God himself to take this triplet mango. The benefit of this fruit will be the power to disappear and reappear at will. In ***Kali Yuga***, since ***Adharma*** will be rampant, the ***dharmic*** person will be given the power that will enable him to wage a guerilla war and win it in an invisible mode.

'Now Arjuna, take out the arrow that lies beneath the tree, near the snake hole. This was the arrow Lord Rama left behind, when Bharatha departed the forest.

'Use this arrow and make this triplet fall in my lap. It should not fall on the ground.'

Arjuna did as commanded. The mango fell in the lap of the Rishi Markandeya. Everyone clapped and shouted in joy.

The rishi gave it to Dharma, telling him, 'Give this triplet mango to the lady who can give birth to an extraordinary warrior. He will be able to command the ***Pancha Bhoodha*** – land, water, sky along with fire and air. He will be extraordinarily competent in land, water and space battles.

God bless you, Pandavas. Arjuna, your act of using the arrow to make the triplet fall in the lap of a Rishi like me may have to be repeated in the Great War to follow. Bless you all.'

They returned to the ***ashram*** with the sacred, blessed mango.

*** ***

11. Back to Dwarka: The Triplets Arrive

Although the day had been a traumatizing one, it had ended on a happy note and to top it all, the Pandavas had been blessed with the extremely rare mango.

That night, there was a discussion between them. Draupadi started the conversation on a playful note.

'You won me at my ***swayamvar***. Dharma Ji mentioned to mother Kunti that he had brought the best alms (***bhiksha***). Without knowing that it was me he was referring to, your mother asked you to share the alms. Now we should not make the mistake of asking her to identify who the beneficiary of the mango should be. Let us decide amongst ourselves.'

Arjuna intervened. 'Why do we need to refer to anyone? This sacred mango is meant for you.' The other Pandavas agreed with him. But Draupadi refused.

'I want to have one son by each Pandav Putra. If I take this blessed mango and get one extraordinarily talented son, the other sons will be jealous. I do not want a rivalry amongst our sons.'

'Draupadi has a point,' said Dharma. 'Which other deserving person can partake of this blessed fruit?'

'The person who is most attached to us, and the person who could bring all of you together to save me from the evil Jayadratha, is Bharadwaj. I can only think of him at this stage. He has not yet been blessed with children. He should be given the blessed mango so that he can have a son,' concluded Draupadi.

They summoned Bharadwaj and gave the blessed mango to him after explaining its benefits.

Bharadwaj could not control his tears. He said, 'I was thrown out of my home by my community. I was not given shelter or occupation or food for the next meal. You invited me to the ***Rajasuya Yagna***, made me the head priest, and are now giving me the most blessed fruit. I do not know how I can repay this kindness.'

'Bharadwaj, do not get emotional. It was you who saved Draupadi. You are a pure soul who sees both prosperity and adversity alike. Only a balanced soul like yours should receive the benefits of this blessed fruit. Please give it to your wife. We will have a great ***brahmin*** warrior adding strength to our ranks when we fight the evil forces later,' Arjuna said.

After thanking them profusely, an ecstatic Bharadwaj went back to his ashram with the glittering mango. The moment he entered, Shakuntala cried at the top of her voice, 'Shyamala and Sharmila, come here! What a beauty! I have never seen such a wonderful mango! Words cannot describe the beauty of this fruit. It must have fallen from heaven. Lord Indra must be eating such fruits. Ji, you have brought the best gift.'

Bharadwaj explained the blessings of the fruit. He also narrated the circumstances under which they had received it.

'Ji, I want to have it,' Shakuntala shouted first, followed by Shyamala and Sharmila. A fight started between the sisters. Bharadwaj could not control it.

'What is this new problem?' he thought. Each one was articulating why the mango should be given to her.

Bharadwaj finally came to a compromise. He would break the triplet into three single pieces. The surface of the first one could be eaten by Shakuntala.

Only the second one's juice had to be taken by Shyamala. The third one could only be smelt, which was done by Sharmila. The deal was struck.

The next few days confirmed the blessings of the mango. All the three of them – Shakuntala, Shyamala and Sharmila -- became pregnant. Their treasure of pleasure was beyond measure. Their joy had no limit. How could Shakuntala explain her joy? She had been yearning to experience the joys of the motherhood for more than a decade.

They were ecstatic. Shakuntala went to Draupadi and shared the good news. Draupadi was very happy for them. She in turn shared the news with the Pandavas. There was a festive mood in the ashram.

The very next day, Dharma advised Baradwaj, '***Panditji***, I thought for a while last night. Since your wives are pregnant, I do not want you to suffer in this forest. You have to go back to the kingdom. I know you have reservations about it, but don't worry. You have met Lord Krishna, haven't you? I will give my recommendation to him. He knows you well. You can go to the kingdom of Krishna, and he will receive you and ensure your comfortable settlement. Do not delay any more.'

Initially, Bharadwaj was reluctant. But he consulted his wives and then made up his mind to go back to Dwarka and meet Lord Krishna with the recommendation of Dharmaraj.

They left for the kingdom of Krishna the next day, carrying the wonderful memories of their stay in the forest.

Before leaving, they bid farewell to the Pandavas and Draupadi with tears in their eyes. Dharma said, 'Bharadwaj, do not shed tears. You are a man with a philosophical outlook. Tears in your eyes do not represent your true character. You are leaving for a good cause. You will be taken care of in the Kingdom of Krishna. Bharadwajji, you will be our head priest when we regain our kingdom. We will meet you soon. Do not worry about anything.'

After saying this, Dharma asked Sahadev, 'Sahadev could you go and drop them in the chariot? Travel through the forests, as we are bound by the verdict of Dhritarashtra. Stop at the border of Dwarka, send a word to Lord Krishna and enable Bharadwaj and his family to reach the kingdom safely. You should not enter the kingdom yourself.'

Sahadev took Bharadwaj and his family in his chariot. After three days of journeying through the forests, they reached the border of Dwarka. Sahadev sent a message to Lord Krishna through the Border Security Personnel. Lord Krishna's son came and received them. Sahadev narrated the details and passed on the request of Dharma, that Lord Krishna would accommodate Bharadwaj in his kingdom. Then Sahadev left to rejoin his brothers.

Pradyumna learned from Bharadwaj why he had left the kingdom of Krishna in the first place, how he knew Pandavas, how he had joined them in the forests and so on. He took them to Lord Krishna. Bharadwaj was thrilled to meet the king. Lord Krishna treated him with great respect. After an exchange of pleasantries, Lord Krishna instructed Pradyumna to appoint Bharadwaj as head of Royal ***Gurukul.***

Further, Bharadwaj was allotted a house in the brahmin colony, the same place from whence he had been thrown out earlier. He received a house bigger than the one he had been staying in as a priest of the ***Samudhra Narayana temple***. Shakuntala was thrilled, as were the other sisters.

Bharadwaj began his new assignment the next day. He went to the Royal ***Gurukul***. The building was new and was the largest one amongst others of its kind. He had to mobilize the teaching staff and start the admission process. The curriculum had been designed by the royal education ministry. Children were admitted at the age of five. There were three sessions.

Between the ages five to eight, they would be taught Sanskrit slokas, mythology and history. Between the ages eight and fourteen, they would be taught war skills - strategic/tactical/operational. Between the ages fourteen and fifteen they would be taught how to retain passion in whatever they did, while also maintaining a philosophical outlook that would enable them to accept the result as it stood.

Both outsourced and in-house experts taught the students. The intake would be one for each year, commencing from the start of ***Uthrayana*** (the phase of the rising sun).

Bharadwaj began understanding the details and interacted with all the teaching staff who had joined. He was surprised to see Matsya among them. He had been teaching swimming in another ***Gurukul*** when Bharadwaj left Dwarka.

'What are you doing here, Matsya?' Bharadwaj asked.

'It was a great pleasure to see you back, ji,' Matsya said. 'I am happy that you are back. It is a full turn of the wheel of fortune. You were banished by the ***brahmin*** community here for no fault of your own, and you came back with a bigger assignment from the royal palace- it is a complete turnaround.

'I will be teaching swimming to the students who join this ***Gurukul***. In fact, as soon as I heard that you were going to head this ***Gurukul***, I requested a transfer here. I gave up fishing a long time ago. I thought my next best strength is swimming. Hence, I will impart my knowledge of swimming to the children who will undergo training here. I am now doubly happy since I will work under you. I am very happy ***Panditji,***' Matsya went on.

Bharadwaj began focusing on his new work. He decided to take the first and last of the three sessions. Teaching ***Vedic slokas*** to the young kids was a divine gift to him. He was busy with the admission process. As the kids literally grow from the ages five to fifteen in the ***Gurukul*** itself, accommodating all of them in would be a difficult task. These activities absorbed most of his time.

At home, his wives were happily waiting for the new arrivals. The same people who had driven them out of the colony now came close to them. They viewed them as people with royal connections. Shakuntala was in particular happy to feel the extra warmth of the same people who had once frowned upon them.

One day, Baradwaj went for a darshan of the deity ***Samudhra Narayana***, the very temple where he had served as priest. He went to the temple and prayed before the presiding deity. With tears in his eyes, he thanked the lord for everything.

As he came out, he met the caste ***panchayat*** head, Rajat Varma.

'Welcome Bharadwaj. You have now become a big man. My judgment of evicting you from the community has been reversed now. You are a lucky man,' he said with a tinge of venom in his speech.

Bharadwaj replied, 'I tried to explain it to you earlier. I will explain it you now as well. Knowledge, weapons, wealth and land are the things assigned to a set of people. The group who owns one cannot have the other. That was the rule. People with knowledge are called ***brahmins***, people proficient in weaponry are ***kshatriyas***, people earning wealth through trade are ***vaishyas*** and the people who till the land are ***Shudras***.

'The one with knowledge cannot have wealth or weapons or land. The same is applicable to the others. In the first of the four yugas, there was only knowledge that was recognized, and all were considered brahmins. As ***dharma*** was diluted in the next ***yuga***, people became possessive, tried to grab ownership of land, and then a new set of people who had good strength were nominated by Brighu rishi to be ***Kshatriyas*** to ensure proper governance, law and order.

'The two groups in the second ***yuga*** expanded into four to address each of these segments. That is how Varna came in. The occupation was never defined as linked to birth, but to proficiency. That is where we are still narrow-minded. We say a Sudhra's son is a Sudhra and we do injustice by recognizing the womb of the mother and not the boy's proficiency and skills. Nowhere in the ***Sastras are we encouraged to*** discriminate against people. Birth may result in skill differences due to past ***karma,*** but the skill set alone determines a person's occupation. In my ***Gurukul,*** I will admit students on the basis of potential and not birth.'

Rajat Varma smilingly said, 'It is your time Bharadwaj ji, carry on.' Bharadwaj left the temple.

As the days passed, the three sisters' delivery date neared. For three consecutive days, there was a mild rain and colorful rainbow in the sky. Bharadwaj observed the changes around him and knew that they were the harbingers of good luck.

He was experiencing a tingling sensation on the right side of his forehead, the corners of his right eye, the right side of his chest and right hand. He interpreted these as signs of good luck.

Finally, the day arrived. It was ***Kartika*** month in ***Vikriti*** year, ***Somavar*** (Monday). The earth was facing a mild tremor; the water in the well was oozing out.

The tidal waves were rising. Rain was pouring. Mild thunder and lightning followed. The wind was blowing. Amidst this sound of the wind and the musical notes of the waves, Bharadwaj received an unexpected guest at his house. Gautama Rishi, a great saint.

Bharadwaj could not control his excitement. "***Rishiji***, I am blessed. A great ***rishi*** like you walking into my house makes me feel that I am reaping the benefit of all the positive karmas of the past. Welcome."

He brought a pot of water and poured it on the ***rishi's*** feet and prostrated himself in front of him, a sort of total surrender.

'Bharadwaj, get up. I was passing through Dwarka on my way to Rishikesh. Something induced me to walk into your house. As you are aware, I generally do not enter any home. Bharadwaj, do you know how blessed you are? All the ***Pancha bhoodas*** – earth, water, sky, air and fire--are going to dance to the tunes of your boys.

'You know their strengths. One boy will be extraordinarily proficient in earth-related matters. He will know the earth's topography, water table, earthquake possibilities, and be able to create tremors in the earth. He can predict the movement of creatures beneath the ground. He can create a hole, go into the earth and come out at another place by navigating below the surface. He can stay beside the earth for months without anyone knowing of it. When he fights on earth, no one will be able to conquer him.

'The second boy will be extraordinary in water. He will swim below the water, stay inside for ages, invoke ***Varna*** and bring rain at will. When he fights on water, no one will be able to conquer him.

'The third boy will be highly talented in the sky. He can invoke the ***Vayu*** (air), change the direction of air, speak to the birds, talk to people at a far distance through the air waves. When he fights from a height, no one will defeat him.

'Above all, Bharadwaj, notice one thing. Only when the three are together will the ***Pancha bhoodas*** obey them. You have to make sure when they reach the age of fifteen, they do not go to the battlefield. Make sure of this, as they will face a hurdle at the age of fifteen. Otherwise they will be well, gaining popularity in all respects. May God bless you, Bharadwaj.'

As he was speaking, the sound of three children crying filled the room. Bharadwaj had become the proud father of three sons. He made his Pranams to Gautama Rishi.

The rishi went in and had a glimpse of these three wonder children, the blessed babies. He blessed them and moved out without saying anything more. The words of the rishi were still ringing in Bharadwaj's ears.

It took a long time for him to come back to the reality. Meanwhile, guests were pouring in, and everyone was wishing them. There was a wave of goodwill sweeping the house.

There was a message with a load of gifts from the palace. Baradwaj realized that he had to conduct his sons' naming ceremony on the eleventh day after their birth. He had to do the ceremonies at the same Samudhra Narayana temple.

In the next few days, he was busy inviting everyone to the function. Matsya ran around to everything ready. After all, he had had his own son's naming function conducted by Bharadwaj.

On the appointed day, all the neighbourhood families came to the temple. Pratyumna and Satyaki came as royal guests. The three children were named in the presence of all the well wishers. They were called:

Bhoomi Sena (Son of the earth)

Jala Sena (Son of the water)

Vayu Sena (Son of the Wind)

The sons of Bharadwaj began a new chapter in their lives. Their supernatural skills came to light very soon.

*** ***

12. The *Gurukul* Bondage

The triplets Bhoomi Sena, Jala Sena and Vayu Sena were growing well. To top it all, these children were actually magical, and they were causing wonders, much to the delight of their mothers.

One day, the three children were left in the main hall of the house. They started crawling. Like all children who have just started to crawl, they also showed an insatiable curiosity. They left things upturned or broken and as a consequence, they were termed naughty. There was a heavy Narayana statue kept on a table. There was a tablecloth that was hanging. Anyone from the ground could reach the cloth. Bhoomi Sena pulled the cloth with surprising strength. The statue started to wobble and fell down towards Bhoomi Sena.

For a second, Shakuntala thought that it would be the end of Bhoomi Sena. She cried at the top of her voice. To her surprise, Vayu Sena blew air from his mouth with such force that the statue fell to the side. An awestruck Shakuntala could not control her excitement when she realized what had happened.

She called her sisters and Bharadwaj. 'Listen, Vayu Sena has certain abnormal mystical powers. The ***Vayu*** (air) listens to his commands. The direction of the fall of the statue was completely changed by him. It is a miracle that Bhoomi Sena was saved.'

Bharadwaj recalled the words of ***Rishi*** Gautama. He said, 'Shakuntala, this is just the beginning. You will see more in the coming days.'

His prophecy came true within the next couple of days. They could see miracles happening around them. While the children were playing, Shakuntala went to the kitchen. In this intervening time, Jala Sena, a naughty child, fell into a big vessel of water. He was totally immersed. When Shakuntala saw only two of the children, she got scared. She started looking for Jala Sena all around the house, as she thought he might have crawled into the open yard. She could not find him anywhere.

Finally, she found him immersed in the water. She thought Jala Sena must have died. She took him out of the water with no hopes. To her surprise, it was business as usual for Jala Sena. He was smiling as though nothing had happened.

It did not stop there. One day, Bhoomi Sena was crawling with his brother. There was a crawling competition amongst the three naughty boys. In the process, Bhoomi Sena fell down from the raised floor of the hall on the ground. But to everyone's surprise, when he fell down,

Bhoomi Sena emerged unhurt. When he fell, the floor became soft, like a feather bed. The earth element embraced him and protected him from injury.

Thus the three sons were entertaining the mothers, keeping them busy with their naughty deeds and surprising them with their mystic skills. Meanwhile, Bharadwaj became busy with his work in the ***Gurukul***.

The three sons started speaking very well early on. At a very early stag,e these blessed sons were able to talk, walk and run.

The days became months, the months became years, and the boys reached the age of four. Shakuntala mentioned to Bharadwaj that the boys were quick in all their activities; she suggested they be placed in the Royal ***Gurukul*** at age four itself, instead of waiting for them to turn five.

It was the year Paridhavi. It was ***Uttarayana***, the phase of the rising sun. The admissions to the Royal ***Gurukul*** would start in this period. On completion of age five, the palace decided to place prince Abimanyu (Arjuna and Subadrah's son) under the tutelage of Bharadwaj in the Royal ***Gurukul***. At the same time Arya Vaisya, the trader's son, also joined the Royal ***Gurukul***.

Kailash Vaisya, his uncle, handed the boy to Bharadwaj and said, '***Guruji***, you were the one who performed the Naming Ceremony for Arya Vaisya. I understand Prince Abimanyu has also joined your ***Gurukul***. Please educate my brother's son and enable him to gain knowledge and wisdom under your tutelage.'

'Your brother didn't come? asked Bharadwaj.

He said, 'My brother was killed two years ago by the fishing community. When my brother tried to force the repayment of their loans, he met an unfortunate end.'

As the new admission process was on, Matsya hesitatingly came to Bharadwaj. 'What is the matter, Matsya?' the priest asked. 'I know you want to say something to me. You come to the door, and then at the last moment you turn back. You have done it three times now. What is the matter? What is bothering you?'

'***Panditji***, I do not know whether I can aspire to this or not, and hence my hesitation. Sagar is still waiting to join your school. Can he aspire to join this ***Gurukul***? We are ***Sudhras***, and even at the naming function, Dhana Vaisya created a big scene. Will he permit my son to study with his? Is Sagar eligible to join this ***Gurukul***? Are we ***Sudhras*** allowed to use the Royal ***Gurukul***? These are the thoughts that bother me. Can you guide me on whether I am aspiring too high by seeking the admission of my son in this Royal ***Gurukul***?' Matsya spoke with tears in his eyes.

'Matsya, stop shedding tears. Your son has a great future ahead of him. He was born to make you proud. The kingdom of Krishna gives equal opportunities to every one of its citizens. Even a lotus blossoms from the mud. Do not worry about your ***varna***. I will admit Sagar. If anyone objects, I will say I am his guardian. Do not worry.'

'***Panditji***, your words are like God's voice. How can I repay you? Please take him under your patronage and give him a life different from the rotten one I have faced,' Matsya said.

Sagar was admitted, and Bharadwaj took responsibility as his guardian. Bharadwaj also asked the admission council to consider admitting his three sons, despite their being only four years old.

He appealed to the admission council. 'My sons can pass any entrance test. They are clever for their age. Since I have a conflict of interest in this issue, I request you to examine them yourselves and consider my application.'

The council appreciated his integrity and conducted certain tests to gauge gauging the intelligence of the three Sena Triplets. Those naughty and smart boys were highly qualified for the entry tests. They were all admitted. Thus the new batch had six persons (only). Bhoomi Sena, Vayu Sena, Jala Sena – the Brahmin boys, Prince Abimanyu, the ***Kshatriya***, Arya Vaisya, the trader's son and Sagar, the ***Sudh Puthra***, son of Matsya. It was a perfect combination of students from all varnas.

The boys resided in the Gurukul with Bharadwaj. The first day the parents came to the ***Gurukul*** to drop them. As expected, Kailash Vaisya made a huge noise once he noticed that the son of Matsya also was going to study with his son.

'Matsya's men killed my brother. The needle of suspicion is still pointed at Matsya. How can I ask my brother's son to study with his killer's?'

Bharadwaj said, 'Don't make accusations against Matsya. He broke out of his community long ago and is no longer associated with them.' Bharadwaj explained the philosophy of equality of opportunity adopted by the kingdom of Krishna. He also emphasized that Sagar was under his guardianship. When Kailash Vaisya continued to protest, he was told he could take away the boy to a different ***Gurukul***. Finally, he reluctantly agreed and left his brother's son under Bharadwaj's care.

On the first day of class, Bharadwaj started teaching the ***sloka*** on the goddess of education.

Saraswathi Namasthubyam Varathe Kamarubini
Vidyarambam Karishyami Siddhir Bavathume Satha

The children repeated this sloka five times. After that they were asked to recite it. Everyone was smart enough to recite the sloka. Bharadwaj was surprised that the best pronunciation of the sloka came from Sagar. Every syllable he uttered was like that of a typical ***Vedic Pandit***. This is the God's infinite wisdom, Bharadwaj thought. The ***Sudhputra's*** parents had been worried about a denial of admission at the Gurukul, but the ***Sudhra*** boy had given the perfect rendition of the *sloka*.

With this, the classes at the ***Gurukul*** commenced. The six children were getting along well. There was excellent chemistry between them. One incident cemented their blossoming relationship.

One day, the children were taken to the ***Samudhra Narayana*** temple. After finishing their ***darshan***, they spent some time in the Gomati. The accompanying teacher left them alone for a while. Jala Sena, wanted to show his skills in the water. He immersed himself for fifteen minutes and then emerged. Swimming came to him naturally. Sagar showed his natural swimming skills as well.

Looking at them, Prince Abimanyu and Arya Vaisya also entered the water.

'You need training before swimming. Please stay back !' shouted Sagar.

But their ego was bruised. When Sagar could swim, when Jala Sena could swim, why couldn't they? They entered the water.

The Gomati was full as it was the rainy season. The river had a massive flow of water. The sounds of the waves created a chilling fear in the passersby. But the children, who did not know fear, were attracted by the deluge. The river had currents in a few places and even the best swimmer had to be cautious in the flooded waters. Abimanyu and Arya Vaisya were new to swimming, just five years old, so how could they hope beat the massive flow?

They were caught by a current and were being taken away by the speedy flow. They started shouting – 'Help! Help! Please save us!'

Sagar looked at Jala Sena. Both being natural swimmers sprang like sea horses and pulled them out of the current. They dragged them to the shore. They had drunk too much water. Their stomachs were pressed by Sagar and Jalasena.

'What happened to us?' asked Arya Vaisya, when he had regained consciousness. 'We thought we would die. Sagar and Jala Sena rendered timely help. We have a second phase of life, thanks to your assistance. How do we show our gratitude?'

Prince Abimanyu thanked Sagar and Jala Sena. They decided not to talk about this episode with the teacher or their parents.

Prince Abimanyu then made a statement like a true statesmen. After all, his was the blood of a great warrior.

From today, we are inseparable friends with a deep bond. Our caste, creed, and color will not come in the way. Nothing on the planet can separate us. We have to take an oath of inseparable friendship.'

They agreed and swore an oath. 'We solemnly pledge that nothing on the planet can separate us. We will give our blood for one another and will protect our unity at all times.'

With this pledge, there blossomed a beautiful friendship amongst them, right there on the banks of the Gomati River, in front of the presiding deity ***Samudhra Narayana*** in Dwarka.

At this point, Sagar raised an issue. 'All of you belong to renowned families. One family holds knowledge as power, one family holds the kingdom as power and yet another holds wealth as power. But my family holds poverty as power. I am a ***Sudhra*** by birth. I could not even enter this ***Gurukul,*** except for the mercy shown by our master, Bharadwaj. It is great that you are admitting me into your friendship. But will it work? Will your families accept me?'

Prince Abimanyu intervened. 'Today I tell my friends: we may be young, but we have a dream, we have a vision. Sagar feels low at the moment. I declare that whenever I have command, you will never be slighted. You will be a key part of the army. Our families may denounce his status, but we should never utter a single word against his family or status that will de-motivate him. This is a promise, Sagar,' he thundered.

The others acknowledged his pledge. Young children do not worry about the differences created by society. In fact, they do not know how these differences came up in the first place. Their friendship was born at a very young age. What the young mind resolves stays strongly in them for ever.

The children returned to the ***Gurukul***. They did not discuss with anyone what had happened. Their bond strengthened further in the days ahead.

Within a few days, the ***Upanayana*** was held. This is the initiation ritual at which boys are invested with a sacred thread to symbolize the transference of spiritual knowledge. It signifies the formal admission ceremony into the ***Gurukul***.

The ***Acharya*** performed the ***Upanayana*** ceremony, and taught the boys the ***Veda*** along with ritualistic literature. After the ceremony was complete, the children had to stay in the ***Gurukul*** with their master till completion of their education. The boys were given a sacred mantra which they were not to share with anyone else. The ***mantra*** came from the ***Vedas*** and the boys had to repeat the ***mantra*** every day so that they would be protected from misfortune.

During the ceremony, a sacred thread called ***Yajnopavitam*** was worn by the boys. They would wear it all their lives. The three strands of the sacred thread had a symbolic meaning. A bachelor wore only one sacred thread, and a married man wore two, making it six strands. If the man had married two or more women, he wore three, which made it nine strands.

<u>Three debts</u>

The three strands symbolized three debts that must never be forgotten:

- The debt to one's teachers, i.e. those who have taught the wearer
- The debt to one parents and ancestors, i.e. those who have nurtured the wearer and made his existence possible.
- The debt to the sages/scholars, i.e. those who discovered knowledge, both spiritual and secular, over the ages, which now enriches the wearer's life.

- After marriage, the man would take on the debts of his wife as well.

Three devis

The three strands would symbolize:

- *Devi Gayatri* (Goddess of mind)
- *Devi Saraswati* (Goddess of word)
- *Devi Savitri* (Goddess of deed)

Upon completion of the ***Upanayana*** ceremony, the boy became a qualified student and renounced all material desires. He became a ***Brahmachari***, entering a phase of self control and abnegation.

The hallmark of having gone through the ***Upanayana*** ceremony was the wearing of the ***Yajnopavitam***. The ***Yajnopavitam*** was circular, being tied end-to-end (only one knot is permissible); it was normally supported on the left shoulder (***savya***) and wrapped around the body, falling underneath the right arm. The length of the ***Yajnopavītam*** was generally 96 times the breadth of four fingers of a man, and was believed to be equal to his height.

The knots in the middle represented the formless ***Brahman***, the pure form of energy which pervades all. The sacred strands of ***Yajnopavitam*** illustrated the fact that everything in the universe emerge from and then merge with ***Brahman***.

The ceremony was performed on a grand scale since the royal family was involved. But Sagar was left alone. He did not understand why he had to be kept out of the ceremony. He could not swallow. For all others, their uncles came along with their families and performed the ceremony under the guidance of Bharadwaj.

Sagar cursed himself, and his birth. His father could not do anything. But Bharadwaj did not forget him. When the others had finished, he came to Sagar and said, 'Come, my dear Sagar. I am here for you. Who said you won't have a thread ceremony? I am your guardian. I initiate the ***Upanayana*** function for you by adopting you. I disregard the ***Varna*** or caste. You are my boy.'

He initiated the ***Upanayana*** for Sagar and spoke the sacred ***mantra*** into his ears to the surprise and astonishment of every person at the function. Sagar could not control his tears, neither his parents could conceal their emotions.

'Bharadwaj is a great soul, and we should never forget his gesture,' said Matsya.

After the function, the life came back to normal at the ***Gurukul***. The boys were taught various ***slokas*** and mythological stories. To every one's surprise Sagar was quick in reciting ***Vedic*** hymns; he could perfectly pronounce the slokas, at times even better than a trained ***Brahmin pandit***.

When the boys had completed the age of seven, it was time to move on to the second phase of their education, learning the skills of war.

*** ***

13. Bravery sessions

The occupation a boy finally chose could be bravery-driven, art driven, technical or trade and commerce-driven. Given their young blood and the stories of bravery every child heard, it was no wonder that the largest number of students looked forward to the bravery session of their education. Society recognized and rewarded bravery more than any other skills. However, admission was not based on choice but on their performance in an entrance exam. One of the trends that emerged was that if not bravery, children often opted to be tested on their suitability for the occupation of their father.

To everyone's surprise, all the six of boys qualified for the bravery session.

The bravery session comprised of theory first, followed by practical lessons on horse riding, chariot driving, elephant riding, archery, ***astras*** and all the battlefield ***vyuha***'s. The theory session was conducted by the ***Gurukul's*** armed forces historians. Practical sessions were conducted by heroes from the kingdom of Krishna – Pradyumna, Satyaki and Krita Varma. On special occasions, Lord Krishna's brother Balaram took special sessions.

The first session began with the story of Arjuna's lessons in his ***Gurukul*** days.

'ThePandavas and Kauravas grew into wonderful children. After their thread ceremony, they all studied in the ashram of their Guru Acharya Drona (also called Dronacharya) – teacher of the royal family. Dronacharya was well versed in the ***Vedas*** and ***Upanishads***, as well as in ***Yoga*** and meditation. He was adept in various martial arts useful in war time, defence and attack. In particular, ***Acharya*** Drona was the supreme authority on training his disciples in the art of archery.

'Out of all the princes, Arjuna had immense liking for the sport of archery. He practiced with great concentration and perseverance. Soon, he became numero uno in this art. ***Acharya*** Drona was very pleased with Arjuna and showed him great love and favour. This caused jealousy in the heart of Duryodhana and his brother Dushasana. Duryodhana, in particular, did not like Arjuna and the other Pandavas and feelings of hatred took birth in his heart.

'One day, they openly criticized their ***Guru*** due to the favour shown towards Arjuna, telling him they were not less skillful in archery. In response to their criticism, ***Acharya*** Drona arranged a test to decide the best archer amongst them all.

'A wooden bird was put on the branch of a distant tree. It was partly hidden by the foliage. An eye was painted on the wooden bird. The teacher called all his disciples and said, "Look, my children, a bird is sitting on that tree. You have to hit the arrow in its eye. Are you ready?"

‘Everyone nodded. First, Dharma was invited to try his skill. He stretched his bow-string and was about to release the arrow when Dronacharya asked him a question, "O eldest son of Kunti, may I know what is visible to you at this point of time?"

‘Dharma replied innocently, "Why, O ***Gurudev***, I am seeing you, the tree, people around me, and the bird!"

‘Similar questions were put to Duryodhana, Bhima, Nakul, Sahadeva and others, and ***Acharya*** Drona got similar answers from them all. He told them to step aside as it was obvious that with such poor concentration, they were sure to miss the target!

‘Finally, it was the turn of Arjuna. He readied himself, his bow and arrow in perfect graceful harmony. The Guru asked him, "O Arjuna, tell me what you see."

‘And Arjuna replied, "***Guruji***, at this point of time only the eye of the bird is visible to me." When asked by the teacher whether he was able to see the bird, the tree, and the people around him, Arjuna replied in the negative, maintaining that he saw only the eye of the bird.

‘Dronacharya was pleased with Arjuna's immense concentration and correct approach. He explained to the others that due to such peculiar yogic qualities and powers, he saw Arjuna as his best disciple.

‘Everyone saw his point, including Duryodhana, but the seed of jealousy was sown in his heart. In his attempt to equal Arjuna and the other Pandavas, Duryodhana fell victim to anger.

‘This incident shows the concentration and the discipline of Arjuna as a humble student. If anybody wants to become a successful student, he must learn from this story,’ concluded the lecturer.

The boys were thrilled to hear it. Everyone wanted to emerge as a hero like Arjuna.

The next session was about astras (weapons).

‘In our mythology, an ***astra*** is a supernatural weapon, presided over by a specific deity. To summon or use an ***astra***, we require knowledge of a specific invocation. The deity invoked would then endow the weapon, making it impossible to counter through regular means. Specific conditions existed involving the usage of astras, the violation of which could be fatal.

‘Because of the power involved, knowledge of an ***astra*** was passed from teacher to pupil by word of mouth alone, and only after the confirmation of the student's exemplary character. Certain ***astras*** had to be handed down from the deity directly. The ***astras*** were generally summoned as arrows, although they could potentially be used as anything.

'For your understanding, children, I am giving you the list of ***astras*** and their effects. The practical sessions will educate you more on this. But before practice you should understand the basics of these ***astras***.

'Children, an astra can be recalled but once released from the bow, and arrow can not be recalled. An astra is to be used only in unavoidable circumstances and not in just any scuffle or brawl.

Astra - Indraastra

Deity - Indra, god of weather

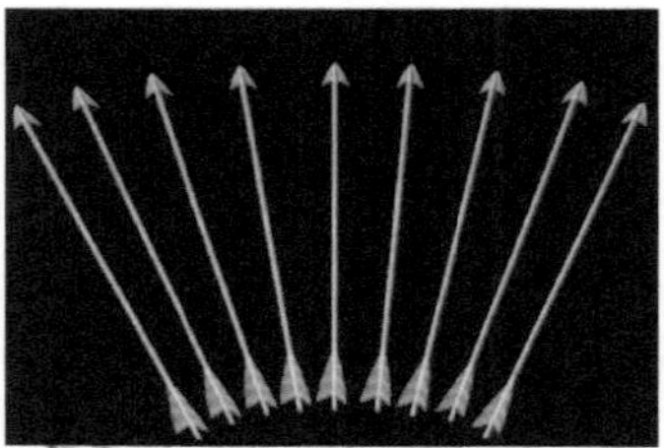

Effect – This would bring about a 'shower' of arrows from the sky.

Lakshman killed Ravana's son Indrajit with this astra.

Astra - Aagneyaastra

Deity - Agni, god of fire

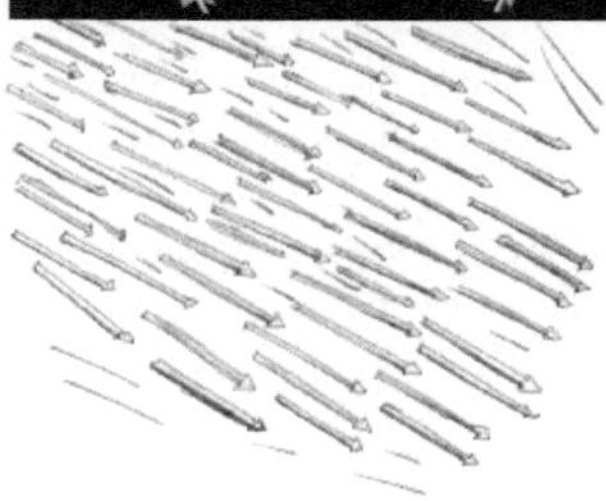

Effect – The weapon would emit flames inextinguishable through normal means.

This fire arrow was used by Lord Rama to destroy the darkness caused by Rakshasas.

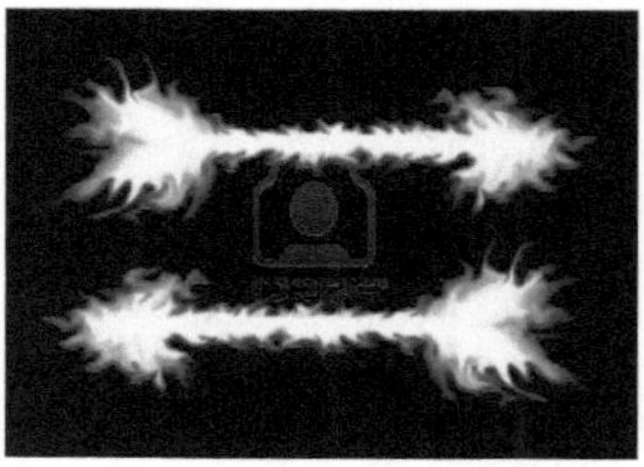

Astra - Varunaastra

Deity - Varuna, god of water

Effect – The weapon would release torrential volumes of water. This weapon is commonly used to counter the Agneyastra.

Great warriors like Arjuna, Drona and Satyaki use this Astra. The usage of this weapon is not possible by inexperienced warriors, as a slight mistake would destroy the user.

Astra - Bhargavaastra

Deity - Bhrugu Maharishi

Effect - It can cause great damage to any army.

Karna got this astra from his guru Parasurama.

Astra - Nagaastra

Deity - The Nagas

Effect - The weapon takes the form of a snake, proving deadly upon impact. When used, thousands of snakes will come down from the sky.

Ravana used this astra against Rama. From a single arrow, thousands of snakes darted towards Lord Rama. Sri Ram in turn discharged Garuda astra. These arrows became garudas and cut the serpents on all sides. Garuda nullified the effect of Nagastra.

Astra – Nagapaasha

Deity – The Nagas
Effect – Upon impact, this weapon can bind the target in coils of living venomous snakes. It was used against Lord Rama and Lakshmana by Indrajit

Astra – Vayvaastra

Deity – Vayu, god of wind

Effect – Bring about a gale capable of lifting armies off the ground.

Astra – Suryastra

Deity – Surya, god of the sun

Effect – Create a dazzling light that would dispel any darkness.

Astra – Vajra

Deity – Indra, god of weather

Effect –Target will be struck with bolts of lightning.

Hanuman tried to catch the sun when he was young. Indra used this destructive astra on him, but he was saved by his father. Vayu.

Astra – Mohini

Deity – Mohini, an Avatar of Vishnu

Effect –Dispel any form of Maya or sorcery in the vicinity.

Lord Rama used it against the demon forces. It drove the demons mad and they started killing each other.

Astra – Twashtar

Deity – Twashtri, the heavenly builder

Effect – When used against a group of opponents (such as an army), this astra would cause them to mistake each other as enemies and hence fight each other.

Astra – Sammohana/Pramohana

Deity – Mohini, an Avatar of Vishnu

Effect – Would cause entire hosts/armies to collapse in a trance.

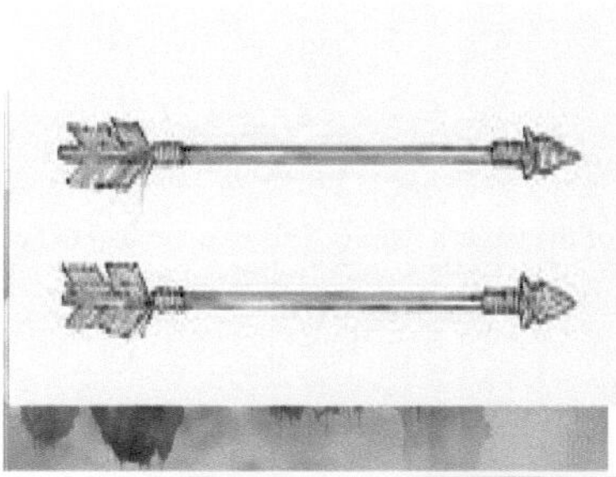

Astra – Parvataastra

Deity – Godess Parvati

Effect – Would cause a Parvata/mountain to fall on the target from the skies.

Parasuram, the Brahmin warrior avatar of Vishnu, used this astra against his targets.

Astra – Brahmaastra

Deity – Brahma, the Creator

Effect – Will destroy entire hosts at once. Can also counter most other astras.

Indrajit, son of Ravana, used this astra against Hanuman. But due to the boon received from Brahma, Hanuman escaped.

Astra – Brahmasirsha

Deity – Brahma, the Creator

Effect –Capable of killing devas.

Only Arjuna knows how to invoke and withdraw it. Brahmasirsha is the ultimate weapon, the improvisation of the Brahmastra.

Astra – Narayanaastra

Deity – Vishnu, the Preserver

Effect – Will create showers of arrows and discs.

This astra's power will increase with the resistance offered to it. It must be obtained directly from Vishnu, and can be used only once. If the user were to attempt to invoke it a second time, it will rebound on him, and possibly, his troops.

Astra – Vaishnavaastra

Deity – Vishnu, the Preserver

Effect – Will destroy the target completely, irrespective of the target's nature. This weapon had to be obtained from Vishnu directly.

Lord Rama used this astra against Ravana's army.

Astra – Pashupatastra

Deity – Shiva, the Destroyer

Effect – Will destroy the target completely, irrespective of the target's nature.

This powerful weapon can be obtained by meditating on Lord Shiva. You cannot get this astra from any gurukul.

'Children, you should be blessed to have these astras. When you go for practice sessions, great warriors of our kingdom, Pradyumna, Satyaki and Krita Varma, will teach you more about them. You should know that it is not just your power but the power received from a god and your own concentration and belief that will propel your arrows into astras. Understand?'

There was a spell bound audience. The boys were mesmerized by these astras and their capabilities. They went to bed that night thinking about them. Being young, the lecture registered in their minds.

The next day, there was a lecture on the greatness of the ***Gurukul*** masters, and the greatest among them - Drona.

'Children, do you know how Drona became the master of the Pandavas and Kauravas? Prince Abimanyu, do you know how your father got his master Drona?'

'No, ***Guruji***, I do not know. Can you explain?' asked Prince Abimanyu.

'Drona's greatness was noticed by the Pandavas and Kauravas one day. I should say that this was their most important discovery d. Here is their story for you, children,' continued the lecturer.

'Drona had great knowledge but no wealth, not even enough to sustain his son. He decided to go to Hastinapur. Kripa, his brother-in-law, was the teacher of the Kauravas and

Pandavas. As he reached in the outskirts of the city, Drona saw some boys playing. While they were playing, their ball fell into a very deep and narrow well.

'The boys gathered around the well, trying to figure out how to retrieve the ball. The boys were the Kauravas and Pandavas. As they were looking at the ball, Dharma's ring fell in the well too. The water was clear and they could see both the ball and the ring in the water. The boys did not see the dark skinned brahmin approaching.

'"You boys of the great clan of Bharat, are you not skillful enough to retrieve the ball and the ring?" he asked them.

'Dharma turned around and replied scarcastically, "If you can take out the ball and the ring, we will make sure you get a good meal at our teacher Kripacharya's house."

'Drona took a blade of grass and aimed it at the ball. The blade of grass stuck in the ball. He then threw a succession of blades that stuck to the end of the previous ones. Soon, Drona managed to pull the ball out of the well. The boys were impressed.

'"Can you remove the ring from the well too?" they asked.

'Drona borrowed Arjuna's bow and arrow. He aimed at the ring and released the arrow. The arrow went through the ring, stuck a stone and rebounded back to Drona, who skillfully caught it.

'Dharma bowed his head in reverence, "O ***Brahmin***, please forgive my boyish impudence. Who are you?"

'Drona said, "Go ask your grandfather Bheeshma about me. I will wait for you boys right here."

'The boys ran to Bheeshma and told him what had happened. Bheeshma welcomed Drona and appointed him to teach the Kauravas and Pandavas. From him, they learned the use of various weapons and the art of war.

'Children, do you know the power of Drona, the great master who taught the Pandavas and Kauravas? He hails from our kingdom of Krishna,' concluded the lecturer.

The boys continued to be thrilled hearing the heroic deeds of the master Drona. They were keen to become great heros. As the days went by, they continued to help their master in their daily routines in the ***Gurukul.*** The work would include fetching water from the well, chopping firewood, helping in the kitchen, washing dishes, taking the cows to pasture and plastering the walls and floor with cow dung.

As they were going ahead with their off class routines along with their lectures, they enjoyed every moment of their stay in the ***Gurukul*** and the bond of their friendship was further strengthened. They became inseparable companions. This was observed by Bharadwaj as well.

The children grew familiar with archery, mace, sword, javelin, fighting on foot, on horse, on chariot, on elephant – all these were taught to them as theory lessons. Lectures were given on military formations (***vyuhas***) and how to strategize and to ride chariots.

The children gained a feel of each of these weapons, and were promised practice sessions. They would put theory to practice in the nearby forest. They looked forward to their outdoor practical classes. The children also learnt the various ***vyuhas*** (military formations).They had intitially thought that the theory sessions were boring. But as they grew older and started the practical sessions, they could appreciate the importance of these lessons.

Prince Abimanyu asked the teacher, 'What is the purpose of these military formations and how many such vyuhas exist?'

The teacher went on to explain the military formations. 'Children, at various times during battle, the supreme commander of either army will order special formations (***vyuhas***). Each formation has a specific purpose; some are defensive, while others are offensive. Each formation had its own strengths and weaknesses. I will list them for you now.

- Krauncha vyuha (heron formation)

- Makara vyuha (crocodile formation)

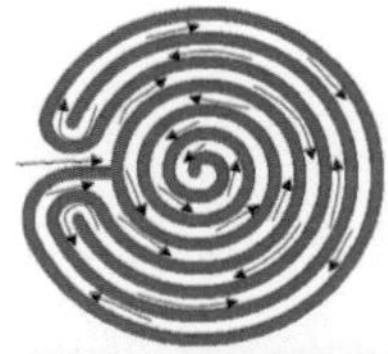

- Kurma vyuha (tortoise or turtle formation)

- Trishula vyuha (trident formation)

- Chakra vyuha (wheel or discus formation)

- Kamala vyuha or Padma vyuha (lotus formation)

- Sarpha vyuha (snake formation)

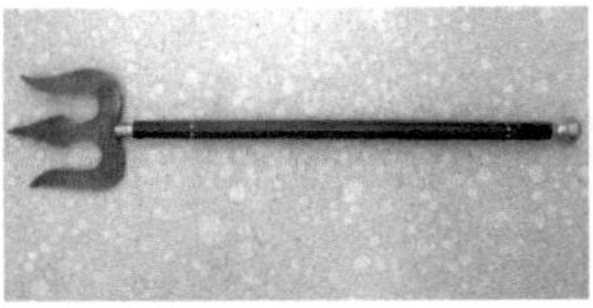

- Garuda vyuha (eagle formation)

- Oormi vyuha (ocean formation)

- Mandala vyuha (galaxy formation)

- Vajra vyuha (diamond or thunderbolt formation)

- Shakata vyuha (box or cart formation)

- Asura vyuha (demon formation)

- Deva vyuha (divine formation)

- Soochi vyuha (needle formation)

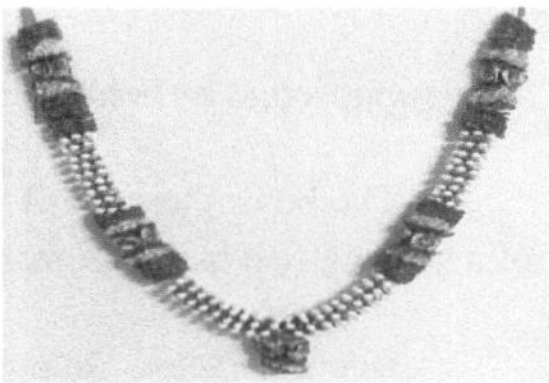

- Sringataka vyuha (horned formation)

- Chandrakala vyuha (crescent or curved blade formation)

- Mala vyuha (garland formation)

'Many of these vyuhas will be explained to you during your practical sessions.

'Most of them will be taught to you, but I am afraid chakra vyuha is known only to Drona and Arjuna himself. Prince Abimanyu, you can ask about your father about it on completion of his exile. You will learn the others in the later sessions,' concluded the lecturer.

The practical sessions were planned in two modules, one in Dwarka ***Vana*** (Dwarka Forest) and another in a camp in the Ravatika hills. The former was conducted by Pradyumna and Satyaki and the latter by Krita Varma and partly by Lord Krishna's brother Balarama.

The first camp started at Dwarka ***Vana***. Here, they learnt practical lessons based on what they had heard in theory classes. Other than the ***vyuha*** (formations), which were supposed to be held at the second camp, the rest of the theory classes were put into practice.

The boys showed off their skills. Abimanyu excelled in archery, and could hit the target of a moving fish in the Gomati River.

Bhoomi Sena, Jala Sena and Vayu Sena were able to control the five elements. ***Agneyastra*** (fire), ***Varunashtra*** (water) and ***Vayusthra*** (wind) could be invoked by them simultaneously when they were together. They could understand that the five elements listened to them, only when they were together and not when they were apart. This was a revelation to them.

Prince Abimanyu could invoke ***Indrastra*** (shower of arrows from sky) and ***Vajra Astra*** (bolts of lighting). Sagar could invoke ***Suryastra***. This might have been due to his being born at sunrise, he thought. Arya Vaisya could invoke ***Mohini Astra***. Thus, each of the boys was proficient in one or more of the astras.

One day, they were left alone to play in the forest. They played hide and seek, but could not find Jala Sena. It had been more than half an hour, and everyone was worried.

Then Vayu Sena recalled his brother's mystical power, of being able to stay inside the water for hours. He guessed Jala Sena was in the Gomati River. Sagar volunteered to dive into the river and look for him. Thus, he found him. They all clapped for Jala Sena.

Sagar and Jala Sena then trained the others in holding their breath and diving under water. They returned back to their camp after a lengthy swimming session.

As they were moving through the forest, Arya Vaisya was bitten by a poisonous snake and he fainted. There was foam coming out of his mouth. Abimanyu said, 'We have to quickly find the snake and identify it, only then can we gauge the correct herbs to use. Otherwise this poison will kill Arya Vaisya. How can we find the snake?'

Bhoomi Sena kept his ears to the ground. He could hear the sound of movement beneath the surface. He located the snake a few yards away. Using his lightening quick reflexes, he exposed the snake. After identifying the snake as a common cobra, they let it go.

They found the necessary herbs on the banks of the river. Since the water was flooding the banks, it would be impossible to cross. 'What do we do?' Abhimanyu shouted.

At that time, they observed yet another mystical skill of Vayu Sena. He caught hold of a bird and said something to it. The bird flew across the river and brought the shrubs. They gave the juice of the shrub to Arya Vaisya, who then woke up.

This incident bonded them closer together. Sagar insisted that he be taught the skill of hearing sound and assessing the movement of objects beneath the ground. Bhoomi Sena taught them to him, but he was nowhere near his proficiency level.

They were all taught of hunting as well. Soon enough, their forest camp came to an end. Pradyumna was very happy with the progress of the boys.

*** ***

14. Graduation & Beyond

The boys reached the second camp in the Ravatika Hills. The great warriors of the kingdom of Krishna, Kritavarma and Balaram, would train them here.

The serene environment, the view of the city of Dwarka, the pleasant weather… all this added to the excitement of the boys.

Before the session began, Kritivarma addressed them. 'Boys, before the practical war lessons, you have to familiarize yourselves with Ayurvedic treatment. In the war zone, you have to give first aid to warriors and their horses if they are hurt. An Ayurvedic clinic set up by the saintly prince of the Pandiya kingdom, Maran, must be visited as part of your syllabus. The clinic is located in the Ravatika Hills.'

The boys reached the clinic. Maran was wearing the dress of a saint, a saffron cloth wrapped all around his body. Is he a saint? The boys wondered. Maran introduced himself and addressed the boys.

'It is a pleasure to receive you here. You need to learn the strengths of Ayurveda. I have been cured by this treatment - not once, but twice in this kingdom.

'I decided to stay back in this beautiful hill and run this clinic. You see these herbs. Some of them are poisonous, some of them are anti poisonous. I brought many of these from southern kingdoms and have mixed them with the herbs grown here.

'You have now commenced your bravery sessions. You should know how to treat an injured horse or elephant yourself, and how to give first aid to your own men.You will be amazed to learn that Ayurveda is one of the Upavedas of the Atharva Veda. The four popular upavedas are ***Ayurveda****, Dhanurveda, Gandharveda* and *Artha Shastra.* I was told that the original text of Ayurveda, composed by Lord Brahma, contained 1,00,000 verses that were spread over one thousand chapters and composed long before the creation of beings.

'Sahadev, the youngest of the Pandavas, practices veterinary medicine. He uses neem to heal wounded horses. His proficiency is well known in the field of veterinary medicine.'

The boys liked Maran's friendly approach, and went around the gardens and tried to understand many of the herbs used in Ayurvedic treatment. Then they went back to their camp to rest.

The next day, there was a session on vyuhas. Practical sessions were taught on how to form the vyuha, how to enter it, how to exit and how to decimate it. All but one of the eighteen vyuhas were taught. The one left out was ***chakra vyhua,*** the details of which only Arjuna and his master Drona knew. But of the boys, Sagar emerged as the best in strategising military formations, entry and exit mechanisms. He was hailed as a budding military strategist. Sagar was delighted, as the fear of being rejected based on his ***varna*** continued to haunt him. This kind of appreciation was a big morale boost for him.

The sessions went on for weeks and weeks but for the boys, time was just flying. They quickly settled down in their daily routines - studying, playing war games, doing the assigned tasks, eating and sleeping.

There was a bravery skill comptetion at Dwarka with sports and war simulation games. These games kindled the competitive spirit amongst the students studying at the ***Gurukuls*** of various kingdoms. Competitions such as these were important for both the students as well as their teachers. The winners and their guru would be feted and the guru would never again need to look for a job. Kings would extend invitations to these gurus to come to their own kingdoms. Also, for the winners, a fast track and extra attention to their education was assured.

The boys made a resolution to showcase their talents and bag all the prizes. The sports day arrived. It was Phalguna month, and young boys from the ***Gurukuls*** of various kingdoms arrived to participate.

Anarta, Anga, Magadha, Virata, Kosaleya, Hastinapura, Gandhar, Pandiya - name any kingdom and their representatives were present. Duryodhana's son Laxman, Dushasana's son Durmashana, Karna's son Vrishasena and all the sons of Duryodhana's brothers were there. These boys had received their training from Ashwathama, Drona's son.

Half of the town came to witness the contest. The wards of master Bharadwaj started conquering the prizes. Abimanyu won all the archery contests, Bhoomi Sena won all the long jump and high jump and running races, Jala Sena won part of the swimming competitions – sprint swimming race, high diving and water endurance contests. Sagar casually won the remaining swimming contests – the back stroke and butterfly. Vayu Sena won the kite contests while Arya Vaisya won the dice games. The people of Dwarka were thrilled.

Duryodhana's son Laxman shouted, 'Cheating! These Dwarka boys win everything. We don't agree.' He was exhibiting the jealousy his father had nurtured against the Pandavas and passed on to his sons. History repeats itself. He was so annoyed by his own team's defeat that he could not appreciate the skills of the other side.

While the contests were happening, one young girl was totally mesmerized by Sagar's athleticism in swimming. When he got the prize, she clapped along with the others. She wanted to go to him and congratulate him. She was blushing without realizing it. As Sagar came back from the podium after receiving the prize, she went close to him. Sagar looked at her and she looked at him. Their eyes met . Something clicked and instead of adoring looks, they were staring at each other without realizing it.

Arya Vaisya shouted, 'Varsha, you are here? Did you come alone?' Varsha then came to her senses.

She said, 'Yes ***bhaiyya***, I came alone. But you are always over protective. You do not want your sister to come out and socialize. This is your problem.'

Arya Vaisya introduced Sagar. 'Sagar is one of my best friends in the ***Gurukul***. Sagar, this is my sister Varsha.'

Even when Sagar returned to the camp, Varsha's face remained in his mind. Similarly, Varsha could not erase her memories of meeting Sagar. A new ***sangam*** (confluence) of two young souls had commenced on that day.

The next day, they had simulations of war exercises. This contest was between two sides, decided through random selection. It so happened that the Dwarka boys had to take on Hastinapura team. It was like a mini-war.

The Dwarka boys undertook a ***sarpha*** (Snake) ***vyuha***. The opposing group started hitting the snake formation at head of the vyuha. Bhoomi Sena dug a pit in the earth and entered it. Then came the surprise element. He walked beneath the ground without being noticed by anybody. He was followed by his brothers. They emerged behind the enemy lines. Now there was an attack on both sides on Laxman's troops.

The attack was unexpected. Everyone could see the mystical powers of Bhoomi Sena. His brothers started involving the other elements – Jala and Vayu. Jala Sena invoked ***Varunastra***; Vayu Sena invoked Vayuvastra. There was a torrential rain and the ***Vayuvastra*** almost uprooted the Hastinapura boys.

Abimanyu was pouring a shower of arrows from the sky by invoking ***Indrastara***. The Hastinapura boys could not face this strategy of double attack. This exercise showcased the multifaceted talents of the Dwarka boys.

Laxman surrendered. He acknowledged the skills of the Dwaraka boys and became friends with them. But his soul nourished the pain that had been inflicted on him. The bruised ego is like a fire, one gust of a hurt and it blazes with the flames of revenge. But for now, just for the sake of honouring protocol, he extended his friendship to the Dwarka boys.

After the contest, there was an assessment of the boys' bravery/war proficiency. Each of the boys got an excellent rating in one area or the other.

Abimanyu	-	Best in Archery
Sagar	-	Best in military formulations and strategy
Arya vaisya	-	Best in resource mobilization for war
Bhoomi Sena	-	Best in ground troop management
Jala Sena	-	Best in naval troop management

Vayu Sena - Best in aerial war management

The assessors Pradyumna and Satyaki noted that the group had a good bond; their individual brilliance was enhanced by their excellent coordination. Further, the group was headed by a born leader, Prince Abimanyu. This young group could emerge as a great hope for the kingdom of Krishna, and both assessors recorded their appreciation for the boys.

The military session got over with this assessment. The boys reached the age of 14. There was a philosophy session in the last year before graduation. The objective was to initiate the boys into real life. All the boys were thrilled to be back in the company of their master Bharadwaj for the final year.

Bharadwaj welcomed them back to his classes and lectured, 'Are we facing or we chasing? This question will bother you your whole life, my dear children. You may think the dream is that which you get during your sleep. But the vision is that one dream that deprives you of your sleep. Not all of us achieve our vision in our life time. Why does one man go through a tough life, crossing many hurdles to accomplish his goals, while the other goes through hurdles and never get anywhere? Why do some people always seem to have an easy ride to success and face minimum difficulties? Why these variations? Have you thought about it, children?

'Is it destiny or your disposition that determines your success? Though growing on the same earth and same soil, two plants from the same mother have different characteristics. Even if the seed of the plant is fertilized with the same manure and given the same water, there will still be differences between them. The same applies to man. The way one absorbs knowledge from the same teacher and same parent differs from person to person. A living thing is not piece of mass production. A living thing goes through changes from time to time. These are works of nature. These are nature's wonders. Man is made by his own beliefs. As he believes, so is he. Unless you perceive your worth, you cannot achieve what you desire.

'Take, for instance, two men who look through prison bars. One sees the mud, the other sees the stars. Your thoughts are the architects of your destiny. A positive mind emits harmonious waves of thought, and a negative mind sends discordant signals. The lock is outside the prison, but the lock is inside for many of us. It is your thoughts that lock you in. When you want to reach the top of the mountain, your attention should be focused on it. If you stumble on a small stone at the foot of the hill and you are irritated and give up your quest, then clearly your focus is not on reaching the top. Do not give up when you are faced with small trials and tribulation. You should continue to focus on the top. Is that clear, my children?

'Everyone has talent. Everyone on the planet is a wonder of the world. Everyone has the potential for extraordinary achievement. Small achievements lead to great victories. Positive habits create results. Opportunity is under one's feet. We do not have to keep brooding on being less fortunate. All we need to do is to recognize opportunity. We need to build a positive attitude rather than complain about temporary stress and uncertainties. Is that clear, my children?'

'***Guruji***, but people like me from ***Sudhra Varna*** do not have opportunities; we are not given recognition by the higher ***varnas***. Why?' Sagar started questioning.

'Sagar, you have to be unmindful of the irritants you come across. You are talking only about irritants as if you have no goal. The kingdom of Krishna does not discriminate between people. It is keen to give equal opportunity to all. Past societal practices maybe an irritant, but still, you have received an opportunity to be here in this ***Gurukul***, isn't that so? Do not look only at irritants, as they are a passing phase of life. Look at your goal, your dream, your vision, Sagar,' Bharadwaj said.

Sagar continued with his counter questions. He sought explanations on the birth related Varna discrimination. He asked his master, '***Guruji***, there are many unsung heroes who have a dream, who work hard but do not make it big. What is their sin?'

'Sagar, good question! You are asking questions with an insight that is beyond your age; it shows your maturity is very high. Sagar, many were born to win but conditioned to lose. If an eagle's egg is placed in the nest of a chicken, the eagle will grow up thinking it is a chicken. The conditioning of the mind is catastrophe for many. If you don't trym you will never know. You may be disappointed if you fail, but you will be doomed if you don't try. Most people give up at the last minute. They might have needed just one more attempt to grasp all that they desired. Always remember, the night is the darkest before dawn. Count your blessings, not your troubles. Many of our blessings are hidden treasures. The men who try to do something and fail are infinitely better than those who try to do nothing and succeed.'

Sagar rushed with his question. 'Master, what should we do to chase our goals?'

'Sagar, you cannot teach a man every microstep that you should take – you can only help him to discover it himself. I am trying to do the same thing with you. I am here to awaken the potential in you. Whether a man makes it or not is a matter of his application. Nobody can do it for him.'

'I have another question. Why should a few succeed and get a standing ovation from society while so many just come and go from this world? The world recognizes only the performance and not passion, master.'

'My dear Sagar, many times, even the specialist cannot solve problems. When he cannot solve problems with a small hammer, he looks for bigger hammers rather than different instruments. Many problems cannot be solved by conditioned thinking and a paralyzed outlook. Trust yourself. Create the kind of life you would be happy to live. Make the most of yourself by fanning the tiny, inner sparks of possibility into flames of achievement.

'Sagar, I narrated the success stories of people who have created path breaking changes under hostile circumstances. No one has an easy ride. Great men have purposes while others have wishes. Wise people build homes with stones that were thrown at them. They were not afraid of losing. They never gave up, and that is the spirit I try to inculcate in you.'

Sagar did not give up. '***Guruji***, when faced with bricks thrown at us or with a series of failures, how do we keep ourselves motivated?'

The master continued …

'A good question indeed. This is precisely the problem for many of us today. Now the time has come that I have to talk to you about ***Karma Yoga***. Here are the messages for you children.

'Do thy allotted work, for action is better than inaction, and even the maintenance of the physical life cannot be effective without action. Without attachment, perform the work that has to be done, for man attains the highest by doing work without attachment.

'Work is virtue, work is worship. Do your duty without any attachment thereof, my dear children.'

Sagar looked confused. He asked, '***Guruji***, does that mean that we have a right to our duty and not to its fruits? How is that possible? A student works hard to get a top rank. A farmer works hard to get a good harvest. A warrior fights hard to win against his opponent. Without an objective, there is no incentive to work hard.'

'Sagar, note that the message does not say that you have no right to the fruits of labor! It urges you to do your duty but to learn to accept the result. You may expect one, but you should have the wisdom to accept the result no matter what. You cannot control the result. Hence give priority to your duty and not to the result.

'Being dedicated to work has to mean "working for the sake of work, generating excellence for its own sake." If we are always calculating the rate of reward before putting in our efforts, such work will not be detached. It is not "generating excellence for its own sake," but working only for the reward that may (or may not) come. Working with an eye on anticipated benefit means that the quality of performance of the current job or duty suffers – through anxiety for the future. In fact, events may not always respond positively to our calculations and hence the expected fruits may not be forthcoming. We should not mortgage our present commitments to an uncertain future.

'It has been held that this principle of detachment leads to lack of incentive for effort, striking at the very root of the work ethic. On the contrary, concentration on the task for its own sake leads to the achievement of excellence – and indeed to the true mental happiness of the worker. Thus, while the accepted practices of motivation may be said to lead us to the bond of extrinsic reward, the detachment principle leads us to the intrinsic rewards of mental and indeed moral satisfaction.

'The result can crown you with a kingdom or crucify you on a cross. You should have the readiness to accept the result, while doing your duty. Am I clear, Sagar? Focus on the roots rather than the fruits,' he quipped.

Sagar continued, 'Master, why are people unhappy and desirious of possessing what someone else has? Is comparison bad?'

'Comparisons are not bad, Sagar. If you can compare, you can compete and if you compete, you can win. The competitor's status and performance invigorates you. Comparisons can be used to motivate or correct you. These comparisons become a problem when they are used for the wrong reasons, like making oneself superior to others or when one compares thereby eliciting a wrong response like admitting a sense of defeat. It is only then that the problem arises. In these cases, they destroy souls. Then what do we do with comparison?

'A postitive ideal leading to positive thought is fine, but do not get into negative benchmarking leading to nefarious thoughts. Here is a sample for you. There was a hunter who bought an amazing dog. It could walk on water, and even hunt ducks while running on water. The hunter showed the dog to his friend, praising its efficiency. His friend did not compliment but found fault with the dog, saying that this dog cannot swim, while his dog can swim. This is clearly focusing on negatives rather than positives. See the positive side of such comparisons.

'The creator, my dear son, expects each person to do what he is capable of, at any point at any time. He does not expect an ant to haul logs as an elephant does in the forest. The ant should not compare itself to an elephant and start complaining. There is an ancient story about a mouse who was distressed because it was afraid of cats. A magician took pity on it and turned it into a cat. Immediately, it started fearing dogs. The magician, therefore, turned it into a dog. Now the dog began to fear the tiger. So the magician turned it into a tiger. Right away, it began to fear the hunter. Finally, the magician was so disgusted that he turned the tiger back into a mouse and said, "You've got the heart of a mouse. That's what you are and therefore you shall remain just that." Hence we need to know what to look at and what to overlook.

'You cannot put your feet into another man's shoes and walk. Live your life. There is a proverb – "If you compare yourself with you, then you are living. If you constantly keep comparing yourself with others, then you are only existing and not living your life."'

Sagar ended with a question. 'Master, I don't want a question as a parting shot for the day, but I want a one line as an answer to the question – are we facing or are we chasing?'

'My dear Sagar, you seem to be having too many questions. Fine, I will answer your last question now.

'Chase as far as the input/effort phase is concerned, and learn to face as far as the result is concerned. To put it in another way: do your duty and be prepared to face the result, whatever it might be, don't give up! Therefore, you should stay focused on the purpose and not on outcome. Be passionate at input stage and learn to be philosophical at output stage. Is it clear, children?'

With that life time concept of attachment with detachment, the ***Gurukul*** course ended.

All the boys had successfully completed their graduation. The graduation ceremony was presided over by Lord Krishna's brother, Balarama. All the boys (now men) were dressed in armour like typical warriors. Each one was crowned by Balarama at the graduation ceremony at the ***Gurukul***. All the parents and the people from the town witnessed the function which was celebrated with pomp and grace.

On their crowing, the six boys, now six men, came out and got immersed in the flurry of congratulatory messages. As per convention, each one had a ***angavastram*** on top of his armour signifying that underneath this armour, there resides a learned man. At the conclusion, all of the men took off their ***angavastram*** and tossed it up in the air. The place was filled with joy and friendship.

The next day was the final day in the ***Gurukul***. The boys went into a huddle. They made resolutions that they would never dilute their friendship at any cost, and would safeguard it, even if it is at the cost of the family. Friendship first, family next, they resolved amongst themselves.

They said to themselves, 'Like the birds, we flew with no worry. Like monkeys we jumped across the trees freely. Like the singing birds we sang freely. We wandered together with no worries, and all these stay back in our hearts as fresh as ever. No one on earth can break our friendship.'

With tears in their eyes, they separated from the ***Gurukul***. '***Samavartana***' marks the end of a pupil's period of study and his return home. They did not realize that very soon their resolution of unbroken friendship would be subjected to a severe jolt.

*** ***

15. The Love That Triggered Enmity

The Graduation ceremony ended. Six students graduated from the ***Gurukul*** headed by Bharadwaj. The children had grown into men, but their resolution to be united for ever brought them together again.

Prince Abimanyu presented a proposal to the Royal Palace for the setting up of an elite ***Yuva*** Army (Youth Army). The Defence Ministry headed by Pradyumna cleared it immediately and Prince Abimanyu was given the charge to set it up.

Abimanyu headed the Yuva Army and all his friends were brought together. Sagar became the chief military strategist, Bhoomi Sena the head of ground forces, Jala Sena the head of naval forces, Vayu Sena the head of aerial forces and Arya Vaisya the chief resource mobilization officer. They began recruiting young men for the ***Yuva*** Army.

Abimanyu told his mother Subadhra about the new move. She was quite delighted, but had one lingering doubt. 'Abimanyu, I met Arya Vaisya's mother at your graduation ceremony. She was totally against Sagar's being included. She said that it was Matsya who killed her husband. I am not in favour of your friendship with Sagar, Abimanyu.'

'Ma! You are mistaken. Arya Vaisya's mother feels that Sagar's father was the one who was instrumental in killing her husband. Also, she has a ***Varna*** Phobia. On the day of the graduation, she yelled at Sagar saying that a ***Sudhra*** did not deserve to be in the school. What right does she have to ridicule the caste of a person and ill treat him based on his birth? Sagar is a talented boy, Ma,'. Abimanyu replied.

'Abimanyu, you may say what you will, but I do not want you to bring that ***Sudhra*** boy into our palace. You have to sack him from ***Yuva*** Army'.

'Ma, I am sorry, I beg to differ. Sagar will be my deputy in the ***Yuva*** Army. Nothing on earth can stop it. He will continue to be in my life.' Saying this, he walked out of his mother's room in great anger.

The parents of the boys were averse to Sagar. They did not want their sons to be friends with him. But the boys were getting closer and closer day by day. Sagar was feeling guilty.

'Friends, do not antagonize your parents. I am from a lower ***Varna***. Let me be what I am. Let me live with this guilt and go into oblivion. I take this as a curse from my parents. You should live happily. Why spoil your happiness on account of me?' Sagar asked with tears in his eyes.

'Sagar, don't ever say this. You were born to achieve. Why should you withdraw from society? Your greatness will be proven one day. Don't ever say that you were born to suffer. No my friend, you are born to achieve. We are all with you.'

The friends became colleagues and got busy with recruitment, war drills and so on. One day, they were invited to have food at Bharadwaj's house. The invitation came from the three Sena brothers. They assembled in their Master's house for a nice dinner.

Shyamala had also been corrupted by Arya Vaisya's mother. Bharadwaj was not at home when the boys started their dinner. Shakuntala came out and saw them eating. She looked at Sagar.

Suddenly she started shouting at the top of the voice, 'Sagar, you Sudhra boy, get out of here. How can you come in and eat with the high ***Varna*** boys? Are you not ashamed to come inside our house? Get out from here. I cannot serve you.'

Sagar was stunned. For him, Shakuntala was like a mother. His master had been everything for him. He pleaded, 'Mata, you are everything to me. Till the other day you were treating me like your son. What mistake did I do to earn your wrath?'

Shakuntala continued, 'You are the son of a killer. Arya Vaisya's mother told me everything, that your father killed her husband. We have given you enough privilege till now. From now on, I cannot permit a killer's son into my house. I am ashamed that I fed a poisonous snake like you. Get out of here, you Sudhra.'

Sagar's master was also not there to support him. He felt as though he had been physically thrown out into the street. He was crying in front of the house, and passersby were looking at him. It was the greatest insult he had ever faced.

Shakuntala came out and shouted, 'You ***Sudhra***, son of a killer, get out, don't even come into our street. This is the last time I want to see you.'

Sagar could not control his frustration and shame. He went to his father and asked him, '***Pitaji***, every one of my friend's mothers claims that you killed Arya Vaisya's father Dhana Vaisya. What is this?'

'Son, we came out of the place where we were staying. Since we could not pay back the debts, Dhana Vaisya took our property. The entire fishermen community came with us when we left. We sailed into the sea without knowing where we were going. Your mother jumped into the sea to kill herself. I jumped to save her. Amidst the thunder, storm and waves, we lost our way and were brought to the shore of Dwarka. Amidst this thunder and storm you were born in the sea. We were saved by the Master Bharadwaj.

'The fishermen followed us, but they could not find us. They went back. Late,r I joined the ***Gurukul*** as swimming teacher. I gave up fishing and I have not even been in touch with our community. They selected a new leader. I stopped following their affairs. Later I came to know from Arya Vaisya's uncle, while he was admitting Arya Vaisya into the ***Gurukul***, that his father had been killed. I did not have anything to do with his killing. Bharadwaj knows all this, Sagar.'

'You did not kill him?'

'Yes, my son, believe me, or ask your master about what I told you just now.'

'***Pithaji***, I do not need all that, your word will do. I will not henceforth be bothered by the accusations against you. I am clear now,' Sagar said in great relief.

After these clarifications, he went to the Gomati alone. He did not want to meet his friends. When he was sitting alone, he heard a girl's voice. 'Sagar, day I met you I became your fan. Your heroics in swimming mesmerized me. As the days passed, I realized I am not only your fan. I think I am in love with you.'

Sagar was astonished at this statement. 'Varsha, isn't that your name? Are you in your senses? Your whole family yells at me as the low caste ***Sudhra***. Your mother accuses my father as the killer of your father. We do not have status in society. What are you talking about?'

'Sagar, no matter what people say, my brother is your friend. I am in love with you. Who can stop me? Let them see,' she said with great conviction.

'Varsha, you have had this feeling for one week. Think calmly whether this relationship would ever work. You are a high society girl. Your parents would never allow it. In fact, it will aggravate the ill feelings of your family towards me and my family. Think of all these consequences before you approach me,' said Sagar.

'I will think for a week and come back, but on one condition. You must teach me swimming during this period.' Sagar thought that she would not leave otherwise, and hence he agreed to teach her swimming every day for the next week.

The swimming classes started that very day. Varsha was determined to seduce Sagar. As she learnt swimming, she would deliberately fall on him, or embrace him on the pretext of drowning.

On the last day of the session, she fell into the water, pretending she had fainted. Sagar jumped into the river and brought her out of the water. She had take in a lot of water, so Sagar pressed his lips to hers and blew air into her mouth, pressing her body with a massage.

While he was doing this massage, he felt the beauty of her body, and fell prey to her voluptuous beauty.

Coming back to her senses, Varsha shouted, 'Sagar, one week is over. I have thought about it. Now I know I love you.'

Sagar could not control his emotions. He embraced her, lifted her, brought her close to him and gave her a deep kiss and announced, 'Varsha, I love you.' A new union of love, a new bond commenced between the two young love birds. They were oblivious to the environment, unmindful of what society would say.

As the days passed, their love intensified. For more than ten days the six friends did not meet each other. The day Sagar had been thrown out of the Sena brothers' house, they had been ashamed to meet him. They were ashamed for not having stopped that unfortunate event. They were all feeling guilty.

Prince Abimanyu finally broke the ice. He decided to take his other four friends to the house of Sagar.

They all apologized to him and invited him back to the Yuva Army. Sagar said, 'I respect you all. I also realize that I am at the lower end of the social spectrum. I should not move with the boys from the higher end of society. You may make promises, but they will not work. Please live happily with your parents. I cannot change the stigma of having a killer for a father or being a Sudhra. Why do you people waste your time with me?'

Realizing the gravity of the situation, they went to Master Bharadwaj. He in turn united them and wished them good luck. He demystified the killer tag on Sagar's father. He advised them to continue to have the same bond they had had during their ***Gurukul*** days. Sagar said that he would not come to anyone's house henceforth, as the parents wouldnever accept him. They all agreed to meet outside the house. They pledged their affection to Sagar.

Varsha and Sagar continued to meet and their love gained strength day by day. For Sagar, his time with Varsha increasingly became the one thing in life that made it all worthwhile.

One day, Arya Vaisya came to know of their relationship. He asked his sister to give it up, as their relationship could end in marriage. Even though Sagar was his friend, Arya Vaisya could not approve of the relationship. The seeds of enmity in his friendship with Sagar had been sown by this affair.

He stopped talking to Sagar. He tried to persuade his other friends to do so, but they all continued their friendship with Sagar. Arya Vaisya thought the only way to end the relationship between his sister and Sagar was to send her away to a far off place and get her married. He thought of approaching Laxman, Duryodhana's son. He wanted to leave his sister in Hastinapura and seek Laxman's help, as he had become friendly with him during the bravery sports sessions.

Varsha and Sagar sought the help of Bharadwaj. He gave assurances to support them but advised them to restrain themselves from taking any hasty step, as both were keen to commit suicide if they were not allowed to marry.

Varsha told the master that she had overheard that Arya Vaisya was trying to send her to Hastinapura. If he forced her to marry someone, she would tell him to consult Bharadwaj on her horoscope.

Worried about the lives of the young lovers, Bharadwaj agreed.

Under cover of registering her in the girls' swimming competition, Arya Vaisya took his sister to Hastinapura and sought Laxman's help, which he was more than eager to give. Ever since he had lost all the competitions at the Inter ***Gurukul*** meet, he had been nourishing his bruised ego. He thought that this was a good opportunity to divide the friends of Abimanyu.

He found a friend to marry to Varsha. His name was Govinda and he was asked to meet Varsha frequently to create an impact on her. But Varsha was adamant. Then Arya Vaisya spoke to her, 'Tell me what you want! You can ask for anything other than Sagar - that will not happen. You may change your mind once and for all.'

'Arya Vaisya, I realize that this marriage between me and Sagar is difficult. I can agree to marry the new person referred by Laxman, but only when your master, the great astrologer Bharadwaj, checks the horoscopes and confirms it', she replied firmly.

Arya Vaisya thought this was a reasonable request. He spoke to Laxman and they arranged for Bharadwaj to come to Hastinapura. When word came to Bharadwaj, he told Sagar and his sons about it. Sagar made a plan to elope with Varsha from Hastinapur. Bharadwaj took his sons with him when he traveled. He was well received and they spent a day taking a tour of the grand city. The next day, Arya Vaisya broached the subject.

'***Guruji***, unless you match these horoscopes, Varsha says she will not agree to the marriage. She is adamant about marrying Sagar, the ***Sudhra***. That will not be practical. Please tell us what to do.'

Bharadwaj began examining the horoscopes. He closed his eyes and meditated for a while. Then he told Arya Vaisya, 'See it is a passing phase. She is suffering from a curse. She will be alright once you do the ***parihar*** (remedy). She cheated her husband, a ***Brahmin*** priest, in her last birth. The man committed suicide. His premature ending has left his soul roaming in the nearby forest, Kamyaka ***vana***.

'Varsha has to stay in the forest for one night. In the moonlight, she has to offer food spread on a banana leaf. The soul will be satisfied and stop bothering her. Then she will be alright. I am not telling this from her horoscope, but by looking at her mind through my meditation. You have to perform this procedure. Let us all go to the forest, and I will help you to complete this ***parihar***. Don't worry, Arya Vaisya', the master consoled him. He made Varsha agree to the plan as well.

The next night was a full moon night. Arya Vaisya began his journey towards the Kamyaka vana with Bharadwaj and his sons, Varsha, and his friends Laxman and Govind. They built a temporary shelter. The moon was filling the sky, and the whole forest looked bright even in the middle of the night. Varsha served food on a banana leaf. She kept the food on top of a raised platform near the hut.

Suddenly, an old ***brahmin*** arrived. He had hair all over his body, and seemed not to have taken bath for ages. He was reciting Vedic slokas under his breath.

He sat near the banana leaf, as though he had known it would be waiting for him. Varsha began serving him. As she served him, he spoke to her in a husky voice. 'Varsha, it is me, Sagar. Do not worry. We will leave this place once Arya Vaisya and his friends go to sleep. I will clap three times. You will come out then. I will take care of the rest.'

Varsha was delighted. The Brahmin left after eating his food. Arya Vaisya was happy that the ***parihar*** had gone off as planned. Relieved, he slept deeply, along with his team.

Two hours later, Varsha heard three claps. She came out. So did the three Sena brothers. Bhoomi Sena dug a pit and asked everyone to get in. Together, they walked beneath the surface of the ground. Vayu Sena invoked fire, lighting their way.

Their horses were waiting for them when they emerged. They took the horses and galloped away.

Bharadwaj, Arya Vaisya, Laxman and Govinda were still asleep far away. As Sagar and the group travelled, Varsha asked him, 'How did you recite the ***slokas*** so well Sagar?'

Sagar replied, 'It was the training of Master Bharadwaj, in the ***Gurukul.*** He used to praise me, saying that I recite the ***slokas*** better than a trained ***pandit***. Those skills came to my rescue today, Varsha. Our love has to succeed: that is God's verdict and that is why our plan worked meticulously. Thank God.'

They reached a ***Kali*** temple in the morning, just when the sun had begun to rise. The morning prayers were being conducted by the pandit of the temple. They all went to him. the Sena brothers introduced themselves as Master Bharadwaj's sons. The pandit said, 'Yes, I know your father very well. What do you want me to do?'

The Sena brothers asked him to solemnize the marriage between Varsha and Sagar. He told the two to exchange garlands. Sagar tied the mangalsutra around Varsha's neck. In this manner, man who had been born at sunrise got married at sunrise. The couple prostrated themselves in front of the goddess, took blessings from the pandit and moved towards the kingdom of Krishna.

When Arya Vaisya woke, he could not find Varsha. The Sena brothers were missing as well. He was furious. He realized that she must have been taken away. He asked Bharadwaj about it, but he claimed ignorance. Arya Vaisya was furious, his animosity towards Sagar now spilling over into enmity with the Sena brothers. Unable to do anything else, he returned to Dwarka.

When he got home, he told his mother what had happened. The whole family cursed Varsha. Arya Vaisya denounced his sister and the Sena brothers. He pledged that he would take his revenge against his sister and the man she had married.

Abimanyu tried to pacify him, but though Arya Vaisya agreed to continue serving the Yuva army, the seeds of enmity had been sown. Paradoxically, it was love that had brought about the hatred among the friends.

Sagar was now the most reviled man among his friends and their families. Their hatred spread to the entire community, with the result the newly married couple Sagar and Varsha had no friends to turn to.

Barring Bharadwaj, his sons and Abimanyu, the hatred against Sagar continued unabated. At a young age of sixteen years, he had to face the onslaught of destiny. But he continued to be passionate about his assigned role as military strategist, and his love for his wife never wavered.

*** ***

16. The operation: Rahasya

As Sagar was settling with his newly found life partner, he had to face yet another blow.

Varsha's mother went to the palace and met Subadhra, Abimanyu's mother. She complained about Sagar. Earlier, she had accused him of being the son of a killer, and a ***Sudhra*** boy. Now she had more ammunition in her armoury– Sagar had eloped with her daughter.

Varsha's mother planned to alienate Sagar from his friends. His friends were his only strength and support. As a mother, the emotional appeal came naturally to her. She succeeded in poisoning the minds of Subadhra as well as the mothers of the three Sena brothers.

Subadhra called Abimanyu. 'Abimanyu, you have to end your relationship with that Sudhra boy, Sagar. I told you to do it before, but you did not listen. Now I am ordering you to sack him. If you do not do this, I am not going to speak to you.'

'***Mata***, how can I sack an efficient person on personal grounds? You are being unreasonable!' Abhimanyu said.

'What? You would disobey a direct command from your mother? Don't take my words lightly. You may have a problem in saying this to your friend, but I am your mother and have your best interests at heart. I don't want you to lose faith but I also don't want you to continue your friendship with Sagar. I will ask Prince Pradyumna to execute my orders. There will not be any embarrassment for you.'

Before Abimanyu could react, Subadhra had summoned Prince Pradyumna and forced him to issue the dismissal order for Sagar.

Sagar was called in and served his order. He could not believe it. Had Abimanyu also let him down, and had this taken place with his consent? Any attempt to meet his commander failed.

He thought, 'For no fault of my own, I have been sacked. Is marrying a high caste girl such a great sin in the kingdom of Krishna? A kingdom renowned for its equality and justice? Has this taken place with the consent of Lord Krishna?'

He was told that the post of Chief Strategist had been disbanded. It was a lame excuse, he thought. Moreover, since the new Yuva Army was yet to be formalized, the decision could not be appealed. He was sacked before the formalization of the army's constitution.

He did not wait around for long, and came back home. He had no idea of what he would do now. The future looked dark and gloomy to him.

Varsha greeted Sagar with her usual exuberance. 'What happened, Sagar? You look very dull today. What has happened to my hero, known for his bravery? Which enemy hurt you, or did someone beat you in practice?'

'Varsha, there is bad news.'

'What happened to my raja? Who upset him? Tell me Sagar.'

'Varsha, I have been sacked.'

'What? Who could dismiss you? How can they run the Army without your strategic input? Why would anybody do this?'

'Varsha, I understand your anger, which comes from your deep love for me. But the fact of the matter is that they have abolished the post of the chief strategist post in the ***Yuva*** Army. Since this Army is still in the formalization phase, the royal charter approving the structure is yet to be complete, and any change can be made now. We cannot question the authorities on this.'

'Sagar, did Abimanyu make this decision? What is his take on this? Did you speak to him?'

'Varsha, Abimanyu was not there. He did not issue this order. It was issued by Prince Pradyumna. I suspect he was under pressure from Abimanyu's mother, who in turn was highly influenced by your mother. Abimanyu is not someone who shies away from straight talk. It must be out of his hands.'

'How can my mother influence the decision of the army – what is this, Sagar?'

'Varsha, my bad fate keeps chasing me. Marrying the girl who loves me is a societal sin today. Our society still denounces a ***Sudhra*** boy marrying a high caste girl. The underlying principles of the kingdom of Krishna are still not pursued by society. There continues to be a difference between the royal policy and societal practices. These practices are passed on from generation to generation. Lord Krishna is keen to bridge this gap, and it is happening, but at a slow pace.'

'Sagar, you married me, we loved each other. Is that a crime?'

'Varsha, no one is saying it is a crime. But society stabs us. It creates barriers to our progress. By doing so, they are trying to frighten future generations from pursuing inter-caste marriage.'

'Sagar, we should prove to the world that we can fight these barriers and live prosperously. We have to emerge as a model for future generations. We should be one of the catalysts who encourage inter-caste marriages. We should support the kingdom to accelerate the pace of creating a society unbiased in the caste, creed or colour.'

'Nicely said. But we have several obstacles to face. I have married you, but I have deprived you of the comforts you knew in your parents' house. You were born with a silver spoon, but here we do not even have mud vessels. You lived a life of luxury, and here you have to live a life of misery. We live in a thatched hut far from the township. I am sorry, Varsha, that I could not give the comforts you know. I am an unlucky man and now I have passed my bad luck to you as well. I feel guilty. Now I do not know how we will manage the next meal.' Tears rolled from Sagar's eyes.

Varsha was deeply moved. She wiped the tears from his eyes, embraced him and told him, 'Sagar, your love is far greater than any material comforts. Your wellbeing is more important to me than anything else. Never say that you are unlucky. You are a born achiever, Sagar. You are going to reach dizzying heights in the future. You do not recognize your own strength. You are a diamond among men. Right now, your skills are hidden and not known to this world. You are going to prove your worth soon. All the people who denounce you now will automatically come back to you. They will plead to be associated with you. The day is not far off, Sagar.'

Varsha's embrace and her words partly pacified Sagar. 'We should look at what to do next, Varsha,' he said.

'Sagar, I agree. That is the spirit. Please do not lose your self confidence. As you say –a wounded soldier who has abundant confidence can defeat a large army that lacks confidence. Do not be strained by the discomforts I am facing. These discomforts are the stepping stones to our future prospects. They are not the bricks thrown at us; they are the bricks being provided to us to build the stepping stones for our growth.'

'Varsha, your support gives me abundant confidence. Your emotional support is like a stoic rock that backs me up. When I received the dismissal order, I was shattered, visualizing dark days ahead. But now I am confident, bold and I think I can dismantle the barriers blocking our progress.'

'That is the spirit, Sagar. Now you are back in form. It is time to have some action now rather than just serious talks. We have the lighter side of life too, Sagar,' Varsha giggled with a deep look into his eyes, inviting him to a tight embrace.

Varsha had been using her speaking skills to pacify Sagar. Now with the warm embrace, she flaunted all her physical endowments, giving him an exciting invitation. Sagar lost all his fighting qualities to his own beautiful queen. The lust conquered all his reservations. The couple experienced a different world, an exciting world of intense pleasure.

The couple woke up late the next morning. They slept so late that they did not realize that they were well into the afternoon. Sagar told her that he would go and meet Bharadwaj and plan his next move. He went to the Royal ***Gurukul***, as he did not want to go to his master's house and face another insult from the mothers of the Sena brothers.

While Sagar went to meet his master, Arya Vaisya was celebrating Sagar's exit from the ***Yuva*** Army. '***Maa***, from today I need not come face to face with that ***Sythan*** (Saturn), Sagar. I am sick and tired of seeing his face. The moment I see him, my blood boils.'

‘Son, what is the matter?’ asked his mother. Arya Vaisya explained about Sagar’s dismissal. She was very happy to hear of it.

Sagar met and explained the situation to Bharadwaj at the Royal ***Gurukul***. As usual he was sympathetic towards him. He volunteered to help him. He got him the job of a swimming assistant in another ***Gurukul***, which was headed by his friend. ‘At least I can light up my kitchen with this job,’ Sagar thought.

The people around him came to know of it. They had already isolated him, generally ignoring his existence. But they were keen on gossiping about him. They spoke of the ***Sudhra*** boy who had eloped with a high caste girl and gotten sacked from the ***Yuva*** Army. They thought he thought too much of himself because of his royal connections with Prince Abimanyu. They gossiped about his becoming a swimming assistant like his father. He should go back to his fishing job, his ancestral occupation, they said. The ***Sudhra*** boy was not even fit to be a fisherman. But with the staunch support of Varsha, he persevered.

One day, he got a call from Prince Abimanyu. He was asked to report to the office of Prince Pradyumna at the palace.

Only Pradyumna and Abimanyu were at the venue at the appointed hour. They both looked grim.

‘Sagar, we have a crisis on hand now,’ Pradyumna said. ‘All the top brass – Lord Krishna, Balrama, Krita Varma and Satyaki--are travelling to attend the wedding of the Yuva Raja of Kosala. They will be back only after ten days.

‘Today, we received a message. The ***Nishadas*** (cannibals) and the ***Kerakas*** (one-legged ***rakshasas***) living on the coastal line have entered the island Antar Dwipa. They came in from the sea. They are holding the tourists – the Yuvaraj of Anarta Kingdom Santhan and his newly wedded wife, as well as the governer of the island--as hostages. These wicked tribes have gone into the thousand year old, semi damaged Shiva ***mandir***. They have locked themselves inside with the hostages.’

‘But what is their demand?’ asked Sagar.

‘The tribes had been conquered by Sahadeva during his conquests. They had posed as a problem to the adjacent civilized kingdoms in the south, and hence, Sahadeva had captured the creamy layer of their top administrators and made them his prisoners.

‘He had left them in the prisons of our kingdom. The remaining wicked men have reassembled. They know that Sahadeva is in exile. They knew their leaders were being held here as prisoners. They are thinking of creating wars between us and our neighbours. Therefore, they took our guests from the Anarta kingdom as captives.’

‘But what is there demand?’ Sagar asked.

'Yes, I am coming to that. They want their leaders to be released at once. Then they will release the hostages. This is their demand.'

'What are the issues to be addressed now?' asked Sagar.

'There are several issues here. One, we have to get the hostages released within three days. The invaders threaten to kill them after that. Two, we should not release the prisoners, as that will open new demands from various enemies. Three, we should have the job done before the Anarta King comes to know of it. Finally, we should keep the operation secret, as the invaders do not want to see an army around the temple and we do not want the public to panic. These are the issues we need to address. Moreover, since none of the top leadership of our kingdom is here, the onus of responsibility is on us,' Prince Pradyumna said.

'By the way, are the other devotees being stopped from going to the temple?' asked Sagar.

'They are being told that a slab has collapsed in the outer hall and the structure needs to be examined and repaired. Till then, for the safety of the worshippers, no one is being allowed inside,' Pradyumna answered.

'Now, what is my role? Why am I here?' asked Sagar.

'Sagar, I asked Abimanyu to head this ***Rahasya***, secret operation. But he said that he was not confident without you. In your absence, he has taken his ***Yuva*** Army on two assignments. Both were not successfully completed. He feels the strategic inputs from you, so vital to their success, were missing. Hence, he desperately wants you back as the chief strategist of the ***Yuva*** Army. What do you say?' Pradyumna asked.

'I am honoured. I am ready to take up my national duty. But I do not want Arya Vaisya involved in this operation. I have no grudge against him, but he hates me. His presence would be a distraction. I can handle this with Prince Abimanyu and the Sena brothers. But I need to assess the situation inside the temple, where the hostages are being held. Only then we can strategize our next moves.' Saying this, Sagar decided to go to Antar Dwipa with the Sena brothers, and asked Prince Abimanyu to stay behind in Dwarka.

The Sena brothers and Sagar reached Antar Dwipa the same evening. None of them had the authority to speak about this mission with their kith and kin. They came to the temple. The place was deserted. Sagar asked Bhoomi Sena to make a tunnel below the earth to the inner portion of the temple. They decided not to come out of the tunnel, but raise their heads just above the surface once they had gotten inside the temple.

They surveyed what was happening inside. About three hundred ugly persons were roaming within. Cruelty and wickedness was written all over their faces. They looked half man and half animal. Half of them walked on one leg. Sagar was told they were called ***Keraka***s and the other cannibals were the Nishadas. They listened to their conversations but could not understand anything, as they spoke in some Dravidian language.

At that point of time, Sagar realised that he needed to find a person who understood the Dravidian language. He thought of Prince Maran of the Pandiya kingdom, who was running the Ayurvedic clinic in the Ravatika hills. He came out of the tunnel jumped on his horse and proceded to Ravatika, asking his friends to stay back on the island.

Maran returned with Sagar. He listened to the speech of the men inside the temple. He could understand their language and translated it for Sagar and his mates.

The hostages had been locked inside the sanctum sanctorum, where the statue of Lord Shiva Statue had been placed. The men were waiting for news of the release of their leaders. But what Sagar heard next was a shock. Once the leaders were handed over, the man planned to kill the hostages.This would incite war between the two kingdoms.

It did not end there. An unburnt, closed clay pot filled with poison had been placed in the waters of two lakes – one in the north and one in the south. These lakes provided water for the people of the kingdom of Krishna. The pot would break in three days and the poison would spread. The pot had been placed in the southern lake three days earlier, and another one had been placed in the northern lake just the previous day.

They wanted to sow panic among the public. Triggered by anger, the Anarta kingdom would wage war against the Kingdom of Krishna. It would be a double blow to the Kingdom of Krishna. The men had also scheduled the events at a time when the leaders of Dwarka were gone.

Once Sagar had heard the entire plan, he knew he could not waste any time. He took the Sena brothers and arrived at Dwarka in the middle of the night. Pradyumna and Abimanyu were waiting for them.

Sagar told them of the wicked plans of the invaders. Pradyumna and Abimanyu were shocked. The situation was more serious than they had thought. 'What is the next step, Sagar?' they asked.

Sagar began explaining his strategy. 'First, remove the poisonous pot from the lakes. Second, we have to agree to hand over the prisoners. Third, we need to engage the invaders, and making them believe that we are desperate, that people are dying due to the poisoned water.

'Fourth, while they celebrate their victory, we should use the tunnel created by the Sena brothers to get into the sanctum sanctorum and bring out the hostages and the sacred Shiva statue. Fifth, we should release their leaders and send them into the temple. Sixth, we should burn the old temple. And last but not least, the whole operation should be done so secretively that nobody should come to know of any of it.

'This will be a secret operation buried in the silent chambers of our souls forever. Not even the top leadership should be briefed about this – now or later.'

'Sagar, now I know the stuff you are made of - courage with calmness, clarity even amidst crisis. I salute you, Sagar. You have a great mind at a very young age. We are blessed to have you with us,' Pradyumna said.

The team started their action in the early hours of the next morning, while the whole city of Dwarka was sleeping. The team comprised of Abimanyu, Pradyumna, Sagar and the Sena brothers, along with Maran.

They first went to the lake on the southern side. Jala Sena submerged himself, and saw that the earthen pot had broken open and the water was contaminated with poison. He came out and explained the situation. The team only had ten ***nazhigas*** (four hours) to dry the lake and refill it with fresh water. 'How do we do that?' was the question on their minds.

Since the poison came from herbs, they showed them to Maran.

'This is known as ***Nerium oleander*** from the ***Kolly*** hills of Dakshin Bharath. A single leaf is enough to kill an adult. Nausea, vomiting, dizziness, slowed pulse, irregular heart beat, drowsiness, unconsciousness, paralysis of legs and finally death – these are the effects of these herbs,' he said.

'Ji, we have no time. How do we remove poison from the lake? Is there any way?' Sagar asked.

'If we place ***Arka Patram*** leaves in the lake, it will function as an anti poisonous herb and the lake will be cleaned of poison in the two nazhigas,' said Maran.

'Ji, how do we get them at such short notice?' the tense Sagar asked.

'Don't worry. Take me to my farm in the Ravatika hills. I have brought these poisonous herbs from the south and planted them at my farm.'

Sagar took Maran on his horse, and they rushed to Maran's farm.

With the help of the moonlight, they found the ***Arka Patra,*** the anti poisonous herb. They brought the leaves to the lake and Jala Sena spread them in the wayer.

In a short time, Maran drank the water and certified that the poison was gone. The boys were relieved.

The public did not know of anything that had happened before sun rise. It was business as usual for them. Only a few fishermen were puzzled, as a lot of fish were found dead along the shores.

The next task was the cleansing of the lake on the northern side of the city. Jala Sena went into the water. Fortunately, the clay pot had not broken as it was only one day old. He took the whole pot out and destroyed it. The poison was removed before it could spread through the water.

Meanwhile, Pradyumna sent a pleading message to the invaders, requesting them not to kill the hostages and assuring them that he would return the prisoners in two days.

There was jubilation in the enemy camp. The men were elated and congratulated themselves on their smartness.

While the messages were being exchanged, Sagar took the Sena brothers and created an underground tunnel leading directly into the sanctorum of the temple. He brought out the hostages and the Shiva statue. Sagar ensured their safe passage via a special boat to the city of Dwarka.

Now the last task at hand was destroying the terrorists. They were waiting for their leaders – the prisoners of war held by the kingdom of Krishna.

The prisoners were brought to the temple and let inside. There was a big celebration inside the temple. But the temple was locked from outside by Sagar. Abimanyu invoked the ***Agni Astra*** (Fire missile) with the help of the Sena brothers. Since the statue was not inside, the building was no longer considered a temple and could be destroyed with a clear conscience.

The terrorists went up in flames. The next day, there was an announcement by the governor of Antar Dwipa.

'The ceiling of the thousand-year-old temple fell last night. The moorti was taken out a day before as precaution. After the crash, ***agni*** was used to cleanse and purify the bhoomi.

'After the old stones are removed, the construction of a new temple will be scheduled on the following ***Pournami*** day. The new temple will also face the sea and the moorti of Lord Shiva will continue to protect all of us from its perils. All are welcome to attend the ***Bhoomi Pooja***. Those who want to help clear the stones of the old temple or take them for any purpose should contact the royal architect's station at the site.'

Sagar, the Sena brothers and Abimanyu met Pradyumna after finishing their task. Maran was also with them.

'Sagar, your strategies have saved our kingdom. In the absence of Lord Krishna, I was stumped as to how we get over the crisis. You are the savior of the kingdom, Sagar. You will be the chief strategist of the ***Yuva*** Army. You should always be with Abimanyu and protect him as a shadow for ever.

'I do not hesitate to seek forgiveness for what happened earlier. The opinions of family members, or for that matter anyone outside the army should not influence our decisions in this regard. I am sorry, Sagar. Caste differences should never govern our kingdom. This is the golden principle of Lord Krishna. For a while, I was carried away due to the appeals of my aunt. Please forgive me.'

Sagar had no words. '***Yuvaraj***, your status is such that I am not privileged enough to even come near you. You have given me a big responsibility. Please do not seek forgiveness from me.

I am too small to deserve such praises. I will always be the servant of our beloved kingdom of Krishna.'

Pradyumna was happy to see his deep-rooted patriotism. They took an oath to never speak of the operation to anyone ever again.

Lord Krishna had taken the Yadava Sena away from Mathura, as they were always facing threats from Jarasandh, the king of Magadh. Lord Krishna could have easily tamed them through a war. But he did not want the people to suffer. Hence he brought them away from Mathura and had settled them in the reclaimed land of Dwarka.

Even so, the threats continued. Such instances of terrorism might have caused unjust suspicion among the citizens and unwarranted hardships to the trade happening through Dwarka. This was all the more reason Sagar's operation had had to be carried in the most secretive manner.

The mothers of the friends continued to scold Sagar for gaining re-entry into the ***Yuva*** Army. They were under the impression that he had regained his position by soliciting sympathy. His neighbours said the same.

Sagar's interest in life was renewed thanks to his better half, Varsha. Master Bharadwaj was happy that Sagar had rejoined the Yuva Army. The unsung hero was not bothered that his competence was not acknowledged by the public. He was happy to have served the kingdom of Krishna.

17. Wedding Bells

Along with enmity, marriage was another big event that swept into the lives of the six friends. Bhoomi Sena, Jala Sena and Vayu Sena were getting married to Narmadha, Sindhu, Cauvery, the daughters of the royal priest and his brothers in the kingdom of Virata.

The Sena brothers swallowed the bitter pill of pride and went to the house of Arya Vaisya. They personally invited him and his family to their wedding. Along with Bharadwaj, they went to the royal palace and invited Abimanyu, Subadhra and the whole Yadava clan. Through the royal messengers, invitations were sent out to the Pandavas and Draupadi, but since it was the year of the ***adnyatvaas***, the messengers could not find them.

A big group of people went to the kingdom of Virata with the bridegrooms. The Pandavas were staying in disguise in this kingdom during the thirteenth year of their exile. Dharma was disguised as Kaka, and working as the king's advisor. Bhima took the name Vallabha and was working as a royal cook. Draupadi was posing as the maid of the queen under the name of Sairandhri. She had joined on three conditions- she would not clean dirty utensils, she would not eat leftover food, and she would not wash anyone's feet. Arjuna, disguised as a eunuch, had become the royal musician and dance teacher, taking the name Brahannala. Nakula took the name Granthika and became the keeper of the horses while Sahadeva took the name Tantripala and became a cowherd.

The wedding of Bhoomi Sena, Jala Sena and Vayu Sena to Narmadha, Sindhu and Cavery took place in the royal hall in the palace. Along with the bridegrooms' friends, Duryodhana's son Laxman also attended the function. There was a music programme by Brahanala (Arjuna) in the evening.

All the Pandavas could see Abhimanyu among the guests. Arjuna was delighted to see his son. He was so near, but yet so far, and they could not meet as father and son. In fact, Abhimanyu went to him and told him he appreciated the music, but he could not recognize his father. Arjuna was afraid of disclosing his emotions and revealing his identity, but he controlled himself and kept quiet.

The marriage function was proceeding well. But yet again, Sagar had to face nasty treatment. Arya Vaisya's mother had corrupted the minds of the brides' mothers. When Sagar came onto the stage at the request of the Sena brothers, Narmada's mother shouted, '***Sudhra*** boy, don't get onto the stage. You are not allowed here. What courage do you have to come up to this stage? We should not have allowed you inside the marriage hall. Know your limits.'

Sagar was ashamed, and Varsha also felt bad. He could not control his tears.

‘Oh god, why did you send me to this world to listen to this ridicule? Have I committed so many sins in my past birth? God, please save me from all this ill treatment. I have not done anything wrong.’ he prayed to the Almighty.

At this point, the Sena brothers did something which no one expected. All three brothers got up and declared, ‘If Sagar is not permitted onto the stage, we will not perform the wedding rituals. ‘

Sagar was allowed to stay on the stage. The marriage rituals went off smoothly.

Meanwhile, back in Hastinapur, Duryodhana was getting restless. He had mandated that if the Pandavas were recognized during the thirteenth year of their exile, they would have to remain in exile for another thirteen years. He had sent his spies to various places to try to ferret out the Pandavas’ hideout.

Things seemed to be going well for the Pandavas though, until the queen’s brother, Keechak, the commander of the armies of Virata, became interested in Draupadi. Keechak asked for Draupadi’s hand in marriage. Draupadi refused. Thinking her to be only a maid, Keechak felt insulted at having been turned down. He decided to force himself into Draupadi’s chamber one night. As soon as Draupadi heard of this plan, she asked Bhima to help her. Disguised as Draupadi, Bhima lay on the bed in her room. When Keechak entered the room, Bhima sprang out of bed and killed him.

The next day, Keechak’s corpse was discovered in her room, but no one could figure out who the killer was. To save Bhima from the queen’s wrath, Draupadi told her that Keechak had entered her room without her permission. When she screamed, someone had come in and killed Keechak, but she had no clue to this person’s identity. The queen apologized for her brother’s misdeeds, and never learned the truth about Bhima’s action.

Duryodhana heard the story. He knew no ordinary man could kill the mighty Keechak, and suspected Bhima of being the assailant. He decided to invade the kingdom of Virata, as he suspected that the Pandavas might have been staying there.

His army attacked Virata, and Duryodhana planned to personally attack the palace from the rear. All the Pandava brothers other than Arjuna went out with the king in disguise. When Duryodhana attacked the palace from the rear, the young prince Uttar was the only man left in the palace. When the women teased Uttar for hiding with them, he came up with the plea that he did not have a charioteer and hence could not go into battle.

When Arjuna heard this, he offered his services as charioteer. He first took the chariot to the tree where he had hidden his weapons almost a year earlier in preparation for his last year of exile. No matter what disguise he might have worn, the mighty Gandiva bow of Arjuna would have made him as conspicuous as a wolf among sheep anywhere. Uttar was puzzled but kept quiet. He was afraid of Duryodhana’s army. Arjuna guessed the situation and asked Uttar to take his place as charioteer while he did the fighting. Uttar agreed.

Arjuna blew his conch, and Duryodhana immediately recognized him. He was happy to locate Pandavas. But to his utter disappointment, Duryodhana realized that the thirteenth year had just been completed. Arjuna singlehandedly defeated the army and Duryodhana fled the battlefield.

During the victory celebration, Dharma explained to King Virata the details of the thirteenth year of exile. All the Pandavas expressed their gratitude to the king. Virata was overwhelmingly happy and agreed to give his daughter Uttara in marriage to Arjun's son Abhimanyu.

The news of the Pandavas' return spread. In every kingdom, north and south, east and west, kings and commoners alike spoke of nothing else. A current of excitement surged through the land, and everyone speculated on what Duryodhana would do next. Would he return their kingdom to his cousins?

Meanwhile, the Virata king gave the Pandavas another city within his borders, which was to be their home for the time being: Upaplavya. Once they had settled here, relieved that their exile was over, Dharma sent messengers to all those he loved. The first ones he sent word to were Krishna and Drupada. He told them that the ***Adnyatavasa*** has ended, and Abhimanyu would marry the princess Uttara in the Matsya kingdom.

The Yadavas were the first to arrive in Upaplavya. Dharma and his brothers and Virata and his sons and brothers went out of the city gates to receive them. Balarama alighted from his chariot, and Virata and Dharma came forward to embrace him. The other Pandavas and Virata's family greeted him in turn.

The second chariot from Dwarka drew up and in it rode he whom they had all been waiting for: Krishna.

As always, Dharma was overwhelmed when he saw Krishna, and wept. They embraced, and the Pandava said, 'The exile is over, and now that you have come, I leave everything else in your hands. Krishna, I bless our exile for one reason: it has made me more certain than ever that our fate rests in your hands, and our future depends on what you decide. My lord, I submit to you. Do whatever you will.'

Krishna's eyes were not dry as he hugged his cousins one by one, Arjuna clinging to him. At last, Draupadi came and stood before him. She only said, 'Krishna.'

Then she knelt before him. Her tears flowed, and neither of them could speak for a while. Krishna took her hands and raised her up. Softly, he said, 'Dry your eyes, O Queen. The time for tears is past. Let me see you smile. You have such a lovely smile, one to light up the very world. Do you remember what I promised you, thirteen years ago in the Kamyaka Vana, when you had just been banished? I always keep my word, Panchali. I intend to cure your sorrow, no matter what saddens you.'

Even as they spoke, King Drupada arrived, and with him came his brothers - Dhrishtadyumma and Shikhandi. Drupada had also brought the other Pandava-putras with him.

Druapadi had been blessed with five sons, one from each of the Pandavas. They had all been left with her father, Drupada. Draupadi had not seen her sons for thirteen years. They sobbed with joy and bitterness at the same time. Duryodhana had robbed her of thirteen years of motherhood.

King Virata said, 'Let us not stand here forever. The city has been waiting to receive all of you. Come; let me welcome you to Upaplavya.'

Once they were in the city, their hearts turned to the wedding, and for the moment, the past was forgotten. There were many arrangements to be seen to still, for a host of friendly kings would soon begin to arrive with their armies.

Everything was perfect on the day of Abimanyu's wedding to the princess Uttara. Like a flame himself was that young lion as he sat before the sacred fire, and another flame was his bride.

Dhaumya Rishi was the chief priest for the occasion. The grave and radiant mantras recited by him united the two lives forever. The wedding of Abimanyu and Uttara was like a dream, almost too good to be true.

Krishna and Arjuna sat next to each other. The day had a wonderful auspiciousness about it, as if the sun of fortune had risen again on the Pandavas after the long night of their trials. The solemn ceremony, coming after the privation and shame they had faced for thirteen years, ensured that the ceremony was cherished by all in attendance.

Yet, even while the wedding was underway, there was a certain tension among the other kings who had come at Dharma's invitation. All of them knew the very future of ***Bharata varsha*** must soon be decided. What would Dharma and Duryodhana do now?

None of the royal guests breathed a word of these momentous matters today. This was the day when Arjuna's son Abhimanyu married Virata's daughter, the gem of his crown, Uttara. And how splendid the kalyana mandapa was: with Balaram and Krishna there, like the Sun and the Moon, and the others like stars around them. Upaplavya was like Indra's Amravati; Draupadi and Subadhra were queens of the palace. Enchantment was in the air, and bright, whispering petals fell out of the Devas' realms to bless the young couple.

Abhimanyu looked into his bride's eyes and saw a love there so strong that it startled him. When the last mantras had been chanted, and they were man and wife, singing and dancing broke out in the palace and in the streets, and did not pause for a week.

The friends of Abhimanyu also attended the marriage with their families. Sagar y stayed away from presenting himself on the stage. He did not want another shameful episode, as Abhimanyu's mother would certainly not receive his presence well. He attended the function with his wife, but sat in a remote corner, lost in the huge audience.

All the guests returned to Dwarka, while the Pandavas stayed back in the Virata kingdom. Varsha became pregnant, but there was no one with whom they could celebrate the news, apart from themselves.

Bharadwaj told Dharma that he would join him wherever he decided to stay, along with his family. The place that Dharma chose would be the place in which the Pandavas would finally settle, or so Bharadwaj claimed.

*** ***

18. The War Begins: Tragedy Strikes

While camping at Upaplavya, in the Virata kingdom, the Pandavas started sounding out various other kings. They wanted to try to gain a peaceful settlement with Duryodhana. Who could understand adversity better than them?

But Duryodhana refused to restore their kingdom on the pretext that they had been discovered while they were in exile. Hence, they were not eligible to receive their kingdom as had been agreed to originally.

Before taking the decision to wage war, the disinherited Pandavas, advised by Krishna, tried to find a diplomatic and peaceful solution to the conflict. Balarama advised the Pandavas to send an emissary to gain the support of the elders of the family like Bhishma, Dhritarashtra, Drona, Karna, and even Shakuni, with the message 'Let us avoid armed conflict as far as possible. Only that which is accrued in peace is worthwhile. Out of war, nothing but wrong can occur.'

While the emissary was in the Kaurava court, the Pandavas continued with war preparations. They sent messages requesting assistance to a number of neighbouring kingdoms.

In Hastinapur, their ambassador of peace was insulted and turned away by Duryodhana. He was intent on war, and defied the counsel of elders like Bhishma. After several failed attempts at peace, war seemed inevitable.

In a last attempt, Krishna travelled to Hastinapur to persuade the Kauravas to embark upon a peaceful path. Here, Krishna took his meals and stayed at the house of the minister Vidura, a religious man and a devotee of Krishna. Duryodhana felt insulted that Krishna had turned down his invitation to dine with him and stay in his royal palace. Determined to stop the peace mission, Duryodhana plotted to arrest Krishna.

At the formal presentation of the peace proposal in the court of Hastinapur, Krishna's words were ignored, and Duryodhana publicly ordered his soldiers to arrest him. Krishna laughed and displaying his divine skills and form, radiated intense light and caused the soldiers to fall back.

Furious at the insult inflicted upon him, Lord Krishna cursed Duryodhana, saying that his downfall was certain. Dhritarashtra was alarmed and tried to pacify the Lord. Krishna returned to Upaplavya to inform the Pandavas that the only course left to uphold the principles of virtue and righteousness was inevitable – war.

The Pandavas gathered their armies. Contingents arrived from all parts of the country and soon they had a large force of seven divisions. The Kauravas managed to raise an even larger army of eleven divisions. Many kingdoms such as Dwaraka, Kasi, Magadha, Chedi, Pandya and the Yadus of Mathura were allied with the Pandavas, while the allies of the Kauravas comprised the kings of Pragjyotisha, Anga, Kekaya, Sindhudesa, Mahishmati, Avanti in Madhyadesa, Gandharas, Bahlikas, Kambojas and others.

Lord Krishna's Narayani Sena were given to Duryodhana under the leadership of Kritavarma, while Krishna himself agreed to be the charioteer of Arjuna. Lord Krishna took an oath against using weapons during the war, but he served as a master strategist for Pandavas.

Dharma asked his brothers to organize their army, seeing that there was now no hope for peace. The Pandavas accumulated seven ***akshauhinis*** with the help of their allies. Each of these divisions was led by one leader: Drupada, Virata, Dhristadyumna, Shikhandi, Satyaki, Chekitana and Bhima. The eighth was the ***Yuva*** Army led by Abhimanyu and his five friends. After consultation among themselves, the Pandavas appointed Dhristadyumna as supreme commander of the Pandava army. Kingdoms from all over ancient India supplied troops or provided logistic support to the Pandavas.

The Kaurava army consisted of eleven ***akshauhinis***. Duryodhana requested Bhishma to command the army. Bhishma accepted on the condition that, while he would fight the battle sincerely, he would not harm the five Pandava brothers. In addition, Bhishma said that Karna would not fight under him as long as he was on the battlefield. Duryodhana agreed to Bhishma's conditions and made him the supreme commander, while Karna was debarred from fighting while Bhishma led the army.

Apart from the one hundred Kaurava brothers, who were headed by Duryodhana himself and his brother Dushasana, the Kauravas were assisted on the battlefield by Drona and his son Ashwathama, the Kauravas' brother-in-law Jayadratha, the Brahmin Kripa, Kritavarma, Shalya, Sudakshina, Bhurisravas, Bahlika, Shakuni, and many more who were bound by their loyalty towards Hastinapur. The kingdom of Vidarbha, with its king Rukmi, and Balarama were the only neutrals in this war.

Each army consisted of several divisions; the Kauravas had 11 while the Pandavas controlled seven. A division (***akshauhini***) included 21,870 chariots and chariot riders, 21,870 elephants and riders, 65,610 horses and riders, and 109,350 foot soldiers (in a ratio of 1:1:3:5). Each ***Akshohini*** was led by a commander or a general, apart from the commander in chief or the generals who were the head of the entire army.

During the war, the weapons used included bow and arrows, the weapon of choice for Arjuna, Bhishma, Drona, Karna and Abimanyu; the mace, chosen by Bhima and Duryodhana, and the spear and the dagger or sword.

The two supreme commanders met and framed the 'rules of ethical conduct,' or dharmayuddha, for the war. The rules included:

- Fighting must begin no earlier than sunrise and end exactly at sunset.
- More than one warrior may not attack a single warrior.
- Two warriors may 'duel' or engage in prolonged personal combat only if they carry the same weapons and they are on the same type of mount (on foot, on a horse, on an elephant, or in a chariot).
- No warrior may kill or injure a warrior who has surrendered.
- One who surrenders becomes a prisoner of war and will then be subject to the protections of a prisoner of war.
- No warrior may kill or injure an unarmed warrior.
- No warrior may kill or injure an unconscious warrior.
- No warrior may kill or injure a person or animal not taking part in the war.
- No warrior may kill or injure a warrior whose back is turned away.
- No warrior may attack a woman.
- No warrior may strike an animal not considered a direct threat.
- The rules specific to each weapon must be followed. For example, it is prohibited to strike below the waist in mace warfare.
- Warriors may not engage in any unfair warfare.

On the first day of the war, as would be on all the following days, the Kaurava army stood facing west and the Pandava army stood facing east. The Kaurava army was formed such that it faced all sides: elephants formed its body; the kings its head; and the steeds its wings. Bhishma, in consultation with his commanders Drona, Bahlika and Kripa, remained in the rear.

The Pandava army was organised by Dharma and Arjuna in the ***Vajra*** formation. Because the Pandava army was smaller than the Kauravas', they decided to employ the tactic of each warrior engaging as many enemies as possible. This involved an element of surprise, with bowmen showering arrows by hiding behind the front lines. The attackers in the front were equipped with short-range weapons like maces, battle-axes, swords and lances.

Ten divisions of the Kauravas army were arranged in a formidable phalanx. The eleventh was put under the immediate command of Bhishma, partly to protect him. The safety of the supreme commander was central to Duryodhana's strategy, as he had placed all his hope on the great warrior's abilities. Dushasana was the military officer in charge of Bhishma's protection.

Ajuna had reservations since all the opponents were close relatives of his. He was counselled by Lord Krishna. He was advised that the war was between ***dharma*** and ***adharma*** and it was his duty to slay anyone who propagated ***adharma***. The battle was ready to commence.

Meanwhile, Bharadwaj came with his sons and attached himself to Dharma. But he was reminded of the Rishi's words on the day of birth of his sons: 'At the age of 15, your sons have ***Bala Kanda*** (life threat during youth phase) and you should protect them during this phase.'

Bharadwaj called to his sons, '***Puthras***, make me a promise that you will not go onto the battlefield. You can stay with Abhimanyu in strategy formation sessions off the battlefield.'

'***Pitaji***, how can we stay back without participating in this war? This is a war between ***dharma*** and ***adharma***. We have come here to support Abhimanyu. We cannot promise you that we will not fight on the battlefield. We can assure you that we will not take too many risks on the war front,' the sons said to their father.

Bharadwaj reluctantly agreed. He told Sagar, 'Take good care of my sons. According to their horoscope, they are in danger. Make sure you save them if any threat looms over them on the battlefield. Will you promise me that, Sagar?'

Sagar loved his master. He agreed. 'Master, do not worry. I will shed my own blood before anything happens to them. I will save them. In fact, I will try to ensure that they stay out of the action. Do not worry.'

Bharadwaj wanted to meditate in the forest near the battlefield. He told Dharma, 'Your Excellency, a Brahmin like me has no role to play on the battlefield. I will go to the forest nearby and pray for the Pandavas. Please give me permission to do so.' Dharma agreed. Bharadwaj left, placing his sons under the protection of Sagar.

Day 1-12 of the war

The Yuva Army was very enthusiastic in their strategy formations. Every day, there was a strategy session. Abimanyu would lead the army. Sagar would stand as a guard behind him, strategizing every move for him, as well as lending martial support. He acted as his shadow.

The three Sena brothers were always adjacent to the chariot of Abhimanyu, and would invoke the five elements from time to time, depending upon the need of the hour. Arya Vaisya would generate and coordinate the resource support for the *Yuva* Army. He preferred not to talk to Sagar. Sagar did not worry about it too much.

Day 1

When the battle commenced, Bhishma went through the Pandava army, creating havoc. Abhimanyu, supported by his friends, defeated Bhishma's bodyguards and attacked the commander. They used their coordinated strategy of moving under earth, creating surprise attacks on both sides of the enemy, invoking ***varuna***, aerial ***astras***, ***vayu*** and fire at will. The opponents could not even figure out what was going on. The Yuva army soon became a talking point for the opposition. King Virata's sons – Uttara and Sweta-- were killed on Pandavas' side, which was a setback to Pandavas.

Day 2

Arjuna was on the offensive on Day Two. Realizing that something had to be done to reverse the Pandavas' losses, Arjuna inflicted heavy damage to the Kauravas.

Laxman challenged Abhimanyu. The ***Yuva*** Army in turn wanted to hit at Laxman. Sagar shouted, 'Kill him! Kill Laxman, the son of jealousy!' Duryodhana saw his son pressed hard by Abhimanyu and went to his rescue.

Abhimanyu was as good as his father, and he gave his opponents a breathtaking fight. When Laxman was aimed at by the skilled prince Abimanyu, an unfortunate incident took place. Arya Vaisya went and stood in front of him.

'Prince Abhimanyu, Laxman is as good a friend to me as you have been. You must kill me before killing him,' Arya Vaisya shouted. Abhimanyu had to let Laxman go that day. His other friends were upset.

That night, the mood in Pandava camp was in sharp contrast to what it had been the previous day. Arjuna congratulated Abhimanyu and his team. Then, Abhimanyu introduced Sagar and his other friends to his father. Arjuna was impressed by the *Yuva* army's surprise attack invoking the five elements.

But within the *Yuva* army, there arose a problem. Arya Vaisya opened the conversation. 'Laxman is also my friend. I do not like you targeting him. Sagar is the one who induced you to fight against him. I strongly object to this.'

'Look Arya Vaisya,' Abhimanyu said, 'In war, such targeting is common. Once the war begins, we cannot look at emotions. Who knows, I may die tomorrow. You cannot crib once you enter the battlefield.'

But Arya Vaisya disagreed. He declared that he would only participate in the strategy sessions off the battlefield. He would not accompany them to the battlefield hence forth.

They finally agreed, largely because they did not want to alienate Arya Vaisya at this stage of the war. Sagar did not react at all, as he thought any reaction would only add fuel to the fire.

Day 3

The eagle formation by the Kauravas and crescent formation by the Pandavas were in place on Day Three. The *Yuva* Army defeated the Gandhara forces of Shakuni. Bhishma killed numerous soldiers of the Pandavas.

Day 4

Abhimanyu was surrounded and attacked by a number of Kaurava princes. Arjuna joined the fray to help him. Again, Bhima was attacked fiercely by Duryodhana. Bhima withstood itand killed eight of the brothers of Duryodhana, adding to the latter's frustration.

Day 5-9

The attacks and counter attacks continued. Thousands of soldiers from both sides lost their lives. Eight more of Duryodhana's brothers were killed by Bhima. Arjuna's son Iravan was killed by the Kauravas.

Day 10

Bhishma had taken a vow to not to attack a woman. Shikandi, a woman in his prior life, was placed in front of Bhishma and Arjuna stood behind Shikandi, protecting him from Bhishma's attack. He aimed his arrows at the weak parts of his armour. The great warrior fell from his chariot. His body was held aloft by the arrows protruding from his body. Arjuna placed three arrows under Bhishma's head to support it. Due to the boon received by Bhishma, he could decide the time of his death. He wanted to wait till Hastinapur became safe from all directions.

Day 11

Karna came onto the field, and Drona became the commander of the Kaurava forces. The plan of Drona and Karna was to capture Dharma alive, but they were foiled by Arjuna.

The Yuva army were actively fighting in the war. However, Arya Vaisya came to strategy meetings every day and sat quiet and watched the proceedings. Sagar wondered whether Arya Vaisya was revealing their secrets to the enemy, as he was now biased towards Laxman's father after Laxman had been attacked by the *Yuva* army.

Sagar raised this contentious issue. It created a flutter amongst the friends. Arya Vaisya openly challenged Sagar. 'How dare you suspect my integrity ***Sudhputra***, killer's son? You are the traitor, since your father killed my father. You are from a criminal family. Hence your mind also thinks like that of a criminal. You are the one who provoked Abhimanyu to kill his cousin, my friend Laxman. Come, I will teach you a lesson. I will make sure that you, a ***Sudhra***, cannot enter the *Yuva* army. Watch out, I will show you the exit very soon.'

Abhimanyu and the Sena brothers were taken aback. They tried to pacify Arya Vaisya. For the time being, a patch was put in place and they allowed him to continue to come to strategy meetings, even if he did not participate in discussions. But the rivalry between Sagar and Arya Vaisya was growing unabated.

Day 12

Duryodhana wanted to capture Dharma alive so that the Pandavas would be weakened. When his attempts to capture Dharma failed, Drona confided to Duryodhna that it would be difficult as long as Arjuna was around. The king of Trigartadesa, Susharma, along with his three brothers and 35 sons who were fighting on the Kaurava side, made a pact that they would kill Arjuna or die. They went onto the battlefield on the twelfth day and challenged Arjuna. Arjuna gave them a fierce fight in which the brothers fell dead. Drona continued to try and capture Dharma, but the Pandavas fought hard and delivered severe blows to the Kaurava army.

Day 13 – The Tragedy

Duryodhana announced his wish to capture Dharma. The plan was to be executed that day. It was the 13th day, and it was the third day under Drona's command. Even the sun was late in rising and when it rose, it was obscured by clouds. All the signs foretold a grim day ahead. In such a heavy atmosphere, Drona made up his mind to achieve results rather than maintain his ideals.

Today there would be no rules, and there would be no limits. There would be no looking back for him. He deployed the entire army, except for a few legions, in the formation of a ***Chakravyuh***. All the soldiers were wearing red garlands and red clothes which made it look as though the entire ground were covered by a giant lotus flower, a flower covered in blood. To the trained eye, the nine tiers of the chakra were visible.

Duryodhana formed the inner layer; the second tier was studded with warriors such as Karna, Dussashasan and Kripa. These were followed by a layer of Duryodhana's other brothers. Ashwathama, Shakuni, Kritavarma, Shalya and Bhoorishravas formed the next few layers. Then Jayadratha came with his own army. Standing guard at the mouth was Guru Drona himself.

Duryodhona showed his tactical brilliance and deployed Bhagadutta, an expert in elephant warfare, and the great warrior Susharma to create a diversion for Arjuna. Bhagadutta was from the kingdom of modern Assam. Both of them dragged Arjuna towards the south, while on the other side, the Pandavas had to face the Chakravyuh.

Today the Pandavas were being led by Bhima. He marched towards the mouth of the Chakravyuh. But they were the students, while Drona was the guru. As they started to attack the rim, a flurry of arrows came out of the inner tier. The Pandava warriors could not hold up against this onslaught. None of them knew how to cleave the chakra. Without Arjun, any attack was just an invitation to lose more soldiers. Row upon row of the Kshatriyas were no match for Guru Drona and his perfect chakravyuh.

Dharma was aware that among all those who were present and available, only Abhimanyu knew how to break the chakra. Dharma summoned him and he came with his trusted strategist and guard, Sagar. When Dharma explained the purpose of his summons, Abhimanyu's young blood started to spurt at the chance of glory this opportunity presented.

He explained to Dharma that once he entered the vyuha, he would not be able to break out of it. He did not have the knowledge of how to exit. Bhima and Dharma came up with an innovative strategy. As the tier broke, the key Kshatriyas would take up position and defend the breach from both sides. This would ensure that the chakra would be breached and a clear line of retreat was available to Abhimanyu and his forces.

Sagar and the *Yuva* army also came up with a brilliant plan. They would use the Sena brothers' powers to create an underground tunnel through each tier so that they would be able to retreat in case anything went wrong. Some portion of the army could also use the tunnels so that they could be shielded from the arrows while moving ahead and defending the broken edges of the tier. Also, if the tiers were closed due to any reason, the mouths of the tunnels would provide a ready exit for Abhimanyu.

The innovative tactic had been discussed in the early war strategy meetings, but the students had not been taught the *chakravyuha* in detail in the ***Gurukul***. But now, they had no choice.

The plan was approved by Dharma and Abhimanyu started off with his *Yuva* army division. To relieve the pressure on Abhimanyu, Dharma and Bhima would attack the chakra in a minimum damage mode on its flanks, where Abhimanyu would make his main thrust.

As the kings and warriors who were to follow were falling in line with the plan, and Abhimanyu made his chariot ready. He wanted to keep Sagar as his rear guard so that no enemy would attack him from behind. As Sagar was about to assume the role of the rear guard, one of the kings from the Pandiya kingdom, Mani Maran, objected.

'How do you expect my forces to be lead by a *Shudra* and a killer's son? It's not possible. I will not allow this.'

Abhimanyu and Sagar were hurt by the allegation and the precious time being wasted. The arrangement of forces to counter the vyuha would have taken at least half a ***naziga***. Abhimanyu asked Sagar to stay quiet and said that he would explain the situation to everyone. But no one was listening. As the talks went on between Abhimanyu and the southern kings, an emissary arrived with a message stating that Varsha had given birth to a baby boy.

Abhimanyu immediately wanted Sagar to go and be with his wife, see his son and only then come back. In the meantime, he would make the arrangements for the army. But the southern kings were adamant. They would not fight under a Shudra. Exasperated, Abhimanyu and Sagar gave up. Abhimanyu instructed Sagar to go back and be with his wife. He asked Mani Maran to be the rear guard himself.

Sagar said to Abhimanyu, 'I do not know whether to be happy because of my son or sad that on the eve of battle I cannot be with you.'

Abhimanyu replied, 'Keep the sweets ready. I will come back and we will celebrate the birth of your son together.'

Sagar went to the Sena brothers. 'You should be very careful, and stay with Abhimanyu at all times. While you are around Abhimanyu, I am not afraid. Also, under no circumstances should you be separated. Stay together and ride together. As soon as Bhoomi Sena hits the ground, Vayu Sena, be with him and guard his back as he gets the tunnelling done.'

Abhimanyu and the Sena brothers were clamoring for action. After the formations were complete, Abhimayu commanded his ***sarathy***, 'Take me towards Guru Drona.' The sarathy obeyed, but with a mix of admiration and disbelief.

His chariot was a blur, and the Kaurav soldiers almost believed that Arjuna had come back. They started to waver. Abhimanyu sent out ***Agni astras*** on all sides and created a full wall of fire that no one could overcome. Drona controlled the fire while Abhimanyu streaked past and entered the first chakra.

Quenching the fires with his Jal Astra, Drona removed the barrier and suddenly, before everyone's eyes, Jayadratha emerged with his loyal army through the smoke and water, and blocked the way. The first wave of warriors started their attack, which Jayadratha easily parried. Nakul and Sahadev started to battle him. But today, they were no match for Jayadratha. He easily shot the wheels of their raths and put them on the ground.

Bhima reached the opening first and seeing Jayadratha and remembering the humiliation he had made him go through in the forest, went ahead confidently. But he did not know what hit him, as in a flurry of arrows, he and his rath were tied to the ground. Jayadratha came close and humiliated Bhima by throwing away his bow and shooting down his chariot flag.

Dharma, who was better at archery than Bhima, also tried, but Jayadratha was a different warrior today. He created a wall of arrows of such quality that even ***Pitamah Bheeshma*** would have envied him. When Jayadratha left behind the wall of the arrows, the army came down and sealed the gap. The ***Vyuh*** was complete. Now no one could enter and no one could exit.

The mighty Pandavas were humbled. They first fought with valour, then anger, then despair, then fear as they began to realize the consequences of their failure, and they started to fight out of shame. Time and again they attacked the ***vyuha,*** but the formation did not break.

In the meantime, Abhimanyu's young blood and the heat of the battle overtook him. He began to fight like a warrior who did not value his own life. He moved further and further and ahead, while his army, who could not match his swiftness, began to fall back. All his uncles were stuck far behind near the first tier.

His rearguard was pursued and attacked by Drona. The three Sena brothers were separated in the melee. Because of this, they could not invoke the **Pancha bhoodas**. Plans for the tunnel turned to dust and with them went the last ray of hope for a safe return.

Within the *Vyuha*, Abhimanyu was wrecking havoc. He had almost reached the last tier. Duryodhana proceeded towards him. As they started to fight, Drona came in between them. Behind him came Ashwathama, Kritavarma, Kripa, Karna and Shakuni, and all of them proceeded to engage Abhimanyu.

A furious Duryodhana said, 'Senapati, why will you not allow me to engage him fully?'

Drona said, 'Duryodhana, don't act foolishly. He has God's will behind him today. If you are captured, then the war will end. I am here to ensure that your army wins. You should fight your own ego and let me fight my war. Look at the way he is fighting.'

Abhimanyu had engaged all the maharathis himself. With every arrow, he reminded his opponents that they were facing the son of Arjuna and the nephew of Krishna. He had the Pandava blood, which had grown strong under the divine instruction of Krishna and Balarama. He succeeded in piercing Karna's body armour and inflicted a deep wound.

Karna and Shalya tried to control his arrows, but were quickly surmounted by Abhimanyu.

Seeing that even the mighty Karna had been overcome, Drona cried out, 'Bravo Abhimanyu. You are even better than your father.'

Turning to Duryodhona, he shouted, 'Duryodhana, this young boy has the capacity to annihilate our entire army if nothing is done now. Today he is fighting his first great battle and not yet at his peak. If he sees another he will be invincible.'

Duryodhana and Dushasana heard his words. Dushasana shouted, 'Drona will not kill himm brother, it is we who will have to do it.'

With this, he spurred his chariot towards Abhimanyu. Abhimanyu saw it and with just six arrows, broke Dushasana's bow and rendered him unconscious. The humiliation shook the very core of the Kauravas and they began to waver.

Abhimanyu had become a vyuha; anyone who came near him or attacked him was swallowed by death. He sent a ***Gandharva astra*** into the air. The Kaurav army seemed to see a thousand Abhimanyus around them. Arrows flew in every direction and the army began to destroy itself.

Meanwhile, the Sena brothers had been separated from each other in different tiers of the ***Vyuha.*** Vayu Sena was in the fourth, Jala Sena in the third and Bhoomi Sena in the second tier. They could not use their powers.

Moreover, the strategic master, Sagar, was also not there with them. Hence each of them became a powerless island, with no assistance from their supernatural abilities.

Vayu Sena had to counter Ashwathama, the warrior son of Guru Dhrona. He could never match Ashwathama, who was rated almost on par with the greatest archer, Arjuna. His opponents knew that Vayu Sena couldn't be defeated when he was fighting from above the ground, as he was the blessed child of ***Vayu*** (air). Hence Ashwathama injured the legs of his elephant, forcing Vayu Sena to fight on the ground. With no assistance from his mystic powers, Vayu Sena was helpless.

Ashwathama discharged the ***Agni Astra.*** Vayu Sena could not counter this fire ***astra*** and fell dead with burns all over his body. In his final moment, he wondered if someone had revealed his secret mystic powers to the Kauravas. His life ended with this question lingering in his mind – 'Who would have done this?'

At the same time, Jala Sena was fighting Vrisha Sena (Karna's son) in the third tier of the ***Chakravyuha.*** Since he was fighting on the ground, he was not able to use his special skills in water. Further, his ability to invoke the other elements had been suspended due to the separation of the three brothers.

Having lost in the 'Inter ***Gurukul*** Bravery Meet,' Karna's son along with Duryodhana's had been waiting for years for an opportunity to strike back the Dwarka ***Yuva*** Army. Now they had the chance to eliminate Jala Sena at his weakest moment. Having been taught by his father, Vrisha Sena was well versed in the ***Vayu Astra.*** The astra lifted Jala Sena off the ground, one hundred feet high. Jala Sena could not command or solicit any of the ***Pancha bhoodas.*** Hence he fell down from the great height and died as he hit the ground.

Bhoomi Sena was fighting in the second tier of the ***Vyuha*** with Lakshmana, Duryodhana's son. Sensing his natural advantage on the ground, Lakshmana distracted Bhoomi Sena and attacked him from behind, breaking his leg with his mace. Bhoomi Sena limped slowly to the horse standing on the battlefield. He sat on the horse and continued his fight.

Having lost his prime advantage, he was not at his best. Lakshmana sensed this and launched a quick array of ***astras*** to defeat and kill Bhoomi Sena.

The three Sena brothers were lying dead in each of the three tiers of the ***chakravyuha***. This victory charged Lakshmana with more vigour.

Now, Duryodhana's son Lakshmana rode like the wind from the flank and dispelled the ***astra***. Sense returned to the Kauravas. He took on Abhimanyu and for some time, Duryodhana looked on as his son gave Abhimanyu the fight of his life. But he did not last long. One slip and an arrow from Abhimanyu struck the young throat of Lakshmana. Lakshmana fell back dead with blood pouring out of his mouth and throat.

Again, the Kaurava maharathis renewed their attack. Ashwathama took the lead, but his astra glanced off Abhimanyu's armour easily without doing any damage. Ashwathama took a hit on his cheeks and his armour began to glimmer with blood.

Karna and Duryodhana began to ask Drona: 'How do we kill him? If we don't kill him, he might destroy our entire army.'

Drona replied, 'He is even better than his father. One of us cannot attack him and win. All of us have to attack him. Karna, kill the two guards on his chariot, who look after his back. Then you should break his bow. Then we all attack.'

Karna was an accomplished archer; he could pick a target by sound. He did his job cleanly. Abhimanyu's back, usually guarded by Sagar, was now open for attack.

Abhimanyu's bow was broken next. As his bow broke, his fall began. His armour was covered by the feathers of hundreds of arrows as six mighty archers attacked him. His horses were killed and his chariot destroyed.

Emerging from the ruins of the chariot with a sword and shield, bloody and weak, he roared, 'You cowards, how could you do this? Guru Drona how could you, a guru who teaches rules and discipline, stoop to break the rules in such a dramatic manner?'

Another arrow shattered his shield and sword hilt.

Abhimanyu grabbed the wheel of his chariot and started to run towards Drona. Drona shattered it with just one arrow. Now he grabbed his mace and started to run towards the maharthis. Blood was pouring out of his wounds. He was delirious with blood loss and stumbling. Even so, he rushed at Ashwathama, who was not expecting an attack. He killed both his horses and his rear guard and staggered back. Ashwathama did not fight back; perhaps he felt a tinge of guilt.

Abhimanyu knew that his end was near. He was crying because he knew his father would never see him again, nor witness his bravery. Abhimanyu hefted his mace but this time he was met by Dushasana's son. The strong ring of their maces wiped away the traces of the smiles that had graced the lips of the warriors who had thought that the end was near.

Abhimanyu continued to fight like a man possessed, but his stamina faltered after ten strikes of his mace. He was but human after all. The loss of blood and the heavy mace took its toll. He became slower and slower and his blows became weaker. With an exceptionally strong blow from the opponent, his mace went flying out of his hands.

Dushasana's son thundered, 'This is for humiliating my father,' and with an almighty blow, he crushed the head of the young Abhimanyu.

The Yuvraj of the Pandavas died in the twilight. For some moments the army that had witnessed his heroics was silent, but as realization of the achievement came, the Kaurava army and the maharathis gave a roar of joy that carried across the battlefield.

The soul of the young hero departed the world, unsatisfied. He had fought to the best of his abilities. Had his opponents been honorable and had he had more time, he would surely have destroyed all of them. Drona was satisfied, as he had struck a blow which would hurt the pandavas. The chakravyuh had served its purpose.

As the roar of joy carried across the battlefield, the spirits of the Pandavas and those of Bhima and Dharmaraj sagged. Arjuna had not yet returned from his battle with the Trigartas.

Dharma fainted in anxiety. Bhima stood there, crying silently, too shocked to speak.

When he was finally roused, Dharma said, 'Drona and Kripa, Karna and Ashwathama, Duryodhana and Shalya could not contain him, so the cowards killed Abimanyu through treachery.'

He told the others around him, 'I beg of you, one of you must kill me before Arjuna comes back. How will I face him? How will I tell Subadhra and Krishna of what has happened?'

Sagar heard the shocking news. He went to the battlefield and sobbed uncontrollably in front of his friends' bodies. He was inconsolable.

He shouted, 'Friends, what fate is this? I could not guard Abimanyu today. I consider this cheating. I am sure that it was Arya Vaisya who schemed. Our strategy was known to the opposition. They knew that all three Sena brothers had to be together to invoke the *Pancha Bhoodas*. Hence, they trapped each of one of you in a separate tier.

'Arya Vaisya is a traitor. The day he protected Duryodhana's son from death, we should have known and thrown him out.

'Oh, ***Guruji***, what can I tell you? How can I face you? It was my responsibility to protect your sons. Today I was kept out of the war, and tragedy has struck. I do not know how I will face you.

'Oh mighty Arjuna, just yesterday you complimented me on working like a shadow behind Abimanyu, and guarding him. Today, I have failed in my duty. I could not protect Prince Abimanyu.

'What can I say now?' Sagar cried.

He knew he had to inform Bharadwaj of the developments. He swam across Saraswathi and went to his hut. Bharadwaj was meditating, but hearing the sounds of Sagar's arrival, he woke up.

'What happened, Sagar? Why are you here?'

Sagar told him about the tragedy. The master was shocked.

He roared, 'Sagar, I told you not to send them intto the battle. I told you they faced a a threat at the age of fifteen. You promised to protect them. You are responsible for what has happened. You knew they were blessed children. They were supposed to be extraordinary warriors on land, sea and air. You truncated their lives. They would have at least lived three times longer if you had not let this happen. The story of their lives will always be that of incomplete success. You have nipped their life in the bud by not sticking to your word.

‘I curse you. You will live the forty-five years of each of my sons’ remaining lives. But you will not live it in full. You will have the capability of each of my sons and like them, you will also die at the age of fifteen. Thus, you will take three births for each of my sons. You will take nine incarnations after this birth.

‘You will be highly competent on land, sea and air in each of the three births. You can win a war, but you cannot avail the fruits of it. Let these nine births forever remind you that you killed my sons in the nine tier ***chakravyuha***. Each of the nine circles will represent one birth for you. This is my curse.

‘Even after cursing you, I cannot quench my anger, as you betrayed so thoroughly.’

Sagar was stunned. His guru, the one who had adopted him, who was equal to his own father, who had been everything for him, right from his naming, had turned against him.

‘He is a true Brahmin, and his curse will force me to face miseries in my subsequent births,’ he thought.

He pleaded with Bharadwaj, trying to explain what had happened, how circumstances had kept him away from the battlefield. But ***Guruji*** did not bother to listen to him and turned away.

Two questions were bothering the two men at that time.

Bharadwaj was asking himself, ‘The children were born of blessed mangos. They were blessed to have extraordinary proficiency on land, sea and air. How could they die so early? Can the words of Rishi Markendeya go wrong? I should ask Dharmaraja about it.’ But Dharna was in mourning.

Sagar was asking himself, “Who could have revealed our strategy and the secret of the importance of keeping the Sena brothers away from each other to the opposition camp? Would it be Arya Vaisya, will he be so bad to his friends? He may be against me, but not against Prince Abimanyu. If not him, who revealed our secrets to the opposition?”

His mind was not getting a clear answer. The tragic day ended with these questions constantly ringing in these two minds throughout the night.

Abimanyu’s death marked the end of adherence to the rules of war, as he was cunningly killed by Duriyodhana’s men.

*** ***

19. The Revenge

Sagar returned to his camp. He told Varsha, 'I cannot console myself. The turn of events today has made me sick. I do not know what I will do without my friends, who were the backbone of my life. I faced a double blow today. Losing my friends is one thing, earning the wrath of my master is another. He cursed me with nine more births with premature death at the age of fifteen. I am not worried about the curse, but I am worried about the wrath of my master, who is a pillar of support in my life.

'I have gone through agony after agony. My birth into a Sudhra family was the first agony. Society castigated me as a man from the low caste, and denied me recognition, but by God's grace, I was given a helping hand at every stage by my master, and he has cursed me today.

'At this moment of sorrow, I am unable to enjoy the arrival of my newborn son. I don't know whether to celebrate it or brood over my ill fate. What can I do, Varsha? I know that someone from our camp gave the secrets of our strategy to Duryodhana, and that has caused the tragedy. I cannot refrain from suspecting your brother Arya Vaisya.'

Listening to what he said, Varsha pressed his hands and gave him a warm embrace. She left him to work out his feelings.

In the meantime, Bharadwaj came to the battlefield and sat there meditating in front of the bodies of their three sons. He went to a state of deep meditation, ignoring all that was happening around him.

The Pandava camp looked deserted and silent. The gloom was seen in every one's face and they were all in a state of shock.

Arjuna came back from his encounter with Susharma's Sena. All of Susharma's brothers had been killed, and so had most of his army. Arjuna looked at the omens and realized that they were evil. His heart beat wildly, and he was full of fear.

When he arrived in the Pandava camp, the anxiety reared its head again. Silence ruled the camp. Arjuna asked frantically, 'Why is it dreadfully quiet today? Why are no veenas playing today, and why do the men shy away away as if they want to avoid me? Where is Abhimanyu? He is always the first to run up and embrace me. Something awful has happened, Krishna, and nobody wants to tell me.'

Arjuna came to Dharma's tent. Everybody was sitting with their faces painted with anguish. Dharma had hurriedly wiped his tears, but could not raise his eyes to meet Arjuna's. The sons of Draupadi could not look up. The tent was in complete darkness.

A horrible thought came to Arjuna. 'I heard Guru Drona had set up ***chakravyuha*** today. Please don't tell me that you sent my son, my dearest son, to break it. None of you know how to break it and he does not know how to get out of it. Dharma, don't tell me you sent my sixteen-year-old son into the ***vyuh***.'

Dharma's sobs and pleading eyes told the story Arjuna did not want to hear.

Overcome by emotion, Arjuna cried, 'But how could this happen? Who killed my son? How will I live if my son is dead? What am I going to tell his mother? Who had the heart to kill a sixteen-year-old boy?'

Krishna said, 'You should not feel pain, Arjuna. Your son will be immortal through the ages for the bravery he has shown on the field today.'

Arjuna said, 'But tell me what happened? Who killed my child?'

Dharmaraj began to narrate the story. He had told them that the plan was to have him break the chalravyuh and have all the warriors follow him and keep it open.

'The brave Abhimanyu had broken through the first tier. We were following him, keeping a little distance so that he had enough space to manoeuvre his chariot. He had broken into the first tier of the ***chakra*** as if it were child's play. We saw him turn and smile at us. We could see the elation on his face. His smile will haunt me for the rest of my days. Feeling rejuvenated and highly confident, we started to spur our chariots right behind his. Suddenly out of nowhere Jayadratha came in between and we were cut off.'

'So how many could get through with Abhimanyu?' asked Arjuna.

'None of us; just a few of his friends and some members of the *Yuva* army,' said Dharmaraj. 'We were intercepted by Jayadratha. Even Jayadratha was fighting as though the gods were in him. We had defeated him before in the forests, but today it was as though nothing could stop him. In desperation, we broke upon him with waves and waves of our forces. But to no avail. We simply could not defeat him.'

'What happened to Abhimanyu after that?' Arjuna asked.

'Your son fought like Shiva. He was dancing his own ***tandav nrutya***. It was as though no one could beat him. He started to break open the tiers one after the other and went in deeper and deeper. The few people from the *yuva* army were slowly being killed off or trapped in the layers. He killed tens of thousands of Kaurava soldiers. Numerous ***rathis*** and ***maharathis*** fell before him. Duryodhana's son made a foolish attempt to take him on and was killed.

'In the end, he was alone. It took the likes of Karna, Ashwathama, Dushasan, Kritavarma, Dushasana's son and our guru Drona to kill him. Even then they could not do it by through sheer skill. They had to resort to cheap tactics to kill him. They attacked him from all sides and still Abhimanyu fought them off. Then Karna came from behind and cut his bowstring with an accurately shot arrow.

'His usual guard was not there today. Kritavarma killed his sarathy and Guru Drona his horses. He fought off all attackers but he was exhausted. In the end he fought with the mace with

Dushasana's son and was still the stronger in the battle. The cowards used an arrow and knocked his mace down.

'He then used the chariot wheel to fend off the attacks, but by this time his end was near. Dushasana's son took the mace to his head and smashed Abhimanyu's head. He died a brave death. A death that will be sung about in the ***yugas*** to come. His death was a shame to those who could not protect him.'

Arjuna's eyes were red with a mixture of fury and tears. He picked up his bow and then said something that took away the breaths of many.

'In the presence of the heavens and the earth, in the presence of my elders and sons, in the presence of our army and the mighty Krishna and on my celestial bow and divine astra: I, Kuntiputra Arjuna swear that by the time the sun sets tomorrow I will kill Jayadratha. If I am not successful, I will give myself up to the embrace of ***agni*** and burn myself to ashes. As a warrior fully armed and armoured, I will walk alive into my own funeral pyre.'

Hearing these ghastly oaths, everyone covered their ears and bit their tongues. Krishna raised his ***panchajanya*** and blew a blast on it so strong that it reminded the entire battlefield of thunder and lightning. Arjuna had turned his grief into rage and wrath.

Dharmaraj felt doubly guilty. He was sure that once the Kauravas came to know of the oath, they would keep Jayadratha guarded like never before. It would be a masterstroke for the Kauravas if they succeeded in eliminating Arjuna. With the whole might of the Kaurava army poised behind this single purpose, would there be any difficulty in keeping one person alive? Dharmaraj was disturbed by the thought of losing his brother, but the calm demeanour of Krishna gave him conviction and strength. He spent a sleepless night, but he was not alone. The entire Pandava camp was on edge.

The evening Abimanyu died, there was jubilation in the Kaurava camp. Drona had kept his word. The death of Abimanyu would break Arjuna's heart. Abhimanyu and his *Yuva* army had been a small but prickly thorn in the sides of the Kauravas. They had caused great damage to their divisions.

The nimble *Yuva* army had been the nemesis of the elephant division. Hundreds had been slaughtered or simply forced to rampage through the Kaurava army itself. For such an army and for such a warrior, no price was too high to pay, no sacrifice too dear to make. He celebrated Abimanyu's death, overlooking the grief from the death of his son. Revenge and hate had won over love and grief.

Jayadratha heard the news of Arjuna's vow, and he started shaking. He cried, 'Arjuna has sworn to kill me before the sun sets tomorrow. I want to go back to my father's kingdom. It is against Kshatriya dharma to pursue someone who has fled the field. Arjuna will not come after me.'

Duryodhana knew that Jayadratha had served his purpose, but since he was his sister's husband, Duryodhana tried to pacify him. 'Don't be afraid. You will be safer in my army than riding home alone. The safest place for you is at the heart of my army. All of us will protect you. No one can harm you so long as you are with us. I shall be at your side. So will Karna, Sala, Shalya, Chitrasena, Bhoorisravas, Kripa, Bhoja, Vikarna, Durmukha, Dushasana, Vinda, AnuVinda, Ashwathama, Shakuni and Alambusa. These warriors will form the core ring to protect you. Every soldier will be there just to protect you.

'Today you kept Bhima, Dharma, Dhrishtadyumna, Satyaki, Nakula, Sahadeva and the rest from breaking into the Vyuha, and now you are afraid of just one man? He is not a god, Jayadratha. He is only another man, like the rest of us.'

Softly he continued, 'Tomorrow, you will kill Arjuna. Not by cutting him down in battle, but by staying alive until the sun sets. Everything is turning our way, just as we wanted. When Arjuna burns himself tomorrow, after he fails to kill you, what will the other Pandavas do?'

Jayadratha ran to the Acharya's tent, with Duryodhana behind him. Drona said slowly, 'I will save you from Arjuna. I will form a ***vyuha*** whose mystery he will never penetrate. We will set you at the heart of it. Even if it is fated that Arjuna kills you, what shame is there to die in the battle? We must save your life, not only for your sake, but for that of the war. I intend to form three vyuhas tomorrow. On the outside, we shall have a ***shakata vyuha***, within that a ***chakra*** and finally a ***suchimukha vyuha***. These vyuhas are impregnable, and no one can enter. Arjuna will have to spend time to break all the three vyuhas.

'You will be saved. We will dig a 10 x 10 yard pit in the earth and make you stay in it. You will rest under the earth with no one knowing your whereabouts. You can come out after sunset. Even if the vyuhas were broken, the pursuers will not be able to figure out where you are. Your pit will be 100 yards away from all these ***vyuhas***. Do not worry. I will myself stand over the three ***vyuhas*** and anyone who wants to enter them will have to pass by me. Arjuna has delivered his life into our hands. Even if he breaks past the ***shakata*** and the ***chakra***, it will take him all day. The sun will have set long before he can reach you.'

Jayadratha was consoled. Duryodhana awaited Arjuna's death.

Meanwhile, Arjuna turned to Krishna, 'I cannot face Subadhra tonight. I don't have the strength to console Uttara. I beg you, go and comfort them for me. Tell them I will see them tomorrow, once I have kept my oath.'

Krishna went to his sister's tent to console her. He gave her wisdom and strength based on the fact that Abhimanyu had been a warrior and had died on the battlefield. Then he left Subadhra and Uttara in the care of Draupadi and took his leave. He went into the night where his sarathy, the faithful Daruka, waited with his chariot to take him to his own tent.

Arjuna had a troubled dream that night. He prayed to Krishna. The dark one appeared in his dream and instructed him to pray to Shiva, asking for his Paashupatastra. During vanavas, Arjuna had prayed for the astra from Shiva and had received it, but he had to regain the knowledge of the astra before the forthcoming battle. He prayed to Shiva and fell into a deep trance. He felt the weapon within himself. He was told by Shiva that the knowledge of the Pashpatastra would return to him whenever he required it.

The next day, the Kaurava army placed Jayadratha far away from Arjuna, and every warrior including the ***Samshaptakas*** (mercenaries who vow to return from battle fields only upon victory) attempted to prevent him from coming anywhere close to the king. As planned, three ***vyuhas*** were formed, with Drona guarding the centre.

Jayadratha was kept 100 yards behind all these vyuhas. He hid himself in a pit dug in the earth.

In another corner of the field, Sagar hugged his newborn child and handed him over to Varsha.

'Please take care of yourself, Varsha. I am going into the battle, as this is a do or die fight. I will see to it that Arjuna fulfills his vow. I want to avenge my friends. Make me a promise. If I do not return from the battlefield, make sure you come to me with our son. I will not leave this earth till I have met you.'

Sagar headed the Yuva army in the absence of his friends. Being an expert at military formations, he supported Arjuna in breaking the ***vyuhas***, as Arjuna alone could not have broken all three before sunset. Arjuna hacked through the Kaurava army and killed more than a hundred thousand soldiers and warriors in a single day. With the aid of Satyaki and Bhima, he was able to advance to the end of the Kauravas formation, but could not locate Jayadratha. Sagar also fought valiantly and killed thousands of soldiers from Duryodhana's camp. His expertise in breaking vyuhas came to the fore that day. Moreover, the agony of the loss of his friends added fuel to the fire of his bravery.

He observed that Jayadratha was not to be seen even after breaking the ***vyuhas***. The sun was setting. Then he saw a place a hundred yards from the end of the ***vyuhas,*** which was guarded by a few soldiers, but there seemed to be nothing beyond them. He realized that there was something strange about it. He kept his ears to the ground and listened. He had learnt the art of sensing living objects under the ground from Bhoomi Sena during his ***Gurukul*** days. He recalled how Bhoomi Sena had taught him to sense the snake in the Dwarka forest during his ***Gurukul*** days.

He used the same technique and listened to the breathing that came from below the ground. Through the tumult of the battle and the thud of the horses, he could hear anxious breathing and feet moving underground. He immediately saw through the whole strategy of Drona and surmised that it must be Jayadratha in the pit. He turned his horses and moving swiftly like the wind, came to Arjuna and told him about the hideout below the surface. Arjuna positioned him near the hideout. He decided to eject him out from the ground by using the Vayu Astra which goes inside and permeates the air with poisonous gas.

Time was running out and the sun was setting. At this juncture, Krishna the all-powerful created darkness. He eclipsed the sun in an instant. The warriors were happy and headed towards

Jayadratha. He came out of his hideout . He saw darkness and no sun, and was in an ecstatic mood.

As his laughter roared across the battlefield, Krishna said to Arjun – 'I will make the sun appear, this is the time that you cut off his head.'

Arjuna fixed an arrow to his bow string, and Krishna said again – 'Cut the head of Jayadratha, because the sun is going to set, and listen to what I say about the killer of Jayadratha. The father of Jayadratha, Vriddhakshatra, was a ruler of the Kingdom of Sindhu. After a long time, he had a son, Jayadratha.

'He heard a divine voice at the time of his birth: "This son will be the star of two races (***Soorya*** and ***Chandra***) in respect to blood, behavior and other attributes. But while in the battle, a very famous man will cut his head in anger."

'The ruler of Sindhu pondered for some time and then called his people and declared - "The man who will cause the head of my son to fall to the ground, his own head will break into hundred pieces." He installed him on the throne and went to the woods for ***Tapasya*** outside of his kingdom. So use the celestial weapon and throw his head into the lap of his father himself. If you let it fall to the ground, your head will break into a hundred pieces. Do it in such a way that his father may not know that it has been done.'

At this point, Arjuna recalled the words of Rishi Markandeya at Kamyaka forest. The Rishi had asked him to use the astras to make the mangoes from the tree fall on his lap. He had told Arjuna that one day, he might have to repeat that feat in a war to come.

Arjun released the arrow, which swiftly cut Jayadratha's head and carried it outside the war zone to his father's place. At that time, Vriddhakshatra was conducting his evening prayer and meditating. He could neither see nor feel the head in his lap. As soon as he finished his prayers, he rose and the head fell to the ground. His own head was broken into a hundred pieces.

When Jayadratha was killed, Krishna withdrew the darkness and the sun came out. Duryodhana broke into tears, seeing Jayadratha dead. Krishna, Arjuna, Bhima blew their conches to tell Dharma about it.

The war continued past sunset as well. Suddenly, Sagar heard some one calling him loudly.

'Well done, Sagar. I have been observing you since morning. You are the one who supported Arjuna in breaking all the ***vyuhas*** today. You are the one who saw the place where Jayadratha was hiding below the ground.'

Sagar turned his head to see who was calling him. To his surprise, he saw Ghatotkacha, Bhima's son. His maternal parentage made him half ***rakhasa*** and gave him many magic powers such as the ability to fly.

'Sagar, I have heard a lot about you from my brother, Abhimanyu. I know you were the chief strategist of the ***yuva*** army. You were always standing behind him like a shadow. Yesterday you were not there. My brother Abhimanyu, the pride of our ***Pandava*** lineage, was killed. I am not going to let go any of those cowards who killed my brother.'

'Ghatotkacha, are we going to fight at night? It is against the rules of the war. We cannot fight after sunset. Are you serious? Are we going to extend the fight today?;

'Sagar, what are you saying? Have these cowards followed the rules? My brother was killed by all the cowards. These cowards claimed to be great warriors. What kind of warriors were they? How could they kill a child? He was all alone. He was attacked from behind; he was killed when he was unarmed. Did those warriors follow any rules? From today, all the rules will be broken. I want these cowards to taste their own medicine. Hence I will not follow any rules now. I will kill all of them tonight.

'Tonight my magic powers will be much more powerful. You will see that. I will attack them from the sky. The opponents are not ready for an aerial war. They are all getting ready to return, thinking that the sunset had ended the day's war. Never interrupt your enemy when he is making a mistake.

'Sagar, speed is the essence of war. Take advantage of the enemy's unpreparedness. Travel by unexpected routes and strike them where they have no precautions. Get ready for flash lightening air strikes. Provide the ground support with your ***yuva*** army while I carry out the aerial attack.'

'I agree with you, Gatotkacha. My blood is boiling too. They killed my dear friends the Sena brothers and my leader Abhimanyu yesterday. How can I swallow the cruel end of my friends, my leader and the greatest ***yuva*** warrior, Abhimanyu?

'The world denounced me, but Abhimanyu embraced me. Society gave me the stigma of the '***sudhra'*** tag, but Abhimanyu gave me status. He used to tell me, "Sagar, don't walk behind me; I may not lead you. Don't walk in front of me; I may not follow. Just walk beside me and be my friend." For generations, I will be grateful to Abhimanyu for having given me such a status.

'Gatotkacha, the worst wounds are not the ones that people see on the outside. They are the ones that bleed internally. I like the scars inflicted by society, because they remind me of the past. Anger ventilated often hurries us towards forgiveness. Anger concealed often hardens into revenge. But Abhimanyu motivated me to see that the best result is always the best insult. I was re-energized by him.

'Abhimanyu crowned me with a key position in the ***yuva*** army. He initiated me into this new position with this remark "Sagar, I am giving the role of a chief strategist in our ***yuva*** army. Forget all the scars and the stigma you receive from your caste tag. You are born to excel. Forget all the wars you fought in the silent chambers of your soul. A warrior must only take care that his spirit is not broken. Re-energize yourself. Get ready for the great task."

‘How can I forget the greatest memories of my interaction with my friend, my leader, Abhimanyu? I do not want to spare any of those who killed my leader. You said it right, Gatotkacha, we should not worry about the rules now. We should destroy all those spineless cowards.

‘I totally agree with you. We should attack them with flash strikes. I will give you the ground support. You carry out your aerial strikes. My leader Abhimanyu always said, “When torrential water tosses boulders, it is because of its momentum. When the strike of a hawk breaks the body of its prey, it is because of the timing.” Yes, timing is key. Let us start our flash strikes, Gatotkacha.’

Then the two young warriors unleashed a war of terror on the opponents. From the ashes, a fire woke again; from the shadows sprang the light and from the broken blade, there arose a renewed vigour. The team was unstoppable. Gatotkacha’s flash strikes slaughtered numerous warriors of the Kaurava army. Sagar continued to fight on the ground, inflicting heavy damage to the opposing forces.

At this point, Duryodhana appealed to Karna to kill Gatotkacha, as the whole of his army was coming close to annihilation. Karna possessed a divine weapon called ***Indrastra*** granted by the lord of heaven, Indra. It could be used only once and Karna had been saving it to use it on his archenemy, Arjuna.

Unable to bear the torture meted out by Gatotkacha, Karna used his ***Indrastra*** against Gatotkacha, killing him instantly. This astra emitted a shower of arrows from the sky. This is the same astra which lord Rama’s brother Lakshman used against Indrajit, son of Ravana in the ***Treta yuga.***

The wave of arrows killed many warriors of the Pandava army. The flood of arrows from the sky also seriously wounded Sagar. Sagar, the son born at sunrise, fought valiantly, but was almost killed on the eve of midnight by Karna.

Sagar was lying on the battlefield in a pool of blood. Warriors who were going back to the camp surrounded him. He was holding onto his life to meet his wife and son one last time. He knew his wife and son would come to meet him as promised. He was lying on the same battlefield where his friends had given up their life the previous day. News came to his wife of his heroic acts and she came running to the battlefield to have a last glimpse of her husband.

******

20 The Stunning Revelations
Myths Demystified

Sagar was lying in the battlefield. He was holding his last breath to meet his wife and his newborn son. He realized that in the end what mattered was not the adulation of the masses, but the understanding and appreciation of the people he loved and cared for. He wanted the approval of his guru, he wanted the approval of his wife, he wanted his son to know him as a good father and he wanted to be proud of himself. But one question that kept coming back to haunt his disturbed mind was, who had revealed the ***Yuva*** army's strategy and crucial information about the Sena brothers to the Kaurava Army?

Close to the place where he was dying, Bharadwaj was sitting in meditation. This was right above the place where his sons had died. His deep meditative state was disturbed by this incessant thought, 'Why did my sons suffer a premature death, even though they were born out of the blessed mangoes?'

As though summoned from his own consciousness, Rishi Markandeya, who had given the fruits to Dharma, appeared in Bharadwaj's mind. His voice boomed as he questioned, 'Bharadwaj, what are you seeking from me?'

'Rishi, my sons were born out of the blessed mangoes that you had given to Dharma. Even so, why did they die so soon? Are the blessings not real?' asked Bharadwaj.

'Bharadwaj, what did you do with the fruits?' asked the Rishi.

'I split the triplet mangoes and gave one to each of my three wives – one took the surface, another drank only the liquid of the second fruit, and third wife only enjoyed the smell of the third fruit,' Bharadwaj replied.

'Bharadwaj, that is where the mistake happened. All three had to be consumed by one person. The mangoes were intended for Draupadi, who was supposed to consume all of them entirely. One person doing this would have resulted in a single child proficient in land, sea and air warfare. You split the fruits among three persons, and hence their lives were truncated to one third of what it could have been. While they lived they were highly skilled on land, sea and air. The mystic power of invoking the ***Pancha Bhoodas*** could be exercised only when they were together. Everything happened as intended, Bharadwaj,' the Rishi explained.

A tleast their life had not been truncated by the deed of Sagar, Bharadwaj realized. His anger towards Sagar softened when he realized what had caused the death of his sons.

Opening his eyes, he looked for Sagar, who was struggling for life on the battlefield.

Meanwhile, Varsha came running with her son. Sagar asked her to bring their son near him. He looked at his son closely and said, 'My dear son, you were born to a ***Sudhra***, who struggled at every phase of his life. Society ridiculed him as a ***Sudhra***, as a killer's son. At least you were born from the womb of a high caste woman. You are going to be brought up by your high caste mother. You can live without the stigma of a ***Sudhra*** tag.

'Please do not deprive anyone of their due share due to discrimination on caste grounds. Learn to treat everyone equally, respect every one in our society. In this war, there were only two sides: ***dharma*** and ***adharma***. People from all ***varnas*** – Brahmins, Kshatriyas, Vaisyas and Sudhras--gave their lives on both sides in this war.

'The Sudhras who died in this war number more than Brahmins and Vaishyas. But that does not make the contribution of anybody less or more. At least the death of the people from all ***Varnas*** must make the society understand that there should not be any discrimination on caste grounds. Let the caste differences die with this war. There is no caste in our blood. My son, you will be blessed to live in a society which does not discriminate based on caste, creed or color. May you live in a society where everyone gets an equal opportunity. I have a dream that the future generation will one day live in a nation where their fate will not be decided by the colour of their skin, but by the content of their character.

'My son, I have another piece of advice for you. Focus on the roots and not on the fruits. Focus on purpose and not on outcome. Chase your goals, but learn to face the outcome as it unfolds. You can aim for an outcome, but it is not in your control.

He paused for a moment and looked at Varsha, who was sobbing uncontrollably. He couldn't bear to see it and he said to her in a strong tone, 'I loved you, Varsha. But you cheated me, betrayed me by passing on our strategies and secrets to the opposition. Why did you do this to me? I loved you so much. Why did you do this?' Anyone hearing the words would have thought that it was a sermon and an accusation from a dying man. But his voice was rock steady.

Varsha could not believe what she had just heard. Her eyes opened wide and her face went pale in utter dismay. She stood frozen in shock for a moment and then broke into a loud sob. 'What are you saying, Sagar?' she asked.

'I know everything, Varsha. You were passing on all the secrets through the Brahmin messenger who conducted our marriage at the forest temple, when we escaped from your brother's captivity.'

Varsha retorted 'Why are you laying this accusation against me? This is not fair! There is nothing more important to me than our family and our kingdom. I would never betray our kingdom for personal gain.'

'Yesterday I came running to our house on hearing of our son's birth. As I was about to enter the house, I overheard you talking with the Brahmin priest, Brighu Maharaj. He was thanking you for all the information which you had picked up from the conversations of our

Yuva army. Till yesterday, I thought that your brother was a traitor. But though he may fight us from the front, he would not stab us from behind.'

Varsha realized she could not keep up the blatant lies and tears slowly gave way to anger on her face.

'When I knew that you were passing the secrets and Brighu Maharaj was the messenger, I felt like killing myself. Varsha, to me the thing that is worse than death is betrayal. I could conceive of death but not betrayal. If you stab the body, it might heal. But when we injure the heart, the wound lasts for generations. Why did you do this to me, Varsha? I am holding my last breath only to know the answer to this question.'

Hearing this new twist, Bharadwaj looked up and started listening intently to this conversation. At that point of time the Brahmin priest referred to by them as Brighu Maharaj came to the battlefield looking for Varsha and wanting to see Sagar's death with his own eyes.

At the same time, Bharadwaj realized something very unusual. The Brahmin priest, Brighu Maharaj was none other than his wife Sharmila's first husband. He had left for the Pandiya kingdom the day after their marriage. The ship was assumed to have sunk with all the crew other than the Prince of the Pandiya kingdom. Brighu Maharaj was also assumed to be dead. Even the rescue ships had come back empty. Sharmila had been persuaded to marry Bharadwaj.

Bharadwaj could not believe his eyes. What was this new turn? Before he could get to know more about Brighu Maharaj, Varsha continued her story to Sagar.

'Sagar, let me tell you why. Your father and his fishermen attacked my father while he was asking them to repay their loan. He had a right to ask for his money back, and it was your father's duty to pay it. He was badly hurt; he was on his death bed when my mother was carrying me.

'My father was holding his last breath to see my arrival into this world. Since he was not sure how long he would live, he asked the doctors to deliver me as a premature baby. He was keen to see my face before he died. The doctor obliged and I was shown to my father soon after my birth. He kissed me, called me "Varsha" and then breathed his last.

'My mother brought me up and would often tell the story of my birth and my father's demise. Taking revenge for the wrong done against my father became the sole purpose of my life. I thought the best way would be to enter your family and take my revenge. I acted as your lover, your wife and I had to carry your son with hatred – all for the goal of striking you when you least expected it. Even my brother was not as focused as me . He was carried away by his friendship with you during the ***Gurukul*** days.

'But I never deviated from my mission. I was your silent and most dangerous stalker. I not only wanted your death but also your complete ridicule. Even my own brother does not know that I am the one who wanted revenge. He still thinks that I am in love with you and that makes me a blot on his honor.

'I will have the last laugh and earn the most honors from my community and from my family. I could not do the spying alone, and then came Brighu Maharaj who had his story of grievance against the three Sena brothers, sons of Bharadwaj. I used him as a messenger between me and Duryodhana's camp. Together we have destroyed you.'

'Does that mean the love, the affection, and everything else we had was a lie? Save me God! I thought that I had one soul who was longing for me, that of my wife. Even that turned out to be false - what a tragedy! Not even a single bright spot in my life!' exclaimed Sagar.

Bharadwaj was awestruck by the whole conversation.

Sagar went on, 'Varsha, you did this to me, not knowing my father was never in the picture as far as your father's death was concerned. My father left the property mortgaged to your father, left the island along with my mother who was carrying me in her pregnancy at that time. In the middle of the night, they took their boat, not knowing where to go.

'My mother, unable to control her emotions, jumped into the sea. My father followed her. The next morning, the two who had jumped into the sea became three with me. We were found at the sea shore by Master Bharadwaj. Thereafter we never had any connections with the fishermen. My father gave up the profession. He was under the care of my master for a while before he took up the job of a swimming teacher at the ***Gurukul***.

'The fishermen communities you are referring to were not headed by my father. Had he been there, he would not have allowed them to use violence. Your uncle was also told this, but no one believed it. Can't someone renounce the position of responsibility of a leader and be an instructor? Can't anyone make a fresh start in life? You took revenge on me on an assumed cause, which was baseless. You could have verified my story with Bharadwaj, who would not have lied. You have punished me for no fault of my own.'

Brighu Maharaj looked at Bharadwaj and aired his grievances. 'I went with the Pandiya king the day after my marriage. The ship sank in the sea near Dwarka. Everyone died, but I escaped and landed on the island of man eaters. They imprisoned me. After one year, I escaped and somehow managed to come back to Dwarka. I learned my wife Sharmila had been married to her brother-in-law Bharadwaj. I was very angry. I wanted to take revenge. I went to the forest, got a job as the priest of a Kali temple, and waited for my turn.

'One day, Sagar and Varsha came with the three Sena brothers for their marriage. From their conversation I came to know that Sena brothers were the sons of Bharadwaj and also that they were escaping from the Duryodhana's son's camp. I thought it would be a good idea to administer their marriage. With just one marriage, the enmity would grow between Duryodhana's son camp and the Sena brothers' camp.

'From that time on, I kept a watch on all of you. Once I came to know of the war between Dharma and Duryodhana, I knew Bharadwaj and his sons would be with Dharma. Hence I went to Duryodhana's son offered my help. They asked me what kind of help I could extend. I told them I could be a messenger between them and their spies in the enemy camp. They referred me to Varsha. On knowing Varsha was a spy, I was initially stunned, but later I came to terms with it.'

Bharadwaj intervened here. 'Brighu Maharaj, how can I play with your life when I have administered your marriage with Sharmila? When the news of the ship came, we were shocked. Sharmila was forced to face the stigma attached to a widow. Her sisters could not see her suffering as a widow at such a young age. Society was not prepared to permit her a free life. She became a prisoner of rituals. She locked herself inside. We could not see a young girl living like a corpse right in front of us. We wanted to liberate her from the jaws of this trap. After great persuasion, she agreed to marry me. I reluctantly agreed, as no one would marry her on the ground of ***Mangal Dhosha*** stigma affixed on her.

'Had we known you were alive, why would we go through all this? You have killed my sons for a meaningless revenge Brighu.'

Bharadwaj turned his attention to Varsha. 'Varsha, I am unveiling yet another secret surrounding your husband's birth. Your family and society ridiculed him as Sudhra. I am now telling you the secret that Matsya forbade me from telling anybody – Sagar is a Kshatriya by birth. The baby I found in my hands in the Gomati river during the pooja was dead. When Matsya and his wife were brought to me in an unconscious state, I administrated first aid. Sagar's father woke up first.

'He saw his wife lying unconscious and a baby who had obviously died. He came to me and pleaded, "You look like a god to me. My wife lost her baby in the middle of the sea, while attempting to commit suicide. Now she is safe but her child is no more. When she wakes up and realizes that the child is no more, she will feel guilty. She will try to commit suicide again for killing her own child. Can you please help me to somehow save her?"

'I was sympathetic to his plea. I went to the nearby Royal Orphanage, where I go for social service. That day, a young Kshatriya lady, Vatsala, who had lost her husband while she was carrying their child, had given birth to a boy. She decided to take up ***vanaprasthashram*** and left the newborn at the Royal Orphanage. I took that baby and gave the child to Matsya's wife in order to save her.

'Matsya and I had an agreement not to reveal this during his life time. Matsya did not want Sagar to lose his affinity with his mother. Now that he is dying, let me reveal that Sagar is a Kshatriya by birth, and true to his blood, he showed his bravery in this war today. Also, all of you thought that he was more proficient in water since he was born in the sea. He always heard that he was good in water and hence believed in himself and conquered the element. All are equal but the way you are brought up determines your capability.'

Now Sagar spoke.

'***Guruji***,

- I was penalized as a low caste ***Sudhra*** even though I was a born ***Kshatriya.***
- I was penalized by my wife for a cause to which neither I nor my family was a party.

- I was penalized by you for the death of your sons for which I was not the cause.

'I do not know why I have been singled out by fate and am being punished for no fault of my own. But, I will not curse my fate, for I have lived true to the people around me, I was passionate in whatever I was doing, and I am willing to accept the results as they unfold. I truly believe that I have to chase my goals but at the same time, I have to learn to face the results. My only wish is that no one on earth be denied opportunities on the ground of his caste, creed or color.

'Life may crown a person or make him a beggar on the streets. But no one should deprive anyone of opportunities. All should have equal opportunities. From below the ground comes the diamond, from the mud comes the lotus. Greatness can come from any one. A mother's womb should not determine one's destiny. I am saying this after facing turbulence right from the womb to my tomb. This is my death wish ***Guruji***,' Sagar concluded.

Bharadwaj had tears in his eyes. 'My dear Sagar, you speak like a philosopher. You have matured beyond your age. In the philosophy sessions at the ***Gurukul***, I saw the sparks in you. Today I am seeing those sparks burn into flames. May you live long, my son. I have to correct myself. I gave you the curse of having a short life in your nine future births.

'I cannot take back my curse, as the arrow once out of the bow cannot be retrieved, I have no powers to withdraw it. But just like astras from a bow they can be controlled by sheer will. I can soften the curse. For each of the nine births to follow, I double your years from 15 to 30. That is the best I can do Sagar. But in every one of your births, you will have a great impact on society.'

Turning to Varsha, Bharadwaj said, 'You lived a false life with Sagar, even though he gave you pure love. For cheating him, you will continuously beg for his help as a prisoner of war in your next birth. You will meet your husband, and he will be the army chief and save you from prison. You have the chance to break your own chakras of rebirth. You have to sincerely love your husband in the next birth.'

With tears in her eyes, Varsha tried to beg for mercy from Sagar. She was overcome with grief. She could not even speak. Her eyes were downcast and streaming with tears, and she asked for forgiveness. Sagar kissed her forehead as a sign of pardoning her. Mercy asked mutely was rewarded without words. He gestured to her to bring the child to him. He kissed the child and summoning the last vestiges of lifeforce in him, cried loudly, '***Veer Chiranjeevi***, may you live long! Unlike your father, may you live happily for a long, long time.'

Varsha's brother arrived. Varsha gave her son to him and said, 'Brother, I am going to be burnt in the funeral pyre along with my husband. Now you are the guardian of our son Veer Chiranjeevi. You must bring him up and tell him the truth about his father. Be gentle when you tell him about me as I cannot bear the idea of him hating me.'

Arya Vaisya took the child from her. His tears spoke volumes about his feelings.

Arjuna came with his warriors. 'Sagar, I was told of your heroics on the battlefield. You also supplemented my efforts in breaking the multiple ***vyuhas*** of Drona. You detected the whereabouts of Jayadratha, the killer of my son. You could spot his hide out below the ground right on time, before sunset. I am proud of the *Yuva* Army of Abhimanyu. You are a great warrior. This war has united all *Varnas*, and now no one can be discriminated against on the grounds of caste, creed, and color.

'Who said you are a *Sudhra*? I declare that your fishermen community will be recognized as *Kshatriya* and they will occupy a new kingdom called the "Matsya kingdom" and your son will become the king. He will rule over a casteless society in this Matsya kingdom.'

Sagar was about to breathe his last. Arjuna closed his eyes for the last time and blew his conch. He shouted, 'Sagar, you are a shining star amongst the greatest of warriors. Your bravery will linger in the minds of the people.'

Sagar's soul departed with this final gesture from the great warrior. The warrior's soul departed, but the shackles of the warrior held his soul back from salvation. The soul was left revolving around the earth.

But Sagar's body went to the flames and Varsha was united with him there, making the ultimate sacrifice.

*** ***

Epilogue

Fifty years later ....

The tourists from countries beyond the borders of the Matsya kingdom came in thousands to see something that was always kept hung in front of the palace of King *Vir Chiranjeevi*. Kosalram from Angadesh was one among them.

He wanted to have a glimpse of this wonder. It lured the tourists to Matsya kingdom. All he saw was one very big but ordinary looking bell. It was hanging at a low level where even a child could ring it. It was placed right in front of the palace. They called it 'Sagar's Voice.' He was surprised that a simple bell had created such a huge following. What is so great about it, he wondered.

He sought the answer from an old man standing next to him. The old man was a resident of the Matsya kingdom. 'You look at this as a normal bell. I have been seeing the impact of this bell for the last thirty years. This bell is the "Bell of Opportunity," a bell for shaking social injustice, a bell against oppression, a bell spelling out equity and justice. It is the voice of Sagar Matsya, the great warrior father of our beloved king Vir Chiranjeevi.

'Fifty years ago, our king's father, when dying on the battlefield of Kurukshetra, said his last words to our king. He wanted his son to live in a state that denounces caste, creed or colour, offers equal opportunity to all and instant justice. Our king was too young to understand but his maternal uncle, the very wise Arya Vaishya, ensured that his nephew was reminded of the words as he grew up. Our king has kept those words as his life's ideal.

'Our king installed this bell in front of his palace and declared that anyone can seek justice from him by ringing the bell. In our kingdom, talent meets demand, opportunity is offered to all, character coexists with competence and performance trumps passive speeches. It is not caste but competence that decides our career. It is our disposition and not our mother's womb that charts our destiny. The words **varna**, caste, creed or colour are banned in this kingdom. Once, a tourist from a neighboring state insulted an orphan child. The child went and rang the bell and the tourist was punished for his remarks.

'In our kingdom, all living things have equal rights, not just human beings. You cannot cut a tree, hunt an animal for pleasure or hurt any human being on the ground of economic or social differences.

'You would be surprised to hear that a cow rang the bell once to seek justice for the death of its calf. The calf was killed by our army commander's chariot. His son was riding it at reckless speed. It happened right here on the main road. The cow in her grief started to wander and went near the bell which rang out because of her push. The king and his soldiers followed the cow to the road and saw the dead calf. Our king punished the rider for killing calf. The cow was accommodated in the royal goshala and her expenses were borne by the person who killed her calf. This is the impact of Sagar's voice, which you described as a mere bell.

'This is not just a bell. It is the voice against oppression and social injustice. In the initial years this bell used to ring frequently. With the passage of time, the inequalities in this kingdom began to vanish. We are an egalitarian society where there is no caste, creed or colour that differentiates us.

'When injustice ceased to exist in our kingdom, the bell stopped ringing. And for the last several years, there has been no need for anyone to seek its support.

'The bell might have stopped ringing, but Sagar's voice has created an impact beyond our borders and the citizens of every country want to have a similar redressing mechanism to address social injustice.

'Our king upheld his father's words. He created the society that his father wanted his son to live in. He also made sure that this voice will continue beyond his generation, by strongly planting the background of this bell in the minds of his heirs.

'Our king is celebrating his fiftieth birth day next week. We pray that he lives for a long number of years and administers justice as and when required.'

Kosalram was spell bound by this strong and emotional speech from an ordinary citizen of the Matsya kingdom.

Sagar's voice continued to ring out. Meanwhile, the souls of Sagar and Varsha were wandering the earth, waiting for an appropriate time to make a reentry into earthly bodies. How would they meet again?

A new journey was about to begin for these two souls. The soul of Varsha would next be a prisoner of war, begging and pleading for support from the soul of Sagar. Where would this meeting happen? What sort of people would they be in their next outing?

Their next karmic journey can be viewed from the upcoming release –

"The Indus Challenge"

[Janam One]

Research Archives

Books:

- Astrology for beginners, BR Raman, UBS Publishers Distributors PVT LTD, Banagalore,2009.
- Bagavat Gita, As it is, PrabhuPadha, Iskon Publications.
- 'Jothidamum NavaGrahangalum', Dr Murugu Rajendran, Bharathi Publishers, T.Nagar, Chennai (Tamil)
- 'Jothida Ragasymam', Gowri Shankar, Bala Vasantha Publishers, Chennai (2008) (Tamil)
- 'Jothida Sastram', M.V.Baskar Anuragam, Chennai, 17 (2009) (Tamil)
- 'Jothida Vilakkam', P.L. Muthukumaran, Thirumagal Nilagam, T.N.Nagar, Chennai(1999)(Tamil)
- Mahabharata, C. Raja Gopalacheri Bharatiya Vidya Bhavan, Mumbai (2011)
- Mahabharatham, Sri Math Swami Sidhavanandar, Shri Ramakrishna Thebovanam, Thinparaithurai- Trichy Di (2010)
- 'Palavagai Jothida Podu Palungal', Sagunthala N Layam, Chennai (Tamil)
- Srimath Bharath Saar, Anna, Ramakrishna Mutt, Mylapore, Chennai (2002) (Tamil)
- 'Simple Jothida Mathematics', M.Matheswaran, Vijaya Publishers, Coimbatore(2009)
- The MahaBharata, Ramesh Menon, Rupa & Co 2009, Volume 1 and 2
- A Saint in the Board Room, Dr.R.Durgadoss and Dr.Yerram Raju, Konark Publishers, 2011.

Web Archives:

- www.archaeologyonline.net, Vedicdiscoveries: Krsna & balarama in Greece
- www.ashtangayurveda.com, History of Ayurveda-Ashtang Ayurveda
- www.askastrologer.com, Sakuna Sastra- Astrology of omens.
- www.astrojyoti.com, Introduction to Indian vedic astrology
- www.bhamidi.net, Understanding your Horoscope
- www.burlingtonnews.net , Vimanas- Ancient flying saucers of Atlantis & Lemuria
- www.defenceforumindia.com, Timeline of mahabharat
- www.esamskriti.com
- www.esamskriti.com/print.aspx?topicid=411&chapter=1, Indian culture & Traditions.
- Firstterm.acjnewsline.org- History of prostitution- Kausharni
- www.goelweb.com, Rajasuya Yajna of Yudhishthira
- Groups.yahoo.com/group/gita-talk, Can a Sudra by Birth become a Brahmin priest in temple?
- www.gutenberg.org/files/The Mahabharata, Vana Parva Part 1
- www.handicraft.indiamart.com, Religious products, Sacred- trees
- www.hindubooks.org/dynamic/modules.php, Women in Hindu Dharma- A tribute
- www.hinduis.co.za/caste.htm, The 4 orders of human being, Translated by Shri Kisari Mohan Ganguli
- www.hindunet.org/hindu_history/ancient/mahabharat/mahab_patnaik.html,The Mahabharat Chronology, Dr K.N.S Patnaik,
- www.hindupedia.com/en/abhimanyu , mahabharat

- http://Krsnabook.com, Why Duriyodhana felt insulted at the end of Rajasuya Sacrifice
- www.indiaandindians.com, Later vedic period
- www.Indiadivine.or, Astrology & Mahabharat
- www.Indiadivine.org, Women in the Vedic & Epic Era
- www.india-intro.com, The story of Drona- Teachers of Kaurawas & Pandavas
- www.indianherbs.org, Ayurveda: Indigenous drugs of India
- www.indianetzone.com/39/education, Education in Ancient India
- www.indianetzone.com, Maithil Brahmin wedding, Indian Wedding
- www.indianetzone.com, Somaras
- www.indianetzone.com, Widow remarriage in modern India
- www.indianresurgence.com/history1.htm , Historicity of Mahabharat War
- www.indiaheritage.org/rendez/article1.htm ,One cosmic day of Creator Brahma.
- www.iskontimes.com, Krishna as King
- www.jyotisha.com, calculate your rising sign, Lagna
- www.krishna.com, Dvarka-Lord Krishna's royal home
- www.mailerindia.com, Namakarana
- Mahabharatonline.blogspot.com, Mahabharat-epic of all time
- www.mahabharataonline.com/stories/mahabharata_charater.php, Draupadi's pride crushed.
- www.mahabharataonline.com/stories/mahabharata_charater.php, The story of Abhimanyu
- www.mahabharataonline.com/stories/mahabharata_charater.php, The story of Uttara (Wife of Abhimanyu)
- www.marriagecustoms.org, Hindu weddings
- www.mydestinyplanets.com, Twins and Vedic Astrology
- www.mysticscripts.com, Zodiac Rising Sign
- www.neemfoundation.org, Neem in Animal health
- www.nodsadhna.com, History of Indian dance
- www.oocities.org/mahabharat/katha/6war/22battle143.htm, Mahabharat-Kathaa-6 war.
- www.oration.com, The Kingdom of Krishna
- www.romapadaswami.com, Rajasuta sacrifice was performed much before the battle.
- www.scribd.com, Map of India during Mahabharat period
- www.scribd.com, Brahmin marriage
- Sushmajee.com/mahabharat/mbh-1-ganguli/g-6-war/23battle.htm , Mahabhaarat-Kathaa-6 war
- www.tumblr.com/voluptupus -woman, Painted Lady- and other stories
- Vedabase.com/en/mbk/2/15, Abhimanyu's incomplete power.
- www.wiki.answers.com, Ritual & practice Hinduism sacred elements their meaning
- http://whatnowblog.wordpress.com/
- http://www.shutterstock.com
- http://www.webdesign.org
- http://saishaktigardens.com
- http://files.vector-images.com
- http://www.harekrsna.com
- http://www.trapremix.com
- http://hqwalls.org
- http://www.layoutsparks.com
- http://thewaymarks.wordpress.com

- http://finalfantasy.wikia.com
- http://8tracks.com
- http://narutofanon.wikia.com
- http://www.behance.net
- http://www.inmagine.com
- http://www.hindudevotionalblog.com
- http://satishverma.deviantart.com
- http://www.noahsanimalfigurines.com
- http://www.allempires.com
- http://www.warrenphotographic.co.uk
- http://www.ancientarms.biz
- http://parotasalna.blogspot.ae
- http://www.artfire.com
- http://olivrodanatureza.blogspot.ae
- http://delawaresnature.net
- http://pinterest.com
- http://www.homeschoolastronomy.com
- http://www.socwall.com
- http://www.architecturals.net/
- http://fierycj.hubpages.com
- http://mustachedude.skyrock.com/
- **http://metal-bender.deviantart.com**
- **http://www.dollsofindia.com**
- Wikepedia.org, Abhimanyu
- Wikipedia.org, Anarta kingdom
- Wikipedia.org, Apsara
- Wikipedia.org, Astra_(Weapon)
- Wikipedia.org, Dvarka
- Wikipedia.org, Indraprashtha
- Wikipedia.org, Jayadratha
- Wikipedia.org, Kerela kingdom
- Wikipedia.org, Kuru Kingdom
- Wikipedia.org, Kurukshetra War.
- Wikipedia.org, Mahabharata & India caste system
- Wikipedia.org, Naming ceremony
- Wikipedia.org, Parikshit
- Wikipedia.org, Rajasuya
- Wikipedia.org, Samskara
- Wikipedia.org, Subhadra
- Wikipedia.org, Upanayana
- Wikipedia.org, Yuga
- Abhimanyu's entry into the Chakravyuh was formation is a foolish act or a heroic one?
- A study of Mahabharata- Sai Teja
- Achieving common goals together, The Varna and Jati System
- Ancient India in the time of the Mahabharat

- Astrology and Mahabharat, Tranalation by K Sadananda
- Astrology for beginners
- Ayurveda in Ramayana
- Brave Abhimanyu
- Caste system in India
- Difference between jati and varna.
- Dwaraka, Information about Dwarka, Dwarka Tour
- Draupadi's sons in Anarta country undergoes military training
- Essentials Explained
- Hindu wisdom- Dwaraka
- Hindu wisdom- Seafaring in ancient India
- Hindu website, The Hindu caste system
- Historicity of Mahabharat, Translation by K Sadananda
- Huffingtonpost.com, The caste system of Hindu society
- Is Hindu intercaste marriages- choice of next generation? Intellectual debate- By Satyjit Mishra.
- Krishna-Myth or Man?
- Polygamy in Hinduism
- Position of women in Indian civilization- Sanjeev Nayyar
- Sri Guru Raghavendra Swamy Charithra, Utmost poverty.
- The central philosophy of Mahabharat by Sitansu
- The theme of Dharma in the Mahabharata.
- Trees &Plants during Ancient Era, MarkandyaPuranna, Devi Mahatmya.
- Vedic knowledge online- Dwarka
- Vedic Sanskar

Glossary of Terms

Word	Meaning of the Word/Definition
Chapter-1	
Banarasi Sari	Banarasi saris are considered one of the finest saris in India. These saris are made of finely woven silk and are decorated with elaborate engravings. Because of these engravings, these sari relatively h eavy. Banarasi saris are mostly worn by Indian women on important occasions such as when attending a wedding and are expected to be Complemented by the woman's best jewelry.
Tilak	A mark worn by a Hindu on the forehead to indicate caste, status, or sect, or as an ornament.
Padma Bhushan	The Padma Bhushan is the third highest civilian award in the Republic of India, after the Bharat Ratna and the Padma Vibhushan, but comes before the Padma Shri. It is awarded by the Government of India.
Bohra	A community in India
Atithi devo Bhava	Atithi Devo Bhavah [Atithi devo bhavaḥ] (Sanskrit: अतिथि देवो भवः; English: 'The guest is God' or 'Guest become God')[1] is a Sanskritverse, taken from an ancient Hindu scripture which became part of the "code of conduct" for Hindu society. Atithi devo bhav regards a procedure of the Host-Guest relationship
Aalam Ballroom	A Ballroom at Taj Palace Hotel, Mumbai
Rendezvous	Rendez-vous is the original French word. It means to have a meeting at a specific place at a specific time.
Phulka	Phulka is an unleavened flatbread (also known asroti) from the Indian subcontinent
La Patisserie	A shop where pastry, especially French pastry, is made and sold.
Ciabatta	A type of Italian bread in a long flat shape
Mezzes	The English translation of mezze is appetizer. Mezze is served either before or with dinner. Several mezze are served at the same time, called a mezze table or platter.
Humus	a thick spread made from mashed chickpeas, tahini, lemon juice and garlic; used especially as a dip for pita; originated in the middle East
Baba ganoush	Baba Ganoush', Baba Ghannouj or Baba Ghannoug (Arabic بابا غنوج bābā ġanūj) is an Arab dish of aubergine (eggplant) mashed and mixed with various seasonings.
Falafel	A Middle Eastern dish of spiced mashed chickpeas or other pulses formed into balls and deep-fried.

Sheesh taouk	Shish taouk is a traditional Arabic and Turkish shish kebab, which can also be found in Syrian, Iraqi and Lebanese cuisines, but is made in kabab houses in many cities around the world
Tagine	A North African stew of spiced meat and vegetables prepared by slow cooking in a shallow earthenware cooking dish with a tall, conical lid
Dim sum	A Chinese dish of small steamed or fried savory dumplings containing various fillings, served as a snack or main course.
Wasabi by Morimoto	Name of restaurant
Pani Puri	A puff-pastry ball filled with spiced mashed potato and tamarind juice and then fried
Paya	A type of dish.
Teppanyaki	Teppanyaki teppan'yaki is a style of Japanese cuisine that uses an iron griddle to cook food. The word teppanyaki is derived from teppan, which means iron plate, and yaki, which means grilled, broiled or pan-fried.
Colaba	Colaba (कुलाबा, pronounced) is a part of the city of Mumbai, India, and also a Lok Sabha constituency.
Vile Parle	Vile Parle (वलिपार्ले, Vilēpārlē), also known as "Parla"," is a suburb of Mumbai.
Wadi Bunder	Bandar or Bunder (in Persian بندر) is a Persian word meaning "port" and "haven"." Etymologically it combines Persian بند Band (enclosed) and در dar (gate, door) meaning "an enclosed area" (i.e. protected from the sea).
Bastar	A form of tribal art
Jaali	Net
Kuthey, Kaminey, tumhara aadmi mar gaya. Abhi tumhara instrument bhi marega. Abey gora	Dog, your man dead. Your instrument also will be dead soon.
Chapter – 2	
Andhakas,Vrishnis and the Bhojas	Within the federation of Dwarka these states were included
Bharatvarsha	Collective name for Ancient India
Manasa Guru	Informally adopted teacher
12 yojans	Vedic measure of distance used in ancient India
Sindh Sagar	Arabian Sea

Parijaat	Flower of god

Chapter – 3

Maagha	Maagha (Hindi: माघ maagh, মাঘ) is a month of the Hindu calendar. In India's national civil calendar, Maagh is the eleventh month of the year, beginning in January and ending in February.
Amavasya Punyakala Snanam Karishye	A type of prayer in the memory of ancestors on a new moon day.
PanditJi	A paṇḍit (Hindi; Devanagari:, Sanskrit: paṇḍita) is a scholar, a teacher, particularly one skilled in Sanskrit and Hindu law, religion, music or philosophy. The English loan word pundit is a derivation thereof.
Brahmanic	Brahmanism the religious and social system of orthodox Hinduism
Dhoti	The dhoti also known as pancha, panche or veshti is a traditional men's garment worn in India, Pakistan, Bangladesh and Nepal. It is a rectangular piece of unstitched cloth, usually around 4.5 metres (15 ft) long, wrapped around the waist and the legs and knotted at the waist, resembling a long skirt.
Katamarans	Sort of a country boat used by fisherman.
Amavasya	Amavasya is the Indian name for a New moon.
Mrigashrisha	Margashīrsha/Mrigashira (Devanagari: मृगशिरा) the 5th nakshatra or lunar mansion as used in Hindu astronomy and astrology is the constellation Orion. Its position is described in the Surya Siddhanta.
Samudra Putra	Son of sea
Nizvetana	Anesthesia
Mandi	Market
Mudhra	Seal used by Authorities.
Atithi	Guest
Namaskar	A traditional Indian greeting or gesture of respect, made by bringing the palms together before the face or chest and bowing
Pranams	Pranam is also a traditional gesture for greeting and offering respect to guest and seniors.
Vani	Moneylending community
Adhikari	Office Bearer

Varsha ritu	Monsoon
Chapter-4	
Dharshan	Darśana or Darshan (Sanskrit: दर्शन) is a Sanskrit term meaning "sight" (in the sense of an instance of seeing or beholding; from a rootdṛś "to see"), vision, apparition, or glimpse. It is most commonly used for "visions of the divine" in Hindu worship, e.g. of a deity (especially in image form), or a very holy person or artifact. One could "receive" darshana or blessing of the deity in the temple, or from a great saintly person, such as a great guru.
Dakshin bharath	Southern part of India
Varsh	Year
Sarama	In Hindu mythology, Sarama (सरमा, Tamil: Carapai, Thai: Trichada, Malay: Marcu Dewi) is usually referred to as the bitch (female dog) of the gods (Deva)- generally the god-king Indra, thus called Deva-shuni (देव-शुनी).
Yama	Hindu god of death and lord of the underworld.
Yadavas	Descendants of king Yadu into the community of which Krishna was born.
Three murthy	Murti is a representation of a divinity
Dravida desham	Area comprising of the present South Indian states
Yuvaraaj	Son of the king; crown-prince
Mlechchha	from Vedic Sanskrit म्लेच्छ mleccha, meaning "non-Vedic", "barbarian"), also spelt as Mlechchha, referred to people of foreign extraction in ancient India
Nishaadas	Hunter/Tribal Folk
Karnapravarnas	A tribe that lived in ancient India.
Kalanukha	A tribe that lived in ancient India.
Rakshasas	Race of mythological humanoid beings or unrighteous spirit in Hindu andBuddhist religion. Rakshasas are also called man-eaters ("Nri-chakshas," "Kravyads").
Kerakas	One legged tribes lived during Mahabharat Era.
Rigvedha	The Rigveda (Sanskrit: 'a compound of ' "praise, verse" and " "knowledge") is an ancient Indian sacred collection of Vedic Sanskrit hymns.
Sadhbarani	Description of a kind of coutesans.
Ganika	Description of a kind of coutesans.
Rupajivas	A branch of courtesans

Shakdivipa	Present day Iran
Magi Brahmin	A type of Brahmin community
Pournima	Sanskrit word meaning full moon; also refers to the full moon day or holi celebration in India.
Kaali	A divine godness who destroys evil. The name literally means black.
Pujari	Pujari is an Indian surname which means "priest"
Sura-ras	A form of intoxicating wine consumed in acient India.
Nara Bali	A ritual sacrifice of humans to please the gods.
Surapaan	The act of drinking Sura Ras
Skaldwipya	Sakaldwipiya Brahmins or Bhojaka Brahmins is a class of Hindu priests and Ayurveda teachers (acharyas), With significant concentrations of their populations occurring in Western and Northern India.
Vata	People with a predominant vata dosha display physical and emotional characteristics linked to the elemental qualities of space/akasha and air/vayu.
Pitta	People with a pitta dosha display an inherent fire/agni elemental character.
Kapha	People with a predominant kapha dosha tend to have a heavy and solid, or large build.
Mantras	A word or sound repeated to aid concentration in meditation.
Atharvan	Atharvan was a legendary Vedic sage (rishi) of Hinduism who along with Angiras is supposed to have authored ("heard") the Atharvaveda. He is also said to have first instituted the fire-sacrifice or yagna.
Bhaishajyams	Hymns for cure of diseases
Ayushyams	Hymns for longevity and prosperity.
Shamana	A person having access to, and influence in, the world of spirits
Shodhana	A fundamental aspect of all yogic paths; a category of purification practices in hatha yoga.
Ayurveda	The traditional Hindu system of medicine, which uses diet, herbal treatment, and yogic breathing.
Vrishnis	A sect of Yadava community
Andakhas	A sect of Yadava community
Samudhriga Lakshna	Beauty
Guruvar	Thursday
Natya Nritya	Natya corresponds to drama. Natya means dramatic representation or

	drama with speech, music and dancing.Nritya corresponds to the mime performed to the song. That is in other words, it is the Interpretative dance
Apsaras	Celestial Maiden
Roop Nritya	Abhinaya and dance
Bhav Nritya	Emoting through dance
Raas Nritya	Sentiment and emotional element with dance
Gopis	Gopi is a word of Sanskrit (गोपी) origin meaning 'cow-herd girl'. In Hinduism specifically the name gopi (sometimes gopika) is used more commonly to refer to the group of cow herding girls famous within Vaishnava Theology for their unconditional devotion (Bhakti) to Krishna
Vedic	The language of the Vedas, an early form of Sanskrit.
Sangamam	The confluence of rivers
Chapter – 5	
Gurukul	A ***Gurukul*** (Sanskrit guru "teacher" or "master"; kul domain, from kula, "extended family") is a type of school in India, residential in nature, with shishyas living in proximity to the guru, often within the same house.
Namasthe Guruji	Greeting to Teacher
varna	Varna (Sanskrit वर्ण "", literally "cover, coat; colour") refers to the main division of Hindu society into four social classes.
Haar	A garland
Rishis	A Hindu sage or saint
Karma	The sum of a person's actions in this and previous states of existence, viewed as deciding their fate
Dashas	The horoscope or birthchart, giving basic indication for an individual or event.
Yuga	Any of the four ages of the life of the world.
Lagna	Lagna (Sanskrit ", 'ascendant'.) Lagna is the first moment of contact between the soul and its new life on earth in Jyotisha
Rasi	In astronomy, a sign of the zodiac (as being a certain number of degrees)
Dhanusha Lagnam	An astrological term- the birth lagna
Khumba Rasi	Aquarius Sun sign
Poorvabhadra Nakshatra	A star sign attached to one's birth.
Guru Mangala Yoga	Mars Jupiter conjunction

Shanti	Peace
Cosmic	Of or relating to the universe or cosmos, esp. as distinct from the earth. Or Inconceivably vast.
Sindoor	Indoor is a red powder (Vermilion), which is traditionally applied at the beginning or completely along the parting-line of a woman's hair (also called mang) or as a dot on the forehead. Sindoor is the mark of a married woman in Hinduism
Shastras	The totality of sacred scripture
Yajna	A ritual sacrifice with a specific objective
Panchjanya	The great Arjuna's conch shell.
Om	A mystic syllable, considered the most sacred mantra. It appears at the beginning and end of most Sanskrit recitations, prayers, and texts
Dharma	Virtue, righteousness, and duty, esp. social and caste duty in accord with the cosmic order
Brahm	The ultimate reality or the universal consciousness or the essence of everything. God in the state of being without form or characteristics.
Chathuryuga	One cycle of 4 yugas ie Satya Treta, Dwarpar and Kali Yuga
Kalpa	Kalpa is a Sanskrit word (काल्प kālpa) meaning an aeon, or a long period of time in Hindu and Buddhist cosmology. The concept is first mentioned in the Mahabharata. The definition of a kalpa equalling 4.32 billion years is found in the Puranas (specifically Vishnu Purana and Bhagavata Purana).
Yuga Calender	1 Kalpa = 1 Day for Brahma (The active phase) = 1000 Chatur Yugas = 14 Manvantaras 1 Manvantara = 71 Chatur Yugas (1000/14) 1 Chatur Yuga = 4 Yugas

Yuga	Years	Ratio
Satya	1,728,000	4
Treta	1,296,000	3
Dwapara	864,000	2
Kali	432,000	1
Total	4,320,000	

We are in the 7th Manvantara and 28th Chatur Yuga of this 7th Manvantara.

Balance left = 14 - 7 = 7 Manvantaras +
Chatur Yuga = 71 – 28
Left in 7th Manvantara = viz 43

Hence we have 7 more manvantras (71x7=497 Chatur Yugas) + 43 Chatur Yugas left in the current manvantras. A total of 497+43=540 Chatur Yugas left. That means 540x4.320 Million years viz., 2.33

	billion years left for the planet – 54% of the life of earth is left (2.33 billion years out of a total of 4.32 billion years left)
Manvantara	Manvantara or Manuvantara, or age of a Manu, the Hindu progenitor of mankind, is an astronomical period of time measurement. Manvantara is a Sanskrit sandhi, a combination of words manu and antara, manu-antara or manvantara, literally meaning the duration of a Manu, or his life span
Satya	Satya is a Sanskrit word that loosely translates into English as "truth" or "correct".."
Treta	The Treta Yuga (Devanagari: त्रेता युग) is the second out of four yugas, or ages of mankind, in the religion of Hinduism, and follows the Satya Yuga of perfect morality and precedes the Dvapara Yuga.
Dwapara	It's a type of yuga
Kali (Yuga)	Last yuga in Chathuryuga
Maha Pralaya	In Hinduism, the "great" or final "dissolving" of the universe at the end of a kalpa, or "day in the life of Brahmā"
Guna	Any of the three interdependent modes or qualities of prakriti: sattva, rajas, or tamas
Sattva	Truthful
Rajas	Energetic
Tamas	(in Vedanta) The element or mode of prakriti associated with lethargy, darkness, and ignorance
Jathi	Caste
Rajasika	of the nature of rajas
vanprastha	A Vanaprastha (Sanskrit: वनप्रस्थ) is a person who is living in the forest as a hermit after partially giving up material desires.
Brahmi,vacha and Amalki	Herbal treatments
Smriti Nasaha	Loss of memory
Satvik,Rajasik and Tamasik	Types of Gunas. Saatvik is the good quality and Taamasic is all bad. Raajas are the undecided qualities which waver according to circumstances and environment
Swayamvaras	An occasion where princes and noble men from all parts of the Kingdom are invited to assemble in a bridegroom choosing ceremony

Chapter – 6

Barber	A person who cuts hair, esp. men's, and shaves or trims beards as an

	occupation
Narada purana	The Naradiya Purana, or Narada Purana, one of the major eighteen Puranas, a Hindu religious text
Rigveda	The Rigveda (Sanskrit: 'a compound of' "praise, verse" and " "knowledge") is an ancient Indian sacred collection of Vedic Sanskrit hymns. It is counted among the four canonical sacred texts (śruti") of Hinduism known as the Vedas
Dharmasutras	Dharmaśāstra (धर्मशास्त्र) is a genre of Sanskrit texts and refers to the śāstra, or Indic branch of learning, pertaining to Hindu dharma, religious and legal duty.
Sapthapadhi	Seven steps
Kumbh vivah	Kumbh Vivah is a combination of two Sanskrit words Kumbh which means Mud Pot and Vivah means Wedding in English. A symbolic Marriage.
Harivarmsa purana	The Harivamsha (also Harivamsa; Sanskrit Harivaṃśa हरिवंश "the lineage of Hari (Vishnu)" is an important work of Sanskrit literature, containing 16,374 verses.
Mangalsutra	A Mangalsutra (mangala sutra, mangalasutra or thali) is a symbol of Hindu marriage union in India
Mangalya Dharanam	Wearing of the mangala-sūtra during the marriage ceremony.
Thirumangalya	Tying the Sacred Marriage Pendant.
Swayamvaras	Swayamvara (स्वयंवर), in ancient India, was a practice of choosing a life partner, from among a list of suitors, by a girl of marriageable age. Swayam in Sanskrit means " and Vara means choosing or wanting".
Booloka	The earth and one of the three lokas.
Ammi	A type of grinding stone
Pathivratha	The chaste, devoted and loyal wife
Mangala Aarti	This prayer is offered at the end of the function.
Chapter – 7	
Sanatan dharma	Hinduism is the predominant and indigenous religious traditionHinduism is variously defined as a "religion"," "set of religious beliefs and practices"," "religious tradition" etc.
Sthapna	Foundation

Ayushya Homa	Ritual for the well being of the new born child.
Sudhpudra	Son of a Shudra
Agni	Fire
Somavar	Monday
Namakaran Sanskar	Naming ceremony
Mayye	Khol-black powder used for eye make up
Kanmashi	Khol-black powder used for eye make up
Ghee	Clarified butter made from the milk of a cow, used in Indian cooking
Samapandhi Bhojan	All people treated as same during the meal.
Aryajan	Respected People.
Mriga Shirsha	Margashīrsha/Mrigashira (Devanagari: मृगशिरा) the 5th nakshatra or lunar mansion as used in Hindu astronomy and astrology is the constellation Orion. Its position is described in the Surya Siddhanta.
Asthra	Weapon

Chapter – 8

Agni asthras	God of fire
Sudharma	Yadara court
Mandhi	Market
Bhojas	One form of a kingdom in central India
Andhakas	A particular tribe.
Manglik dhosha	Mars when it occupies certain houses, i.e. 1st, 4th, 7th, 8th and 12th houses, the horoscope is called as Mars Dosha / Manglik Kundli
Adarvana veda	A collection of mantras and formulas.
Jati Bahishkar	A collective ban by the community
Parnasala	A hut made out of leaves and twigs
Panchayat	a village council
Jathi prashta	Someone who has defied the laws applicable to his jati and he is considered impure.
Putra	Son

Chapter – 9

Asuras	A member of a class of evil divine beings in the Vedic period.
Nagas	A tribe from the origin of the snakes
Kokilas	A singer/a song bird

Chakravakas	Brahminy Duck.
Rajasuya Yagna	royal consecration worship
Ashwamedha yagna	royal worship with the horse
Kinkaras	Rakshasas
Kshatriyas	A member of the royal or warrior Hindu caste.
Karandavas	Ducks and swans
Mehndi	Mehndi (مہندی, मेहँदी) is the application of henna as a temporary form of skin decoration in Indian Subcotinent
Mridangas	Percussion instrument from India of Tamil origin. It is the primary rhythmic accompaniment in a Carnatic music ensemble
Veenas	Type of musical instrument
Gangs	Type of musical instrument
Cymbals	A musical instrument consisting of a slightly concave round brass plate that is either struck against another one or struck with a stick.
Agni Suktam	A hymn devoted to the lord of fire.
Varuna Suktam	A hymn devoted to the lord of wind/Sea

Chapter – 10

Vanavaas	Vanvas (वनवास) is a Sanskrit term meaning residence (vās) in a forest (van).
Adnyatvaas	Staying incognito
Surya Namaskar	Salutation to the Sun
Tapasya	Meditation
Dvapara Yuga	Dvapara Yuga or Dwapara Yuga(Devanagari: द्वापर युग) is the third out of four yugas, or ages,
Adharma	Adharma is the Sanskrit antonym of Dharma. It means 'that which is not in accord with the law'
Pancha Bhoodas	Pancha indicates Five, Bhoota means elements
Kali Yuga	Kali Yuga (Devanāgarī: कलयुग, lit. "age of (the male demon) Kali", or "age of vice") is the last of the four stages that the world goes through as part of the cycle of yugas described in the Indian scriptures.
Indraprastha	Capital City of Pandava Kingdom
Kamyaka Vana	A forest
Treta Yuga	Treta Yuga is the second out of four yugas of mankind, in the religion of Hinduism.

Dharmic	Is a term of great importance in Indian philosophy and religions.
Ashram	A hermitage, monastic community, or other place of religious retreat for Hindus

Chapter – 11

Bhiksha	Bhiksha is food obtained by asking for alms. Bhiksha signifies a Hindu tradition of begging for alms with the purpose of self-effacement or ego-conquering.
Sasthras	The totality of sacred scripture
Kartika	A Hindu calendar month
Vikriti	A Hindu calendar year
Uthrayana	It is the six-month period between Winter solstice (around December 22) and Summer solstice(around June 21), when the sun apparently travels towards the north on the celestial sphere.
Sakuna Sastra	One of the branches of Astrology where an astrologer can predict the outcome of a question just by observing the changes in the environment is called 'Sakuna Sastra' or Astrology of omens.

Chapter – 12

Saraswathi Namasthubyam Varathe Kamarubini Vidyarambam Karishyami Siddhir Bavathume Satha	A hymn or goddess Saraswathi.
Upanayana	Upanayana (Sacred Thread ceremony) (lit. "near sight"), also called "sacred thread ceremony",” is commonly known for being a Hindu Sanskara,
Yajnopavitam	A sacred thread worn by the children after the Upnaya ceremony.
Brahmachari	Is a person who is usually a novice of a monastic order and who dedicate his entire life to humanity and God
Brahmacharya	Brahmacharya means leading a life of pure thoughts, pure actions and pure aspirations.
Dvijas	A person who is twice-born: a distinction made between the first three classes of society and the lowest class, the Shudra. Only the dvijas may study the Vedas.
Gayatri Mantra	The Gāyatrī Mantra is a highly revered mantra, based on a Vedic Sanskrit verse from a hymn of the Rigveda
Savya	The right way of wearing the sacred thread. From left shoulder to right waist.
Srishti	The natural world encompassing all that is around us.
Sthithi	The position in time and space of a specific thing.
Vinasa	Destruction

Tithi	In vedic timekeeping, a tithi (also spelled thithi) is a lunar day, or the time it takes for the longitudinal angle between the moon and the sun to increase by 12°. Tithis begin at varying times of day and vary in duration from approximately 19 to approximately 26 hours.
Gunas	Skill sets
Karmic	Karma(Hinduism and Buddhism) the effects of a person's actions that determine his destiny in his next incarnation
Nakshatras	Nakṣatra Generally a star, constellation, or any heavenly body; sometimes collectively, the stars.
Chapter – 13	
Gurudev	Literally meaning teacher is god
Vyuhas	Military formations on the battlefield.
Agneyastra	Agni (अग्नि) is a Hindu deity, one of the most important of the Vedic gods. He is the god of fire and the acceptor of sacrifices.
Varunashtra	The Varunastra (Sanskrit वरुणास्त्र) is the water weapon (a storm), incepted by God Varuna, master of the oceans, rivers, and lakes.
Chapter – 14	
Bhaiyya	Brother
Sangam	Confluence in Sanskrit
Sarpha	Snake
Karma Yoga	Karma yoga (Sanskrit: कर्म योग), (also known as Buddhi Yoga) or the "discipline of action" is based on the teachings of the Bhagavad Gita, a sacred Sanskrit scripture of Hinduism
Angavastram	The piece of cloth that is worn on the upper part of the body by males.
Samavartana	The Samavartana (समावर्तन) is a Hindu sacramental ritual (Saṃskāra) that was performed at the close of the Brahmacharya period and marked the end termination of the student life.
Chapter – 15	
Maa	Mother
Pitaji	Father
Parihar	Negating the evil effects through ritual
Slogas	A couplet of Sanskrit verse, esp. one in which each line contains sixteen syllables
Chapter – 16	
Sythan	Saturn
Nishadas	Nishada was the kingdom of the Nishada Tribe, a tribe of people who

	the Vedic people considered as out-casts.
Mandir	Temple
Rahasya	Rahasya A secret doctrine or teaching; any subtle idea or recondite point of thought; mystical or esoteric teachings. Also a name of the Upanishads. As an adjective, secret, mysterious. The form sa-rahasya also means secret wisdom.
Bhoomi Pooja	The worship(Puja) of the land (Bhoomi)
Nerium oleander from Kolly	Ayurvedic herbs
Arka patram	Ayurvedic herbs
Pournami	Full moon day
Chapter – 17	
Brahanada	The dance form of Arjun
Upaplavya	A place on the border of modern day Indian state of Haryana and Rajasthan.
Adnyatvaas	Living in camouflaged identity
Chapter – 18	
Akshauhinis	An Akshauhini (अक्शौहिनि), was an ancient battle formation that consisted of 21,870 chariots (Sanskrit ratha); 21,870 elephants; 65,610 horse-mounted warriors and 109,350 infantry, as per the Mahabharata
Vajra	Indra's thunderbolt.
Phalanx	A group of people or things of a similar type forming a compact body or brought together for a common purpose. Or A body of troops or police officers, standing or moving in close formation.
Bala Kanda	Life threat during youth phase.
Akshohini	Ancient battle formation
Varuna	Rain god
Vayu	Wind god
Sarathy	Charioteer
Pitamah Bheeshma	The grandfather or grandsire
Maharathis	Capable Warriors
Puthras	Son
Chapter - 19	
Manoeuvre	Maneuver: act in order to achieve a certain goal

Chakra	Wheel
Tandav nrutya	The divine art form, is a dance performed by the Hindu god Shiva
Panchajanya	Panchajanya is the conch of the Hindu god Vishnu.
Shakata vyuha	Formation of a cart wheel
Suchimukha vyuha	Formation in the shape of a needle
Samshaptakas	Mercenary to vow to return from battlefield only upon victory else death
Soorya	Sun
Chandra	Moon

Chapter – 20

Ram Rajya	Kingdom of Lord Ram
Vanaprasthashram	The act of renouncing worldly bonds and going and living in the forest.
Veer Chiranjeevi	Literally meaning brave and long living

www.ingramcontent.com/pod-product-compliance
Ingram Content Group UK Ltd.
Pitfield, Milton Keynes, MK11 3LW, UK
UKHW041351190726
13845UKWH00026B/543